A SMALL GUN . . .

I don't know what woke me: I certainly didn't consciously hear a car engine. I got up, yawning, made my way into the living room and, just to check on the weather, looked through the curtains to a still, white, snowbound land-scape—

Keir's car parked in the drive.

I ran to the door, changed into my boots, flung open the door, and raced across the porch and down the steps, around the hood of the car . . .

But it wasn't Keir. The tall figure in the gray parka, her hair in a woollen cap, was Erica.

I felt my heart stop, falter, in disbelief. Where was Keir? And why was she here?

I walked to the driver's door, unsure what to do. She stared straight ahead. I tapped on the glass of the driver's window but she refused to look at me.

Finally she turned her head and stared at me, then lowered the window. Desperation, utter misery, and exhaustion—all of these were written on her face—but oh, God, she was still lovely.

I waited for her to speak. She looked at me with dark-rimmed, tragic eyes, and I think it took a few seconds for her to recognize me.

Then she said, "Sally," and lifted her left hand—and there was a small gun held within it. I just stood there in shock and watched her squeeze the trigger and shoot at me.

BOOK YOUR PLACE ON OUR WEBSITE AND MAKE THE READING CONNECTION!

We've created a customized website just for our very special readers, where you can get the inside scoop on everything that's going on with Zebra, Pinnacle and Kensington books.

When you come online, you'll have the exciting opportunity to:

- View covers of upcoming books
- Read sample chapters
- Learn about our future publishing schedule (listed by publication month *and author*)
- Find out when your favorite authors will be visiting a city near you
- Search for and order backlist books from our online catalog
- Check out author bios and background information
- Send e-mail to your favorite authors
- Meet the Kensington staff online
- Join us in weekly chats with authors, readers and other guests
- Get writing guidelines
- AND MUCH MORE!

**Visit our website at
http://www.pinnaclebooks.com**

A TURN OF THE BLADE

Veronica Sweeney

Pinnacle Books
Kensington Publishing Corp.

http://www.pinnaclebooks.com

PINNACLE BOOKS are published by

Kensington Publishing Corp.
850 Third Avenue
New York, NY 10022

First Printing: October, 1998
10 9 8 7 6 5 4 3 2 1

Printed in the United States of America

To
Colleen Clifford
1899–1996

who told me she couldn't wait to read this book—
and then didn't—

this novel is lovingly, sorrowfully dedicated.

Acknowledgments

My thanks to Jill Hickson for her continuing belief in my work, and to Louise Thurtell for her faith in my being able to make the giant leap between genres.

Thanks to my friend Valerie Newstead for her advice on matters *kosher*.

I owe a special debt to Inspector Eric Fiander of Fredericton, New Brunswick, for sparing the time to answer numerous questions—from Canadian Police procedure to ornithology—with unfailing patience, and for his invaluable help in checking the manuscript.

My thanks also to my family, for their support and encouragement in the years of writing this book.

Hast thou found me, O mine enemy?

The First Book of Kings

Chapter One

I suppose I fulfilled the secret fantasy of every editor in the world of publishing the day I killed a writer. Yet until I killed Erica Tudor I don't think anyone would have described me as an overly assertive woman, let alone an aggressive one. Keir would tell you—and Beth—that I lack that competitive edge, that necessary ambition, to carve out a truly brilliant career. "You have no killer instinct," Keir would say.

Yet I killed Erica.

It still bothers me. And not just the *wrongness* of what I did, but the waste. Not the loss to the world of a gifted writer, for Erica wasn't all that *good*. But she might have improved. What if, had she lived to be fifty or so, the sum total of all her years of experience came spilling out over the keys of her Macintosh and Erica turned out something vivid rather than glossy, truthful rather than glitzy and shallow? Writers with less style than Erica have written classics; the tortuous metaphor isn't for everyone.

For Erica was only twenty-five when she died. *Twenty-five.* At twenty-five you think people are staring at you if you don't shave your legs for a week. At twenty-five you're thinking of what *he's* thinking in the middle of lovemaking. At twenty-five you look in the mirror and *search* for wrinkles. It was a pity that Erica had to die before finding her true potential. She was searching for it, I know that. I feel as if I understand Erica—now. I didn't understand her, or even know her well, when she was alive.

Erica was not one of my writers, she was one of Beth's. Beth had discovered her, "made her," as Beth often muttered over cocktails at Little Nell's after work on days when Erica was proving incalcitrant or demanding—or both. My writers could be as sensitive, as difficult, as Beth's, but were more literary in style. Beth's life's work was The Blockbuster. I didn't envy her; my writers didn't sell as many books but the pressure on deadlines and style was not as great, and the books were *shorter,* too. Beth, on the other hand, had a special gift for finding and marketing writers whose work appealed to those millions who wanted, primarily, A Good Read. Beth's stable of best-selling authors made her the envy of other editors, but she rarely lost an author to a rival publisher. Writers *like* Beth. So do I. She has the kindest heart beneath her professional veneer and she's been my best friend for twelve years. But if Beth knew I'd killed her best-selling author, I doubt she'd ever speak to me again.

I finally met Erica at the "housewarming"—as Sammy Thorne called it—that excuse, as if publishers needed one, for champagne and honeyed chicken wings when a company moves from one building to another.

And it was not a move to celebrate—any more than Jonah would have yelled Yippee as he went down the gullet of the whale. Brambles Thorne had been swallowed—*merged,* the *Wall Street Journal* would have it—and was now part of the great international media group Inter-tel Global.

Editors are a floating population, constantly on the move from publishing house to publishing house, either voluntarily, in search of better money and better prospects, or involuntarily, when we're fired. Perhaps that's why we've been known to cling sentimentally to our little cubicles while we have them. We spend most of our working lives staring at manuscripts or writers, and while we have the benefits of long lunches to break our routines, we like to feel *cosy*, to have our own things around us, to have a sense of *proprietorship* within our four walls.

The original offices, home to Brambles Thorne Publishing since its formation in 1922, were in a converted mansion on Washington Square. My office had been at the back, its single window half-filled with the bulk of an elderly air conditioner. If it hadn't been for this grumbling metal monster I'd have had an uninterrupted view of the brick wall of the neighboring building, four feet away. But the walls of my office had been of mahogany and the bookcases, also mahogany, rose thirteen feet into the air to touch the ornately plastered ceiling. The office was thirteen feet high, and thirteen feet square, a perfect box. I had loved it.

The new offices on Second Avenue had a plain, smooth ceiling, and a lot of it. The outer wall of each office was glass, and I was privileged, as a senior editor, to have one of those that looked over the shoulder of the UN building to the East River. My bookcases were of limed pine and the lighting was discreet and scientifically adjusted to maximize human ophthalmic efficiency. It was a pleasant room: it would have been called Bright and Airy in the days when one opened windows instead of turning knobs to get air.

That evening, the evening of the housewarming, I was feeling depressed, as much about the relocation as the merger, and I wasn't the only one in the editorial staff to regret this move to brighter, more modern premises. The secretaries, sales staff, marketing and art departments were all in moods of enthusiasm—their jobs were safe, we had, praise the Lord, passed down the gullet of the whale without a single crunch of grinding jaws, without the single rolling of a head. But we editors huddled in dissatisfied groups, tossing off our champagne in a serious manner and watching our authors, those top earners who were invited to this celebration, moving about the room.

"I don't like this," I muttered to Beth. "Why did we have to move into the Inter-Tel Global Building? They've got six imprints, now, counting us—all fighting for the same elevators and car spaces. I liked life when it was civilized—when you had to cross town to hunt a head. These guys will be ambushing my writers on the way from the lobby. 'James Hammel, Booker Prize winner, last seen between floors fifteen and twenty.' " I took a healthy gulp of champagne.

"Mm," Beth murmured. I doubt if she'd heard me. Her attention was fixed on Sammy Thorne, our managing director, as he brushed past an attractive, slim woman in her fifties who had smiled and greeted him. He gave her a polite nod, a distracted glance—already he was searching the room for more interesting, more promising company.

"Poor Eleanor," Beth said. "Sammy didn't have to be so damned obvious."

Eleanor O'Brien was one of the top literary agents in New York, but a recent and bitter split with her agency partner had meant upheavals in her office, and the loss of some clients.

"An uncharacteristically dumb move for our leader," I noted. "Eleanor will bounce back." Eleanor had recovered quickly from Sammy's snub; she threw one dark look like a dagger at Sammy's back, then turned to chat brightly with James Hammel, one of the several prestigious literary novelists whom Eleanor represented and I edited.

"Ross took all their big earners with him when he left her, the rat." Beth turned to the suave form of Ross Gilbert with something like disdain. Ross was ploughing through the crowd in Sammy's wake like a sleek yacht following a fat little pilot boat through dangerous shoals. "I don't know why Erica left Eleanor—I'm not going to agree to any more money no matter who's representing her."

Beth stiffened and raised her head, her gaze towards the entranceway. "There's Erica now."

She moved forward, across the room, and I would have followed, keen to catch my first glimpse of the fabled Ms. Tudor, when James Hammel appeared at my elbow. "Sally, I have to speak to you." James stood close, his normally controlled features now showing some signs of distress or agitation. "I know I said *The Baron of Fifth Avenue* would be ready by July, but I'm having a dreadful time with Andrew—"

"Oh, no—" My dismay was real: when James was unhappy, he didn't write.

"My dear, I think sometimes he's determined to destroy me and my work—and the terrible thing is I still love the little—"

"Sally!" It was Beth's voice. I could just make her *out*, pushing her way through the knots of people talking loudly, earnestly into each other's faces.

James said, quickly, "I really need to talk to you *soon*. I'm thinking of leaving Eleanor as well. Do you think she's losing her touch as an agent? Even Erica Tudor left her—"

"I wouldn't do anything rash. Erica might find she misses Eleanor's experience and encouragement—"

"Sally!" Beth closer.

"I'll call you tomorrow," I promised James. "We'll do lunch."

Beth was beside us, looking pleased. "James, can I drag Sally away? I want her to meet Erica."

James had never hidden the fact that he regarded Erica's work as pulp fiction at its worst. Beth must have known his feelings, for she smiled wickedly at him as she spoke. James rolled his eyes and said in his clear, upper-class English accent, "I was just going to speak with the enfant terrible over there." He adjusted an already geometrically straight bow tie and went to speak to Sammy Thorne, grandson of the founder, and the man most responsible for pulling—and pushing—Brambles Thorne into the nineties.

Beth was already ushering me back through the crush,

and I went happily enough. Erica had given up a successful modelling career on the west coast after the overnight sensation of her first novel, *Traces of Heaven,* three years before. She had moved to a large country house in New Hampshire and rarely came to New York. I had been on a skiing holiday with Keir in Colorado at the time of her first two book launches, and overseas at the time her third and current bestseller, *Gaining,* was published.

She was very tall, taller than I expected, close on six feet in her low-heeled Italian shoes. All heads turned as she approached and remained gazing at her after she had passed.

I had seen pictures, of course, for she enjoyed a friendly relationship with the press, but nothing had prepared me for Erica in the flesh. She had the even, startling bone structure of a young Marlene Dietrich, the perfectly straight nose, the well-defined but delicate chin. Only the mouth was different, her lips were full and wide, but not too wide. My lips, too, were full, but wider than they had been at Erica's age because facial surgery had given me that faint, secret and permanent smile that Erica had seemingly been born with. I was fortunate to be married to one of the country's—possibly the world's—finest cosmetic surgeons: Erica had no need, no need at all for Keir's gifted hands. I looked at Erica and thought, *even her breasts look real. . . .*

She saw Beth, and her smile widened, showing white and even teeth: it was a lovely smile, it had the guilelessness that had made a star out of Farrah Fawcett, and her hair, like Fawcett's, was worn long, in loose and glossy curls. Again, I knew that hair was real. I knew because mine looks very similar, but is not real. My hair is bleached and permed and fussed over by the most expensive hairdresser in Manhattan. Sometimes even he fails me and I have eight wigs, all long and blonde and glossy and looking almost as good as Erica's did, coming as *she* just had, from a windy September afternoon, and running one hand impatiently through it to flick it out of her eyes as she walked.

I didn't resent her beauty, though it must sound as

though I did. No, it was her *kind* of beauty, it was the way she chose to accentuate it. And still I hadn't worked out this sudden antipathy, until Beth, who had been about to walk forward, suddenly said to me, in a lowered voice, "Hey, I've never realized this before." She looked at me, at Erica, at me, at Erica, then she whispered to me, "You guys look so alike! Erica could be your little sister! I mean . . ."

And Beth blushed. Who has seen a New York book editor blush?

"You mean younger sister," I said. "That's okay. Face it, she *is* young enough to be my daughter."

Erica was almost upon us. I too have a smile like Farrah Fawcett, I have been told more than once. I turned it, now, upon Erica and tried—oh God, how hard I tried!—not to dislike her.

But I didn't want to move forward to this young woman, to have her eyes—blue eyes, not gray like my own—fully upon me, to have to stare into that face and be forced to realize that she was everything I had ever aspired to be: she was my "type," she was my "style"—even to the earth tones of her clothes—and she was natural, unforced, and *young*.

And yet, despite that smile, there was little warmth to Erica, though her words were courteous and her handshake firm and friendly. It was not, I felt at the time, a coolness towards me, particularly, but an overall guardedness. Yet she was young, beautiful, rich, and famous. In my naïvté—I was forty-two at that time and still I could think this—I believed this woman should be at peace with all the world. Surely she had it all.

We didn't speak for long. I congratulated her on the success of *Gaining* while Beth stood by, smiling proudly. *Gaining* had sold its two millionth copy the week before.

Erica was modest. It was a success, she admitted, perhaps more than it deserved. "One of these days I might become a real writer, produce something of lasting merit. A social document on American values—that's what I'd like to write. Does that sound ridiculous ?''

Both Beth and I, simultaneously, reassured her that her novels *were* documents of social history.

In a way it was true. Erica's readers of the future would be able to gain much more detailed insight into what America wore, drove, ate, drank, and injected itself with in the late twentieth century than many an award-winning writer of literature would provide.

That was one way of looking at it.

And her books were making the company tens of millions of dollars: who were Beth and I to say, ''Yes, change your style, get *earnest?*''

At this point Sammy, thirty years old, married but forgetting himself, galloped across the room to us and began to monopolize Erica's attention. He stood at a little distance from her, not too close, and with his back very straight, so that his glossy dark head would reach its absolute maximum of five feet eight.

I left them standing there, a little trio, Erica, Beth, and Sammy, author, editor, and publisher, happily talking of their success, and went to the women's room. I was just taking out my makeup to retouch my face, when Erica came into the room.

''Hi,'' she said.

''Hi.''

She didn't go into a cubicle but stood at the mirror beside me. I recognized her perfume; somehow I would have thought she'd choose something more earthy than Miss Dior. We stood there side by side, reapplying our lipstick, checking our eye makeup, fluffing our hair, and trying to study each other without being seen to do so.

She was one of the few women I'd seen who could wear a brilliant red lipstick and not look like a tart. The woman was stunning. Beside her, I looked like her mother from L.A.—and overdressed, at that. I stood there at the mirror trying to busy myself and all the time I was thinking, *What did I do, that this girl should be the one to come share the mirror with me?*

I didn't know why Erica Tudor should be studying me. Except maybe to ask in horrified self-honesty, *This is the best I can hope for, after I'm forty?*

And then she said, "We have to talk."

She turned to face me, one hand gripping the edge of the bench. "We have to talk," she repeated. "Will you have lunch with me tomorrow?"

I stared at her. My first thought was that she was unhappy with Beth's work on *Gaining*. But I had left her not ten minutes before, telling Sammy—in front of Beth—what a joy it was to work with her, how supportive Beth was.

"It's about Keir. But you realize that, don't you?"

And such was the trust between my husband and myself that I had to ask, bemusedly, "What about Keir?"

And Erica Tudor said, "We love each other. We've been lovers for eight months. Are you trying to tell me you weren't aware?"

There are women, I know, who can think very quickly, whose minds can sum up a situation and act upon their instincts almost immediately. I should be like that. As it was I was still facing the mirror, my brain lagging a good five seconds behind the conversation. My mascara wand was in my hand and I was gazing at Erica Tudor's famous and perfect profile. My first thought was, *I gotta tell Beth, she's been working too hard.*

Then I turned and gazed directly at her, and I saw that she meant what she said.

And my second thought was, *Keir's been flirting with her.* Somewhere, somehow, he's met Erica and he's been flirting with her. She thinks it's serious, real. How do I handle this?

There was no archness in Erica's manner, no spite, no sense of victory. She still looked anxious, wary. And when I didn't speak, she became agitated, turned away and put her lipstick and small hairbrush back in her handbag. Her hands were shaking.

Then she said, speaking quickly in that pleasant voice which, despite years in L.A. and New Hampshire still bore traces of her Mississippi roots, "I had to tell you. To get it out into the open. He said you knew, but that you hadn't talked about it, that you were both avoiding discussing it. He's so desperate not to hurt you. *Did* you know? You didn't, did you." Not a question, a softly spoken statement that informed herself as much as me.

I found my voice, and it sounded very remote, very cool. "I don't know what you're talking about."

For a moment Erica looked close to tears, then, with sudden resolve, she said in a harder voice, "You've known your marriage was over for years. Keir is very fond of you, he's grateful to you—maybe he even still loves you, in a way. But you've been growing apart all these years, it's become a marriage of habit and convenience. Is that what you want for him? He's so desperate to *live*. And the two of you—why you hardly have any sex life . . . Look, I'm sorry!"

I found I'd moved away, had stepped back, away from this mad woman. I groped behind me for the door handle.

Erica was saying, "We didn't mean it to happen! These things aren't *planned*—"

"You're crazy, Erica," I flared back. "The strain of producing two hundred thousand words in twelve months has given you a problem in dealing with reality."

Erica said, in a cold voice, "Ask Keir. Ask him tonight when you get home."

"Let's ask him together. He'll be calling for me at eight." I looked at my watch. It read seven forty-five. I looked up at Erica and had a momentary and pleasurable victory in the look of panic and doubt that was suddenly written on her features.

"He's coming *here* tonight?"

"He often picks me up when I'm going to be working late."

"I know. He leaves from my hotel to call for you."

And she pressed on, seeing my shock, filling the silence with words that had obviously been considered, long-suppressed, and were now unstoppable.

"We met at the launch of James Hammel's book, last fall. You flew in from London that day and your plane was late. You came straight to the Marlborough Regency, where they were holding the launch, and Keir was to meet you there. We spent two hours talking, Keir and I, and we arranged to meet the next day. It was Wednesday, the day he usually plays golf. I left the book launch early, because I didn't want to meet you. I knew then, already, you see? So did Keir."

I thought, *Beth would have told me if my husband had spent two hours talking in corners with an ex-model.*

"I'm not listening to any more of this," I said, and turned to open the door. I was beginning to believe her, and I couldn't bear it. I had to find Keir. To find my husband and have him assure me: No, it's not true. It's not true.

I came through the door into the corridor and walked quickly towards the large main reception area where every-one was gathered. But Erica was close behind me; now she was beside me; like a gliding wraith, like a reflection in a flattering mirror, like the doppelgänger I feared she was, Erica Tudor kept pace with me with her longer stride, speaking all the time in an urgent undertone that became more Mississippi with each phrase.

"I know you're feeling upset right now, Sally, I truly do. I can understand what you're going through. But it's best to get it out in the open. Then we can start making decisions—"

And just as I was about to step through the open doorway, she took my arm with a grip that physically prevented me from moving forward without shaking her off and making a scene. I was forced to stop and look up at her.

Still keeping the pressure on my arm, she said, "We *will* talk. In a friendly manner or with lawyers around a table.

Your marriage is over. Keir loves me and he's asked me to marry him.''

Pulling my arm forcibly out of her grasp, I said in a low voice, "Your brain is as full of third-rate crap as your novels." Then I turned to walk into the reception area—and stopped.

For Keir was over at the champagne table, talking to Beth. Beth was looking up into his face, her smile alight. She wasn't alone; every woman in the room was looking at Keir in the same way that every man had looked at Erica. Over six feet tall and slim, with the finely bred bones of a young Gregory Peck, the same straight black hair, the same devastating, direct dark gaze, Keir wore his background of money, privilege, social acceptance, as if he walked constantly under an invisible banner, like a Roman patrician. Keir was one of the New York Stanforths. He was even related, but not so closely as to cause embarrassment, to the Boston Stanforths. And Keir was successful and wealthy in his own right.

He looked up and saw me, and smiled.

He loves me. Of course he loves me. Look at him, it's there on his face.

But then his gaze slid past me and his smile froze, his face paled. He looked back at me. He looked at me with all the love he had for me, there in his dark eyes, and such sadness, such wretchedness, that I knew that there was truth, some truth, in what Erica Tudor had been telling me.

How often have you said to yourself, you wouldn't blame him, couldn't blame him? So many lovely young women, smiling at him, vying for his attention. And he'd smile, and look at me, as if the attention was amusing, but puzzling. For he belonged to me. And I to him. For nineteen years of marriage.

He didn't move towards me. He seemed unable to move, despite his innate good manners, let alone his love for me, the concern for me that was written on his face.

And Beth, clever Beth, quick Beth, was gazing between me and Keir and could sense that something was wrong.

I could see the puzzlement in her eyes as I moved past her, without saying goodnight, or goodbye. I left the room, and Keir followed me. I managed to keep walking only by repeating over and over to myself: *It can't be true. It can't be true. . . .*

Chapter Two

I don't remember coming to myself until we were in the car and on our way home. I pressed the button to lower the window and took great gulps of the not-always-pleasant air of a New York evening.

Keir was silent. Too silent. There was an atmosphere of constrained emotions, of words unsaid, that made the roomy old Mercedes feel small, stuffy.

We'd turned on to Central Park South. "What's happened, Sally?" Even the tone of his voice was different, as if what he was really asking was, *How much do you know?*

"I had a talk with Erica Tudor." My voice sounded too light, as if it came from the top of my head. I cleared my throat. "She said . . . she said that you two have been lovers for eight months."

I heard Keir inhale, preparing to speak, and added, "She gave details."

Don't lie to me, Keir. Please don't lie.

We'd reached our apartment building, and Keir slowed the car. He turned into the garage, used his key, and we waited while the metal grille of the door rolled up. Like a drawbridge; this had been our castle. Ours. Impregnable.

I thought, *Did he bring her here?*

Keir didn't speak until we were inside the apartment. I dropped my handbag on the hall table. Behind me I could hear Keir locking the door. In the living room he dropped his briefcase and headed for the liquor cabinet. I stood at the windows, watching the city shining below and around me. Behind came the sound of two stiff drinks being poured. Even the *clink* of the ice had an ominous ring to it.

"Sally . . . ?"

I hadn't heard him move towards me across the thick rug—I hadn't even noticed his reflection. When I turned he was standing there, holding a scotch in each hand, holding one out towards me, gazing at me. The look contained—what? Love? Pity? Both, I suppose, looking back on it.

I accepted the glass. He drank from his own, watching me over the rim, the love still there in his eyes.

"Tell me," I said, and there was a kind of plea in my voice that I hated to hear, hated him to hear.

He sighed, ran his hand through the thick straight hair, looking suddenly, utterly miserable.

"It wasn't supposed to happen," he said.

And I burst out laughing.

The next thing I remember was that we were sitting on the settee, and I was laughing, and crying, and Keir was holding me—how did that glass of scotch end up on the floor?—and he was trying to tell me of Erica Tudor, how he had seen her, and loved her, and how he could not bear that she would not be in his life.

I'd like to be able to say that I was calm, that I took all this in with maturity, acted with the dignity that befitted a woman of my age, the wife of a New York Stanforth. But I wasn't. I was like a little girl, immature, utterly vulnerable, not possessing any strength or resources of her own. I cried, I pleaded with Keir, I held him and I would not let go.

But Keir didn't try to let go. His arms were around me

just as tightly and he let me cry, soothed me and told me everything would be alright. He said he still loved me. But he didn't answer when I asked how he could love me and Erica Tudor at the same time. He didn't answer when I asked him—begged him—not to see her again.

"Why won't you say something?" I sobbed. "At least be honest with me . . ."

"I'm trying! I just don't know."

"You don't . . . *know?* You don't *know?* What's to know? You can't love her *and* me! You can't!"

"She possesses me, somehow. Maybe the . . . the need for her will stop one day. Then I can forget her. I'll try. Really, Sally . . . dear God, you mean more to me than anything in the world. I'll try to get over her."

I gazed up into his face. We had known each other since I was sixteen and Keir eighteen. Keir and I had had each other's love for nearly twenty-five years, nineteen of these married to each other. I don't see that it was a weakness to try to hold on to that love, knowing that with its loss would come an emptiness I would never be able to fill.

Keir said, "I think I'd better leave, Sally, go away for a while until I've sorted this out."

"Leave?" I stared at him. "What do you mean? You don't *leave* to sort out problems in a marriage. You stay and sort them out together. We'll get some counseling. I've let you down somehow—or you feel I have. You must feel that, or you wouldn't have needed to go to Erica." A sudden thought chilled me. "Keir . . . She was the first, wasn't she? Have you ever—"

"Of course not!" he said, vehemently. "And I didn't want to now, with Erica—but I've *fallen in love,* Sally." And he spoke the words through clenched teeth, as if it were a disease, a kind of breakdown of his immune system.

He kissed me then, fondly, gently, on the lips, and then he stood and moved towards the bedroom. I followed him, crying, desperately trying to think of something I could say or do that would stop him. He disappeared into the dressing room and I could hear him unfolding the little aluminum ladder that we kept for reaching the suitcases at the very top of the closets. I didn't want to follow him into the smaller room, and I sat on the foot of our bed. Keir was dropping suitcases down on to the carpet. They made a sound like a branch falling onto the forest floor.

He moved the suitcases to the bed and I tried to talk to him as he packed, unhurriedly, methodically. He answered me as best he could, but it was horrible that this conversation could sound so trite, so clichéd; every word we spoke we had both heard on so many screens, in movies and on television. And still we struggled.

"How can you do this? I thought you loved me . . ."

"I do, but . . . I have to go, Sally."

"She can't love you as I do! It can't last!"

"But I'll have to find out. I can't *not* see her again, I just can't."

He carried his two suitcases through the apartment. I trotted close behind him. "But what will happen to me? You don't care what will happen to me." I was sobbing so hard I was choking, choking so badly I was almost fainting. If only pity would hold him, then let him stay out of pity. Only let him stay.

"Keir!" as he opened the door.

"Goodbye, Sally," he said. "I'm sorry, my darling, I'm sorry . . ." and he was out the door, closing it gently behind him.

I walked back into the living room and sat down on the sofa. I was still sitting there when the little antique French clock Keir had given me for our tenth wedding anniversary *ping*-ed nine o'clock. I stared at the tiny swinging pendulum behind its glass case. Nine o'clock. A little over an hour ago I had had a husband, a marriage.

A telephone rang, somewhere far away, in someone else's life. It rang and rang, and just as I came to the realization that it was my phone, by the side of the bed, the ringing stopped. I had fallen into another deep sleep when it rang again and I started up, reaching my hand out blindly.

I knocked over several objects on the bedside table; the clock, a glass—and bottles. One still contained liquid. I could hear it glopping and shooshing onto the carpet. I didn't bother to pick it up.

Into the receiver I said, "Hello . . ." hoarsely, hopefully, for memory was returning with a rush. It had to be Keir.

It was Beth.

"Sally?" she said, and there was a strange, constrained note to her voice. "I . . . I've heard from Erica, Sally— about Keir." A pause. "Sal? I had to ring to see . . ." Again she paused. My pal Beth. "Are you okay, Sally?"

I tried to talk, but couldn't. I was shaking too much; my body didn't seem to belong to me at all. It was more than weeping, it was paroxysms of sobbing that robbed me of all movement, of all thought except that *Beth knew*. And I had to say something, speak of what had happened, announce the facts. And when I told her, I would have to acknowledge the truth to myself at the same time. But it was impossible. No sound came from my mouth and my frozen limbs could barely cope with holding the receiver to my ear.

Beth said, "Stay there. I'm coming over. *Now.*"

And she hung up.

My head hurt. There were two bottles of champagne that testified to the cause, one prone on the bedside table, the other on the floor. Tissues scattered the bed like a heavy fall of snow, all damp with the outflows from eyes and nose. Across the room, despite the dimness of the drawn shades, I could see myself, when I sat up, reflected in the dressing-table mirror. I hadn't changed my dress from the night before. Above my string of pearls my face was white and puff-eyed, like a body that had been underwater for several days.

Minutes went by and I calmed. Beth was coming. It was an incentive, and I stood and tried to tidy myself a little. I changed into another dress, and brushed my teeth and splashed my face with cold water. I didn't bother with makeup. You'd have to have a practiced hand with painting corpses to do anything with this face.

I grimly contemplated my reflection in the bathroom mirror. I pulled back my hair and looked at the white lines of scars about my ears and up into my hairline. Even the faint, faint lines under my eyebrows were visible this morning. You should see me, Keir, all your good work wasted.

And I allowed myself to wonder, for the first time, what I would have looked like, today, without Keir's cosmetic surgery. Would I look like Aunty Shirley? Or Aunt Miriam? No, all my aunts were fat. With or without Keir I would never have allowed myself to get fat. Maybe I'd look like Uncle Ira . . .

When I was young I wouldn't have been taken for Erica Tudor's sister as I had been yesterday. I had chosen this face. That was the irony of the situation. Keir had always indulged me in cosmetically improving my looks and, brilliant surgeon that he was, he had given me the face that I'd always wanted, my idea of beauty. He must have liked my creation: the blonded hair, the high cheekbones and rounded chin, the taut jaw, my perfectly straight pert nose. A few chemicals here, a few transplanted fat cells there. Clever Sally, clever Keir. And what did we create? The experimental model, the prototype, of Erica Tudor.

I bent over the bowl and vomited.

When I finished I straightened and looked at myself with hatred. "I hope you're pleased," I said. But the forty-two year-old woman in the mirror looked too sad and tired even to hate. The gray eyes gazed back at me with the impassivity of a goldfish looking out through a glass bowl.

The intercom buzzed.

When I opened the door to Beth she stepped inside and wordlessly held out her arms to me. We backed into the living room in a kind of tearful fandango, both speaking over the top of each other. I was trying to tell her what had happened and she was saying, "Honey . . . honey, I know. I got this this morning. She sent it by messenger."

She took an envelope, heavy, expensive lavender-colored stationery, and handed it to me.

Sit down. Read it," she said. "I'll make us coffee."

I pulled two sheets of fat paper from the envelope.

Dear Beth,

    This will come as a great surprise to you but I thought I should let you know immediately. I have fallen deeply in love for the first time in my life, with the most wonderful man I have ever known, and he returns my love.

    Normally, I would expect you to be thrilled for me—how often I talked over lunches about how I needed the stability of a long-term relationship, and how much I have always envied your wonderfully happy marriage to Malcolm. Please try to be happy for me.

I felt my gorge rising and swallowed hard several times. Even when she was genuinely moved she sounded like a cheap romance writer.

"You okay?" Beth appeared in the doorway.

"Yes. Still reading."

Beth disappeared.

Please try to be happy for me, even when you find that the name of this man is Keir Stanforth.

    I know that you are Sally Stanforth's coworker and friend and this must place you in a difficult position. I have wanted to tell you sooner—for I regard you as my friend, also, and it's been hard keeping my happiness to myself. Keir and I have been meeting clandestinely in New York for eight months now. As of last night, Keir told Sally of his love for me and left their apartment. He is now with me in New Hampshire.

"No!" I cried out.

Beth came back into the room.

We will stay here or in a hotel in New York (address to follow) until the divorce, when we will marry.

Beth, I would hate to lose you as an editor. We have had such a warm rapport and profitable results from our association. I hope you can remain friends with Sally and with me.

Fondly, believing in your understanding,

ERICA

"Are you?" I shot the question at Beth.

"Am I what?" She'd been gazing at me worriedly, and now looked startled.

"Can you remain friends with Erica Tudor and with me?"

"I'm not her friend, Sally. After all these years I don't think I know Erica any better than on the first day I met her. What do you say we have that coffee—you look like you need it bad." I followed her down the hall to the kitchen. I think the pause gave Beth time to phrase her reply. For I knew what she would say, what she *had* to say. I sat numbly at my own kitchen table while Beth poured the coffees.

"It's just business, honey. You know that. Sure I could say, 'I won't edit your books anymore.' But Sammy would give her another editor—hell, he'd get up off his ass and edit her work himself if it meant keeping her." Beth had sat down opposite me and now fixed her gaze upon me. "But he wouldn't keep her."

I nodded tiredly. "She'd get her revenge by going to another publisher. Erica's only offering a choice in a mood of nobility—or what she sees as nobility. It's really a test." I looked up at Beth. "A test to see if she can trust you. You can't refuse, Beth, I know that."

Beth's eyes filled with angry tears. "I wish this wasn't happening, Sally. God, I wish this wasn't happening as much as you do!"

"It's okay, Beth. Really."

Beth stood and came around the table and we embraced. I felt no bitterness towards her. She had no choice.

Beth insisted on making lunch for us both. I took a couple of aspirin with my meal. I was calmer, now, though my head still felt fuzzy. Knowing someone else knew, understood, was helping me more than I had thought.

"And don't worry about Sammy," Beth was saying. "I've already told him the basic facts. He said for you to take as much time off as you like." Her eyes sparkled. "But he suggested you take Ann Varvison's manuscript with you."

"Take it with me?" I murmured. It hadn't occurred to me to *go* anywhere. But I looked around the kitchen, and I thought of the large, empty rooms that lay beyond . . .

"I might," I said. "I'd like to get out of the apartment for a while. Move into a hotel, maybe."

"A busy one," Beth said. "Spend his money—he's got enough of it."

"Yes, I will go to a hotel," I said, with growing determination. "I'll disappear for a few days—let him come look for me. So what if he worries? So let him worry. What's he done to *me*, Beth?" And to my chagrin the tears were close once again. "What's he done to *me*, leaving me like this after nineteen years of happy marriage? I could be floating in the East River even now for all he knows. The bastard!"

"Good, you're getting angry. That's *good.*" Beth stood and fetched a box of nearby tissues and put them in front of me. "Keir knows you're strong, Sally. He knows you wouldn't do something like that."

And, as she seated herself again, "Sally, I'm as surprised as you are about this. It's just . . . not like Keir. An *affair*— it's got to be temporary. A midlife crisis on his part. You guys were too happy, too close, for Erica to come between you permanently. She couldn't replace all those years you had together—she's not a giving person, like you. She's too self-conscious, too insecure for a man as complex as

Keir. If it hadn't been for you, Sally, he'd be with wife number four by now, like the rest of his siblings."

I had to smile, I even laughed, despite myself. The Stanforths—the younger generation of Keir's brothers and sisters anyway—were a restless lot. His sister Katherine, a year older than Keir and closest to him, was about to marry what would be her third husband.

Katherine's never satisfied, Keir had said when she'd divorced, his own satisfaction evident in his voice, in his eyes as he looked at me. Only . . . a year ago. By the fire at our cabin in Beaver Creek. *Before he met Erica.*

Suddenly remembering Erica's remark about Keir's and my sex life, yet not wanting to admit this to Beth, I said, "Maybe . . . it was all meant to happen. Maybe we were growing apart without me knowing it. You can get used to each other, get into a rut. And . . . maybe he's changed his mind about having babies."

Beth had three beautiful children whom she adored. This hit home for Beth and she said in a low growl, "Catch my Malcolm telling *me* we wouldn't have babies. You should have just gone ahead and had that operation to clear your fallopian tubes—gone to Europe to have it done and come home and had his baby willy-nilly. It's your *right,* girl!"

Beth always made me feel better. Beth could always make me smile. "It wouldn't have been honest," I said.

"Honey, this is *marriage* we're talking about here. There is such a thing as being *too* honest."

I pondered the horrible possibility that Keir had, secretly, changed his mind only recently, and wanted Erica because she was the right age for them to have children.

"Keir is forty-three," I said. "Time's not running out biologically for him like it is for me, and he is a little vain. He'd want to be able to make a reasonable showing when his son challenged him to a set of tennis."

His son. Keir's son.

We had been married five years when I had finally succeeded in persuading Keir into fatherhood. But a year passed and there was no baby. So I went to Keir's gynecologist friend, Jeremy Camberwell, and had tests. All those years on the pill and for nothing. My fallopian tubes were as tightly closed against my monthly descending egg as if I'd had my tubes tied at puberty.

"Tell Keir," Jeremy had said. "I think I can clear them without much trouble. But tell him what you want, Sally."

I had told Keir, and he had said no, he'd changed his mind. I'd pleaded, he'd remained quietly adamant. There was room in his life for only two things, his work, primarily in reconstructive surgery with only occasional cosmetic work, and me. He reminded me that I'd continued working as an editor because he was home so seldom. And he was right, there. He would never have had the time to be a really good dad. But I'd have been a really great mom. It had been a sadness for me but one which I'd filled with Keir and work. And now, with Keir gone, I'd have had something, *someone* to remind me of those years. I could see myself ringing some exclusive girls' school in Virginia and screaming down the line, "Pussycat? It's Momma— do you know what your father has *done?!*" Pussycat would have sorted him out. Anyone with a bloodline the likes of the New York Stanforths and the Brooklyn Feldmans would be formidable.

Beth was saying, "Why not get right away, go on up to the Cape for a week or so? Reading Ann's manuscript will help take your mind off waiting for Keir to come to his senses."

Maybe Beth was right. I didn't know where I was going, but work might be the best antidote to the long hours of the night asking *why?*

Before she left, Beth asked if I'd like to come to her place to stay, rather than a hotel. She has a lovely house which she shares with her music-teacher husband, Malcolm, their two sons and baby daughter, and two cats. But I didn't trust myself, my own emotions, not to break down, make an idiot of myself, make that whole loving household miserable with my presence. So I thanked Beth, but said no.

I had to be alone, to sort out my confused thoughts; I had to find out where my marriage had gone wrong.

And no matter what happened, I vowed to myself as I packed my belongings after Beth had left, no matter what lay in the future, I would not let Keir see me break down again.

I packed too much luggage, but each time I looked around the apartment, I had a strong presentiment that I wouldn't see it again for a long time. Had he brought her here, I wondered, on the Wednesdays when he usually played golf? Had they played here, instead, their own games?

I booked into the Marlborough Regency, just down the street, for the few days I thought I'd need. The old hotel had a warm atmosphere that just might help me decide what the hell I would do next. The following day I called in to the office and collected Ann Varvison's manuscript, *Blood Will Tell*. But I couldn't work on it, didn't even glance at the first page. I was barely functioning. I spent seven days in that hotel room. Seven lost days.

I thought only about Keir. I spent hours with my comfortable armchair pulled up to the window, studying this city that I loved so much, the bustle of the days, the lights at night, the sleepy awakenings when even New York seemed fresh, reborn.

I realized I had taken my old life too much for granted. There must have been changes happening, within Keir, within our relationship, that were so subtle that I couldn't see them. Or had I chosen to ignore them, because it was more comfortable to do so?

I didn't know. I only knew that I loved him, had never stopped loving him, had never been bored, resentful, could never even stay cross with him for more than a day. We always made up. We could see each other's point of view. We tried to give each other what we needed.

So what went wrong?

It bothered me, Erica claiming that Keir and I hardly ever made love. So okay, it wasn't as frequent as in the first years, but it was tender, passionate and ... once a fortnight, once every three weeks. Is that bad? Is that the sign of a bad marriage?

And—okay, maybe lately it had been once a month or so. But that was *lately*. How could we make love as often, I thought viciously, when he was taking matinees to sleep with Erica, make love with Erica, spend all his spare time and energy and passion *on Erica*.

I would come to myself with my nails pressed into my palms, sitting there by the window, and wish I'd brought Keir's revolver with me.

I fantasized about driving up to New Hampshire to find her house, seeing the look in her eyes as she opened the door and saw me pointing the deadly little barrel right at her face.

Surprised to *see* me? Why, sugar, she was just blown away.

I grew a little strange in those days at the hotel.

I kept expecting a call from my secretary, Serena, at Brambles Thorne; should Keir ring, I'd instructed her she was not to tell him where I was but to phone me immediately. She was an efficient woman, Serena, and discreet. But three days passed, and four, and the phone rang only with queries regarding my writers, or calls from Beth to find out how I was feeling.

I was beginning to be afraid. Surely three days was enough for him to see that he belonged back home, with me. Where was he?

At times of utter despair I'd try to comfort myself with the thought that I had only Erica's word, in her letter to Beth, that Keir was with her. What if she'd been lying, indulging in wishful thinking? Perhaps Keir, too, was languishing alone in a hotel room high above Central Park, knowing what a mistake he'd made, wondering how he could come home.

I phoned his office, finally, feeling sick with anticipation, hearing, or imagining I heard, guarded coolness in the accents of the receptionist when she recognized my voice. I didn't, mercifully, have long to wait.

"Sally? Where have you been? I've been frantic with worry!"

My emotions spilled over, relief, joy . . . "Keir, I'm sorry . . . I just had to get away . . ."

"Where are you now?"

"At the Marlborough Regency, I've been here all along. Keir, you could have left a message with Serena—I'd have called you . . ."

"I only spoke to the receptionist. I didn't want to leave my name. Too many people at Brambles Thorne must be gossiping about us without a joke going around that I can't find my own wife."

"You should have thought of that earlier. Do you realize how you've compromised our careers? Mine, Beth's—even Erica's when the press . . ."

"Oh, God, we've got to keep it out of the hands of the press . . ."

"Then come home."

There was a silence. Then, "I don't . . . I don't know if I'm ever going to be able to come home again. I've decided to let you have the apartment, Sally. I've been back and moved out all my things. I've left the furniture, except for the Art Deco I collected—and the paintings—just a few special pieces you wouldn't—"

"Moved them out? Out where? *Out where?*"

"Up to Erica's place in New Hampshire, just for the time being. Your car's still in the garage, Sally, that's what frightened me. I would have thought you'd have taken it. I've got the Mercedes, I'll keep that. I've been to a lawyer, Sally, I've kept two million and given you the rest . . . I'd like to keep the cabin at Beaver Creek, but you can have it if you like. And the Paris apartment—do you want that?"

Erica's place in New Hampshire. I knew a little about it. I'd seen a picture spread in *Vogue*. Erica had dogs and horses and a groom and housekeeper and butler and two secretaries . . . Keir *had* been living in Erica's house. His clothes, his *few special pieces,* were in Erica's house.

"Sally? The Paris apartment . . ."

"How could you do that?" I could barely breathe. "How could you move everything you own from our home—to hers?"

His voice was gentle in the silence. "Sally . . . darling . . . there is no 'home' any more. We've changed too much. We have to move on."

We've changed too much.

I've changed too much. I was no longer twenty-five. I had become middle-aged.

"Then you lied," I said finally, "the night you left. You said you needed time alone, time to think. But it was a lie. Erica was the one who told me the truth. She said you wanted a divorce, that you wanted to marry her. Is that the truth?"

"I don't know what I want! Christ! Do you think I don't know what you're going through? What I'm putting you through? I want it to be over—as quickly as possible, to cause you the least pain . . ."

Keir, ever the surgeon. "Finest knife work in the country"—at a hospital function I had overheard another surgeon praising Keir when he wasn't listening. How proud I'd been.

Finest knife work in the country.

Quick and clean.

Very little blood. Nice, Stanforth. Very nice.

I don't remember replacing the receiver.

I packed my bags and took a cab the short distance to the apartment. I went to the garage, not up to the apartment itself. I couldn't bear to see it. There would be great spaces of white wall where his Few Special Pieces had stood or hung for most of our married life. There were too many spaces within me already. My whole psyche was reverberating, like an empty room, an abandoned place.

My car was in its usual space, a neat little two-year-old Volvo, comfortable and small enough to park easily on New York streets. I piled my bags into the trunk and drove out of the garage of that luxury apartment block for the last time, headed for East River Drive.

It was Friday. He would take the Mercedes—possibly with Erica in it, if they were together in New York—and drive to New Hampshire. I would take my time, have a leisurely dinner somewhere en route.

For I knew where Erica Tudor lived, had known ever since that first enormous advance for *Traces of Heaven* had paid for the house. Beth had shown me photos that Erica had sent her, of a big blue-gray clapboard farmhouse on a hill. "It's just west of a town called Meadowsweet—isn't that cute?" Beth had enthused. I had studied the photographs with interest, and agreed. I had even thought that perhaps Keir and I might one day get a country house. I'd always liked the idea of living in the country. Somehow weekends in Colorado weren't the same thing.

And since then, of course, there'd been so many photographs of the house, interiors and exteriors, in nearly every interview that Erica gave to the press. I would know it when I saw it, though I didn't know the exact address. Just west of Meadowsweet. East of Eden. North of hell.

Why didn't I think to bring the gun? I should have brought the gun. Nothing like a gun to let people know the seriousness of your intentions. *What, this little thing? Just ignore it, let's talk business here.*

Yeah.

Chapter Three

I drove competently enough, and with part of my brain this surprised me. I was, in so many ways, coping very well, I congratulated myself. After all, seven days ago I had had a life: a husband, a home, a future. Now my world had contracted to the interior of this little Volvo and the contents of two suitcases and an overnight bag. The future was this highway, heading . . .

Where? To confront my husband and his mistress; to reclaim what had been taken from me. So this was a voyage as much towards my past as towards my future.

Even the car journey northwards.

I had been sixteen, seated beside Uncle Zachary, so nervous that it was hard to keep still in the deep leather seat of his old Bentley. This was 1969 and the Bentley was already embarrassingly old to Geoff, my brother, and me. All our friends' parents drove Caddies and Chevies. Yet here we were, anyway, on our way to Maine, all three of us in the front seat, me next to Zachary, and Geoff on the window side. Our bags were in the trunk; mine were filled with a complete new summer wardrobe, dresses in the latest "empire" line, in all the colors of sugared almonds, delicate materials that were reminiscent of Zeffirelli's *Romeo and Juliet.*

We had often visited the Fifth Avenue apartment of Zachary's partner, Dr. Roger Barton, but this was the first time we'd been to the Bartons' summer residence in Maine—a big house by the sea—and we were to stay for two weeks.

We usually went to Florida for six weeks, and to separate summer camps for the rest of the holidays. That is, Geoff and I did; Zachary returned to New York and his vital work in cardiac surgery. Uncle Zachary, who seemed as old to Geoff and me as the Bentley did in car years, could not have been more than fifty, then. He, in turn, had elderly uncles and aunts, and although, strictly speaking, they were our relatives too, they seemed removed in a very real sense of the word. They were all frail, critical, and had large, very white teeth which they showed in most disagreeable smiles when they weren't telling Geoff and me disagreeable things.

From the time of our earliest memories of Florida, we were told to speak up, be quiet, pay attention, keep out from underfoot, to stop eavesdropping, to listen when we were spoken to. Aunt Lou kept cats and her condo always smelt of their urine. Uncle Gus dribbled when he talked about the War. We hated listening to Uncle Gus's stories. We knew what had happened to our grandfather, to other aunts and uncles. We remembered as much as we could bear. But it was like the stories of vampires and werewolves and the fears that came in the night. It was best not to think too hard on these things. Even today, news footage, a conversation, brings nightmares.

Our parents had died violently, too. Not in the vortex that had swept over Europe, but right here in the USA, in a plane crash en route to L.A. It was to have been their first holiday alone together since their honeymoon. I was three and Geoff was seven.

Florida, of course, meant more than elderly relatives and bad memories. Florida meant the beach, and boating and fishing and long mellow evenings strolling on the boardwalk eating ice cream. Florida was Uncle Zachary, no longer in pinstriped suit but in bright shirts and baggy shorts, from which his thin white legs protruded like the limbs of figures I made at school from pipe cleaners.

On that trip north to Maine and the beckoning, mysterious house called Seahaven, I felt very grown-up, very mature. I only hoped Geoff wouldn't spoil it by calling me Minnie Mouse—an allusion to my school uniform's black stockings—in front of any boys.

Like Geoff, I'd attended P.S. 91 until eighth grade, when we'd both gone on to boarding schools in Connecticut. It had been reading and swapping magazines with the other girls that had enabled me to gain the knowledge to choose the wardrobe Uncle Zachary had provided, and my hair had been cut in the latest "helmet" style, fitting close to the head and suiting my thick, straight, dark-brown hair and the rather round little face underneath it. I would not disgrace myself in my looks nor, I hoped, in my behavior. But would that be enough? Uncle Zachary had assured Geoff and me that as well as Roger's two children, Brett and Sandra, there would be many other young people our age at the estate.

"Jews?" Geoff had asked. His Jewishness had always been more pronounced than mine, even than Zachary's.

"Perhaps," Uncle Zachary had answered. "What difference does it make? These are *people*. Are you looking for a wife already?"

Jewish or gentile, I didn't care. These two weeks meant, for me, a wonderful possibility. *Boys.*

Attending the Cherryvale Stables Academy, the only time we girls mixed with boys was three times a year at the school dances, when we mingled embarrassedly with the students of Fairbairn Military School. Geoff attended this establishment and for years had avoided me when the two schools met. But lately we had found a favorable benefit in being related. Until I was fifteen I was interested only in horses. When I began to find boys interesting I realized also that my brother not only was one, but had friends who were often very cute indeed. And Geoff found benefits to my existence also: I was one of those outgoing, confident kids who noticed everything about everyone. I was therefore a walking encyclopedia on the senior girls of my school.

A year later, Geoff had his first real love affair—that's what he called it—with a senior from Cherryvale. He'd just graduated and I knew his silence in the car as we drove northwards was because he was thinking of Dee Samuels and composing letters in his imagination.

I tried to regard these two weeks as Geoff did, at worst, a temporary setback in our normal year's timetable. But I couldn't suppress my high hopes: would Brett and Sandra be friendly? Would there be a boy there who would find me pretty? Would I discover romance for the first time? I tried not to indulge in daydreams, but they crowded in on me as I sat between my brother and uncle on that trip north. A boy, with blue eyes and sun-bleached hair rose from the sea like a Greek god to pause and smile at me— me, Sarah Elaine Rebecca Feldman, as I stood on the beach in my pale-blue Juliet dress of spotted voile, its frail fabric pressed back against my body by the wind from the sea and floating behind me like a cloud, a wave . . .

Then would follow long walks hand-in-hand, along the beaches, through the deep green woods, long kisses stolen under the moon while we could hear, far away, from a window of the house, someone playing Chopin on the concert grand.

Life so very rarely measures up to one's expectations, and how often does life measure up to the expectations of a teenager? Yet on the second day of my stay at Seahaven I had my wish. I came out of my room and was walking towards the stairs when Keir Stanforth came abruptly through the doorway that led to the library, and into my life.

We kept walking towards the stairs, and all the while glancing at each other awkwardly, quickly; long enough for me to realize, with heart-stopping clarity, how handsome he was.

"I'm Keir Stanforth. You'd know my sister Katherine."

"Of course."

Of course. You would have to be the wonderful brother of pretty, dark-haired Katherine with the knowing black eyes and the supercilious smile. Katherine who shared my room and fingered my clothes between thumb and forefinger and made comments about girls who slavishly follow Carnaby Street trends.

Keir was standing with one foot on the top stair and leaning back against the wall to regard me, his head on one side a little. "What's your name?"

"Sarah Feldman," I managed.

"Sarah," he smiled. "Do they call you Sally? Can I call you Sally?"

Why was this beautiful boy poised on the stairs talking to me? *Me.* I didn't know where to look, and had an excuse, in the next moment, with the sound of low thunder outside. I looked down towards the open door and saw the view of the lawn and path was dulled, as if leached of color, and the lavender bushes by the door were being tossed by more than mere breeze, it was a wind that preluded a storm. Already one of the maids was coming briskly along the hall. She closed the front doors and returned towards the back of the house.

The hall was darker, more intimate. I looked back at Keir, and his gaze was still upon me. Oh, the perfection of that face, even there in the gloom of the wide upper hall. And what made it astonishing—what never, through the years, ceased to astonish me—was that he seemed so unaware of his attractiveness.

He was so close. So close to me, this perfect boy. His features sobered, and he studied my face, then moved back a little. "Well?" he said, for he must, by now, have noticed my silence, my painful blushing. "Can I call you Sally?"

"Yes," I said.

I thought that when all the cousins and friends returned

from their outings he would forget me. I was prepared for it. We were sitting on the broad porch, watching the sun struggle through the grey clouds, when the girls came back from sailing. They huddled around us, damp and happily breathless and smelling of salt and clean skin, and laughed up at Keir with their perfect smiles. And the boys—including Geoff—returned from the pool. And still Keir sat beside me, and included me in whatever conversation was made.

The following day was fine and hot and we all swam in the sea. All the families came, running down from the house to the beach; all of us, smaller siblings and most of the grown-ups, running over the tufted dunes, squealing, laughing, and Keir was beside me, Keir took my hand. We splashed into the water, and still Keir held my hand.

The group accepted me, then, with surprising ease. There were small snipings of jealousy from one or two of the other girls—Katherine herself behaved with good grace, and Keir's mother smiled upon me, albeit a little tightly. For Keir and I were accepted, as were so many other young couples, as Going Steady. Just for those magical nine days. It was transient, it was innocent, it was unforgettable.

We wrote to each other, Keir and I. Once a week, at first, then the letters were crossing, then we'd stopped counting. When Zachary, Geoff, and I returned to Seahaven, Keir was seated on the stone wall by the big iron gates, waiting.

He was even taller, and had filled out more, no longer an awkward boy but a confident, mature-looking med student at Harvard. Geoff, gallantly, seeing Keir spring down from the wall on sighting the ancient Bentley, gave up the front seat and sprawled in the back, his large feet against the window ledge. Keir scrambled into the front seat to sit beside me.

Nothing had changed, I saw, as he gazed at me, then

said a warm hello to Zachary, calling him Sir, greeted Geoff in the backseat—and turned to gaze at me once more.

That was the summer I dared to say to myself *I think he loves me.* That was the summer that he told me so himself.

I returned almost every summer to Seahaven for five years. The only year I missed was 1971. Uncle Zachary and I stayed in New York that summer, waiting for them to send Geoff's body home from Vietnam.

I had to pull the car over to the side of the road; overtaken with a renewed sense of loss, from which I had never really recovered.

Zachary had stoically refused to show his grief, but something went out of him, his humor, his very interest in life, when Geoff died. Never a large man, he seemed to shrink still further, until he seemed a small, wizened shell of himself. Only a few years later, expert heart surgeon that he was, his own heart failed him. I don't think he fought very hard, at the end, to stay alive.

Only I remained. Alone. But Keir was close. Through years of medical training he had had to harden himself to the fragility of life, the unfairness of death, but he nevertheless always *understood.* He who had never lost anyone close to him still possessed that empathy of spirit that went beyond his grieving for a close friend, when the sniper's bullet had taken Geoff. Then, and over the years when I would break down with the memory, with my grieving, it was Keir's arms about me, Keir's words of comfort spoken softly against my ear, Keir's presence my only real solace for the remembrance of the horror of my brother's death, for the empty place Geoff left behind.

Sitting there in my car, rocked slightly by the roaring passage of passing cars and trucks, I realized what had affected me most over the past days since Keir had left me: except for brief conversations with Beth or my secretary I had hardly spoken to a soul. Certainly I had no one to whom I could unburden my rage, my fear, my grief. Even with Beth I had held back; she had been distressed enough.

And my sense of loss plummeted to new and darker depths with the realization that the only human being with whom I had ever felt safe enough, comfortable enough, loved enough, to unburden my soul, lay bare my fragile psyche, was Keir. Keir who had held me when I had cried, as a girl, for Geoff; who had been my strength and comfort through Zachary's illness and death; Keir who, since that first moment on the stairs at Seahaven, had been my best friend. It had been Keir, all my adult life, who had always been there for me, willing to be put out, bored, railed at, wept upon; gazing at me always with loving tenderness that told me, even without words, that I was the most important person in his life.

And now it was Keir who was wounding me, his love turned to a kind of dispassionate pity.

The sense of betrayal twisted like a knife blade within me. I tried to find some instance of his growing impatience, boredom, displeasure—each time failing to find anything but his fondness, his affection.

And this road north was so filled with memories, the returning visits every year or so to stay at Seahaven: we had stopped at this gas station, had eaten at that truckers' restaurant, had stopped by this bridge on a warm spring day and walked for two miles beneath the willows.

There were worse thoughts even than this—and whoever it was who said that the worst was remembering the best at a bad moment was so very right—for I realized that this was the first time I'd taken this road alone.

No, I must have driven north like this by myself. Hadn't I? I had to think, really consider. No, I hadn't. On the roads that led to Maine I had always been with Keir, and he had done most of the driving. I liked to be free to look at the scenery, to fiddle with the knobs of the radio, to change cassettes or CDs. And to hold Keir's hand.

We always drove like that, I thought now, with a lost sense of wonderment, on all long-distance trips; on the open road Keir drove with his left hand on the wheel and his right hand enclosing mine. It was second nature to us; we found comfort, in those long hours of driving, with that physical connection between us.

Did he drive to New Hampshire with Erica Tudor's hand in his? Needing the contact of *her* skin against his, as he had once needed mine?

I tried to tell myself, to inform myself coolly, brutally, that he no longer needed any closeness between us, not emotionally, let alone physically.

But this was impossible. *Impossible.* He was *my Keir.* I couldn't ever remember wanting or needing the touch, the *feel* of another human being other than Keir. It had been Keir from the first.

But for him? What else had he needed, and why didn't he ask? We could talk about anything, everything—but this. How could he change so much? How could he come to need Erica so wholly, so completely, until there was no longer any room for me?

What had I done, that he could cease to love me?

And how could I not notice that it was happening?

Chapter Four

I stopped in Hartford and made myself eat something—I think it was fish—in a small cafe, with tables set out under a vine-covered pergola. I do remember that there was a view of a park, and several children were floating boats upon a pond.

It made me think, with a start, *who gets custody of the Flotilla?* Every spring we bought a new model boat, Keir and I, every spring since we married, beginning with a little red child's yacht on whose stern Keir had painted *Sally,* and underneath, *NYYC.* From that year on, we had added to the fleet, becoming more and more high-tech as the years passed. Only a few months ago we had bought an imported remote-control submarine.

Will he go to the pond in Central Park with Erica?

Will he do all the things we loved to do together, with Erica?

What had she done to him? Keir and I had been so happy together. I hated her so much. I wouldn't have thought it possible to hate somebody so much.

Erica and me in Central Park, at the pond. I show Erica my new model ship, and she is polite, for she can afford to be: she has Keir.

Look, Erica. Look, look, look. See the new model ship. See it sail towards you across the pond. Sail, sail, sail. She is the biggest model ship in the world, and this is her maiden voyage. She is called the Titanic. *She is perfect in every detail, Erica, just like you. Perfect, perfect, perfect. See how she sails towards you, see the real smoke from her funnel. Pick her up out of the water, Erica. See, see, see. See Sally press a button.*

BOOM.

Titanic *blows up with all hands.*

Browsing in an antique shop I found a model ship, about ninety years old. Fragile, exquisite, too expensive, I nevertheless bought it. I somehow felt an affinity with the little vessel. Both of us dry-docked, earthbound. Not like the Flotilla.

Keir in a pair of old shorts, faded denim. He ran from one side of the pond to the other, long legs brown against the bright summer grass, white teeth flashed at me in frequent grins of communion. We would talk to other model boaters, many of them children. Keir, who never wanted his own but was so good with children. He let them steer the Flotilla, too. Kind Keir, generous with his toys. The boy in him.

Lying on the grass together, arms about each other, kissing, surreptitiously fumbling with each other's bodies when we thought we weren't being noticed. Like lovers, like teenagers. The boy in him.

Was he immature? We had grown up together, there was no way for me to judge either of us. When were we All Grown Up? When were we Mature Adults? Did we make it all the way?

Was Keir, with Erica, yearning backwards for his youth? That *would* be immature. That would be weak.

Keir, weak?

These were the thoughts that kept me company on that journey. Or was I trying to fault Keir, now that he had rejected me, because it was easier to let him go, if he were less worthy of me?

I found a growing sense of trepidation, the closer I came to the moment when I'd confront Keir and his mistress. I scolded myself for postponing the moment but used my tiredness as an excuse and spent the night in Hartford. In my exhaustion I managed to sleep, and that night I had a vivid dream.

I lived at Seahaven. Seahaven as it had been. Lived there alone amidst its beauty and its peace. The gardens, in the dream, were even more lush than they had been in reality, lavish to the point of being almost tropical.

Keir came, one day. He drove up in his white Mercedes and asked to see Geoff's toys.

This made perfect sense. I led him up the narrow stairs to the attic and there were all our toys, Geoff's and mine. The room looked like a Christmas display at F.A.O. Schwarz.

Keir, in the dream, behaved as if we'd never met. In the dream I loved him, but he seemed out of my reach, a handsome stranger. I wanted to say, *Remember me? I'm Sally.* But a kind of shyness held me back.

"I'd like to buy the toys," Keir said, "for my sons."

I felt my heart sink. He had sons . . . And then I remembered Erica. Dear God, he'd married Erica. *They had sons.*

Keir moved to the little attic window and called down, "Darling, bring the children in to see the toys!"

I moved to stand beside him. Outside and below the window I could see the garden and the drive. From the Mercedes a beautiful woman emerged. She was pregnant. From the passenger doors at the rear two boys aged about seven tumbled out and ran laughing up the path.

Erica stood in the garden, raised her lovely head, and blew a kiss.

I looked at Keir, so close beside me. He smiled down at her with such love on his face.

I woke, sobbing dryly. My chest hurt, my grief a physical thing.

The dream stayed with me all the next day. Then I took my laptop out into the little courtyard garden behind the old coaching inn where I was staying, and sat down with my back to the warm sunshine and wrote:

> *Man with family comes to sale of deceased estate because of vintage toys. He's a collector. Finds house belongs to his former teenage love. Inside the house, belonging to her late brother, are toys the man remembers from his own childhood.*

I paused. What was the name of the central character? He was a doctor, a famous pediatrician called (this took half an hour of wordplay) Piers Danforth.

> *Piers had been best friends with (another name search) Scott. Piers had fallen in love with Scott's younger sister, Deborah. When Scott is killed in Vietnam, her family move to a different part of Maine arid Piers and Deborah lose touch. Piers is married with two little boys. Deborah is a writer who has never really forgotten him. Tell their story in flashback!*

I finished with an almost triumphant flourish of keys.

It was quite cold. I hadn't noticed the sun retreating behind the roof of the inn, the growing chill. While I hadn't written much, I'd been sitting here for two hours or more, thinking, planning. The dream, of course, had begun it. A story was now running through my imagination like a film across a screen. I was about to turn off the laptop when I had a last, sudden inspiration.

I scrolled back to the beginning of the text and wrote, very bold,

SCOTTY'S THINGS

and beneath that I wrote,

A NOVEL BY SARAH FELDMAN.

Insulated within the little Volvo, I meandered around Connecticut in the rain. Unable to bear thoughts of Keir-and-Erica, Erica-and-Keir, I was thinking of those far-off years at Cherryvale Academy, the dances with the boys from Fairbairn Military School. And I cried anew; for me, and for Geoff, and for Uncle Zachary, and for my parents. I would have liked to have my parents around today. I missed them, the serious, gentle blur that was all I remembered of my father, the perfumed dream that was my mother. But mostly I missed Geoff, and Zachary, who had died when I was twenty-four, his obituary printed in *Time* magazine, and mourned not only by the medical fraternity across the country, but by the hundreds whose lives he had saved. I cried for them all, selfishly, for I needed them. I needed someone to run to, and they were all gone, my parents, Geoff, Zachary—and Keir.

I must have been driving faster than I thought, for it seemed only a short time before I'd crossed both state lines and found the turnoff: *To Meadowsweet.* Less than a mile west of the little town—there it was, up on a rise to my left, appearing so suddenly that if I hadn't glanced that way I might have missed it.

The soft blue-gray of the painted timbers, the white-painted shutters, looked comfortable in the dusk. Only the downstairs lights were on. Even from this distance I could tell that the curtains were a warm apricot pink, the light behind them, through the square panes of the windows, glowed cosily. It was the kind of sight that drew one, even a stranger passing on the road would have slowed to admire it.

But for me there was only bitterness. This picture of old-fashioned charm and hospitality was built on deceit, on corruption. The two people at the heart of that house were living a lie, living a life that had been built upon my pain. It was not honest. It was not *right*.

I had turned the car into the driveway, and parked before the large, electronically locked metal gates. I had turned off the engine without realizing I had done so, and now sat gazing at the house. To enter the property I would have to press the intercom button and announce myself.

This is Sally Stanforth. I've come to collect my husband.

It began to rain once more. It made me feel even worse, the streaming windshield before me blurring the storybook home, washing it away to a few lights in the watery dusk. By now my grief was beyond tears but the skies wept for me. I couldn't bring myself to turn on the windshield wipers, for it was better, I decided, like this. The distance, the gathering night, the waterfall down the glass before me, all served to isolate me from Keir and his new life.

That was the moment. The physical barriers between us were suddenly more, so much more, than a windshield, a gate, a driveway, a rainy night. Like the indistinguishable shapes of light before me, unrecognizable, now, as well-lit rooms, Keir had blurred, become unrecognizable in my mind. Whoever had done this thing, whoever had hurt me so deeply, scarring me, I knew, for the rest of my life, it was not Keir. Not *my* Keir, the man I had loved and married. Somewhere in the past year, so subtly I had not seen the metamorphosis, he had changed into a stranger. A stranger who could leave his wife and twenty-five years of shared past, to run off with a woman almost half his age.

Where was Keir—*my Keir?* And where was the woman who had lost him?

The affair had been going on for *eight months.* How could I not notice? We were so close; he never spent a night away from me.

So he made love to Erica in moments snatched between his work—and his time with me.

How could I not notice that his thoughts, his feelings, were with someone else?

Outside the Volvo, the rain turned to sleet, and I remembered . . .

The warmth of our cabin on vacation last February. Our days were spent skiing, tobogganing. *Keir was happy.*

We made love—

Only once, okay. Only once in two weeks. And afterwards . . .

Afterwards I slept, and woke to find him gone from the bed beside me. I found him wrapped in overcoat and cap and scarf, standing on the balcony, in the cold clear night, looking at the stars.

I'd said, "What are you doing, darling? What are you thinking?" I wasn't worried, understand. Just concerned. He wasn't often moody, wasn't often low in spirits.

"Thinking how small we are," he'd answered me. "How little choice we really have in the scheme of things. How hard it is to be happy."

I'd taken his arm gently, but remained silent. There was very little to say to console him without sounding trite. So I remained silent. I thought I was Communing with him. On some Deep Level. I thought he knew that I Supported Him.

But he hadn't turned to look at me. I held his arm and pressed my body close to his but—and I see it now—Keir remained alone.

The next day he went for a long walk in the forest by himself.

He went for a lot of long walks in those two weeks.
I didn't notice.
I didn't mind.

I started the car and backed out of Erica's driveway. I headed back through Meadowsweet and, once on the highway again, I turned north; not south, towards New York, but north, towards Maine. I would begin at the beginning, I thought. It had been twenty years since that last summer I had spent with the Bartons. By then I was engaged to Keir. We had visited a few times, in summers since, but never for more than a few days, and that, seven or eight years ago. Roger had died, and the family was scattered.

But I felt I had to see Seahaven. I needed to touch the

past. I needed its comfort, and perhaps only then would I discover what had gone wrong.

I spent the night in Green Bluffs, and I felt like a stranger, for there were high-rises—in *Green Bluffs*. And there were more houses, many more than I had ever seen or expected to see. There were houses, too, all along what had been the narrow country road leading north from the village to the Seahaven estate. Only now the road was no longer narrow but wide, and it was tarred and guttered. And at the very end . . .

The gates were still there, but the trees beyond, on the property itself, were gone. I could see the ocean, and one could never, in previous years, have seen the ocean for the forest of beech and larch and pine that crowded either side of the long drive.

There were houses here, too. I could see them, huge brick and clapboard mansions almost as large as the old house had been. I strained my eyes to see down the hill, but in amongst the park-like lawns, the tarred road, and what looked like warehouses down by the shore, I could see no sign of the sprawling white clapboard house.

And here, against the stone wall, where Keir had once waited for me, was a sign: SEAHAVEN ESTATE.

I climbed out of the car and went to stand in front of the sign. Underneath Seahaven Estate, it said: COUNTRY MANSIONS AND CONDOMINIUMS. YOUR PRIVATE PIECE OF MAINE. And below the words was a map, a colorful and highly stylized cartoon map of cartoon roads and houses, each with its own little patch of green. I half expected one of the little doors to open and Porky Pig to come out and stand upon his stoop, or to see Mickey Mouse mowing one of the flat green lawns.

I noticed a boom gate had been constructed, just inside the wrought-iron gates, level with the little stone gatehouse that had always been empty. The gates, well-oiled, never left open at any time during my years of coming here, were wide open, and looked as if they now stayed that way. Someone was approaching from the gatehouse.

"Can I help you?" the man asked cheerfully. He wore a suit and a little name tag that said *Seahaven Estate*, and beneath it, the word *Ken*.

"I. . . I used to stay here, I knew the former owners," I managed.

"The Bartons?" He seemed delighted. "Mrs. Barton, that's Dr. Barton's widow, still lives here. She has the place down the slope there, with the green shutters, closest to the water. Bayhaven, it's called. She's not there at the present, though."

"I haven't seen her for some years. I hadn't realized she'd sold the place."

"Sold it five years ago." Ken looked mighty pleased about it.

I was noticing, now the trees had gone, that I could see no sign of the old house at all. "There's nothing left of the old house," I said.

"Oh, you mustn't say that," said Ken with gentle reproof. "The name lives on, as you see." He waved an arm expansively at the Loony Tunes map.

"But the house itself—"

"Dry rot." Ken's voice suddenly serious. "Under the paint it was rotten. It wasn't worth saving. And the design, you must admit, was of no real architectural interest."

"No . . ." Wistfully.

"Quite a, well, an ugly house, really. No style. Just an overgrown weekender."

An overgrown weekender.

"It was a practical house," I defended it. Found I had to defend it. "And inside it was magnificent."

"Well, yes, as you say, and you'll be glad to hear this." Ken was grinning, happy again, warming to his subject. "You'd know the house very well, of course —"

"Of course."

"Well, some of the woodwork was salvageable—the panelling in the library."

"It was cedar," I said, "all cedar."

"Yes, and we've incorporated the timber into the dining

room of number seventeen, Greenhaven. That's it, second on your left—hasn't been sold yet, I can show you over it— and into the main hall of Summerhaven—a Japanese couple have bought that. The main staircase—you'll remember it was two storeys."

"Yes."

"We had enough of it to build the staircase in Blue-haven—that's the blue-gray clapboard place with the shingle roof. The Italian marble tiles have gone into the entrance halls of Springhaven and Beachhaven—you can only see the roofs, they're out of sight down the slope there."

And so it went on. The mahogany bookcases here, the marble fireplace there, the oak kitchen here, and the chandeliers . . . Ken paused like a magician, tantalizing, hand poised over the top hat, "You remember the chandeliers?"

"Yes." Numbly.

"Each of the condominiums has one of the original Seahaven chandeliers." He waved a triumphant hand at the seashore as if he had made the warehouse-like block of apartments appear even as he spoke. "You see? Seahaven lives on. Each of the owners of these beautiful properties has a piece of history within their walls."

"But . . ." I stared at the warehouses, "how many condominiums are there?"

"Thirty-six."

"But there weren't thirty-six *rooms* at Seahaven, let alone chandeliers." For most rooms had had old-fashioned ceiling fixtures, dating from the time the house had been built. They must have been all the fashion in 1920, and I'd always thought them elegant with their brass chains and tulip-shaped glass shades. Some had been beautifully etched, but they were certainly not chandeliers. Only the entrance hall, the living room, and the dining room had possessed chandeliers.

I had upset Ken. He looked distressed. As if the rabbit had died at the bottom of the hat. "Well," he said, "we had to refurbish some apartments in the same style."

I said nothing.

"With exact copies," he said. "Can I show you any of the houses? Are you interested in buying a summer place?"

"No."

"I just thought, since you seemed to have such strong memories of the place, you'd find you wouldn't be disappointed in the interiors of any of the houses. You'd find the *ambience* is just the same. Well, almost the same ... I imagine."

Driving again, on through the dark and not caring where. Not lost, for that state presupposes a direction, a destination or, at the very least, a point of departure. I had nothing, I realized now, and I drove as if I had come from nowhere, was heading nowhere.

Keir gone to Erica, a prettier, younger version of me. And more, a writer just as I had always planned to be— but I'd never quite managed to *do* it. And she was a millionairess in her own right. She was more of a success at twenty-five than I would ever be.

Not only was there no one to run to, there was no *place*. The house in Brooklyn where Geoff and I had lived with Zachary was now an art gallery and French restaurant.

And now Seahaven.

I was like Seahaven. It was like me, in pieces, the foundations destroyed. All that was left was fragments. There was no safety for me anywhere. No *haven*. There was no center to my world at all.

Chapter Five

Through the fog I realized there was water. I could smell it, the faint sea smell. The line of traffic was still there in front of me, and I would have kept following it but for the realization that I had reached the sea, and couldn't understand how, or why. The signs, TO FERRY, appeared out of the fog. The other cars seemed to know where they were going. I pulled over to the side of the road and parked.

There was a building nearby and I went in, used the rest room, had a cup of coffee, and realized I was in Bar Harbor. I had almost driven off the edge of the United States and not noticed.

People near me were talking about Nova Scotia, about Canada generally, the best places, the best views, the best hotels.

I'd been to Bar Harbor once, touring with Keir. Staying at Seahaven we'd explored most of Maine. But I'd never come this close to Canada before. Odd, but Keir and I had never been to Canada. And here I was, almost driving onto the ferry without a ticket.

A voice over the sound system announced that the ferry

would be three-quarters of an hour late due to the fog. And I thought, suddenly, *why not?*

I bought a ticket, the best day suite available, and when the boat finally arrived, I drove the little Volvo on board the *MV Bluenose* for the six-hour trip to Yarmouth, Nova Scotia.

Once in my cabin I lay on the bed and fell into my usual fitful sleep. I woke with a steward tapping on the door, and when I answered it he informed me politely that we were now docking and did I want him to take my bags. I thanked him and watched him go, not daring to talk because I knew I'd sound like a madwoman. I looked at my watch—it was afternoon—but on what day? And what on earth was I doing here? I should have bought a return ticket. If I drove off this ship, I'd be in Canada. What would I do in Canada? What was there for me here?

Something new. A respite. Not the past, that fled before me each time I reached for it. This would be a hiatus only. A blank time, not filled, thank God, with memories, for I had none in this place—that place—that shore I could see drawing closer through the cabin porthole.

Nothing could touch me here, the only pain was that which I brought with me. There could be no new assaults. I would drive around Canada, I thought, drive around that great country of dark forests that was even now coming closer, closer.

Into the woods, I thought, like Uncle Zachary's fairy-tale figures from Grimm and Andersen. I tried to forget, as I drove the car off the boat and waited for Customs, that every character in every fairy tale I'd ever read had met with more problems in the woods than they'd had before they entered them.

Nova Scotia was a blur of green and autumn-toned scenery, blue-gray sea and quaint little guesthouses and restaurants whose staff were far more kind and talkative and interested than I would have liked. After two days I took the ferry to

Saint John, New Brunswick, and from there on I stayed at large hotels where I was more anonymous. I drove north, until the climate became uncomfortably cold, then I drove south, and I slept when I was tired and ate when I was hungry and nothing, nothing, meant anything at all.

Part of my brain told me that I was almost out of control. My hands shook constantly. I either talked too much to shop assistants and driveway attendants, or, more often, I was noncommunicative, even surly, driving around Canada giving Americans a bad name.

It was in Montreal, staying at a large but comfortable hotel, that, brushing my teeth one morning, I really studied my reflection for the first time in days. My hair looked a mess—I'd taken to wearing one of my wigs because I simply couldn't be bothered with my hair. Now I noticed that not only was my perm growing out, but my blonde hair color was, too.

I strode back into the room, called a hairdresser, and made an appointment for that morning. Two hours later I'd had my hair cut off and dyed so dark a brown as to be almost black. I chose the style and the color from a book, quickly, carelessly. All I knew was that I didn't want to look like a poor imitation of Erica Tudor any longer.

What I wasn't expecting to find, when I finally looked in the mirror, was that Sally Stanforth had disappeared, and the woman looking back at me was Sarah Feldman.

The mouth was my own, the eyes were my own. And I saw Sarah-that-was, there in the mirror. And I saw Geoff, too, and the few images that I had of my mother.

"Don't you like it?" the hairdresser asked, in French.

My French is very good, and I murmured that I liked it very much indeed, that I was moved a little because I was surprised to see how much like my mother I was. She tutted sympathetically and asked, helpfully, if I would like a facial, also.

Why not?

I lay back and gave myself over to the pampering, feeling my body coming alive a little, just a little. It wasn't so much the facial: I think it was the memory of seeing my mother, seeing Geoff, there in the mirror. Realizing that they hadn't left me altogether. In a way, they were still with me, would always be with me.

I became more aware from that point. I kept giving myself shocks when I'd pass a mirror, or see myself reflected in a shop window. I actually began to enjoy Montreal, enjoyed speaking French again, touring the old section of the city, dining on real French food. I even took out Ann Varvison's manuscript and did a little work, up in my hotel room, one night when I couldn't sleep.

I should go home.

But where was home? I wasn't ready to face New York. I left Montreal at last, but unwilling to leave the comfort of this country, I drove northeast once more, across the Quebec border and back into New Brunswick. I would go back to New York. I must. But slowly. Very slowly.

The little town of St. Claude was a pretty spot, built on the curve of a river, and I stopped and spent a few hours there. I avoided lunching in restaurants, feeling vulnerable dining alone; feeling that people were staring at me, that my defeat and unhappiness must be written on my face. That day in St. Claude I wasn't very hungry. I bought a small order of fries from a McDonald's outlet and wandered up the main street, looking at the window displays of buildings that must have been well over a hundred years old.

A dress shop, very chic, as French as anything in Paris, displayed only two items in its beautifully dressed window, a black suit trimmed with red, and a dark red blouse. It was silk, the blouse, and I stood there on the pavement and scrutinized it closely. I wasn't the sort of woman who wore red, I didn't have any red in my wardrobe. With my hair light-blonde for so many years I'd felt I'd look too pale, that the color would overwhelm me. But the reflection in the glass, the woman looking at the red blouse, was a slim brunette with gray eyes. Brunettes look good in red.

I decided suddenly to buy that blouse. It was a crazy idea. I'd probably never wear it, it would be doomed to hang at the back of my closet, a reminder of that time of madness, that hysterical flight to Canada.

But I would buy it. When I'd finished my french fries, when I'd wiped the grease from my fingers . . .

Moving on in the meantime, I noticed the next shop was a real estate agency. I stopped and stared at the window, and found myself smiling at one of the display photos.

It was a small, single-storey house with a high-pitched roof. It had a background of pines, against which its log walls melded; it seemed to grow out of the very forest that surrounded it, and it probably had. It was an unusual shape, little rooms leading off to either side, the eaves were trimmed with cutout work, and there were scarlet geraniums in the window boxes. The windows themselves were made of tiny diamond panes, as if they'd come from a very old house, and none of the windows, that I could see, were exactly the same shape or size. The house, eccentric and charming, reminded me of childhood images. It was the Ponderosa and the witch's gingerbread house, it was Walton's Mountain and the cottage of the seven dwarfs.

Fully furnished cottage of old-world charm, read the caption around the large photograph, above in English, beneath, the same words in French. *Includes barn, garage, and sheds, plus one hundred and thirty-two acres, fifty acres of cleared, fenced pasture and eighty-two acres of virgin forest backing onto nature reserve.*

I stood entranced before the window, the french fries going cold in my hand. It was such a pretty property, conjuring up a way of life that was foreign to me, but held a promise of a peaceful existence.

Fifty acres of cleared, fenced pasture. There was a smaller photograph of what must have been the view from the house, for I could see a corner of the barn in the picture. The land sloped away to more trees in the distance, an earth road ran in a gentle curve through the cleared land, the fences were rustic, unpainted, and looked to be split rails.

Eighty-two acres of virgin forest. What would it be like to own one's own forest?

But the price was outrageously high.

I ate a cold french fry, and that was when I saw, in the shop, beyond the window display, a man sitting behind a desk, quite close to the window. He was speaking on the phone, but his eyes were upon me. As our gazes met, he smiled.

He was a well-dressed businessman, round-faced and solid. He looked approachable. I hesitated and, as I did, he finished with his phone conversation and replaced the receiver. I opened the agency door and put my head through, not willing to go any further, not willing to look too interested, for I was not.

"Why is the little log farmhouse so expensive?" I asked in French, for seeing him closer, without the glass between us, he seemed suddenly very French. Perhaps it was merely his clothes, but my instincts were right.

He leaned back and smiled. "If you saw it, you'd understand," he said. In French the words had a sense of poetry and mystique about them that I was sure he was not unaware of. Yet he didn't seem in any hurry to impress me, to make a sale. He didn't even invite me in, so I went in anyway.

There was only one other person in the room, a girl in her late teens in very high heels, standing over a photocopier that hiccuped out printed matter. She was staring at it as if it mesmerized her.

"I'm Frank Dufour," the man said, and held out his hand. "You're American, *Madame?*"

I was a little hurt. In Paris I passed as a French woman. I had had difficulty with Quebec French, and New Brunswick French is slightly different again. But American? "Does it show?" I asked.

"Only in your business-like approach," and he said the

words with such charm that I wasn't insulted. I *had* been abrupt. I had been very New York. No *Bonjour,* no *s'il vous plaît.* I'd been alone too long, I was forgetting my manners.

I took his hand, smiled and said, "I'm . . ." And why I did it I don't know, perhaps it was part of the changes I was undergoing, "I'm Sarah Stanforth." Not Sally. No one called me Sarah any more. No one except the second generation of aunts and uncles in Florida, whom I rarely saw. But suddenly, for this brief time in this little town of St. Claude, I was Sarah. And I liked the sound of it.

I sat down in the chair opposite Frank Dufour's desk as he said, "The property you were looking at was owned by a writer, Otto Hahn. He designed and built the little house."

The hair stood up on the back of my neck.

Frank continued, oblivious, "His work is better known in Europe . . ."

"My own background is Austrian," I said.

"Then you'd know his work." Frank looked pleased. "He and his wife Frieda are great friends of mine."

If only Uncle Zachary were alive to hear this.

Zachary had had—and I had inherited—copies of all Hahn's works. I was very familiar with his novels, essays, and poetry, in translation. I knew he had migrated to Canada before the war—and he was here in St. Claude, now. So close.

"I suppose it's the fact that the house belongs to Otto and Frieda Hahn that makes it so valuable —" I began.

"Oh, no! On the contrary, in this district his work is not well known. They were just Otto and Frieda, and well loved for themselves."

"You say 'were.' " My spirits sank.

"After the Berlin Wall came down, they walked in here one day, very somber, and told me they wanted to go home. It was unbelievable for many of us here. They were so much a part of St. Claude. They write to my wife Nanette and me. They miss the place, but they feel they've made the right decision. But they left everything, all their furniture. To see the house you'd think they'd just stepped out for a walk."

I was silent.

"You do want to see the house, don't you?" Frank smiled gently.

"Yes," I said. "But I can't buy it, of course."

"Of course. But you are an admirer. I think Otto wouldn't mind. I'll just ring Merlin to announce we'll be coming."

My brain suddenly pictured an ancient family retainer, with, perhaps, magical powers, standing guard over the fairy-tale cottage.

We drove south, towards Fredericton, in Frank Dufour's car. On the way he told me a little more about the house.

"The main reason for the price is the inclusions. The Hahns brought their own furniture with them, from Germany, before the Second World War. It would have been valuable then, but now . . . That's why Merlin and one or two dogs are staying on the place. The furniture is very valuable."

"Why didn't they send it to Christie's or Sotheby's?"

"They're quite determined that the house should be sold exactly as it is—and the furniture does suit the place. But someone will buy it for a weekender and, as you say, the furniture will then go to auction in New York. It's inevitable."

I felt saddened at his words, and yet I shouldn't. It was like Otto Hahn—from the gentle wisdom of his writings, I felt I knew him—to make such instinctive decisions from the heart rather than from any monetary consideration. I hoped someone would buy his home and keep it intact as he and his wife had wished.

"Perhaps the town could buy it as a museum?"

Frank shook his head at my suggestion. "St. Claude is not a wealthy town. We have little industry. In the winter we have skiers, in the summer, fall, and spring we cater to tourists. There's no money to buy the Hahn place." He paused. "They had a name for it. It was on the gate, many years ago. I must ask them what it was—I could put it on the display."

Why was I bothered, bothered already, about the name of the Hahn property going on the display? But I *was* bothered. It was a kind of irritation that Frank Dufour was looking for further incentives to tempt buyers. I was surprised to find some sense of proprietary feelings within me. Someone might buy the farm who didn't understand the Hahns, didn't realize what a national treasure they owned.

Now, when I look back, I think it was already happening to me, on the way south out of St. Claude that September day. The countryside had been working a kind of magic upon me ever since those first confused days in Nova Scotia. How could I be so close to the United States, and yet so far away? And what was it about Canada that I needed, and it was giving me?

James Hammel, tired of journalists describing him as an "expatriate Englishman," once said to me, "Someone wrote somewhere that everyone has two homes, a place where one is born, and a place where one's heart belongs. I don't think many people would disagree with that. Why then can't people accept the second home, the *chosen* home, as the real one? I've lived in New York for thirty-two years; I was nineteen when I left London. I'm now an American citizen. Why doesn't someone ever write, 'New York novelist, James Hammel'? Surely *choice* is what's important. My heart is in New York."

Coming out from the trees that grew thick to the edge of the narrow drive, seeing the little house there above me for the first time, James's words came unbidden to my mind. Until then I'd never understood what he had meant.

Now I did. We came up the drive in Frank Dufour's red Jeep and I saw the house and its outbuildings and fields and forest and I felt such a sense of *belonging,* as if I'd been living in this place for years. It was as though the house were shouting at me; not that it belonged to me, but, as James had said, that I belonged to it.

The second surprise was Merlin. Not a grizzled old groundskeeper but a tall, dark-haired young woman in her twenties. She wore a T-shirt and jeans with the elegance that many very tall women possess, and her features, though not in the least beautiful, were large and very striking; she could have been a New York model on vacation. She was weeding the garden bed near the porch when we drove up, and she straightened and smiled a welcome. Two enormous mongrel dogs came dashing from the trees behind the house and positioned themselves protectively in front of her, but she stood there, calmly, speaking to them gently, then called to us in English, "They won't hurt you, promise!"

We climbed out of the car and waded through the dogs, as enthusiastic now as they'd been suspicious a few seconds earlier. Frank switched to speaking English, and he and Merlin kissed on both cheeks, obviously old friends.

I was another matter: Merlin shook my hand, and though her smile was genuine enough, I was aware, as we approached the house, that both she and Frank were watching me carefully, noting my reactions. Frank had introduced Merlin as the property's closest neighbor to the north, who was kind enough to stay and caretake the place until it was sold. A neighbor; so she, too, would have been a friend of the Hahns.

They both love the place, I thought. This middle-aged businessman and this young girl; both of them love this place, and they'll judge me by my reaction to it.

But then I forgot Merlin, and Frank. The front door was opened, and I crossed the porch and stepped through the doorway into a living room of comfortable proportions, the walls of the same rough logs as the house exterior. It smelled of old timbers and leather and furniture wax, like a temple, a church. I walked from room to room as if I knew my way.

Only the large living room was of natural logs, the rest of the house was walled with rough plaster, painted off-white. It was a perfect setting for the ancient pieces of heavy furniture, black with age: there wasn't a piece that was under two hundred years old. But my predominant feeling wasn't one of avarice, even of admiration. I wandered about sensing such a strong feeling of déjà vu that I was almost frightened. I had known these rooms, this furniture . . .

And then I remembered. The old photograph albums that my great aunts and uncles had brought with them from Austria of my grandparents' house in Vienna. Not many pieces of furniture were as old as these, but they were of the same *type*—big, bulky, highly carved. That's what it was; the Hahns' taste in interior decoration was that of my own forebears; this was pre-turn-of-the-century Vienna. It was my own roots, transplanted in their entirety to the backwoods of Canada.

"I've made no changes," Merlin said, behind me, as I entered the broad kitchen with its stone-slab floor and dark-stained timber cupboards.

"No, I can see that," I agreed. Copper-bottomed pans hung from the walls, there were flowers in a vase on the windowsill. It was as if Frieda Hahn would come through the back door at any moment, her hands full of fresh beets, smelling of the earth that clung to their roots, and ask us if we would have coffee and strudel.

I heard Frank say, "The kitchen cupboards came from an old convent that was demolished about the time the Hahns built the house. They were recycling long before it became fashionable." He then went on to tell me of the valuation that Christie's had made, only six months before, that I would find, truly, that the price of the house and its contents was more than fair, given the value of the furniture.

I wanted to say to him, *You don't have to sell me the house.* There was no need for him to say anything at all. I wished he'd be like Merlin, perch upon a tabletop, lean in a doorway, and let me absorb the atmosphere. But the house itself made even that a difficult task. I tried to look at it as a curiosity, as an outsider, a *New Yorker*, would look at it. But the house was shouting at me, very loudly: *You're mine.*

My longing for this house was so strong it was a kind of physical hurting. I turned and caught the gaze of Merlin, leaning against a window ledge. We looked at each other and she smiled a little, as if she understood.

All the way along the drive I had my head turned to look back at the house, until it disappeared within the thickening forest.

The old, white-painted front gate seemed to be permanently open, so there was no need to get out of the car, but I asked Frank to stop, and he did so. I climbed out of the front seat and stood by the gate post, looking back up the drive, feeling the silence, the sense of peace, hearing the sound of the wind in the trees. From here one couldn't see the cottage; the only sign that a house lay at the end of the little dirt road was a letter box made of an old cream container, turned on its side, a flap cut in its base through which to reach the mail, and *Hahn* and *578 Spring Mill Road* written on its side in green paint.

The drive rose in a slope and curved through the trees. And though at Seahaven it had dipped down, towards the sea, the trees themselves were the same pines and larches and maples and beeches . . .

What are you doing, Sarah? Trying to find your past, any past? Taking on Otto and Frieda Hahn's memories? Wanting to become part of their happiness and contentment in this place, because you have none of your own?

Frank and I were silent for most of the journey back to St. Claude. On the edge of the little town, Frank finally said quietly, in French, "What are your thoughts, Mrs. Stanforth?"

I took a deep breath, and muttered, "I have to make a few phone calls."

He nodded, slowly, but didn't comment.

He parked his Jeep behind his office and we walked

through to the front of the agency. Frank paused by his desk and handed me his card and, from a desk drawer, a copy of Christie's valuation of the Hahns' furniture.

"If you're staying in St. Claude," he said, "I recommend the Brunswick Inn—it's on King Street, on the northern edge of town. It's an old coaching inn—beautifully restored and the food is excellent. French, of course," he added.

I smiled my thanks and walked out into the bright sunlight. An autumn day in St. Claude, New Brunswick.

Very nice, Sarah. But winters here will freeze your little butt off.

There would be so many things to see to: the complexities of this plan were enormous.

And even if I could afford to buy the farm, could work as an editor for Brambles Thorne from the farm . . .

What happens when Keir and I get back together? As we will, as we must.

And what does a New York editor do, hurled in a farmhouse in the middle of a Canadian forest?

Someone will ask, Sarah. Get your answers straight. Write.

The answer came boldly. It would surprise no one back in New York. I'd always wanted to write. Lots of editors regard themselves as writers, biding their time, looking for the right subject.

And hey, I don't need money. Keir had promised me that I'd want for nothing.

I booked into the pretty little Brunswick Inn, as Frank Dufour had suggested, and immediately phoned the New York accountant who had handled Keir's and my affairs. Yes, Dr. Stanforth had been in touch and matters were already underway. He went on with details, but I'd stopped listening. So, Keir had wasted no time-in trying to disengage us from each other.

There was more than enough to buy the farmhouse. That was clear. I told him to expect the check for the amount to be drawn against what was, now, my own account. It was obvious that my accountant thought I was a little deranged with shock over the ending of the marriage, but he gave me the information I needed, and I drove back into St. Claude and signed the papers for the farmhouse that afternoon.

It was madness, I often thought, over the next few weeks, while waiting for the sale to go through and for my belongings to arrive from New York. I had no trouble with gaining residency status, as I was self-employed, but matters had moved so *fast*. "You're making rash decisions when you're vulnerable," Beth said repeatedly, each time we talked on the phone. And, secretly, most of the time I agreed with her.

In my room at the Brunswick Inn I continued to work on *Scotty's Things*. The growing manuscript was my solace, a private place where I could go and escape even my pain over Keir's betrayal. For what grew out of *Scotty's Things* was Keir as I had known him. I was rediscovering our past, our love and that early happiness we had found together. Yet like a dream, certain things changed, metamorphosed. The house where Keir/Piers comes to buy the toys looked a lot like the Brunswick Inn, with its mellow brick and garden trellises. Seahaven ... was Seahaven. But it belonged to Sarah/Deborah's family, in the same way that I had, I realized now, always wanted Seahaven to be mine. *I can rewrite history,* I thought happily. I can redefine my past. I was reliving, with Scotty and Deborah and Piers, the best years of my life. And I was having fun.

Can I actually do this? I'd ask myself sometimes. Is this a story that people will respond to, will they start to read and want to turn pages to see what happens next? Will *Scotty's Things* get to be pages, real, honest-to-God *pages*, bound down one side, *turnable* pages, not just a printout that Beth will read and tell me, wryly, regretfully, "Honey, don't give up your day job"?

And I wanted to continue my day job. I liked being an editor. I didn't need to be based in New York: my writers were a far-flung bunch anyway—only two in New York, one in Saskatchewan, two in California, one in New Mexico, one on a farm in Cornwall, England, and one in a beach house in North Queensland, Australia. Between editing these longtime clients, I'd maintain contact with agents regarding new and established authors. Sammy Thorne saw no problem with me continuing to buy for my list while living in St. Claude, so long as I kept in close contact with him. So I invested in the most up-to-date business equipment until my room at the Brunswick Inn began to look like my office back at Brambles Thorne. It was good to know that Sammy had faith in me at this low point of my life: he knew I was an excellent editor, that my writers liked me—several agents had negotiated out-clauses on behalf of their clients should I ever leave Brambles Thorne. And my new Canadian address had this benefit— it solved any problem he might have of keeping Erica and myself apart at the frequent publishing functions.

There would, of course, be visits to New York and meetings at the office, but I was looking forward to these. I'd get a loft apartment in the Village, decorate it my own way. On hearing this, Beth again declared that I was out of my mind. "Keir gave you that beautiful apartment. What are you going to do with it? Sell it? You'll never get another one like it."

"I'm giving it back to him."

"What? Sally, it's worth millions!"

"He was the one who chose it. He decorated it. I put a lot of Uncle Zachary's money into buying my share of it, sure, but Keir's more than made up for it with the settlement. I have the farm, enough to buy my own place in New York when I need to, and more than enough to live on for the rest of my life. I'm giving him back the apartment."

And Keir and I might yet need it again.

"Sally, honey, this is *divorce* we're talking about, here. This is *war.* You have to think of your future."

"No I don't."

I changed the subject, went on to give her another list of things I'd need sent up from the apartment. Beth and Malcolm were doing my packing for me, for I couldn't bear to return to New York just yet, and I certainly couldn't face the apartment.

Keir did not call me during this time and in all those weeks, which became a month, there was never a phone call or letter from Keir's parents, Bill and Barbara, nor from Keir's sister Katherine. I shouldn't have been hurt, but I was. When I finally called Bill, and later, Katherine, they were cool. The sorrow they expressed at "these unfortunate events"—they both used the same phrase, as if they'd decided at a family enclave exactly how they would handle my call—did not really ring true. I couldn't fault their words, their expressions—but something was wrong.

Had they only accepted me because of Keir, I wondered. Had their friendship and fondness of twenty-five years been an act? Were they happy that Keir was filling the newspapers and gossip magazines with pictures of himself and Erica Tudor, that without my speaking to the press at all, the word was out that Erica had destroyed our marriage and smeared the respected name of Stanforth with innuendo and scandal?

I tried to avoid reading any of the articles, they filled me with such rage and misery. I turned my mind to the Hahn property, often driving out there to walk about the place and absorb some of its atmosphere and peace.

Sometimes Merlin was there, sometimes not. I would park the car and knock on the door, and if there was no answer I simply explored the fields or the woods. I was familiarizing myself; I was a landowner. It felt odd, and rather wonderful. I wondered what Keir had said when someone—and there would have been many keen to do so—had told him that I had decided to resettle in Canada. I somehow expected him to call me, but he never did. Beyond my pain was a sense of surprise that he could so easily sweep more than twenty years from his life, and go on as if those years had never existed.

I thought often, in these days, of Uncle Zachary. With

his love of literature he had often suggested I make my career as a novelist. He'd praise each of my articles and stories published in college magazines, would phone all the aunts and read my work aloud to them. And yet I had drifted into editing, loved the *busyness,* the lifestyle, even the stress. I had been too busy to notice that Zachary was saddened by my decision. Now I confronted the fact and gained comfort that Zachary, were he alive, would approve of my move to Canada. Zachary would encourage me in any endeavor that led to my writing.

Even this wild escape to the woods, I thought—on one visit to the farm in the sleety rain, stomping through the forest above the house—Zachary would probably be highly amused to see me occupied like this, dressed in a dark-green raincoat and galoshes, bought especially for such days as these.

Zachary had always told Geoff and me: "Simplify the problem. When you break it down to its simplest forms a problem is often not a problem at all."

This is what I'm doing, Uncle Zachary. My very life was a problem, so I've simplified it down to bare existence in a beautiful place. Do you think it'll work? Stepping back from the trees so I can see the woods?

I smiled around at the ancient trunks, the dripping branches. Somewhere a bird called, a bright complaint against the gray of this autumn day.

"I'm simplifying everything," I told Zachary. "Maybe that way I'll find an answer. When I know what my life means, maybe I'll find a purpose."

For I didn't have one. Keir had been my major purpose. I could see it clearly now. It wasn't Keir's fault, it was my own. The sensible, mature side of me knew that life for a woman doesn't end at divorce. But all my emotions denied this. My life—the life I had always known—*had* ended.

I marched on through the woods, once again, as on so many occasions, brooding about Keir's defection, hating Erica . . .

Erica in the woods. Lost in the woods. Chop down a

tree and make it fall on her. *Splat.* Whoops. The forest makes a statement, revenges itself upon all writers for the trees that became woodchips that became pages in novels both memorable and forgettable.

Where's Erica Tudor? She's under a lot of pressure right now . . .

I had turned back half an hour ago, and should have seen, down there to my left, the clearing and the farmhouse by now. But it seemed this was the wrong ridge, for there below was a stream, but no clearing. Had I climbed too high, moved too far south? Was this the stream that ran through the southeast corner of my property? If so I had only to follow it . . . but was it the same stream?

I hesitated for some seconds, then, panicking despite myself, I plunged down the slope, needing to move—in some direction, any direction. And it was later than I had thought—or was it my imagination that the sky was really darkening, that the trees were filling with shadows? I was mistaken, surely; my own dark thoughts had overtaken me, that was all. Serves me right.

I wondered suddenly if I were being punished for the murderous plots I kept hatching against my husband's mistress. For I was lost, here on my own—well, almost my own—property. My body, not Erica's, would be found next week, next year, moldering amongst the leaf litter. Going back to nature.

Not funny, Sarah. Not funny.

Finally I found a worn track, cut across my own downward, scrambling path. I stopped, breathless, frightening a tiny chipmunk who had been skipping homewards along a branch overhanging the track. We stared at each other for an instant, then he was gone. I didn't even see him turn. One second he was there, and the next there was only a flurry of leaves to show where he had disappeared, off along the branch up into the tree.

I was shaken. For an instant the chipmunk had startled me as much as I had frightened it. I turned along the worn path, following it downhill, praying my house—or any house, for that matter—was not far away.

The path levelled out, but just then the sun disappeared behind a mountain and the pines and firs, the birches and maples, seemed to crowd together, there before me where the track wound itself away into the trees.

I was too tired to run, but I walked faster, hearing no birdsong, now, no sound at all but my own ragged breathing. My feet in the heavy rubber boots felt leaden. I paused and leaned against a tree trunk.

I mustn't panic. Here was a path—a path led somewhere, didn't it?

Something moved to my right so slightly, so quickly, that my subconscious was the only part of my brain to react. That part of my brain that was responsible for instinct, for the possibility of danger, that primitive part of my brain labeled *Perils,* subheaded *Dark Parts of the Forest.*

I looked to the right.

And the hairs stood up on the back of my neck, on my arms, even the backs of my hands tingled.

A dark shape, an inhuman shadow, separated itself from the equally dark yet recognizable shapes of the trees. It moved *towards* me, lurching a little, and hissing. It came at me, down the slope, dark and purposeful and *hissing* as it moved.

Chapter Six

I froze to the spot in terror, all my Great Aunt Becky's ghost stories and the tales of evil spirits and woodland fiends that had haunted her own childhood in Austria came back to me now. I clutched my tree trunk while all the time the apparition moved closer . . .

It was near enough, now, for me to see that it was human. The face that peered towards me in the gloom was nut brown and wrinkled as any children's book illustration of a malevolent gnome.

Yet there was intelligence there, and the features themselves were even. The face could have been described as handsome, if it wasn't for the look of demonic fury that contorted it.

"Can't a man piss against a tree without damn tourists crashing about? Piss off, you! This is private property!"

"I . . . I know . . ." I began, edging downhill, backing away from the spitting fury of the man.

"You know, eh?" He followed me a little. I noticed, inconsequentially, that even in that dim gray light his clothes were neat; browns and greens like the forest itself.

No wonder he had appeared to metamorphose from the very trees.

"You know, eh? You know this is private property, yet you wander about just as you please, eh? Bloody careless, lawless hitch! Bloody . . ."

I ran.

His voice was louder, as if he were shouting, but at last it seemed to be receding behind me. He wasn't following.

Where was I running to? Where? It was dark and I was running and . . .

A fence.

Thank God, a fence, a gate. And beyond, a broad pasture, and a stream running through it.

I saw the lights, then, far away to my right. I didn't open the gate; heavy galoshes and all, I clambered over it and half ran, half stumbled towards the lighted house. The sun was gone, the sky dark gray, and it began to rain, suddenly and heavily. The layout of the place, the barns, sheds, and the log walls of the house—I knew this farm. The little man in the forest had been wrong. I wasn't trespassing. This was the Hahn property. The *Stanforth property.*

I managed a semblance of calm as I came around the house and up the steps to the front porch. Inside I could hear someone playing the piano, a piece by Liszt, accurately but not very confidently. There was another car parked beside my own, not the blue pickup that I had seen Merlin driving.

At my knock. the music stopped. There were female voices, then the door opened.

It wasn't Merlin, but a pleasant fair-haired young woman, about my own height. She looked surprised to see me, and concerned, stepping back immediately to usher me inside.

"Mrs. Stanforth? We were getting worried about you. It's almost dark. . . . You're drenched!"

Merlin hurried out from the direction of the kitchen and she, too, seemed relieved to see me.

"I was . . . exploring," I said, still breathless.

"You look exhausted," the blonde girl said. She wore

overalls and a faded denim shirt. She was rather plump and pretty in the way one imagines Scandinavian country girls to be. Her expression was open and friendly, and I smiled back at her, wondering who she was.

Merlin said, "You haven't met my partner, have you? This is Natalie Newman. I don't know if Frank told you— Natalie and I live together."

"No," I said, as Natalie and I shook hands.

Merlin was saying, "Take off your boots—the fire's lit. Why don't I put some scones in the oven?" And when I protested at this being too much trouble, she continued, "The freezer's full of food. Frieda gave it to Natalie and me but we left most of it here since we come backwards and forwards so much."

In the end we all three peered into the freezer and decided to stay and have a meal. I had a chicken chasseur, Merlin a small chicken pot pie, Natalie a traditional roast turkey dinner, and we followed it with apple pie, served, like the coffee, with long-life cream.

In my socks before the fire, scraping the last of the apple pie from my plate, I said, "I met a man in the woods just now."

They stopped eating and looked up at me. "A small man, neatly dressed but woodsy—not very friendly. He thought I was trespassing."

Natalie rolled her eyes and Merlin went back to chasing the last of her pie about her plate with a wry look on her face. "Alby Gresson," Natalie informed me.

Merlin glanced at her, then at me. "Didn't Frank tell you about Alby? I suppose he thought it wasn't important."

"It is if he's going to jump out at Sarah every time she goes for a walk in the woods," Natalie put in. "At the very least, he's her neighbor, like we are."

"Is he dangerous?" I asked.

"We-ell . . ." Natalie considered.

"No, Nat, of course he isn't. Stop trying to scare Sarah." It was "Sarah," now. Had become "Sarah" when I set the sixteenth-century refectory table near the fire. Somewhere between the cutlery drawer and the table, padding about in my socks, I had come to be accepted despite the fifteen or so years' difference in our ages.

"I'm not scared," I told them, smiling. Then I remembered the handsome, narrow face, twisted in dislike. "He gave me a fright, that's all, appearing out of the dark. Though to be fair," I conceded, "I think he was relieving himself and I embarrassed him."

"Relieving himself?" Merlin looked puzzled.

"Peeing, Merlin. Where have you been?"

"Obviously a medical term," Merlin sniffed. "Why don't you just *say* he was pissing up against a tree and you stopped him mid-stream?" She glared as we both erupted into laughter. "Well? Am I right?"

Natalie sprawled across the table, laughing. I said, "I can understand him being embarrassed—though I didn't actually *see* him doing what he was doing. But he seemed hostile. Even taking his affronted modesty into account."

"Hostile. That's the word for Alby, alright, eh?" Natalie turned to Merlin.

"But not dangerous. He's just a sad little man," Merlin countered.

"And *nasty.*"

"He seemed very possessive of this place," I told them. "We met only a short way up the slope from the upper pasture gate. What was he doing there?"

Merlin said, "There's no fence between his property and yours. It used to be the one property, you see. Alby used to work for the Hahns. Before they left, they sold him fifty acres along the road—it adjoins his family's property. But he knows where the boundaries are, he shouldn't be on this place. I think he still feels responsible for it, in a way."

"Was he the Hahns' foreman?"

Natalie shook her head. "This was never a working farm—the Hahns ran a couple of cows and goats—just for a hobby, really. No, Alby was hired occasionally to do odd jobs."

"An odd little man for odd little jobs," Merlin quipped. She turned to me. "Do you know, he was one of Canada's most highly decorated pilots—one of the youngest, too. He came back from the war in the Pacific quite a hero."

"And time went on and people forgot about the war," I suggested.

"Exactly," Merlin nodded, "and Alby became bitter, got a real chip on his shoulder. He made so many enemies he lost his job with City Hall and had to go back to farming. He'd managed to quarrel with just about everyone in town by the mid-fifties, Dad says. He did marry, finally, a local girl, and had two sons. His wife left him and he divided his land to give his boys a small farm each. The only friends he ever had were the Hahns. But they were loved by everyone."

Almost to myself I murmured, "I hope he won't continue wandering about the place like that."

"Killing your trees," Natalie muttered.

"He won't bother you," Merlin reiterated. "He probably won't speak to you unless you speak first."

"And whatever you say, he'll disagree with you," Natalie put in.

"Did you offend him in some way?" I asked.

"I backed into the main gate one day. I was still learning to drive Merlin's pickup and I put it into reverse by mistake. The Hahns weren't worried, they thought it was funny— but that's why you can't shut the front gate properly. Alby happened to be walking by—he walks everywhere—and he saw it. Came running up and abused me, swearing at me, going purple with rage. I'm a nurse—I work in the intensive care unit at St. Claude Hospital—and I swear I thought he was going to have a stroke. And it wasn't even *his* gate."

It was late when we locked up the house and left—every few days Merlin went home to Natalie at their own home, never on any particular day. When buying the house I had taken over paying Merlin's wages for the caretaking of the property, and she had also agreed to come and stay should I have to return to New York at any time.

Coming down the porch steps in the dark, looking around at the silent shadows of the barn and garage and the distant woods huddled against the road below the fields, I was glad to know that Merlin and Natalie were close—only a kilometer away. And they were looking forward to having me as a neighbor. They had already invited me to their own farmhouse on the day I moved in. "You won't feel like cooking dinner for yourself in the middle of unpacking," said Natalie, giving me a hug goodbye.

As I waved and drove off I realized that the two women would become—if they weren't already—my friends. And I'd already developed friendships with several people in St. Claude, Frank Dufour and his wife Nanette, Monsieur and Madame Ambroise from the Brunswick Inn, who insisted I call them Louis and Marie-France. I had not wanted close friends here, initially, I hadn't wanted to become too close to anyone.

I made a decision on the drive back to the Brunswick Inn that night. As soon as I was the legal owner of the farm I would have a fence erected between Alby Gresson's place and my own.

The farm was mine, finally and completely. I dressed in my new red silk blouse and Frank and Nanette took me to lunch at *Chez Jacques* on Queen Street to celebrate. I liked Nanette very much, but she seemed overly concerned that I'd be lonely at the farm. "You must not bury yourself away in the countryside, Sarah. You are still grieving over the end of your marriage, are you not?"

"A little," I said, unwillingly, for I had told the Dufours some of my history.

"But you must socialize—we will make sure you are not left alone and sad in your pretty little house. You must come to dinner with us."

I thanked them warmly for their concern, and accepted

the invitation. But I wondered, again, with my new and caring friends, whether I would be allowed much time for the silence and *aloneness* I needed to try to learn to live without . . .

Keir.

During lunch I had looked up from the table, glanced out the window and across the street—and he was there, on the other side, just turning away to disappear into the crowd of Friday afternoon shoppers. He was wearing one of his usual dark business suits . . .

I had to be mistaken. It couldn't have been Keir.

I must have looked shaken, for Frank said, suddenly, kindly, "Are you alright, Sarah?"

"Yes," I smiled, "I just . . ." My eyes had found the spot in the crowd across the street where the man had disappeared.

"It is hard, Sarah dear," said Nanette. "There is a time for grieving, and a time for healing. I think you were right to follow your heart and stay with us in St. Claude. Who knows, my dear," she went on, "you may even discover you can love again, and marry a big tall Canadian and have many children."

I looked into her eyes and tried to smile. It wouldn't matter if he were Canadian, Colombian, or Congolese, there would never be any other man in my life but Keir.

Frank had already given me the keys to the farmhouse and notified Merlin. She had left a message with Frank that I was expected for dinner with herself and Natalie at seven, and to wear old clothes as, besides the two dogs I had already met, they had two others, as well as seven cats.

After leaving the Dufours, I turned back towards the center of town. I would do some shopping, buy some supplies for the house. And all the time, walking along the street, past the shops and into the mall, I was searching for that dark-suited, dark-haired figure, my heart thumping with anticipation, with a wild hope that I had not been mistaken. Keir had come to find me.

I was loading the contents of my shopping cart into the back seat of the Volvo when I saw him again. He was standing only ten meters away along the pavement. But this time, with no plate-glass window or passing traffic between us, I could see that it was not Keir.

I stood there, leaning a little on the roof of the Volvo, and had to swallow hard against the rising, threatening tears. I had made myself not believe. And yet . . .

I turned away and busied myself with the minutiae of stacking all my groceries—but I couldn't resist glancing again, to make sure.

The handsome, slim man with dark hair was arguing, quietly but vehemently, with Merlin.

Now I definitely turned away and continued with loading the car, embarrassed lest I be seen staring. But I had noticed, this time, the difference between the man with Merlin, and Keir. This man was older. Though his hair was black, it contained some gray and there were lines on the strong-featured face. He had larger features than Keir possessed, his nose more aquiline, his jaw heavier, his mouth broader, the eyes deep-set under heavy dark brows. In his late forties or early fifties. Like Keir, he dressed urbanely, was tall and slim.

I pushed the cart to a nearby collection space, and when I got back to the car, Merlin and the man had moved a little in my direction, but were still arguing heatedly.

It was none of my business, and I climbed behind the wheel of the car—but paused before I started the engine. As I watched, Merlin ended the scene, saying something that must have been particularly vicious. The man looked taken aback, and in that moment of surprise, before he could retort in any way, Merlin stormed off down the street.

The man was left looking after her, but finally he, too, walked away, to climb into a car parked at the curb, about four cars along from mine.

I sighed and wondered who he was. No doubt I'd find

out some time, if he was a native of St. Claude. Still wondering about him, still coping with my own feelings about Keir, sparked so strongly by merely seeing a man vaguely like him, I started the engine and pulled out from the curb.

The man was still sitting in his car, a current model Buick LeSabre staring grimly before him, as my car drew almost level.

It happened suddenly; he pulled out in front of me so abruptly that I had to stamp on the brake. There was a squeal of brakes behind me and a shout as a driver coming along the street had to swerve. I gave a short toot on the horn, cross now, for he really hadn't checked the traffic: I know, for I hadn't taken my eyes off him.

He lowered his window and began to shout at me. "Are you blind? Couldn't you see me coming out?"

"You didn't indicate at all!" I yelled back; fright and relief that we had not collided making my voice shrill.

"Well?" he demanded. "Get moving, then!" He glared at the front of my car, uncomfortably close to his door. He must have had a clear view of my license plates, for he added, "New York driver—should have known."

The unfairness of the attack had me almost wrenching the little Volvo into reverse. But having given the man room, I waited and forced myself to be calm: I waved the bad-tempered stranger on.

He muttered something, looking away a little and then turned back to me, insisting with a wave of his hand that I precede him. Perhaps just to irritate him further, I did not move, but gave an almost regal wave of the hand to indicate that *he* was to go first. He did so, now looking almost comically embarrassed.

Like me, he headed south of St. Claude, and watching the back of his head, the way he moved, even in that narrow space, it was like driving behind Keir in his old Mercedes. I was disappointed when he turned off to the right on the outskirts of town. I watched his car go in my side mirror, again wondering who he might be—

And ran straight into the back of the car in front of me.

The same vehicle had passed me during the debacle in the street, but I'd been too intent on my quarrel with the man in the LeSabre, and I hadn't really noticed it. I noticed it now, in great detail, for my car stopped with a jolt that shook me, stunned me, the sound of the impact tore at my nerves, and there was the back of a dark-green Jeep Cherokee close—oh, so close, to the hood of the Volvo.

In the moment of displaced sensibility that followed it seemed as if the driver in front hadn't noticed, for he made no effort to move.

Maybe he's stunned. Maybe he's really hurt.

My hand was on the door handle, ready to climb from the car, when the driver ahead opened the door of the Jeep.

If I'd felt shaken before, I felt even worse now, for unfolding himself from the driver's seat of the Jeep Cherokee was the largest policeman I'd ever seen.

He must have stood at six feet five or six, as heavily muscled as a wrestler but without an ounce of self-indulgent fat on his huge frame. He looked at me for a moment, hands resting on his hips, then jerked his head towards the side of the road. I nodded, understanding, and started the engine once more. With a final glance at the place where our cars joined, he turned and climbed back into the Jeep.

I waited until he had moved forward a little, then pulled the Volvo over to the side of the road, bracing myself for the sound of glass beneath the wheels—but there was none.

He parked the Jeep a car's length in front of the Volvo and, with an official-looking little pad in one hand, walked leisurely along the roadway towards me. With the other hand he placed a cap on his head. All business. I felt myself shrinking down in the seat. *This wasn't happening . . .*

Oh, God, he was big; I had to turn my head to look from the point of one shoulder to the other. He had a face that even the fondest mother could not call handsome;

it was all angles, not a gentle curve or soft line visible anywhere, not a hint of any warmth or emotion having ever lit that face from within. Strength was there, and determination, definitely. I felt sorry for the criminal population of St. Claude—if there was one. If there wasn't, I could very well see why.

He leaned brown arms on the open window of the Volvo, and it *moved* with his weight. I saw that the skin of his knuckles was marked with ancient scars. I noticed other things: another scar on his upper arm that ran up into the sleeve of his light-blue shirt; the plastic name badge on his right breast that read *P. D. McGarret;* the metal and blue enamel police badge over his right breast that said *Sergeant;* I saw the red braid around the brim of his cap. I couldn't see his eyes, as he was wearing very dark sunglasses, but judging from the rest of his face as he leaned it close to mine, the eyes wouldn't give me any reason to relax.

He said, "Two near accidents in two blocks, and compared to New York we have short blocks—Miss . . . ?"

The accent sounded totally incongruous. It was not Canadian—my ear had attuned itself to the Canadian way of saying *oat and aboat* for *out and about*—but *this*. This man spoke as if he came from south of the Mason-Dixon Line—way south.

"Stanforth," I managed to stammer. "Mrs. Sarah Stanforth."

"Would you like to show me your license, Mrs. Stanforth, and can you give me one good reason why you just ran up my ass?"

"Yes . . . I mean . . ." I gave up and turned away gratefully to hunt in my handbag for my license. By the time I found it, he had moved to the front of the car and was gazing at the damage—and there must have been damage—to the front of the Volvo. Then he examined the rear of the Jeep.

I climbed out and came to stand beside him, holding out my license. He took it and studied it.

Cars were passing us. It was a broad road and we were

now well past the little shopping center and between large houses on broad stretches of lawn. Most of the cars that passed slowed a little, and some of the drivers lowered their windows to call at the cop—"Hi, Barry," or "Perry," or maybe "Paddy," it was hard to catch the name over the sound of the engines. No one seemed impatient here. I even earned a few glances of sympathy. But at least there wasn't much damage. None at all to the Jeep Cherokee, but his tow bar had folded my license plate in on itself like soft taffy.

"I'm afraid I lost concentration just for a minute," I said.

"Sure looks like it." He walked back to the Volvo, pulled a pen from his pocket, and opened the citation pad.

"I've got the only damage done—there's no sign of anything wrong with your car at all," I said, desperately.

He was leaning on the roof of the Volvo to write, but looked up. "I'd like you to remember today," he said, calmly.

We both heard a car come to a halt behind the Volvo, a car door slammed, and we looked up. Merlin had parked the blue pickup and was striding towards us.

"I almost didn't recognize you!" she said to me, gaily. And in the same breath she demanded, "What are you doing?" of the police officer.

There was a second's pause, for he must have been as taken aback as I was. Then, "What does it look like I'm doing?" The tone a little testy. He turned back to the citation pad, but had barely touched pen to paper when—

"You can't give her a ticket. She's new in town. It doesn't look good to book newcomers."

He straightened, slowly, and turned to her. I looked at Merlin's obdurate young face and edged along to stand a little between them. The cop's dark glasses masked any hint of emotion in his eyes but beneath them the large features looked even more grimly set. "It's alright, Merlin," I murmured in an attempt to defuse the situation.

Addressing Merlin, the officer said, "Supposing you get

back in your car and mind your own business, ma'am?"
The tone was polite enough, but he leaned ever-so-slightly
on the word *ma'am*. Was he baiting Merlin? Being a local,
did he know she was gay? I could sense his mood was ugly,
tried to think of something to say, but Merlin would not
back down.

"No, Mrs. Stanforth is my friend—this was just an accident that could've happened to—"

"Let me be the—"

"*You.* You're just being officious."

"Merlin!" I warned through clenched teeth, but she was
talking over me. I had to repeat her name several times,
growing more and more alarmed each time I glanced at
the big silent cop with his steely patience.

"You've just finished a bad day and you're taking it out
on the first member of the public to—"

"Merlin . . . Merlin!"

"—annoy you. It's called victimization."

"Would you just get your butt out of here and let me
do my job?" Despite the coarseness of his words they were
spoken in a deadly calm voice. I sensed that this was a man
who never raised his voice. Perhaps, when you're six feet
six, you don't often have to.

"Your job? Your *job?* This is your job? Harassing helpless
women—"

He took a step towards her; I moved closer between
them. Merlin was very tall, almost six feet, the cop was very
tall indeed, I came up to the second top button on his
shirt. Between them, I felt very small.

"Merlin, that is *enough,* " I said in desperation.

Perhaps it was the schoolmarm tone of voice, but they
both stopped and stared at me.

"Shut up, Sarah," Merlin said. And to the cop, "She's
the one who's bought the Hahn place."

"So?" But he turned and glanced at me.

"So she's more than just a source of public revenue,
Perry. She's a local, now. Give her a break."

"Don't try to tell me my job, Mel. Friend or no friend, Mrs. Stanforth was driving in a manner—"

"Give her a break, Perry. This once. Her husband's left her only six weeks ago, she's come here for a new start—don't let her think St. Claude is full of narrow-minded zealots. Or is it? You can check on her license if you like, but she's been driving all over Canada and never even got a parking ticket. Look at her, man, does she look like a danger to the public?"

He looked at me. I avoided his gaze. I felt mortified at Merlin's well-meaning description of my pathetic personal life.

When I finally glanced at him, the big police officer still had his granite features and the black lenses of his glasses turned towards me. I met my own reflection in them, distanced, dwarfed. I hated his quiet scrutiny, wanted to be away from here, away from those black lenses. I had time to notice other things, that he was not naturally dark-skinned, for there were freckles across his large hooked nose; and beside the deep grooves that ran from his nose to the outer edge of his mouth, there were faint creases in the skin, as if . . . as if the man might smile occasionally.

"Look," I said, frantic, now, to get away, "I'll take the ticket, I don't want to cause any—"

He snapped his pad shut, and placed his pen back in his pocket. "I'll let you off with a warning. This time. Be more aware of your surroundings, Mrs. Stanforth. And get that license-plate straightened out." He held my license out towards me.

I took it, my hand shaking a little. "Thank you, Sergeant."

The officer turned to Merlin. "Don't get in my way again." Quietly.

"Don't try to frighten me." She glared up at him.

"I'm warning you, Merlin."

"Yeah? Are you going to arrest me? That'd really look good in the *St. Claude Gazette,* wouldn't it?"

They hate each other, I realized, watching them. *What the hell is going on?*

I felt I should say something, anything, to break the tension between these two, but Merlin said, "See you this evening, Sarah," and walked away, back towards her vehicle.

The big cop watched her go, moving after her a step or two then standing with his hands resting on his gun belt with his back to me. I didn't know if I should move to my car or not. I felt like a schoolgirl waiting to be dismissed.

He turned back to me when Merlin's car was well on its way, and again the black lenses considered me, detached, impervious.

"Get that license plate straightened out. Soon," he said, finally, and moved past me towards his own car.

"Yes. And . . . thank you."

He was halfway to the Jeep and looked back at me with what might have been a look of contempt or merely tolerance for a pathetic driver; it would have been possible to tell if I could have seen his eyes, but all I had to judge with was a slightly bitter twist to a wide, grim mouth, and a tilt of the big head.

But I wasn't thanking him for letting me off. "For not taking it further with Merlin," I explained. "She was wrong to interfere like that."

"You think I showed great restraint." The black lenses unreadable, the deep, flat voice unreadable. This man was *scary.*

"Well . . . yes. It was very kind of you."

He grimaced a little, and lowered his head. It took me a few seconds to realize he was trying to hide the fact that he was amused. But by then he had turned back to his vehicle; speaking as he opened the Jeep's door, I barely caught his words.

"I couldn't very well run her in, could I?" He glanced back at me over his shoulder, and actually smiled. "Merlin's my baby sister. She always was a brat."

And he folded his great height back down into the car, closed the door, and started the engine.

As he pulled out onto the road, I found myself staring after him.

Chapter Seven

"*Peregrine* and *Merlin?* Your parents named you *Peregrine* and *Merlin?* How could they do it to you?"

"Why?" Merlin looked up from stirring the custard, mock-outraged. "They're great names! Well, Merlin is. Peregrine is a terrible name—and Perry deserves it. I'm delighted he's stuck with Peregrine.

"Anyway," she added, "what choice did Mamma and Dad have? They've both got big beaky noses."

"Aquiline," Natalie said, kindly, from where she was basting the chicken at the wall oven. "Aquiline noses."

"I'm intrigued," I admitted to Merlin. "How do you and your brother not look in the least alike, not to mention his Southern drawl?"

"Easy," she said. "We're both tall, but looks-wise I take after Dad's side of the family. He takes after Mamma's. Mamma comes from a family where anyone, including the women, who was under six feet was regarded as a bit of a runt."

"It's true," Natalie put in. "Merlin's mom is six foot two. Not," she added dryly, "as if she's ever spoken to me."

A silence.

"Ah." I said.

" 'Ah,' indeed. You'd think in this day and age people of my parents' education and sophistication would be able to accept having a homosexual child—not Mamma and Dad, though. Oh, Mamma is alright with it, but Dad wouldn't talk to me, hasn't had me in the house, ever since I moved in here with Natalie three years ago."

"That's a real pity. And your brother?"

"Oh, Perry's so uncomfortable about it he's almost funny. He's so *straight*, you see. Everything about him. And yet *he* doesn't get on with Mamma and Dad either. They can't forgive each other. We're a messed up family, I guess."

I helped dish up the food and carry it into the dining room of their little farmhouse. It was comfortable and homey, the house they shared—everywhere were the rag rugs and crocheted throw-overs that Natalie had made. We kept talking while we ate. Merlin seemed happy, eager, almost, to discuss her estranged family.

"Mamma and Dad have always expected too much of us. We have a family company, you see, and Perry was groomed from childhood to take Dad's place as chairman of the board. They sent him away to a really strict English-public-school type of place down in Boston when he was ten. He loathed it. He wasn't good at his studies, hated the discipline . . . I was only tiny, but I can remember the scenes when he'd come home from school on holidays. All Dad could do was yell at him, tease him, ridicule him—try to make Perry fight back, prove him wrong. It worked for a while; he stuck it out until he was fourteen, then he ran off."

"Ran off?"

"Yeah, just . . . disappeared. Turns out he'd got caned by a 'master' as they called the teachers, and Perry had punched him—knocked him cold with one blow. He was over six feet even then, you see."

We were quiet a moment, Natalie was busy eating, Merlin

seemed lost in thought, and I was trying to digest the idea of a frustrated, emotionally wounded young boy, lashing out the only way he knew how, and then disappearing, filled, perhaps, with shame for what he had done, unwilling to face a father he had loved and failed.

"I never forgave him." I was startled to see the look of bitterness distorting Merlin's young face.

"But," I said, "how old were you when he ran away?"

"I was four. There's ten years between us. I was four, and I remember everything. Because I loved him. He was the one who carried me on his shoulders, who laughed with me, and listened to me, and told me stories. He was the one who taught me how to tie my shoelaces and climb a tree, and how to put a worm on a hook. Mamma, she's not a demonstrative woman. She can't help herself, that's just the way she is. And Dad—he was never there, and when he was it was to exhort us to be smarter, cleverer, better than anyone else. Perry only ever wanted to saddle up his pony and ride off for days at a time into the woods. He really was misnamed, wasn't he?" she said suddenly, lightly, as if to distance herself from her pain. "He should have been called Buck, or Slim, or Tex. Instead he gets lumbered with Peregrine David Willingham McGarret."

It was Natalie who continued, "Janice—Mrs. McGarret—was discovered to have cancer of the stomach seven years ago. She had to have an operation to remove the tumor—Perry came home straightaway. Janice has recovered, with treatment—and Perry didn't go back to Georgia He was a cop down there, too. He knew a guy who's a police inspector here, that's how he became attached to St. Claude Police Station."

Merlin ate stolidly through this.

"Did you and your parents see much of Perry after he ran away?" I asked.

She shook her head. "By the time we found him he was fifteen, practically adopted by this redneck family in a place called Slow River—can you believe it? He refused to come home, and my father said, to hell with you then."

Natalie answered my question directly. "He'd phone them at Christmas and Thanksgiving, wouldn't he, Merlin? But he'd only talk to Janice or Merlin. David refused to speak to him."

"Nat, can we drop this subject now?" Merlin scowled up at her partner. "It must be boring Sarah—it's sure as hell boring me."

You're not bored, my dear. You're grieving.

After dinner, we sat in the little living room and watched a video of *Waterloo Bridge,* both Natalie and Merlin being fans of British cinema. While she was setting up, I said to Merlin, "I saw you in town today—just before I ran into Perry I almost ran into the guy you were talking to."

She looked up, her eyes wide, a delighted smile spreading across her face. "That was *you?* My mother phoned me later to tell me how upset Dad was. He and Perry and I had coffee together to try to settle our differences, and it just failed miserably. Then he almost collided with someone on the way home. He took it all out on Mamma. . . . And it was *you.* I should hire you as a hit man—hit person. You almost wipe out my father *and* my brother, all within a few minutes!"

She collapsed with laughter, and even Natalie thought it was amusing. "What are the chances?" she grinned wonderingly.

"It wasn't all my fault," I insisted.

But all through *Waterloo Bridge* Merlin kept giggling quietly to herself.

The first few days in the new house were a little strange: the *silence* of the place—for even the Brunswick Inn had been built on a main road. And the *darkness;* walk outside on any night except the brightest of full moons and one could walk into a tree in no time at all.

And I was lonely, in those first days. I'd stand on my front porch of an evening and watch the lowering sun send lengthening shadows across my fields towards me and wonder, *What am I doing here?*

But there was only one answer: *Where else?*

And there was no answer for that. I simply had to trust my instincts, the feeling of safety and belonging I had been given by this house, this land, when I had first set eyes on them.

What I was missing most was Keir. But I forced myself to keep busy, for I had chores to do, and I went about them with my mind set against my pain; filling the linen closets in the hall with my own linen, unpacking my clothes and hanging them within the enormous, carved seventeenth-century armoires in the main bedroom. I even accustomed myself to the feather mattress and quilt on the Louis XVI four-poster bed.

It was on the third day of my residence on the farm that I took my morning coffee out onto the porch, and since a rare clear blue sky and sunshine beckoned, I walked into the yard and wandered about the outbuildings for the first time.

I'd parked the Volvo in the garage, but it was some distance from the house: it would be a good idea if I could clear the old barn in front of the house and park the car in there.

The barn was a wonderful building, very European in style, its vertical timbers weathered a lovely pale gray. Inside it was a real mess, the repository of fifty years of the Hahns' occupancy of the farm. There were odd lengths of timber leaned against the wall, unrecognizable pieces of machinery, and in the center of the floor, an ancient, dust-enshrouded Buick that looked as if it could have been a getaway car for John Derringer. The backseat was missing and, when I raised the hood, so was the engine. The wheels were all in place: the car stood on wooden blocks. It was as if someone had begun to work on it and lost interest.

I was at the back of the barn, looking for the missing backseat when a bell rang, deafeningly, just above my head, so loud and sudden that it was an assault upon my ear drums, an explosion of sound, and I screamed a little, starting forward and whirling to face the huge electrical bell attached to the wall. It was an extension of the phone bell.

I ran, back to the house, up the stairs, across the porch, and into the big living room. The phone was on a table against the wall; out of breath, I reached for it.

"Hello?"

"Sally darling, it's Aunty Miriam. Have your fingers frozen so you can't dial a number and let your family know where you are?"

"Oh, Miriam, I'm sorry. I did tell you I'd be moving into the house this week."

No matter how welcome the voices of my relatives, my friends, there was always that sense of disappointment. I was waiting for Keir's voice.

I let Miriam talk, and heard what my problem was, what her problems were, and through her words came the sound of footsteps on the porch floorboards.

When I looked up, Alby Gresson was standing in the open doorway.

He stopped there, and saw me, and leaned forward and knocked, four times, very slowly, on the open door, watching me all the time.

"I'll call you back, Aunty Miriam, Mr. Gresson, one of my neighbors, has just called."

I hung up on Miriam, who was saying, "Just let me tell you about your Aunty Shirley and—"

I walked to the door. Before I could say anything, Alby said, "How'd you know it was me? We were never introduced."

"Merlin McGarret told me it must have been you, that day in the woods."

I didn't want to invite him in. There was nothing *wrong* with him, he was a pleasant-looking, well-dressed man who could have passed for being in his early sixties. It was the memory of his rage in the forest that day. He looked at me benignly enough, now, waiting to be invited in.

"Won't you come in, Mr. Gresson? I was just about to make coffee."

"No. Won't stay." He leaned both his hands in the doorway. It wasn't a threatening gesture at all, so why did I feel a little trapped, as if he were blocking my way of escape, as well as the sunlight?

"I just came to give you an apology. Didn't realize you were the new owner. Wouldn't have thought it, young woman like yourself. Expected one of them doctors or lawyers from Montreal or Quebec to buy it for a weekender. Didn't expect a woman." And he looked at me carefully, as if to make sure the rumors were true. "You should have said, up there in the woods. As 'twas, 'twas me that was trespassing, eh?"

"Not at all," I said, "the sale hadn't been finalized." I thought for a moment. "I didn't hear your car—did you walk up here?"

"Walk everywhere, that's how I keep trim." The touch of a boast in his voice.

"I wanted to see you, actually. . . . Shall we sit on the porch in the sun?"

We went out onto the porch, where the sun was slanting in, and sat on a bench. I continued, "I'd like your permission to put up a fence along our boundary."

"Our boundary?" He looked blank.

"The boundary between your farm and mine."

Still I thought he hadn't understood, for his puzzled frown hadn't changed. Then he said, "Read much Robert Frost, Mrs. Stanforth?"

I understood immediately. "Yes, I like Robert Frost's poetry very much."

"He wrote one that begins, *Something there is that doesn't love a wall.*' "

"I know it well. One neighbor's apples won't eat the other man's pinecones, or vice versa, but—"

"I'm growing berries, Mrs. Stanforth. Blueberries, raspberries, you name it. You got nothing but forest on your side."

"That's beside the point, Mr. Gresson. I may wish to run . . ." I thought quickly, "Angora goats in the near future."

"This was the one property. The Hahns' place and my fifty acres. It's always been the one property."

"But it isn't any longer. You have a separate title."

He glared at me.

"Costs a lot of money, fencing. Can't afford it. Can't afford it now, nor in the future. Got two sons out of work—these are bad times for farmers. Got no money to put up fences where there's no call to have them."

I considered, then said, "I'll pay for the fence."

He gazed at me for a long moment. I saw changing emotions behind his bright green eyes. I wanted to look away but felt I'd lose something. What? Some kind of edge, some ground, some face? What?

"So be it." Alby Gresson stood up, and remained looking down at me. "You're a tough little woman, Mrs. Stanforth. Do you always get what you want?"

"No, of course not," I replied.

"Oh, I expect you do." He touched the brim of the soft tweed cap he was wearing and moved off, along the porch towards the front steps. "I expect you do."

I called a fencing company that morning, and they said they would send someone out to survey the area in the afternoon. When a car drew up in the driveway at two-thirty, I went out to meet the contractor: he was a young man, surprisingly well-dressed in a gray suit.

"Mrs. Sarah Stanforth?" he said, with a worried look I couldn't fathom.

"Yes," I said.

"I have some papers that I have to deliver to you . . ."

I didn't hear the rest of what he said, for I opened the papers in my hand to find that I had been served with notice that Keir was divorcing me on the grounds of "irreconcilable differences."

* * *

Later, much later, it seemed, two neat but casually dressed middle-aged men arrived in a pickup with *Fredericton Fences* written on the side of the cab.

I somehow coped with talking to them, providing them with plans of the property and choosing fences that would match as closely as possible the fences that already existed on the farm.

I watched the pickup drive off, down through the fields towards the woods to the left, where Alby's boundary met mine.

I went back to drifting about the house. That's what I did, simply moved from room to room, looking at the walls, the furnishings, as if I had never seen them before.

And I *was* seeing them from a different perspective.

Though I had loved the farmhouse from the very first, with part of my mind I had always believed that Keir would come back to me. I had supposed we would return to New York, set up house once more in the Central Park apartment, that we would keep the farmhouse as a weekender, an alternative holiday home to our places in Paris or Beaver Creek. A place to snatch three days, a week, here and there during our busy year. A place to be ourselves, together; yet somehow a reminder of my independence, of the time I had been forced to cope alone, and succeeded. I would have succeeded because waiting, out there, all the time, was the day that Keir would want me back.

Now what?

Now what, Sarah?

I drove into St. Claude for something to do.

In a cobbled, French-looking lane that ran between King and Queen Streets, I found a bookshop. I love a good bookshop and this was a wonderful little place, dark and smelling of sandalwood incense that blended nicely with

the smell of new paper and print. At the back of the shop
a young man played the guitar. There were several people
browsing so I didn't feel out of place, and no one bothered
me, asked me if they could help me, if there was anything
I needed. I couldn't even have said who were customers
and who were bookshop staff, as everyone seemed to be
happily reading books.

And then I saw the stand. It was beside the cash register,
prominently placed, though not as prominently as Maeve
Binchy's new work. Still, Erica's dump bin—as we carelessly
call the elaborate cardboard display stands of new
releases—was large and glossy, predominantly blue with a
lot of gold lettering. The illustration on the top of the
stand, a blowup of the cover, showed a raven-haired woman
standing looking out to sea, a blue dress blown back against
her body by the breeze, a pair of sandals held in her hand.
Surely the damn hook wasn't *still* selling well . . . yet here
it was, *Erica Tudor's latest glorious bestseller,* Gaining.

The top section of the dump bin was given over to copies
of *Gaining,* while the lower sections held copies of Erica's
earlier works.

I hadn't read *Gaining.* I'd had such a busy year with my
own list, and had been involved in an auction for one of
the biggest new literary talents at the time of its release. I
remember Beth and I had talked about how we hated the
title: Beth had told Erica repeatedly that it sounded like
a diet book, but Erica had been adamant, and Sammy had
sided with her. Diet books, he said, sold very well, and had
even suggested to Erica that she change the career of the
heroine from the owner of a chain of exclusive boutiques
to a chain of weight-reducing salons, something Erica had
thought a great angle. So, *Gaining:* and while I stood glaring at the gold copperplate name of my young nemesis,
three women bought it.

I waited until the last of the customers had abandoned
the dump bin and went over to it. I picked up *Gaining* and
began leafing through the pages.

His body was a perfect V, narrow hips broadening to wide powerful shoulders.

His hair was black, his eyes so dark that they, too, seemed black. They gazed at Fern steadily, asking questions of her that she dared not face. Give me a break.

It was a story of two women, a blonde and a brunette, both beautiful, both rich, both in love with a man, dark-haired, dark-eyed, rich . . . There were doctors involved—the brunette was sick . . . tests, tests . . . a marriage out of pity . . . adultery with Fern, the blonde.

The brunette wife finds she is suffering from Huntington's disease. By now she is pregnant. She goes to their favorite remote beach . . .

"Are you alright?"

I looked up from where I was leaning, gripping the edge of the counter.

The young man who had been playing the guitar—soft, long brown hair and brown eyes behind glasses—was looking at me with real kindness and concern. He spoke with a slight and charming accent.

"I'm okay, thank you. I think." Forgetting myself, speaking as if I were alone. "The bitch wants me dead."

He introduced himself as Eugene Boillot. I muttered my name, that Erica Tudor was having an affair with my husband—he knew all about it, for he read the *New York Times,* not to mention *Who.* He gave me coffee, good, strong coffee and he let his business partner, his sister Lisette, serve any customers. We sat talking for three hours, myself and this kind young man—though at thirty-three he was older than he appeared. There was a naïveté to him, an openness, that made me trust him instinctively.

Books were his great love, and he was fascinated by publishing, quizzing me about the whole process. And to hear firsthand a sordid tale of deceit and betrayal involving a best-selling author must have been captivating.

Sometimes you can talk to a stranger where you can't talk to a relative or a friend, and I think that's what happened on that October afternoon in Boillot's Bookshop.

I made an arrangement with Eugene that he would let me know of any new books that came out on the Vietnam War, and made a decision. I would buy all three of Erica's books, *Traces of Heaven, Strings,* and the latest, *Gaining.*

Eugene asked me to have lunch with him on the following Friday: I looked at him, startled, and thought: *This is a date. This man, nine years younger than me, is asking for a date.* For I could see more than empathy in his eyes— Eugene Boillot found me attractive. It astonished and delighted me even while it frightened me a little. He found me desirable.

How long had it been since a man had looked at me like that?

Even Keir.

When I returned to the farmhouse, there was a message on my machine, from Keir.

"I just . . . wondered how you were. I guess you've received the divorce papers by now." A long pause. A sigh. "Oh, God, Sally, I only . . . I wish there was some way that this could happen without hurting you . . ." Another pause.

"Beth told me about your farmhouse. It sounds like a beautiful place. I can see you there, windswept, sunburnt. Maybe . . . maybe you could phone me. Tell me about it."

There followed another long pause, so long that I thought he must have hung up, quietly. Then his voice again. "Phone me."

I was on my knees by the little table on which the phone stood, my head down, weeping.

In an effort to control my life, my feelings, I decided not to call him back. I told myself it was because I was busy, and this was true. Stephanie from the library tracked down several excellent reference books on Vietnam for me, and Eugene and Lisette faxed details of two brand-new titles I hadn't yet seen.

I enjoyed my lunch with Eugene, but refused another date, explaining that I wasn't yet ready. . . . He nodded, understanding.

Still I didn't phone Keir.

Was I punishing him, knowing he wanted to hear from me? Was I trying to cause him to worry? How much would he worry? What would it take for him to come to me?

It would take Erica being out of his life.

And out of mine.

I could *kill* Erica.

I wouldn't even need a weapon. Find her at one of her literary lunches . . . Erica in a pale blue silk dress, signing copies of *Gaining*- out on the balcony. *Yes.* Such a crush around the popular young authoress you wouldn't believe. And who would notice two eager hands come out and push the blue silk figure over the balcony, out into space. The look of surprise on her features, growing smaller and smaller, the blue silk fluttering about her, a copy of *Gaining* clutched in one well-manicured hand . . .

Erica Tudor's new novel hits the streets.

Chapter Eight

Several days later, I was awakened by Brendan Jones of Fredericton Fences Ltd. He and his brother and employees were in my south field, working on the fence. and Alby Gresson was there, waving a shotgun around and threatening to shoot the workers.

I pulled on jeans and a sweater and raced off down the drive, cutting through the fence and across the south field, puffing now, to the trees, and a twenty-meter jog through the woods to the boundary. The trucks belonging to Fredericton Fences would have had an easier job, Alby having given his permission for them to cross his property, it being almost entirely cleared. He had, Brendan Jones had informed me, been most cooperative.

And why not? I'd thought, wryly, with two hundred meters of free fencing at stake?

But any cooperativeness had evaporated by the time I broke out of the woods and tramped across to the stationary men and machines. Admittedly, Alby carried his shotgun pointed at the ground and spoke quietly, but the very sight of it, the metal of its twin barrels catching the early-morning sun, made me shiver.

Holes had been dug down the hill towards the main road, and I failed to see what the problem could be. But as I approached, Alby was only too pleased to let me know.

"We didn't come to any agreement about cutting down trees, Mrs. Stanforth. Won't have it. You tell these fellows right now, or they can clear off my land."

I looked from Alby's determined face to the patient, suntanned features of Brendan Jones and his partner, his brother, Matthew. "I don't understand," I said. "You said nothing of chopping down trees, Mr. Jones."

"Three trees, Mrs. Stanforth—you can see them down there." And I could, now. They lay in a dip in the slope where they'd have collected more water and were better protected than on the slope. They were about thirty feet tall. Not giants of the forest by any means, but still . . .

"I don't want to cut down any trees, Mr. Jones."

"But ma'am, they're little more than saplings."

"You heard her," growled Alby. "That's both of us, now. We don't want any trees cut down, you hear?"

Alby had edged closer to me, was standing at my shoulder. We were just the same height and must, at that moment, have been alike in our expressions. The Jones brothers looked at each other helplessly.

"What are we to do, then, ma'am? Do you want a straight line of fence, or not?" Brendan Jones asked.

"A straight line of fence," I said carefully, "is the ideal, I suppose." I felt Alby bristle, glare at me. "But it's only aesthetic, isn't it?"

The Jones brothers looked at me with their mouths slightly open. Alby gave a gnome-like chortle of laughter.

"What are you saying, Mrs. Stanforth?" Matthew, the younger of the two large men, scratched his sandy-colored beard. "Are you saying you don't care if the fence isn't straight?"

I nodded.

"Well, you're paying for this, ma'am," said Brendan. "We're here to do as you say. Just tell us what sort of a fence you want us to build, and we'll build it."

"Take the line back onto my property, just before the first tree. Mr. Gresson can have the extra few meters. Bring the fence back into alignment farther down the slope, after the last tree."

"Is this a curve you want, ma'am, or a sort of rectangle shape?" Matthew asked with barely disguised sarcasm.

I met his gaze. "Rectangles are cheaper than curves, aren't they, Mr. Jones?"

Alby was chortling so hard he forgot to breathe and came out with a snort that made us all look at him.

I noticed Brendan Jones was trying to hide a smile. "We can do it, Mrs. Stanforth. It shouldn't cost too much more." He met his brother's frowning gaze. "Rectangles *are* cheaper than curves, Matt."

"I'll have to order more timber," said Matthew and turned away, but not before I heard him mutter something about a lot of trouble and money for three lousy little trees.

Alby said, "Would you hold my gun for a moment, Mrs. Stanforth?"

And I found myself holding the heavy weapon, so awkwardly, so unprepared for the weight of it, that I nearly dropped it. Alby had gone over to one of the trucks and, leaning back against the hood, was removing his boot and seemed to be shaking a stone from it.

Or, at least, that's what I thought he was doing, until I heard two car doors slamming, one after the other, and turned to find a police car parked on the grass nearby, and Perry McGarret and a young officer with a head of thick, blond curls walking towards us.

He was slim, with a strength that seemed more wiry than the heaviness of bone and muscle evident in McGarret's frame. He looked to be only in his early twenties, but he nodded pleasantly to Alby, and spoke his name. Then, approaching the Joneses and myself, "Matthew, Brendan . . ." He didn't know my name, but smiled—a warm smile, showing very white teeth—and touched the brim of his cap.

McGarret was beside me. He said, "You have a license for that weapon, Mrs. Stanforth?"

I looked at him and tried to think of something to say.

The men—all the men, even the workmen who were standing idly by—burst into laughter.

The young officer reached up and punched McGarret on the upper arm. "Stop it, Perry—don't you know how scary you look? He was joking, ma'am," he said to me.

I looked at McGarret. The corners of his mouth were pulled a little. "I *was* joking," he said.

I felt myself blushing

McGarret held out one enormous hand towards me. I stared at it, then realized he wanted to take possession of the shotgun. I handed it over, almost gratefully. He broke it, peered at it, cradled it over one arm, and sauntered over to Alby by the truck.

"Constable Peter Copely." I turned and the blond young officer was holding out a hand also, to shake my own in a warm and friendly grip. "I gotta admit Perry and I were worried when we got the call to come out here, Mrs. Stanforth, but you've managed to defuse the situation here."

If he was laughing at me it was done so good-naturedly that I couldn't take offence.

"We've solved the misunderstanding, yes. There was never really a problem."

I looked over at Alby: he was standing calmly enough, his hands in his trouser pockets as he listened to McGarret. The big man was leaning back against the body of the truck, the shotgun held negligently over one crooked elbow and his cap pulled down low against the bright sunlight. The two looked extremely incongruous, the difference in their heights and builds so exaggerated. But there in the morning sun they seemed to be chatting quite amicably. Even when McGarret walked off, still carrying the weapon, Alby watched it go with equanimity.

McGarret approached me. Once again one of his hands was held out. I saw, as on that day he had leaned on the edge of my car window, the scarred knuckles.

"We were never properly introduced. Perry McGarret."

I shook his hand. "Sarah Stanforth."

He nodded, and looked over at Constable Copely. "You coming?"

Peter Copely had been discussing salmon fishing with the Jones boys and dragged himself away with some reluctance.

"You got a car?" McGarret asked me.

"No. I walked. Or ran," I added dryly.

"Hop in." He was walking towards the police car.

"It's not far." But he was already holding the back door for me. I climbed in and he shut the door and put the shotgun in the trunk.

Peter Copely got into the driver's seat and grinned at me in the rearview mirror. "Looking forward to driving to your place—haven't seen it since I was a kid."

"You know the place?" I asked.

"My grandparents were friends of the Hahns. I used to visit when I was about six, seven. That old car still in the barn?"

McGarret sank into the passenger seat, and looked at Copely.

"The Buick? Yes," I said.

"Haven't seen the place for a long time . . ." repeated Peter Copely rather wistfully, as he started the car and turned it around.

"If you have time, I'll show you around," I offered, not thinking they would, being on duty.

Through the window, Brendan and Matthew Jones were waving. The oddest sight, however, was Alby Gresson, also smiling, also waving.

"Sorry?" I asked, for McGarret had rumbled something in his bass voice that I hadn't quite caught.

He took off his sunglasses and turned to me, and I was struck by the sight of very dark blue eyes, his father's eyes, warm eyes, intelligent, perceptive.

He said, in a slightly louder rumble, "We could manage that."

The two men even stayed for coffee, sitting at the big oak table in a kitchen I had thought was very large until filled by two policemen over six feet tall. I showed them around the house, and Peter Copely ran on ahead rather like the boy he had been when he had last seen the place. McGarret lumbered along beside me or just behind me, not saying much.

I showed them the garage and the barn, and they walked round and round the old Buick, and round and round the aborted engine, and back and forth between the Buick and the engine, their heads together, muttering mechanical jargon. Peter Copely even found the missing backseat. "It's probably where my brother Dan and I left it." And he led us towards a manhole in the wooden ceiling. He found a ladder, too, and we all, one by one, climbed it, though it creaked dangerously under the weight of the men.

There was the car seat, its brown leather stained with bird droppings, in front of the loading door of the loft.

The two police officers carried the car seat back down the ladder for me, and propped it in a corner.

Constable Copely said, "I'll ask around, if you like. Might know someone who'd buy the car from you."

"Great, I'd like to get rid of it."

McGarret scowled at the Buick, seemingly lost in thought. Then he said, to no one in particular, "Come on," and left the barn abruptly.

Copely and I followed him out into the sunshine. He was climbing behind the wheel of the patrol car.

"You said I could drive," Copely complained.

"You can choose lunch."

"Luigi's Burgers."

McGarret groaned.

"Then let me drive."

"Luigi's then—but none of them garlic burgers."

"You're the boss."

I thought they'd forgotten me in this exchange, but both

paused, halfway into the car. "Thanks," McGarret said, and disappeared.

Copely leaned over and took my hand. "Nice to meet you, Mrs. Stanforth, thanks for the tour and the coffee. We'll see you again, I'm sure."

I watched the car begin to leave, then it stopped abruptly and reversed, expertly, to pause on the other side of me.

The black sunglasses back in place, McGarret said, "Better get a lock for the garage and the barn. We don't like to encourage thieves round these here parts."

And he drove off once more.

Roun' these heah pohts. More and more I had the feeling that the man had somehow strayed off the set of *In the Heat of the Night.*

It snowed during the night, and in the morning I went out to the wood heap to cut some kindling; I liked to keep the fire in the big hearth set and ready, despite the cottage having excellent central heating. I was becoming quite capable with an ax—something I'd never touched in my life. Keir had always cut the firewood at our place in Beaver Creek.

When the voice spoke behind me, suddenly, destroying my aim and sending two splinters of wood flying in opposite directions, I knew it was Alby Gresson. I swung around and glared at him.

"Sorry, didn't mean to scare you. I'm light on my feet, always have been. Makes for being a good hunter, come the season. But I do tend to scare folks sometimes."

I looked at him: he wore a clean blue-checked shirt and well-scrubbed, faded denims, but above the mud and snow on his boots there was a shine to the brown leather. He must be kept busy, with his own farm and helping his sons, yet I didn't know a farmer in the district who was as consistently well turned-out as Alby Gresson.

"How come you don't have anyone to do that for you?" Alby asked now, with a jerk of his head in the direction of my ax leaning against the chopping block. "A woman can't do everything around a place this big," said Alby.

"Why not?" I didn't like his attitude. I don't know why it was, but I sensed, still, the proprietary feelings he had towards this farm.

"You need a man around. You need a man around for a lot of things." And he smiled. It was a leer, really.

I looked away to throw more kindling into the basket. I hoped I was mistaken, but when I looked back at him and caught his gaze . . . It was definitely a leer.

"I'm coping very well, Mr. Gresson, thank you very much."

"Just concerned about you, that's all. A woman out here. All alone. Just being neighborly. I used to work for the Hahns, you know. Did everything for them. A good man, Otto. And Frieda—fine woman, that. Treated me like one of the family. Ate with them in the kitchen many a time. We'd stop work and have coffee most mornings. In the kitchen."

I didn't reply to this. In the silence, I realized that he was waiting for me to note that it was mid morning, that it was time for coffee, and today he obviously had the inclination to accept an invitation—if I would give one.

But I was silent.

Why didn't I like him? He'd lived a sad and lonely life. There was no harm in being kind to a lonely old man, was there?

But the silence had lasted too long, my hesitation had somehow communicated itself. His handsome, small features tightened, his eyes narrowed.

"Place like this," he said, almost resentfully, "it's too big for a woman to run all by herself. You'll need a hired hand. I came over to offer—any jobs you need doing, I'm available. Only live two hundred meters down the road. There's the phone number." He brought out, from his shirt pocket, a neatly folded piece of paper. On it was written, *Albert Gresson, Esq.* and a phone number.

"Thank you," I murmured, holding the paper helplessly. "But just now . . ."

"Front gate's in bad shape. Never been the same since that dyke from over the way backed into it. Otto had me fix it but it was only temporary. And the nameplate won't fit on the new top bar I had to put on—too narrow."

"Nameplate?"

"This place has a name. Got the nameplate at home—copper, it is. Frieda had it made by one of those artsy types in town."

"Could you bring it back?" I asked, and then was sorry I had spoken. I didn't want to give Alby an excuse to come back.

"Gave it to me, they did, before they left," Alby said tightly. "Don't forget, my fifty hectares was part of this place—got just as much right to be called . . ." and he muttered a word I couldn't catch.

"What did you call it?" I queried.

"Never you mind!" His voice was suddenly loud. "Maybe I'll give it back, maybe I won't. Anyway, you need me to work around here? Eaves need clearing out already. Windows'll need painting before winter. Pasture gates need painting now. I got other people waiting on my services but thought I'd give this place first option, for old times. What do you say, Mrs. Stanforth?"

What do I say? I didn't like him, I didn't want him hanging about the place, nor did I want an implacable enemy.

I had to stand up for myself. This was a new country, a new Sarah. "I'm sorry, Mr. Gresson, but I've already made arrangements with someone from town to do any heavy work I can't manage."

He didn't speak for some seconds, his expression one of complete surprise, even shock.

"Who?" he said, the one syllable a hostile, even violent demand.

"Someone from town," I said, picking up the basket and turning towards the house.

He moved in front of me. "Who in town? I know everyone in town."

I took a breath to gain time, and held his gaze. "I don't think that is really any concern of yours, Mr. Gresson. You should have spoken sooner. I presumed you'd be busy with your own farm."

He didn't want to deny that. "Am," he said, grudgingly, "but I thought I'd help you out, being a neighbor. It's not the money, don't need that. Always been a careful man and I got plenty. Wasn't asking for charity—just like to do a bit of work elsewheres for a change, get off my own place."

He turned and stumped off along the drive.

"I wasn't suggesting . . ." I started to say, but he disappeared round the barn, and a little later I saw his small, upright figure stalking away down the drive. I wondered if he'd come that way. Or had he cut across country, through the woods?

It was being unneighborly, perhaps, but I didn't like that thought. Already, they were *my* woods. Even on a visit—and I hoped there wouldn't be too many—I wanted Alby Gresson to come up the drive like normal folk.

I returned to the house, and rang Frank Dufour: he recommended a man named Larry Carey as a handyman and I phoned and asked if he'd come round the following day and clean out the guttering. He was a brown, wiry young man in his early twenties, and he seemed keen to work. When I brought coffee out to him, we sat on the porch and he told me why. "Two sets of twins and another baby on the way. Marie says this one has to be a single—won't know for another three weeks. Not that I mind twins, but . . . as it is, it'll be five babies in four years."

I sat there with him, drinking coffee, and found myself feeling a little nervous, edgy.

It was nothing to do with the man before me, speaking so fondly of his tired young wife and growing family. It was the fact that the house—except for where the barn blocked some of the view—was so exposed. Anyone lurking in the woods down by the boundary that adjoined Spring Mill Road had a clear view up the fields to the cottage. What if Alby had seen Larry's battered pickup turn in the gates? Or . . . maybe he watched the house anyway.

No. Surely he had better things to do. A berry farm needed a lot of work in the fall.

Didn't it?

One of the nice things about living alone is that one can wear what one likes, dress for comfort and not have to take anyone else's opinions into consideration. That night, before I went to bed, I curled up on one of the twin settees in the living room and watched the late news. I wore an ancient, almost threadbare pair of flannel pyjamas, purple ski socks, and two new purchases—a white terry cloth robe and a pair of slippers, big, very pink, very fluffy creations that would make a good present for a yeti. What really sold me on them was the little faces on the toes, black shoe-button eyes and whiskers and very long ears, which I sometimes jammed in doors when going from room to room.

I had been out with Merlin and Natalie, and I was just debating whether a hot chocolate would help me not to have a hangover in the morning, when the phone rang.

"Sally?" Keir's voice, hesitant, as if unsure of his welcome.

I carried the phone to its furthest extent and sank down on the arm of one of the settees. "Where are you?" I asked, hoping he was close, coming to me.

"New York. I'm back in the apartment. It was good of you to say you wanted me to have it, but I've put it in your name. I'll stay on, if that's alright, and pay any expenses."

He was still in New York.

He was still talking of property division.

"Are you well, Sally?" Keir was saying. "Tell me how you are."

"I'm . . . fine," I said. "I'm coping."

*My life is in shreds, you stupid prick. You've taken from me
everything that was sure, everything that was safe, and left me
with chaos. I am lost. That's how I am, Keir. Lost.*

"And you?"

"The same. Coping." A pause. "It's not easy."

I held my breath. What isn't easy? Let it be *life without
me.*

"Erica's in New Hampshire, she didn't come down with
me."

In the pause, soaring hope.

He seemed embarrassed. "I felt I should . . . at least get
divorced. Make it look as if it's *serious.* I feel as if I've
compromised her, Sally. She's getting hate mail, did Beth
tell you?"

"No." Beth trying to sit on the fence. But she was my
friend, she should have realized how much I'd have
enjoyed the idea of sacks of hate mail arriving for Erica
Tudor. If she was really my pal, I thought sullenly, Beth
would have sent them all up to me. If so many people had
taken the trouble to write, then *someone* should get some
gratification out of it.

"Will you call me, Sally? During the week I'll be here
at the apartment. Call me anytime."

"I'll try, but I'm very busy. I have a social life up here,
Keir. And . . . I'm writing."

"Wonderful! That's wonderful! What's it about?"

"Loss, grief, anger . . ."

I was holding the receiver with both hands, my body
stiff with self-control. "I have to go now, Keir," I lied.
"Someone's at the door." Then, "Is she going to join
you?"

"Yes," he said. "She's working on the new novel. She
said she'd be busy anyway, and I should come back to New
York, and drive up on the weekends."

Some relationship.

He went on, "I'm glad to be alone so I can call you, talk
to you. Are you happy, Sally? Are you alright?"

"I'm not going to fall apart, Keir," came my cool, almost downright cold, little voice.

"I know. I know how strong you are."

I closed my eyes against the pain, against the wilful stupidity of this beloved man.

I said, "Does there have to be a divorce, though? Can't you just live with her?"

A sigh, sharper, a touch of exasperation to the sound, yet I couldn't tell if it was directed at me or at himself. "It's the newspapers, the media coverage. I guess they see this affair with Erica as irresponsible."

So," I said, "you're getting divorced in order to legitimize your relationship with Erica?"

"Please—" he started. But I hung up on him, stumbled to the liquor cabinet, and poured a glass of gin.

I went to bed and took the bottle with me. I drank myself to sleep for the first time since the night I had discovered Keir had been having an affair with Erica.

Sometimes a hot chocolate just isn't enough.

Chapter Nine

Kate Millett records in *Flying* how she advised an unhappily married artist friend that if she wanted to leave her relationship she should do so in order to *work*. That the work would always be there to depend on, more reliable than love.

Why remember that now? I'd read *Flying* in the early seventies. Why these words? Now.

Because of *Scotty's Things*. I was finding myself, the girl that Sarah had been.

And I was losing part of myself, too. Losing the edge of my pain over Keir. A pain I had lived with for so many months and in such uncomfortable proximity, that to come to myself and find I had not been grieving over Keir for an hour or more, was a kind of enlightenment, like breaking out of dark woods and suddenly knowing the way home. I found myself waking up in the middle of the night thinking about the manuscript, and, during my days, rushing through my chores in order to get back to it.

Hi, this is Sarah. I'm close by but I can't get to the phone just now, so please leave a message when you hear . . .

I was dreaming of Keir. I woke up, hearing his voice,

and scrambled to the phone in the living room with such haste that I ran into the door and bruised my forehead.

"Call me when you can. I *have* to talk to you, Sally."

"Keir, I'm here!" breathlessly.

"Oh, God."

"What's the matter? What?"

"I thought . . . I . . ." He was silent for some seconds, then, in a calmer voice, "the divorce came through—did they tell you yet?"

"No, I had a message to phone the lawyers but I've been busy."

"I was going to drive up to see you. Would you see me? Talk to me?"

"Yes. Yes, of course."

"I don't . . . I don't know if I should come, now."

"What do you mean? Why not? Keir, what's the matter, have you and Erica split up? Keir?"

"She's pregnant, Sally."

The desperation, the pain in his voice, meant, at that moment, nothing at all. I heard only his words, and their meaning.

Erica was pregnant.

Keir's son, Keir's daughter, was at this very moment growing inside Erica Tudor. Not me. *Erica*. Once again, Erica had taken what she wanted.

"I didn't . . . for *you.*" I could barely get the words out. "I did what you wanted . . . and I lost you. I don't . . . *a child.* A child to remind me of you . . . of *us* . . ." I stopped, wondering if I was making any sense. It was suddenly so hard to put my words, my thoughts, in order. For even if Keir still loved me, he now belonged to *them,* to Erica and their child. He would not abandon them.

"When's it due?" Such a cool voice; was it really mine?

"The last week in July. She's only six weeks pregnant . . . Sally—I didn't want you to read it in the newspapers. Someone from her gynecologist's office has leaked the news to the press."

He sounded wretched, but I couldn't gather my thoughts, couldn't think of anything to say.

Keir continued, "It wasn't supposed to happen. She always talked about her career coming first. Now she tells me she planned it, as if that makes it alright. *I didn't want this, Sally.*"

"It's alright. It doesn't matter. You must be pleased *now*, though. You must. Your little girl, or your son . . . you must be pleased. Aren't you?"

A long pause. Unwillingly, "Yes. Maybe. Now it's a reality. Pleased for the child, the baby itself. Not . . ." Another pause, *"as something to share."*

I closed my eyes against my tears.

Keir said, "Do you understand?"

"Yes," I said.

"I can't . . . I can't ask you what I should do."

"No. Don't." Quite definite, almost hard. For I didn't care. Later, I knew I would, but here, now, on this bleak morning in early December, holding the telephone receiver in my own living room, hundreds of miles from Keir, I didn't want to know anymore. Later, my coldness would amaze me. I'm certain it surprised Keir.

"Look, Sally, I want to see you. We've always been there for each other, for twenty-five years. I'm realizing that I can't throw that away—I don't *want* to throw it all away."

His words were like a blade, twisting inside me. I had used almost the same words to him that night in New York when I'd discovered the affair with Erica. *You can't throw away twenty-five years of love, Keir! You'll come to regret it. You can't throw it away.*

But he hadn't listened, he hadn't wanted to know.

And now it was me. I didn't want to listen, I didn't want to know. Not because I loved him less, I didn't. But I felt myself being destroyed with each word he uttered.

"This is your decision, Keir. It has to be all your decision."

"I love you, Sally. I haven't stopped loving you. I want to see you."

I replaced the receiver, quietly.

Despite the solid months of work, after Keir's call, I found I couldn't write *Scotty's Things*. I simply could get no further with the plot. When I tried, my sentences were stilted, the conversations clichéd. I could no longer *see* my characters, let alone know them; they had become strangers. So I mailed what I'd completed—eight chapters—to Beth, with a note that said, *Dear Beth, be honest. Love Sally.*

The answer came in a phone call three days later, at one in the morning. "Yes!" before I said more than hello. "Sally," and a catch in her voice, "It's beautiful. It's *beautiful.*"

"You're interested?" I breathed, still bemused, groggy from sleep.

"Yes! *Yes!* Now finish it. Start tomorrow. Tonight! I want to read the rest of it! And Sal?"

"Yes?"

"I can't wait to tell Erica."

The friends I saw the most during those weeks that led through Hanukkah and Christmas were Natalie, Merlin and her parents, and the Dufour family. Merlin and Natalie bought me a pair of ice skates, and Frank and Nanette presented me with an enormous red and blue sled. Janice and David McGarret gave me a small original watercolor that had struck them as looking rather like the hills above the farmhouse.

And I was even pleasantly surprised to receive a card from their son, signed briefly, with a heavy hand, *Regards, Perry McGarret.*

With skates and a toboggan for presents, it would have been very churlish not to use them when invited out with the kind people who had given me these gifts. So I found myself, that winter, learning to dance on ice with the Dufours' eldest boy, nineteen-year-old Jerome, on skating trips with the family, and tobogganing down the slope at the back of the house with a shrieking Merlin and Natalie and their four mongrel dogs tumbling about with us in the snow.

From New York—an odd silence. I'd had so many friends, and Christmases with the Stanforths had always been the central event of the year's calendar. Now, not a phone call from anyone—except Keir.

His call on December twentieth brought the Keir I had lately come to expect, caring, unhappy, embarrassed. He didn't know what to send me as a gift, he said. Was there anything I would particularly like?

"Erica's head on a platter."

"Sally . . ." A touch of exasperation.

"Keir, we're divorced. Divorced people aren't supposed to give each other presents."

"We're not the usual divorced couple."

"No." Both our voices heavy. It was painfully true. It would have been comforting to say, *No, you are my enemy. I hate you now. My love has turned to hate and you will be my enemy until we die.* But I loved him still.

"I'll put some money in your account for you," he said.

"Not a lot, Keir—"

"Three hundred—only three hundred dollars. Buy yourself something fun. From me. Something silly. Promise?"

"Okay," I managed.

"I'll call you again soon."

"Okay."

It was on one of the shopping days between Christmas and New Year's that I drove into St. Claude to buy my gift from Keir. I couldn't think of anything "fun" or "silly" I really wanted. I'd left my frivolous side in New York, along with the woman who had been Mrs. Sally Stanforth.

No, today I was being extremely practical. I was going to replace my old briefcase, one that Keir had bought me for a birthday present. It was now sixteen years old, and sentiment and good care could no longer hide that it was falling apart.

But replacing the briefcase would be yet another break with Keir, with my old life, with the rushed mornings and manuscripts that were now published novels, with the memories that that ancient black briefcase contained.

I liked the atmosphere of the leather goods shop, the wood paneling, the expensive imported goods and their scent of leather and polish. I found myself seduced by a square-cornered, beautifully crafted Italian briefcase in dark green.

The sale done, I was just wondering whether the briefcase's color would really be practical, how much of my wardrobe would tone with its British Racing Green shade, when the gunshots began.

They came from some distance, three in quick succession, then a pause—and two more.

I looked up at the shop assistant, an impeccably groomed woman in her late forties. Her face had paled. "Oh, my heavens!"

Gunshots now, police sirens . . . *I know some policemen. I know them by name . . .*

I hurriedly paid for the green bag and left the shop, turning towards King Street, where my car was parked.

King Street was being cordoned off, there were two ambulances coming along from the direction of the local hospital, sirens wailing. My car had narrowly missed being part of the cordoned-off area, and I stood by it, in a gathering crowd on the civilian side of the yellow tape that pronounced every few feet, *Police line do not cross* . . .

And then I saw McGarret striding purposefully from the shattered glass doors of the St. Claude branch of my American bank, over to where . . .

A group of people were gathered around a man's body lying on the roadway, lying very still.

McGarret spoke briefly to another policeman, older, shorter, stockier, then glanced up and moved back towards Copely, now leading a young man, handcuffed, from the bank. A young female bank teller came out the door immediately behind them, and McGarret spoke to her before looking up at one of the several approaching ambulance attendants and guiding her towards them. Someone covered up the man on the ground.

More police arrived, and an officer asked the crowd to please pull back, please go about their own business . . .

McGarret was standing once more by the fallen man, discussing something with the older and obviously more senior officer.

And none of this, disturbing sight though it was, would have been out of the ordinary, given the man's job, were it not for the dark stain at the shoulder of his navy blue overcoat, and the bright red blood that dripped, dripped, dripped, from the scarlet fingers of his left hand, held awkwardly, carefully, a little way from his body.

"Move back, please . . . Come on, folks, go on back to work, everything's under control here," the young policeman said to the crowd around me. I started to turn away, with one last worried glance at the wounded McGarret.

Then he looked over, and saw me.

I had to stand still, then, for he was walking towards me. The young policeman saw him coming and stepped out of his way. The crowd parted like the Red Sea, and he didn't take his eyes from mine. I could see the bullet hole in his coat, such a small hole . . .

The police cordon was strung between us, and he stopped at the flimsy barrier. His blood dripped, tapping, onto the plastic tape and he moved his hand a little, so, instead, it made a dark puddle on the road's surface.

"Mrs. Stanforth?" Startled by the deep voice speaking my name, startled away from the sight of his blood falling from each of his fingers, I dragged my gaze up to his face and found myself thinking, *He's been shot. Someone has shot him. And he hasn't lost his hat.*

"Mrs. Stanforth, I'd like you to do something for me."

"Yes?" He was pale under the brim of his hat, the pupils of the dark blue eyes were dilated a little, and the deeply grooved lines that ran from his nose to his mouth were white. He was probably going into shock.

"I'll have to go to the hospital, I guess." *I guess.* "Will you go on out to my parents' place and tell my mother you've seen me and that I'm still standing?"

"Yes. I'll go now. Your parents will be worried if they hear."

"Someone at the station'll phone my father—it's my mother I'm worried about. And tell them we caught both of them." He jerked his head back towards the man lying on the ground. The ambulance attendants were even now lifting the body. A police car started up and drove off.

One of the ambulance attendants moved towards McGarret. "Perry!" with professional heartiness. "Don't stand there bleeding all over the street!" Like two tugs he and Copely came alongside and nudged the big man towards an ambulance stretcher now being pushed towards him. He watched me go to my car, not turning away until I started the engine. I wondered if he wanted me to be able to deliver the message literally, *Tell my mother I'm still standing.*

If John Wayne never said that, then he should have. John Wayne, come to think of it, never lost his hat either, that I can remember.

My hands shook and sweated on the wheel, all the way up into the hills to the big white house made of glass.

Chapter Ten

When Janice McGarret greeted me in the hall, I could tell instantly that a phone call had already alerted her. Her large face was a ghastly, pasty white, and her dark eyes were red-rimmed.

"Raoul—Inspector Raoul Gerlain—he was still at the scene, but he phoned to let me know. He said you were coming straight over. Thank you, Sarah."

"Perry said to tell you he was alright. He said, and I quote his words exactly, 'Tell my mother you've seen me and I'm still standing.' He smiled when he said it. He's very tough—I'm sure he'll be okay, Janice." I hoped I sounded confident.

"Sarah, could I presume on your kindness again? Will you take me to the hospital? I think I'm too upset to drive myself."

"Certainly."

The maid was standing at the door, holding Janice's handbag, a fur hat, and a luxurious woollen overcoat.

"David's playing tennis. I left a message for them to tell him to get to the hospital immediately."

We left the house and she almost ran towards my car. I

still felt shaken by what I'd seen, but I had to describe everything to Janice McGarret as I drove, every little detail, from hearing the gunshots, to my last sight of her son, his body held stiffly, determined not to collapse until I had driven off.

I wondered what would happen at the hospital, whether—and how soon—I could escape to go home. I wanted a brandy, or a gin and tonic at the least.

"I called Merlin. Natalie's on a day off, so she won't be at the hospital. I told Merlin to meet us there. I do hope David won't lose his temper—this will upset him."

If the accident made any hidden resentments and smoldering blame come to the surface among the McGarrets tonight, it was going to be a bumpy time indeed. I wished I could desert them. And even as I was thinking that, Janice put out a hand and placed it over my own on the wheel. Her touch was icy—she, too, for all I knew, might be going into shock.

"I can't tell you how grateful I am that you drove out to see me," she said.

Did soldiers in the field feel like this? Officers who had to lead men through heavy shelling? Suddenly caught up in circumstances beyond their control, in a drama beyond comprehension, drawn further and further into the conflict by an overwhelming sense of duty? I had problems of my own, my husband loved me but was staying with a woman with whom he was fast falling out of love, out of a sense of . . .

Duty.

We were mad, I decided. All us really nice, well-brought-up people of the world. We were all mad.

At the hospital we were ushered into a waiting area outside Intensive Care. I fetched a cup of tea from a nearby machine for Janice and told her, for the twenty-third time, not to worry about her son.

Janice was still trembling with the frustrated urge to

heal, protect, nurture him, as she had done a third of a century before. He's her baby, I thought suddenly, wonderingly. That great overgrown slab of granite in there is her little boy.

If you'd been a mother, Sarah, you'd understand.

Merlin arrived, and the two women embraced, Merlin barely controlling her tears. "Natalie sends her love—I thought it best if she stayed at home with the dogs, just in case Daddy—"

"I know, darling. Thank Natalie for me. I understand. . . . And here's Sarah, who was there almost when it happened. She's been so kind."

Merlin and I embraced, and she really did cry now. Her own handkerchief was already wet, so I gave her mine. After she calmed down a little, we sat in a row on the uncomfortable vinyl chairs, mother and daughter holding tight to each other's hands.

"Why did he have to do this?" Janice asked no one in particular. "He had so many opportunities. He's a bright boy. . . . Why choose to do this? Chasing bank robbers, cutting dead bodies out of car wrecks, going to houses where women and children have been brutalized—Oh, I know what he does, though he won't talk about it. How can he *do* it?"

"I don't know, Mamma. It's just the way he is. He knows the risks. Maybe he *needs* the risks. Even as a kid he had such a strong sense of right and wrong, remember?" And Merlin turned to me, half-laughing. "I used to tag along when he'd play cops and robbers with his friends. Perry *never* wanted to play the villain. Perry always had to be the cop, the hero, the good guy—" her voice broke.

"A man died today," her mother said. One of the bank robbers. Raoul Gerlain told me. He died in the street. Perry and Peter's car was the first on the scene. The robbers came out shooting when they saw the car pull up. They still don't know if it was Perry or Peter who shot the man. The other robber ran back inside when he heard the backup cars arrive. He surrendered."

I had wondered how it had happened. But it only made me feel worse. Quick footsteps on the linoleum made us look up in the direction of the elevators. David was striding towards us. He embraced all of us in turn, Janice, Merlin, and myself. I was beginning to feel very odd, included—however temporarily—into this family of disturbing and inimitable people.

David looked drawn, as if this attempt on his son's life had aged him. I felt a wave of pity for him.

I glanced at the clock on the wall. When would someone come and tell us he was alright? He *would* be alright. He had to he. He was built—as Collette Palmer, my Australian writer, would have it—like a brick shit house. He had stood there in the street, talking to me, hadn't he? Covered in blood under that blue regulation overcoat, okay, but standing and delivering orders—well, requests—in a calm and confident manner that belied the sizable hole in his shoulder.

A doctor appeared, and David, Janice, and Merlin sprang to their feet. I rose a little slower, hung back, not wanting to intrude.

There was no need to worry, the surgeon said, the bullet had chipped bone and there'd been some bleeding, but he was not in any danger, and he'd recover the use of his arm without much more effect than a touch of rheumatism when he was older. Right now he was conscious but drowsy. We could see him if we liked.

As the family trooped for the door, I excused myself, saying I'd come back the next day and visit.

David McGarret turned and scowled at me, "We're taking you to dinner." The invitation like a threat.

"No, really . . ." over Merlin and Janice's insistence. David hooked his arm in mine and would have escorted me through the doors to his son but I was stubborn in this, and held back. "Okay, I'll accept the dinner invitation. Thank you. But I insist you go in there without me. It should be a family thing. Go on."

They left, and I sat down again on one of the vinyl chairs

in some relief to be alone. It wasn't that I didn't care about these people. I did. Somehow, unwillingly, unwittingly, they had become my friends. But I'd done enough, and wanted to be away from here, back at my little log cabin, back to my telephone and my novel and the hope that Keir might ring tonight.

Yes.

"Sarah?" Janice's voice dragged me back from more thoughts of the past. I looked up, startled. Not only Janice, but David and Merlin were smiling at me. "Perry would like to see you."

He must be exhausted, they all must be very tired, it was getting late and the nurses might . . . But David put his hand beneath my elbow and ushered me towards the door, towards the room where his son lay. We entered—and I turned, surprised, when David smiled and left me there. He closed the door behind him.

The room bristled with intimidating medical equipment, and there were two beds, one empty. McGarret lay on the bed farthest from the door, and I was relieved to see that his eyes were closed and he appeared to be sleeping.

I moved to leave but thought, no, I'd better stay a little bit longer for the family's sake. So I walked to the window on the other side of his bed, watching the sleeping man all the while. He'd still be recovering from the anesthetic, of course, and they'd probably given him something for the pain. Once his family had left the room, he had quite naturally dozed off. *I could* speak his name, wake him . . . but why? And what would we talk about?

I turned to the window: it was thick glass, but I could faintly hear the wind keening past the building. Like the McGarret mansion, the hospital was built on slopes and there was a wonderful view, there before me, of the river and the lights of St. Claude, just beginning to twinkle in the dusk. The low clouds, pregnant with more snow, threw a gold reflection back at the little town.

I suddenly felt very lonely, very distanced from everyone. The afternoon, filled with death and the fear of death, had me wondering. What was I doing with my life?

These people I had befriended—all the people I knew in that little town there below me—lighting their lights, living their lives . . . They *had* lives. I seemed—even today, even now—to be living my life vicariously through others. When was I going to be happy again? How long was I going to remain, like that Sarah in the glass before me, on the outside, looking in?

The dark outside threw the reflection of the entire room onto the glass. There was a dull light over Perry McGarret's bed, and I saw that he had moved his head. His face had been turned slightly more towards the door, as if he had dozed waiting for me to enter. Now his face was turned away from the light, from the door, towards the window, the features in shadow.

I looked over my shoulder and, yes, he was watching me.

I opened my mouth to say *How do you feel?* but he spoke before I could do so.

"What are you thinking about?" he asked.

"The town. You can see the lights of almost all St. Claude from here. The river is just a dark curved line."

"I know what you can see. I was asking what you were thinking about. Seems to me it didn't have much to do with the view."

I looked at him directly, at the heavy brow that threw his eyes in shadow. I didn't need questions like this right now. What was he made of, anyhow, that he could come out of a general anesthetic and hold a conversation like this?

To gain time, I walked around the bed to the side where the light was attached. He turned his head to follow me, so now his face was no longer in shadow.

Finally I said, "Days like today make one thoughtful. Standing on a hilltop looking at one's town always makes one feel detached."

And he said, gently, "Is *one* lonely?"

Gratingly, "No, Sergeant McGarret, *one* is not. One is a writer. Writers often indulge in seemingly time-wasting introspection which, in *one's* particular profession can be helpful and, ultimately, lucrative."

He didn't say anything. He lay there quietly with a smile lurking somewhere behind his still features. Yet he was pale, the white lines between his nose and mouth as evident as they had been that afternoon.

I said, "You're hurting, aren't you?"

It was an opportunity to study Perry McGarret debating how to lie. Somehow I knew he didn't like doing it and wouldn't be good at it. The man was refreshing in some ways, I'd give him that.

I thought he'd close his eyes once more, but he seemed content to lie there and contemplate my face, still looking rather dreamy. I wondered if he were fully conscious.

"Sergeant . . . I'll go. I'll let you sleep."

I'd turned away when he spoke again. "Don't go."

I watched him helplessly. "Can I get a nurse?"

"Nope."

"They might be able to give you something for the pain."

"Nope."

I came back to the bed. "What are you trying to prove, Sergeant?"

His gaze upon me was calm. "I know it'll pass. It reminds me I'm alive." Then, "How about you?"

I said, firmly, "You need your rest," and turned towards the door.

"Mrs. Stanforth." The voice held a little of its old strength, the authority that he was used to having respected, obeyed.

I stopped, but didn't turn. And the bastard waited. Waited and waited, while I stood with my back to him and silently cursed him.

Finally, I looked over my shoulder, a concession in order

to get out of the room, away from him, with his power of pity over me.

"Thank you." He spoke only when our eyes met directly. "For your kindness."

"I delivered a message," I muttered. "Anyone in the crowd would have done the same."

"I don't mean today. I mean what you've done for my sister, my parents. You made me see that even my father's capable of change. Some."

"I didn't do anything. I was the stranger here. They befriended me. And as for your father, of course he can change, anyone can change. He knows he's made mistakes. He's trying."

He made no rejoinder to this.

"I'll go," I said, and backed towards the door. "But I'll . . . come back if you like."

Something stirred in his eyes. "If one wants," he drawled softly. "If one can spare the time."

I walked smartly out of the room.

Outside the family greeted me with smiles, "You were so long, what were you talking about?" Merlin asked.

"Nothing. Nothing much."

We were heading for the elevators, I was slightly ahead of everyone else, eager to get out of there. David grinned, pressed the Down button and said, "Where would you like to eat? We were thinking of the Brunswick Inn."

I drove home alone from the Inn, about midnight. It had been a pleasant meal, the McGarrets so obviously relieved that Perry was alright. Yet I still felt edgy and uneasy; I kept starting at shadows on the road and even beside the road. I made myself drive extra carefully, watching my way with greater concentration.

"These people are too demanding." I was surprised to hear the sound of my own voice, complaining above the soft purr of the Volvo's engine. "Let them work out their own problems. I won't go back to the hospital. This is one tough pilgrim—he doesn't need me.''

And why the hell was I even thinking of him? Why did I keep seeing him on the street, swaying a little with shock and pain, determined not to move a step until I'd left the scene? And his eyes as he watched me from the hospital bed, summing me up as I stood by the window, watching my discomfort as I kept edging towards the door. Quietly absorbing. Filing away.

I was tired, that was all. I needed to be home. And I saw with gratitude, over to my left, the white-painted fence posts of Merlin and Natalie's place. Only another two hundred meters.

I turned into my own drive and immediately had to brake furiously. As it was, the bumper struck the closed gate—closed for the first time since I had seen the place—and I was forced forward sharply against my seat belt. The engine stalled. In the silence I thought I must have made a wrong turning, that this wasn't my driveway at all. But there was the old milk can with its new lettering that said *Feldman-Stanforth* in my own neat little letters.

I looked back at the gate. It was a five-bar, brand-new, painted white. In the center of the top bar was a highly polished copper plaque.

I climbed out of the car and moved closer. The plaque said *Jaegerhalle*.

I knew, of course, as soon as I saw the copper plaque. I should have been angry, wildly angry, but I was too busy, in those moments, being nervous. The Volvo's headlights were bright and comforting, but all around me—and I dared not look all around me—was darkness. That very *black* darkness of the countryside at night.

Hurriedly, now, I went to the latch on the gate; it was new and stiff and I had to fumble with it. That's when I heard the car approaching.

I kept struggling with the catch, finally released it, and watched the gate swing inwards, smoothly.

The car pulled in just behind the Volvo and the headlights of both cars shone directly on me, but I was beginning to lose my nervousness; this was an enemy—if he was an enemy—that I could at least see.

Alby Gresson climbed out and stood by the open door of his station wagon. I moved away from the direct beams so I could see him more clearly, though it was not as clear as I would have liked. His face had too many folds, and I couldn't tell whether his face creased in good humor— or something else.

"Is this your doing, Mr. Gresson?" I asked, calmly enough.

"Just coming home from my sister's place on Orchard Road—saw your car pull in." Yes, the smile was there, in the voice. Either he hadn't heard my question, or he had his own script so well memorized he could not be deflected. I hadn't heard his car approaching from any great distance. There were shadowy places along Spring Mill Road where a car could park unnoticed. "Thought I'd see what you thought of it," he added.

"You mean the gate. The gate was your doing?"

I edged towards the open door of my own car.

"Fixed it. Yeah," he said.

"Replaced it. You replaced my gate without my permission, Mr. Gresson."

I should be careful. I really should be careful. Yet I was furious. The man had no connection with my property, no right of way over my property. And here he was, putting up a new entrance gate, a new—for me, anyway—name. It was a presumption, a violation.

"Felt I owed you," he said, sulkily.

"Owed me?"

"Yeah. Didn't believe you, 'bout hiring another fellow. But I know Larry Carey. Good man. Good Catholic. Struggling to make ends meet with all those kids. Good of you to take him on. And you *needed* a new gate."

"No, it. . ."

"Wasn't any trouble—had the timber and paint at my place. Measured it up last week, while you were out. Made it in the shed, drove down with it on the trailer when I saw you leave this afternoon."

Saw me leave. He had been watching the place!

"I can't accept something like this!"

"I can't take it back. Don't need any new gates, nor do my boys. All my gates work fine. Never let anything fall into disrepair on my place.

"Besides, I wanted to give you back the nameplate. I was being unreasonable about that. Put out a bit, by your attitude. Oh, the Hahns gave it to me alright, but I don't need it. Too grand a name for my little place. You seen my house? *New Colonial,* the design's called. There's nothing of the German fairy tale about it. Not like this place."

And he was admitting, suddenly, "Wanted to buy this place—but the Hahns had this crazy idea that all the furniture should stay with it—that someone'd come along who'd be crazy enough to like it the way they had it. And they were right. And I'm glad. Glad you got it and you're keeping it like they wanted on the inside."

How did he know? How could Alby Gresson know?

Almost as if he'd read my thoughts, "I talk to people," loftily. "Frank Dufour and Larry Carey. I know the Ambroises at the Inn—and lots of people more important than them. I've got a lot of important friends in this town, don't think I don't."

"I wasn't suggesting—"

"Know everyone there is to know. I can move in any circle. Once moved with the very best of 'em. Dead, now, though, all that generation. Things were different then. A lady was a lady and a gentleman was a gentleman."

He looked over at me. "You wouldn't have known this town then. Built on timber it was, and thriving. People in the big houses—they knew how to entertain their friends. Now! Look what's happened to those houses: museums, offices, drug centers, shelters for battered wives . . ."

I was proud of St. Claude's sense of community, noting the converted large mansions dotted around the town's squares. These houses had been given over, for the most part, for the public's benefit. Seeing it through the eyes of a nostalgic Alby was to see it as a sign of moral and social decay.

"They're replanting trees now," he was saying, "instead of chopping them down—and they may as well, won't bring this town back the way it was. New people coming in, some richer than the old families, maybe, but no sense of *style*. No breeding."

He nodded sadly, "Blood will tell. Look at the McGarrets. Self-made money. Why, I knew old Davey McGarret when he had a little workshop down River Bottom Lane. New money. No *breeding*. And look at the third generation—has all that money made any difference? Nah. Daughter thinks she's a man, and the son runs away like a little heathen vandal at fourteen. Comes home after all these years and what's he got to show for his life? Nothing but a policeman's badge, and only a sergeant at that. Not too bright, if you ask me."

I broke in finally, hopping from one foot to another for warmth, "Thank you for returning the name plaque, Mr. Gresson. I'll write out a check for the cost of the gate and put it in your mailbox."

"I didn't do it for money!" His rage, as I had seen on other occasions, was swift and disproportionate.

"I know, but I won't have you inconvenienced." And, as he started to bluster, "I can't accept gifts from strange gentlemen."

Alby Gresson regarded me, quietly.

Finally, I said, "Can I trouble you to close the gate after me, Mr. Gresson?"

He nodded, slowly. "Yeah."

"Then I'll say thank you, and goodnight."

"Goodnight, Mrs. Stanforth." And he stood watching as I got behind the wheel of the Volvo and drove through the entrance. I drove carefully, partly watching the icy mush of the potholed drive before me and partly watching the rearview mirror, in which I could see Alby Gresson walk towards the new white gate and close it.

I drove on, having to pay close attention to the steering, as the road curved a little and the mud and slush were thick and slippery. Each time I looked back, until the curve of the drive and the trees hid him from sight, he was still there, the headlights silhouetting the new gate and the narrow-shouldered figure standing behind it. Only when I could no longer see him, with the sense of relief, came the realization that I'd forgotten to ask him the meaning of *Jaegerhalle*.

The phone was ringing as I came in the door.

"Hello?"

"It's Keir. Sally, I've been trying to call all evening—"

"Is everything al—"

"I wanted to tell you as soon as possible—"

"You're marrying Erica?"

"For the sake of the child." His voice very strained, very strange.

"When's the magic day?"

Can I get to the bitch beforehand? Run her down with the Volvo, poison her? Mossad had poisoned an umbrella tip, once: what you can do with umbrella tips you can do with almost anything. Someone, sometime in history had poisoned a wedding dress, I seem to remember—or was that in an opera?

"We were married today. We just flew back in a few hours ago."

"From Vegas? Oh, tell me you didn't."

The line was silent for a long time.

"Keir."

"Yes. Las Vegas. Erica wanted it."

"Where's Erica now?"

"In the bathroom, having a shower."

"You're in New York?"

"At the apartment, yes. She loves it here. She's got the place full of baby things—furniture, clothes, everything."

"Keir—"

"It *should have been you*, Sally. I was stupid, and so selfish. It should have been you. *Ours.*"

Regrets? Now? *NOW?*

Keir went on. "I've never fallen apart before, have I?" A cool voice. "I've always managed to stay detached. I always thought I was pretty tough."

"You were. You are," I told him.

"Thank you." As if I'd said, *nice tie, kid.* "I suppose I was tough because I had nothing to be afraid of. Everything in my life was so sure . . . so *assured.* The only thing in my life that ever made me question anything was Geoff's death . . ."

The old pain settled around my heart. I sat down slowly on the edge of the table.

"I'm so sorry, I've hurt you so much," Keir said.

"It's alright. Keir . . ."

"You expect to understand everything when you're older, don't you? There's always a time *out there* when you think you'll have all the answers, don't you think?"

"Yes—"

"But they don't come. The answers. Not with success, certainly not with age—"

"Keir, you must get some help! There's Hal Abraham, or . . . who was that nice English psychiatrist you used to play golf with sometimes?"

"No, they don't understand. Every psychiatrist I know is a worse emotional mess than I am. *Erica's coming,*" he said in an urgent voice. And, louder, "So that's the way it is—"

"Goodbye, Keir."

"Sally . . ."

"Congratulations. Be happy."

I hung up. I considered getting drunk, and thought, no. No. Why should I? What do I have to blot out, to forget? I was tired. I went straight to bed in the tall, narrow French mahogany four-poster with its rose-colored curtains. Before I turned out the light, I looked around the room, at my life. I was quietly surprised to be pleased with it, with myself.

Chapter Eleven

I spent the next few days phoning people in New York, trying to find out more of what had been happening with Keir, seeking some explanation for his disturbed state of mind.

I was normally in touch with Beth every week. We talked about the progress on *Scotty's Things,* but we usually tried not to talk about Erica and Keir. Now I phoned her especially, but she was at a loss to explain matters. Erica had rung her only that morning and told her about the wedding. She had been "deliriously happy," according to Beth, who had also spoken to Keir, to give him her congratulations. He had sounded bright enough, and they talked about plans for their honeymoon in Paris in a few weeks.

Paris. Our old apartment in Paris. A honeymoon. Keir hadn't mentioned *that.*

There was a silence, while we both pondered what to say. Then Beth said, "If it's any comfort, she's been making things really difficult around here."

My editor's brain took over from my worry about Keir. "What do you mean? Is she refusing to finish the new book?"

"Oh, she's finishing it alright—said she's just polishing it now. But she's trying to get out of her contract—you know we gave her a five-book deal after her first book—there's still two more to go after this one, *Catwalk*. She doesn't want to write anymore. She wants to buy out her contract."

"What? But it'd be worth—!"

"I know, I know. But married to Keir—sorry, Sally—she can afford to get high and mighty. She's already had cards printed. Pale apricot with raised gold lettering, *Mrs. Erica Stanforth.*"

"Oy, please!"

"See what I mean? It's as if she's suddenly become aware of the Stanforth name and what it represents and wants to become a society matron or something. Mind you, I wouldn't care, but you know how much this company has invested in her. We stand to lose a bundle. Her paying us back a lousy couple of million isn't going to make up for the projected loss of income if there aren't any more Erica Tudor novels.

"And there's something funny about *Catwalk,*" Beth added.

"What? You've read it chapter-by-chapter, haven't you?"

"Not this time," a sarcastic singsong voice from Beth. "We'd worked out the synopsis, and Sammy checked it—you know how interested he always is in our little money-spinner. But this time she said she didn't want to let me see the progress on it. She wants to hand the *whole thing* over. And she's saying already that she doesn't want a major edit."

"What does *that* mean?"

"God knows. I'm braced for her turning *Catwalk* into *grand litchitchure*. Something she'd imagine would please the Stanforth clan."

"Has she pleased the Stanforth clan?" I found myself asking in a low voice.

"Hell, honey, I don't know. She never mentions them.

"Somehow, if she was welcomed into the bosom of the family, I think she'd have let me know."

I was silent.

"When are you coming to New York, Sally?" Beth said, gently. "I miss you. Don't stay up there in the snow, brooding. Come down here where you can meet some handsome and eligible men . . ."

"Soon, Beth. Soon. In the meantime, send up Collette Palmer's new manuscript as soon as it arrives, won't you?"

"Will do. Maybe we should both go and visit her. Life in Queensland, Australia, sure sounds good to me right now."

"Me too."

"And Sally . . ." A pause. "Don't worry about Keir. Go on with your own life, honey. Keep working on *Scotty's Things*. Sammy and I can't wait to see it finished. Just don't brood about Keir. If he loves you, he'll come back to you, somehow, some way. Even Erica won't stop him. Even having *ten* kids by her won't stop him. But . . . don't hold your breath, kid. Don't put your life on hold."

"Too many metaphors, Cosgrove."

"Stop listening to my words, my friend. *Hear* me."

"Frankly, Sally, I don't think Keir's state of mind has very much to do with you anymore." The coldness of the words matched the tone of my former mother-in-law's voice.

"I care about him, Barbara. I always will. He sounded so depressed—"

"Perhaps he was depressed at having to call you. So like Keir, trying to do the gentlemanly thing, rather than have you read of the marriage in the tabloids."

Tabloids. Who, besides Barbara—and maybe Bill—Stanforth, would say *tabloids?*

"He often phones me, Barbara. We're still friends."

"And do you think that's *wise?* Do you think that's *kind?* He has his new life, now, Sally. I think you might be the

one who's depressed, my dear. Are there any good psycho-
therapists in Canada?''

"Barbara, I don't need a—"

"I think you should leave him alone, Sally. Your marriage
to Keir is over. Try to be adult about this. Try to keep your
dignity, my dear."

The only person to listen to me carefully, very carefully,
was our psychiatrist friend, Hal Abraham.

"So if you could just keep an eye on him, check for any
signs of depression."

"Sure, sure."

"I mean, he was very down."

"Yes, yes."

"Yet he seems to be hiding his state of mind from people
in New York."

"I see. I see."

"Hal, give me one more double affirmative and I'll blow
a whistle in your ear."

Hal laughed. "I'm sorry, Sally. I was just concentrating.
I can see why you're worried about Keir."

At last! *"Thank* you!"

"And I'm playing a lot of golf with him lately, so I'll try
to talk to him a bit, draw him out. Though, to tell the
truth, he seems very happy. Is that hard for you?"

"No, of course not! I *want*—"

" 'Cause there's another reason for his phone calls to
you, perhaps."

"What?"

"He's very fond of you, Sally. He hated hurting you.
We've talked a lot about that. He feels guilty. Very, very
guilty. Phoning you to check on you, to see if you're okay—
that's understandable, given the fact that you were married
for so long, and it was a very amicable breakup."

Oh, was it, my friend?

"Keir feels he can still talk to you. In a very real way, he
still needs you in his life."

Yes. Yes!

"But it might only be a kind of transition phase, while he's settling in with Erica. It might not be anything more than a temporary holding of the hand, till he can walk by himself, so to speak. You might leave yourself open to a lot of grief, if you read anything more into it."

"But he's unhappy! He said!"

"What could he say? Could he phone you every few days to tell you how *happy* he is? He's made you miserable, Sally. He's broken up a twenty-year marriage to run off with a girl young enough to be his daughter. He *does not feel good about that.* And he doesn't want *you* to feel that he's callous, that he's unaware of your hurt, your loneliness."

"You're saying . . . Keir rings me up and pretends to be miserable and depressed because he doesn't want me to believe he's *enjoying himself?*"

"That's oversimplifying a bit. I think what you're picking up from him, what he's letting you hear, is a very real side to him. It's the guilt-ridden, unhappy side of him. But, Sally . . . I can't say it's the real side of Keir. I can't say it's the *main* side of his personality at the moment. If it is, he's one hell of an actor."

"I see."

Gently, "He is being honest with you, Sally. I'm as certain as I am of anything in this life, that those feelings he expresses with you are genuine."

"Thank you. Thanks, Hal."

"How're you getting on up there, Sally? You got someone to talk to? You seeing someone to help *you* through this?"

"I've got friends. Very good friends. I'm fine, Hal."

"You're a strong girl. You'll be okay. And Sally?"

"Yes?"

"You get too lonely . . . get yourself a cat."

"*What?*"

"A cat."

"Are you *nuts,* Hal?"

"Don't knock it. Cats are great therapy. Cats *work.*"

"I'll keep it in mind."

"Do that. See you, Sally."

I don't know about cats, but Hal Abraham was great therapy. I hung up the phone laughing.

I may have had friends in St. Claude, but there was one I neglected during that time.

I told myself McGarret wasn't really a friend anyway. I couldn't see that I'd have anything much in common with him or that I'd have much to say to him, if I visited him in the hospital.

So I sent a dozen red roses and, two days later, a big bowl of out-of-season fruit, and conveniently came down with a bad case of the flu.

I phoned The Aunts in Palm Beach. Specifically, I wanted to speak to Aunty Miriam.

I knew The Aunts—and The Uncles, though there were fewer of them—loved to hear from me, but it was hard to sit through the questions, candid and persistent, about my health, my emotions, the divorce, and That Marriage—for all The Aunts read The Tabloids. But now there was something I wanted to know.

"Aunty Miriam, you studied German history as well as the language, can you tell me what *Jaegerhalle* means?"

"What?"

"Jaegerhalle."

"For a start, you pronounce it with a *Y. Yayger-hahl.* Didn't Zachary teach you anything?"

"What does it *mean?*"

"It's part of Prussian mythology. A hunting lodge in a magic forest, where the spirits of hunters go when they die. And not just any hunters—not hunters who killed for *sport,* only those hunters who killed from necessity, to stay alive. It was a place where it was always spring or summer, and the game was always plentiful and came back to life immediately after it was killed. Sort of a hunter's heaven. Come to think of it, the lodges looked a little like your little house in the pictures you sent your Uncle Gus and Aunt Sadie. Why do you want to know about *Jaegerhalle?*"

"I found out it's the name of my farm."

"Otto Hahn called his farm *Jaegerhalle*? Find a nicer name, darling. Something pretty, that suits you."

Still worried about Keir, I rang him at his office, and was told by his secretary, with some embarrassment—for we had always liked each other—that Dr. Stanforth had gone on vacation the day before.

This was three days after I had spoken to him.

Had they left for Europe already? I phoned Beth, who said she didn't know. But surely, she said, Erica would have told her if their plans had been put forward. *Catwalk* was expected on Beth's desk any day now.

I phoned the house in New Hampshire, not once but over a dozen times. The housekeeper or one of the other servants answered. At first, yes, Dr. and Mrs. Stanforth were in, but not taking any calls. The best they could do would be to take a message.

"Have Dr. Stanforth call Mrs. Sally Stanforth."

"I see, madam. Yes. I have the number." Coolly.

And later, when no one returned my call, "Can I speak to Miss Tudor, please."

"*Mrs. Stanforth* isn't accepting any calls at the moment, madam. May I take a message?"

And I would leave a message for Erica.

Finally, when the housekeeper told me that Mrs. Stanforth had returned to New York to join her husband, I gave up.

Maybe Hal was right. Maybe I was reading too much into Keir's phone calls.

Maybe even Barbara, his mother, was right. Maybe I needed help.

Yet I wasn't to be allowed to forget. I suppose it's the price one pays for being married to a media personality. And overnight that's what Keir had become. Because of Erica. The women's magazines were filled with pictures and stories about Keir's marriage to Erica Tudor. I read all about it, every painful word.

My only refuge was *Scotty's Things:* I took my pain back to my computer and started work on the novel again, writing long into the nights, sometimes until three or four in the morning, and then sleeping late. The messages piled up, but I ignored them for the most part, though it was hard to ignore the McGarrets, who were worried more than most about my health.

"I wish you were well enough to visit Perry. Maybe you could talk some sense into him," Merlin grumbled, when I returned one of her calls.

"Me? Why me?"

"Well, he *talks* to you. He must like you. He's such a taciturn bastard.

"When are you going to be well enough to come to the hospital?"

"I don't know, Merlin. I'm aching all over and can only eat just the tiniest bit." I coughed pathetically.

"But he's talking about discharging himself, and it's only been five days. It's all Raoul Gerlain can do to keep him there."

I remembered the solid-looking inspector at the scene of the bank robbery. "Merlin, I wouldn't make a dent in your brother's resolve, I assure you—"

"He thinks he's so tough. I worked it out yesterday, he's got a John Wayne complex."

Two days later she phoned to say that "the big ox" had discharged himself from the hospital and gone home. "Mamma's furious with him. She's driven our there with an overnight bag intent on nursing him back to health herself. What fun, eh? Can't you just *see* it?

"And how are you feeling, Sarah?" she added.

"Oh, I'm feeling a lot better."

"Yeah, I thought you might be." But before I could react, shc said, "Nat's asked Eugene Boillot and Lisette to dinner Wednesday night—she's working odd days lately—but can you come?"

I'd been shut up for so long, with just the book and my murderous thoughts of Erica, that dinner with friends sounded appealing. I was just about to accept when there was a commotion of voices at Merlin's end of the line. I could almost think I was speaking to a gathering of The Aunts.

Finally, Merlin's voice returned, clearer. "I'd better go. Mamma's just arrived, dragging her suitcase behind her. They had quite a scene." She was speaking in a hushed voice and trying not to giggle. "So I'll see you about seven on Wednesday."

I agreed, and we hung up. I was smiling myself. So Perry McGarret hadn't wanted his mother's presence at "his place." And yet he must be finding it difficult to cope. I could just see him, pointing the way back down the drive. Go *home, Mamma—a man's gotta do what a man's gotta do.*

Collette Palmer's new historical saga arrived by special delivery the next day, and I started work immediately, propped up in a corner of the settee by the fire. I had my new slippers on, the ridiculous twin confections of pink fluff with rabbits'' ears. In New York I wouldn't have been caught dead in them, but here I could please myself. The warm fire, a cup of hot chocolate at my elbow, and getting paid to read a really good, ripping yarn set in the days of the clipper ships on the China Run . . .

Look at me, Keir! Look at me coping!

On Tuesday, January twenty-fourth, I went to a ballet performance in Fredericton, with the Dufours, and didn't arrive home until very late. On my machine was a message from Keir.

"Sally . . . I've been trying to reach you all night . . . I don't know what to do. I've compromised myself over and over and over . . .

"And what I've done to you—" His voice broke.

"That's the worst part of it. I'll . . . call you back later. What I really want is to see you. *I tried,* Sally. I tried to do the right thing, but . . . You *can't make everyone happy.*" He stopped.

"I love you, Sally."

I didn't care what time it was, I phoned New York: the phone in the apartment rang and rang.

I didn't ring the house in Meadowsweet, New Hampshire. For I knew now—though there was no sense of victory, just a sick sense of worry—that Keir was almost definitely not there.

No one in New York seemed to know where Keir had gone. Finally, on Wednesday afternoon, I gave up, dressed, and went to dinner at Apple Tree Farm, and tried to have a pleasant evening.

We all ate too much, and drank too much, and told silly anecdotes about our childhoods and tried to solve the world's problems.

Lisette and Eugene left at eleven-thirty. I stayed on— we were talking about feminist literature by now, sitting cross-legged in front of the fire discussing whether Fay Weldon had sold out to commercialism, when a draught from the front door had the fire billowing smoke and sparks into the room and we looked up, chilled and sobered by the sudden icy blast and its flurry of snow.

"You really are stupid, Merlin, leaving your front door unlocked!"

We were further sobered by the sight of Peregrine McGarret, standing just inside the door, in boots and jeans and parka, pushing the hood back and scattering snow down his back and onto the rug.

The four dogs, until now asleep by the fire, scrambled to their feet and barked furiously. Merlin and Natalie tried to calm them.

"Perry, you idiot—what are you doing out on a night

like this? *Heel,* Chloe!" Merlin yanked on the collar of the leggy rottweiler-greyhound cross, who was straining towards McGarret. The two smaller dogs, Honey and Rat, were rushing in circles around his ankles. He watched them, tolerantly.

"Come in Perry, and close the door." Natalie hauled Olaf, the German Shepherd cross, out the door towards the kitchen.

Gradually, the room settled down. The dogs, except for Olaf, grudgingly accepted the large man in their midst and dozed fitfully by the fire once more. The humans in the room repaired to the chairs by the fire.

"You should be locked away, going out in this weather!"

"Raoul called me to ask for some advice on Sam Norman—"

"Raoul wouldn't have needed you there. You just have to play the hero. Sam won't kill anyone."

"One of these days these midnight shooting sprees will. And lock that goddamned door, Merlin."

"We don't need to, we've got the dogs . . ."

"Oh, and they were just right on the ball, weren't they?"

"Alright, we'll lock the door—we usually do—we just saw the Boillots off, we forgot."

"Don't forget."

"Alright."

"Well . . ." Natalie smiled brightly at each of us in turn determinedly. "Can I get anyone a drink? Coffee?"

I should have left with the Boillots. I felt very sleepy, and not a little fuzzy around the edges. And it was affecting my emotions, too. Half an hour ago we had been happily and deeply in discussion on literature: McGarret's uncomfortable presence had let in more than a swirl of icy snowflakes.

For a few hours I had managed to forget about Keir. Now I realized that the sound system in the corner was playing Rachmaninoff's *Variations on a Theme by Paganini.* It had always been one of Keir's and my favorites. And this was the first time I had heard it since the breakup of my marriage. I tried hard not to think about it. . . .

Natalie returned, bearing the coffee. I came to myself only when the McGarret siblings stopped speaking, only then realizing that they'd been discussing Janice's well-intentioned visit to her son two days ago. At least, Merlin had been speaking; McGarret's replies had been mono-syllabic.

"I'm really glad you called in. Merlin wanted to ask you to join us tonight, but I vetoed it. I felt you should be resting," said Natalie.

"So he goes out in a snowstorm instead," growled Merlin.

McGarret didn't answer the accusation, but sipped his coffee. Merlin said to me, "Sam Norman is a Vietnam veteran. He suffers from war nerves, and every few months he gets a bit confused and thinks he's back over there. He has a couple of hundred acres, fortunately, and he hasn't caused any hurt yet, but he'll run around all night, letting off round after round of ammunition at the trees, the moon, his own house, once. Blew all the windows out."

"Where is Sam now?" I asked McGarret.

"In the hospital. They'll keep him a few days and he'll be okay—for a while."

Our eyes met across the hearth. He looked fatigued, but held my gaze. I couldn't see why his regard should be discomforting, but it was. Perhaps it was because the man didn't blink very often. That can be unnerving.

How tipsy was I? Could I risk driving home? I did want to go home.

"So what brings you to call on us tonight—not that we're not glad to see you." Natalie smiled warmly at him.

"Saw the lights still on as I was passing. Thought I'd ask Merlin how Mamma was taking it." When neither Merlin nor Natalie spoke, he continued, "She won't answer the phone. Mrs. Kelly takes messages from me, but she won't call back." He grinned a little, wryly. "I don't want her worrying. But I don't want her over at my place fussing, either.''

"She'll get over it," Merlin grinned.

"Won't make herself sick or anything?" Unsure.

"Mamma? No. Getting cross will probably do her good. She doesn't get mad often enough. What's really funny is that Dad's taken your side."

McGarret's big head came up.

"He's telling her she was interfering and that you're the sort of man who knows his own mind and she should respect that."

"No fooling." He looked wonderingly at his sister. "The old man said that?" He was quiet for a long moment, then, abruptly, he turned towards me.

"I'd better drive you home, Mrs. Stanforth, when you're ready. Or were you going to spend the night here?"

Natalie said, "Why don't you *both* spend the night? We've got two spare rooms, you know."

McGarret and I were unlikely allies. No, we had things to do first thing in the morning . . . I wanted an early start to finish the editing job. McGarret had to feed Patsy and exercise her.

Patsy? His horse.

Well, the girls were saying, if Perry would drive me . . .

"I can drive myself," I said, and then looked up into the strangely opaque eyes of McGarret.

"I don't thing so," he said. That was all. But I read in the words that he suspected I might be over the legal limit of alcohol. I didn't argue. I wanted to go home. I was suddenly very depressed. Maybe there was a phone message at home, maybe Keir had called again. Pulling on my coat and boots while Natalie and Merlin fussed over a tolerant and noncommittal McGarrett, I was already thinking—with that clarity that alcohol can sometimes give—that I didn't believe the thoughts of all my New York friends. I believed what I heard in Keir's voice.

Suddenly we were outside in a cold wind that hit like a blow from an iron glove, drawing the breath from my body in a gasp and pushing me back into McGarrett, walking slightly behind me. I moved forward before he could steady me, but his solid bulk had given me the impetus I needed and I made a steady and straight path to his Jeep.

It had stopped snowing, thankfully, but the wind was freezing. At least I'd be able to drive the Volvo home tomorrow. Merlin had promised she'd come over to pick me up. She and Natalie leaned on each other's shoulders, and grinned. I grinned back, happily, and waved. McGarrett kindly helped me up into the Jeep and we drove off. The girls stayed on the veranda, waving, their arms around each other's waists.

It struck me that they were *too* happy, almost amused. At me? At McGarrett?

Oh. At me *and* McGarrett.

Merlin would be really enjoying this. When I had told her, during a discussion on families, of Keir expecting a baby with his mistress, that he'd possibly marry her, she'd said that if I really missed having a man as my raison d'être then I should consider taking on her brother. His rehabilitation as a living, breathing human being would give me a life's work.

I had giggled, highly amused. How could any man compare with Keir? After twenty-five years with the best, you don't compromise.

I realized I should be being polite, making conversation. But one sneaked look to my left at the stiff, unattractive features of the giant beside me and I quailed at the thought. His eyes were fixed on the road, and he drove competently with his one undamaged arm.

I cleared my throat and tried, "This is very kind of you."

He didn't answer. But just then the wheels hit an ice patch and slid a little. He controlled the car surely, expertly. In the dim, colored lights of the console, his face looked very grim.

I turned back to the view before me and to my right. It was probably the red wine, but I felt as blurred, as insubstantial as the night out there. Reality shifted about like

the few snowflakes that were falling, whipped past us by
the wind and our forward motion, seeming to rush towards
us as the headlights picked them up, turned them golden,
then discarded them, back behind us into the dark silence
of the woods as we passed.

Keir.

"Go ahead," McGarrett said. "I won't tell."

"What?"

"Cry," he said, to the billowing snowflakes that were
falling faster, now. "You've been trying not to. Shoot, why
don't you just let it all out?"

And then he looked at me, the change of expression in
his usually impassive features one of gentle pity, and I felt
myself start to dissolve.

No-no-no, Sarah. NO.

"I don't want to cry. I'm just getting over the flu." I
fumbled in my handbag for a handkerchief, needing to
blow my nose, to wipe the sudden tears away, to hide my
face from this sudden and inexplicable source of empathy.

"Thank you for the roses you sent—and the basket of
fruit," he said.

"That's alright."

"You're a nice woman, Mrs. Stanforth."

I looked at him. His big face was once more scowling
out at the road before us. I murmured "thank you," not
knowing what else to say, feeling instinctively that in this
man's rather limited vocabulary, to be described as a "nice
woman" was to be something rather special.

He said, now, in a low voice, "That husband of yours
must have been one hell of a man."

Gruffly, "He still is." And then, hating myself but not
able to prevent my correcting him, "But he's not my husband. He's my ex-husband. And he's just remarried. And
they're having a baby in July."

A small pause, then he made a sound deep in his throat;
it might have been "ah," it might have been a grunt. I
couldn't tell whether it was a note of sympathy or impatience with me for dwelling on it.

"Read about it in the papers some," McGarret said. "Seemed to me like pretty low behavior for a man."

I flared. "You don't know him!"

Again a little pause. I would have thought, if this was the first time I'd met him, that he was concentrating more on the road than his words, but I realized that there was nearly always this slight pause before he answered, as if he liked to choose his words carefully.

"Do you always jump to his defense like that?" he murmured.

"Do you always talk as if you stepped out of a western?" *Low, Sarah. Low.*

But there was no noticeable change in his demeanor, nor in the atmosphere between us. He said, "I found myself in Georgia when I was fourteen, stayed sixteen years—still go back there for three weeks every year—I don't apologize for the way I talk."

"Sorry, I was out of line—"

"I have to work at my grammar, though." And there was the trace of a smile about his mouth. "Them—those—what-do-you-call-'em, double negatives. Everyone at the station gives me hell about *them.*"

A sense of humor there, I thought. Who'd have believed it? He can actually laugh at himself.

"And I mean what I say." He spoke without explanation or preamble, and looked at me. One serious look, for emphasis.

And through my still tipsy haze, I looked at him and felt ashamed. I realized he was speaking the truth. The man had not really spoken an unnecessary word in my hearing. That was why he thought everything out so carefully before he opened his mouth. It he didn't have anything worth saying, he wouldn't speak. And he wouldn't lie.

"I envy you," I said, and was irritated to find tears of self-pity close again. Why couldn't I be stoic, strong, take consolation from my moral superiority?

"Me? There's nothing to me. Sure isn't anything to envy. No education, no wife, no family. Envy . . ." He shook his great head over the word, then looked at me. "You're a funny woman."

"You're tough," I said, almost fiercely. "You're surviving in possibly the most difficult job in the world, and against a lot of opposition. Merlin's a survivor too. Both of you . . . you're tough. I'm not."

He had scowled at me a few times through this, then we reached a curve and the car slewed slowly and gracefully to the right; round we went, in a complete circle in the middle of the road, then kept going, without a pause.

"Sorry about that," McGarret said.

"It was fun," I muttered.

And it had been. I don't know why, but even feeling the wheels go, sensing the sudden tension in the man beside me, I had felt utter confidence in his ability to handle the vehicle.

He looked over at me consideringly. "You have to go right home?" he asked.

"No. Why?"

"Want to show you something . . ."

"Okay," I said, feeling reckless. And, as I said, trusting him. I knew—I just *knew*—that I was safe with him.

We turned off to the left after a few hundred meters, and seemed to be climbing a little. The road wound through dense forest, and then began to dip, and came out at last into open country once more. I was comfortably, utterly lost, but it was warm and cozy in the Jeep and it didn't matter. Even the silence between us didn't bother me because I was accepting the idea that McGarret didn't talk much; the quiet in the car was cordial. I was so comfortable I'd even forgotten that we had an objective, I was just happily driving through the snow.

And then McGarret said, "You got to promise not to tell *anyone* about this."

"Okay."

"Here we go. Hold on , . ."

We'd reached a crossroad in low, open country. Our lights, on high beam, picked it out. They were the only lights for miles around, and McGarret, in the center of the crossroads, suddenly braked.

It was mad, dizzying, magical, round and round and round we went, the snow passing sideways across the windshield, now, and I was thrown against the door of the car and closed my eyes, and made myself open them—for we were still going around—around and around and around and I didn't want to miss any of this madness.

We finally slowed, and stopped, still smack in the center of the crossroads. McGarret stopped the car, and looked at me. I was still laughing, and he grinned broadly.

He leaned his good arm on the steering wheel, looked out into the snow, still smiling, and said, "Shoot, I haven't had so much fun since I don't know when."

"Do you do that often?" I asked, catching my breath.

"That? Hell, no! Lady, I'm a policeman! I haven't done that since I stole my daddy's Pontiac, winter of sixty-nine."

"You stole your father's car when you were . . ." I was too confused to calculate.

"Twelve," and he had the grace to look a little shamefaced. "Brought it back without a dent. He never did find out about it."

He glowered over at me. "And don't you go telling him, hear?"

"Seems to me I have a lot of information you'd rather not have revealed, Sergeant."

"I trust you." He started the car.

He drove me home, then, and parked outside the house, and there was, oddly, a moment of awkwardness. I didn't know what to say and neither did McGarret. He avoided looking at me, gazed through the windshield, instead, then, catching sight of the barn, "You get those locks put on, like I said?"

"Yes, sir."

He glanced at me with a scowl.

I said, "Thank you for the ride . . ." and I couldn't help smiling. "Both of them."

He growled as I was opening the car door, "Just don't let Raoul Gerlain hear about this."

"Goodnight," I said.

"Goodnight, Sarah."

He waited until I was inside and had closed the door before he drove off.

I liked the way he said my name in that accent of his.

I slept late the next morning. A smiling Merlin woke me, hammering on the door, and made coffee for me. My head was still thumping as she drove me back to Apple Tree Farm to collect my car. I ignored any hints that she threw out about the drive home with her brother.

I stayed for lunch with her—Natalie was at work at the hospital—and helped her feed some antibiotic tablets to a struggling Chloe, who was suffering from a bad ear infection.

After that I was allowed to escape home, and I took two aspirin and went straight back to bed.

I don't know what woke me: I certainly didn't consciously hear a car engine. I got up, yawning, made my way into the living room and, just to check on the weather, looked through the curtains to a still, white, snowbound landscape—

Keir's car parked in the drive.

I ran to the door, changed into my boots, flung open the door, and raced across the porch and down the steps, around the hood of the car . . .

But it wasn't Keir. The tall figure in the gray parka, her hair in a woollen cap, was Erica.

I felt my heart stop, falter, in disbelief. Where was Keir? And why was she here?

I walked to the driver's door, unsure what to do. She stared straight ahead. I tapped on the glass of the driver's window but she refused to look at me.

Finally she turned her head and stared at me, then lowered the window. Desperation, utter misery, and exhaustion—all of these were written on her face—but oh, God, she was still lovely.

I waited for her to speak. She looked at me with dark-rimmed, tragic eyes, and I think it took a few seconds for her to recognize me.

Then she said, "Sally," and lifted her left hand—and there was a small gun held within it. I just stood there in shock and watched her squeeze the trigger and shoot at me.

Chapter Twelve

It was unthinkable. It was impossible. It was some dream, or a nightmare. I wasn't really awake . . .

But the noise was deafening, I felt it explode inside my head, against my ear drums.

And it woke something within me. I can only think of it as a survival instinct, for I didn't even know whether I'd been shot. I ducked, and ran, across to the barn, and round to the doors—and realized then that the doors were locked. Damn McGarret!

Erica was coming after me now—I heard another shot, and at the same time *something* went whistling over my head.

I ran around the barn, considered climbing the gate and trying to run for the road, but it was so exposed, this field, fifteen acres of untouched snowy space against which I would have been an easy target.

I kept running around the barn, had reached the back of it, beneath the loading doors, where the woodpile was . . .

And there was my ax, carelessly left there since the night before, leaning against the barn wall.

I grabbed it up as I passed, and whirled, dodging back against the barn wall—and then turning—but Erica was not behind me.

How many shots had she fired? But it didn't matter. If that had been Keir's pistol, she might have brought extra ammunition with her, could've paused, just around the corner of the building against which I huddled, refilling the clip. Keir only kept a few bullets in the little Beretta.

Three shots . . . she'd fired three—hadn't she?

I heard her footsteps approaching, along the side of the barn that faced down the hill, away from the house.

"*Sally.*"

Not a question, not a request.

"*Sally!*"

I heard the squeak of the snow beneath her boots as she walked towards my corner of the barn.

And then the footsteps stopped, and I heard them retreating, back the way they had come. Did she think I'd doubled back?

I was having a hard time controlling my breathing. My heart was beating so hard it was difficult to take breaths of the cold air.

Where had she gone? Maybe I could come up behind her . . .

I gripped the ax and ran around the corner—and ran smack into Erica.

We bounced off each other. The little Beretta in her hand exploded again, harmlessly, the bullet winging off to my left. She took a step back and raised the gun once more, this time sighting along the short barrel. I saw her lips pull back against her teeth in concentration.

It all happened in an instant—as she aimed the gun, I brought the ax up with one strong movement of my right arm.

Why did I do that? Why not duck, why not drop the ax, grapple with her for possession of the gun? I'll never know if there would have been time—it happened too fast, Erica aimed the gun, and I brought the ax up, swinging on the fulcrum of my shoulder and weighted by the heavy blade.

The gun exploded somewhere in the space beneath my left arm, and the ax kept going in its deadly sweep and the sharpened head of it buried itself in the side of Erica's skull.

It made a sound. I should have been deafened by the blast of the gun, but I heard the sound of the axe biting home, and I felt along the length of its handle the hideous feel of the impact.

I let go immediately, stumbled sideways and fell over in the snow. Erica fell too, to my right, towards the wall of the barn, taking the ax with her.

I scrambled to my feet, and screamed. I screamed and screamed and couldn't stop. Erica was hurt, badly hurt. Her eyes were open and staring and there was snow on the blue irises and still she didn't blink as the flakes melted. She kept staring up at the sky and the eaves of the barn, though her body trembled as if she were cold, and her gloved hand opened and closed, on the gun, on the snow. And then she lay still.

And I remained there, on my knees, trying not to look at the ax, still there, fixed in Erica's woolly cap, just above her left ear. And still I screamed Keir's name.

Chapter Thirteen

I was inside the house. I don't know how I arrived there, but there I was, my knees only now giving way. I slid down the door until I crouched against it, my knees near my chin, so I held them, hugged them, and listened to a voice, my own voice, moaning a little.

There was no thought, not for a long time. What brought me to myself at last was a splash of color, off to my right. My bright pink rabbit slippers, there by the door, eyeing me with two sets of good-natured rabbit eyes, as if they didn't know what I'd done.

What I'd done.

Once, in a different age, a woman had stepped out of them into a pair of shoes, to run out a door into the arms of the man she still loved.

What had happened?

There was blood on my hands. Not much. Spatters. On my cuffs, too, on my sleeves, on my jeans. There were also two holes beneath the left arm of my sweater where the sleeve met the body. That's where the bullet shot from the car window had narrowly missed me, and the second hole had been the last bullet, just as I'd—

But panic was overtaking all rational thought. I was already distancing myself from what had happened, denying even the proof, there in front of me. The blood was horrible, horrible. I wiped my hands on my jeans, wiped most of the blood off my hands, onto my jeans and then stared at the stained denim in horror. I felt contaminated, filled with panic, hysteria.

I stood up. Some blood had spattered on my boots, too, and I'd somehow wiped a little of it off onto the small rug just inside the door. Things were getting worse and worse. My little house had been a haven, a sanctuary. Now the horror of what had happened was invading the house.

I tore off my sweater, and my boots, and my jeans, and after a hesitation, I wrapped them all up in the little rug and padded through the house with it rolled up under one arm. I propped the rug up in a corner of the laundry.

And then I had a shower, and washed my hair. I simply didn't think. I had to get clean. Clean of the blood, clean of what had happened. I dried myself and powdered myself and sprayed myself with perfume, and only then I thought of Lady Macbeth, and realized that it was not over.

It had really happened. Erica had tried to kill me.

Erica is dead. And the child. Oh, God. *The child is dead.*

I needed time to think. I dressed in jeans and shirt and another sweater, and wandered into the living room.

I must do something. Something must be done.

I looked out the window. The white Mercedes still sat there, blending in with the snow.

Erica is dead. Erica and the child within her are dead.

I curled up in a corner of one of the sofas, curled up and put my arms over my head. The voice persisted. I blocked my ears and moaned to cover the sound.

I killed Erica. She's dead. I killed her. And the child.

I had to do something. But still I crouched there, biting my clenched fist to stop my moans from breaking out into a wailing, into a screaming.

I looked over at the phone. I could call someone . . .

The police. I should call the police.

Veronica Sweeney

I stood and made my way to the phone. I looked up the number of the St. Claude Police Station, and dialed half the number . . . Then I replaced the receiver. What if the receptionist put me onto Perry McGarret? Or Peter Copely? Or Raoul Gerlain?

These people knew me. What would they think of me if I told them what had happened?

I'd ring the emergency number. Maybe, given the seriousness of the offence, they'd send someone from Fredericton or Saint John . . .

But they wouldn't, I knew they wouldn't. They'd phone St. Claude and a police car would be sent out from there. Even if I'd never met the officers before, word would soon get around. I'd be brought to the station . . . across the room Peter Copely and Perry McGarret would turn and stare . . .

Don't dial yet. Get your story straight. Think. Don't get on the line and blubber and scream. Stay calm. What to say?

"My name's Sarah Stanforth. I've just killed someone." Or, "Hello, please have an ambulance sent to 578 Spring Mill Road. There's been an accident." Or, "Hello, this is Mrs. Stanforth at 578 Spring Mill Road. Someone just tried to shoot me and I had to defend myself with an axe."

How had I done it? Who takes on someone with a gun and wins, carrying only an ax?

I had my hand on the phone, ready to press 911—and again I stopped.

If I dialed they would answer. They would send for the police. The police would come, and see Erica lying there, my ax in her skull.

"It was an accident, Officer."

"Who is she, ma'am?"

"My ex-husband's new wife."

"And what's she doing here, Mrs. Stanforth?"

"She just . . . arrived."

And at the trial—thoughts rushed, crowded in on me— the prosecutor would say, "Didn't you make several calls to Miss Tudor's house in New Hampshire, as well as the apartment in New York? Only a matter of days before she arrived at your farm?"

"Yes, I did, I was worried about my husband."

"So you told a lot of people. But to everyone else, your husband was very happy to have married Erica Tudor. But you were not, Mrs. Stanforth. You were very unhappy about it, were you not?"

"Yes."

"One could say you were obsessed with the thought, when your husband phoned you and told you he had married again. You were almost insane with jealousy, Mrs. Stanforth, weren't you?"

"Yes."

"Why did you finally stop calling the apartment and the house in New Hampshire? Was it because you finally managed to get through to Erica Tudor and asked her to visit you in Canada?"

"No!"

"There was still the matter of the New York apartment, which your husband had placed in your name, but which Miss Tudor wanted very badly. She'd already bought nursery things to decorate it. Did you promise to discuss handing over the ownership of the apartment—an apartment worth upwards of two million dollars?"

"No, I—"

"And having lured the pregnant Erica Stanforth to the farmhouse, did you not attack her with an ax?"

"No!"

"She had brought her husband's revolver with her— a small .25 caliber pistol. She tried to use it to defend herself."

"She shot at me!"

"You claim you were acting in self-defense, Mrs. Stanforth?"

"Yes! Yes, it was self-defense!"

"Then why didn't you *turn the blade of the ax*? Why, in the time it took you to run around the corner of the barn not once but twice, did you not think to turn the blade of the ax? You could have struck her with the *blunt end of the ax, Mrs. Stanforth*. But you didn't. You struck the deceased a deadly blow to the side of the head, with the very sharp blade of an ax. You wanted her dead, Mrs. Stanforth.''

I screamed then. I screamed and screamed, and I ran through the house to the bathroom, and I vomited into the toilet bowl. Stayed crouched there and kept dry-retching even when my stomach was absolutely empty.

I had killed a pregnant woman.

You wanted her dead, Mrs. Stanforth.

I must have passed out. I woke lying on the bathroom floor in utter darkness.

But I was allowed no confusion. Memory returned immediately.

I washed my face and stumbled out into the living room: the grandfather clock against the wall had just struck seven.

What was I doing, what had I been doing all this time?

I went to the cabinet, poured myself a stiff brandy and sat down with it, gripping the glass with both hands to try to stop them shaking.

I had to make my brain *work*. It strove constantly to wriggle out from beneath my will, to flee away into numbness, seeking oblivion and escape.

But I couldn't allow that to happen. I had to think, to try to find some way of convincing the authorities that I couldn't have helped what had happened. I had to convince them of the truth. I thought of Keir—the scandal would ruin him. It would tear him apart to think I had killed not only Erica, but their child. I had killed Erica with the sharp blade of the axe. How could I be *sure* people would believe me? How could I be sure Keir would understand? I wished there were some way I could turn back the clock so that Erica hadn't come here. Why did she do it? There was no reason for her to come here . . .

What if she didn't come here?

I took a large swig of brandy. Now I was being really stupid. You can't hide a murder. You can't hide a body . . .

Who, after all, knew she was coming here?

It was the start of an insane series of thoughts, yet these thoughts brought with them a rush of warmth, as if real life, the normal world, was here after all.

Who knows that she came here?

If she'd taken off, wildly upset—as she must have been—anyone, the part-time maid at the New York apartment, Clorinda, or the housekeeper or staff at the New Hampshire house, would have contacted Keir. If Keir knew she was coming here, here to New Brunswick, he'd have phoned to warn me. So would Beth.

But Keir hadn't phoned. Nor had Beth.

Neither Keir nor Beth knew.

And even if she had told someone she was driving to Canada to see me—which was highly unlikely given her obvious intention—who was to say that she ever arrived?

Put yourself in Erica's shoes. . . . I took another large swallow of the brandy, feeling its warmth beginning to spread through my trembling limbs. More and more I was coming back to myself. *Put yourself in Erica's shoes* . . .

Erica drove over six hundred miles to kill me. Violently. Passionately. And carelessly. She didn't care if she was caught. I might not have been alone in the farmhouse, Larry Carey might have been mending some tiles on the roof. She hadn't cared about witnesses.

And I had no enemies here in Canada. When my body was found, the first place they would go would be to Keir. To Keir and to Erica, for it would come out that Keir and I were still debating the disposal of a two-million-dollar apartment. The fact that we'd been trying to be noble and foist it onto each other would be overlooked. I'd had my will changed only to take note of the divorce. Everything I owned, except for a few personal things for The Aunts, still went to Keir. Keir knew that. Did Erica?

No, it couldn't be money—Erica had her own money—and she'd know that I'd allow Keir to buy my share of the apartment if he really wished to. The police might always look first for a disgruntled spouse in a murder case, but there was no ill will between Keir and myself. Quite the opposite . . .

I had to stand and move about, beset suddenly by another wild thought.

Could it be possible that she wanted me dead out of jealousy?

Hal Abraham would ask me, gently, if I wasn't fantasizing, needing to believe that Keir still loved me . . . and one couldn't blame him. Keir was going to be a father, he had just married a beautiful young woman who was to be the mother of his child. Why would he wish to return to his first wife, only days after his wedding? But the phone messages, the calls . . .

What else would drive Erica to hate me so much? Why would she risk everything, *everything* to wipe me from the face of the earth?

But where was Keir, and why hadn't I heard from him since the cryptic phone message of two days ago?

I should call the New York apartment again, I even walked to the phone. But I didn't trust myself. I was afraid of what I might say when Keir answered. I was afraid of going insane if Keir did *not* answer, if Keir could not be found.

There was a sudden noise, a scratching at the window, and I screamed. I ran and turned out the lights, and approached the window, carefully. There was another noise, now, softer, persistent. It was snow, a sudden shift and strengthening of the wind. It had veered a little in its direction and was striking the window with scurries of flakes: the noise had been a branch, a wind-driven twig, that was all—and the snow was being blown in under the porch roof, was striking the window at the front of the living room, obliquely, with a sighing, hissing sound.

I could see nothing outside but the snow. The white Mercedes was invisible. And even though I knew the sounds were twigs, were heavy, sleety snowflakes, still I was afraid.

I was afraid to stand at that darkened window, and I was afraid to turn my back on it, to take my eyes from that darkness. For I knew what was out there, in that icy wind, gradually being buried under the snow. By tomorrow the horror would be covered, the blind eyes buried.

But the ax would still be there. Beneath the snow, sightless and out of sight, Erica was still demanding my attention. The nightmare could not be forgotten, hidden.

Or could it?

I owned a hundred and thirty-two acres of land, and eighty-two of those acres were virgin forest. A body could be hidden anywhere in all that space. Murderers were always burying bodies. I could do it, too. But I'd have to hide Erica until the spring thaw. Until the ground was soft enough for digging . . .

The car. What about the car?

No thoughts came. I'd finished my drink, and went to the cabinet for another. Then I changed my mind. I went instead into the kitchen and made coffee. I had to be awake, and sober. I only had tonight to decide the rest of my life, to try to escape.

What was clouding my thinking was Keir. I realized it as I stood at the table waiting for the coffee to percolate. If the truth of Erica's murder came out, then Keir would be ruined. I would go to jail, but I was guilty, I would deserve it. Keir would be ruined and, knowing Keir, he would wish for death before that.

And Zachary. Some alert journalist would eventually connect Sarah Feldman Stanforth with Dr. Zachary Feldman, pioneer in the field of heart and lung transplants. Everything Zachary had achieved, everything he and all The Aunts and Uncles and my parents had struggled for in the United States would be for nothing. The Feldman line had all but died out. It finished with an ax murderess, who would end her life in a Canadian women's prison.

No!

Zachary had devoted his life to me and Geoff—I owed his memory more than this. And Keir . . .

I stayed in the kitchen, unable to eat anything, but drinking cup after cup of coffee and filling up the notepaper I used for shopping lists with ways to escape from having to go to prison. Somewhere around five o'clock I burned the entire notebook in the fuel stove and fetched my copy of Erica's latest published work, *Gaining*. There was method to my madness, though I passed out on the open pages about six-thirty.

It was still dark when I woke, and I knew what I had to do. Anyway, I told myself, it was already too late. Stupidly, in my shock, I had waited too long. I had even had a shower, for Christ's sake. Now it was morning, though still dark, and I was committed to my actions.

I taped a new message onto my message machine, explaining I'd reached a really difficult part of the novel and not to worry if I didn't get back to the caller for a short time. Anyone who knew me would know, from previous messages, that this was nothing out of the ordinary.

Then I went to my room and packed the clothing and other things I'd need for the trip. I shoved everything into my largest leather handbag.

I changed into a beige ski jacket and black slacks, and pulling on gloves. I took the key to the barn and went outside.

It had stopped snowing, but the wind hadn't dropped. It bit at my lips and nose and even found my ears within the close-fitting hood of my jacket.

I forgot the discomfort immediately as I circled the front of the Mercedes and rounded the side of the barn. The wind howled and whistled around the eaves, through the gaps and knotholes in the timbers. I paused at the corner, then took three steps out, rounding it in a broad arc, as if something, or someone, like yesterday, could be waiting for me.

But the scene, lit golden by the first rays of rising sun, was one of pastoral calm. This side of the barn was more protected, since the wind's shift. It was as still as a photograph, a painting. There were the textured, weathered gray timbers of the barn, the snow-covered slope dipping away gently to a snow-topped fence. And a robin sat on the handle of the ax, which leaned there, at an angle, its blade buried in the snow that had been piled against the barn wall during the night.

I stopped abruptly. The robin hopped about a little the ax handle, fluffed up its feathers, and watched me with its bright small head turned on one side.

I felt angry towards it. Didn't it have any sense, any instincts at all? Why did it sit there, the ultimate touch to this picture-postcard scene, mocking the reality of what lay beneath that snow?

That was when I almost changed my mind. I could go back inside and call the police and when they came I could refuse, refuse in screaming hysterics, clinging to the front door handle, if I had to, to view what lay beneath that snow, beneath that ax. If I called the police I would be spared that, at least. But the arrest, the questioning, the jail, the trial, then jail forever . . . all that would lie before me.

Could I risk turning my back, accepting the pretty winter-scape scene as my final view of Erica; risking, too, that a jury might believe that I had been mad with jealousy, had lured Erica here and murdered her in cold blood? If I couldn't risk that then I had to go to the barn and find a shovel, uncover Erica's body, and remove the ax from where it was embedded in her skull. And that was just the beginning.

I stepped from one foot to the other in indecision and, almost mimicking me, the robin did the same.

He made up my mind for me in the next second. He flew away. A flutter of wings and he was gone, his brown and scarlet blurred into a russet ball as he dipped and swung and headed off towards the east, over the rooftop of the house, towards the forest and the hills, into the blinding light of the rising sun. I was left alone with the horror beneath the snow. Suddenly I was trembling violently. I knew that once I began to try to hide this crime

I would be irrevocably committed. The robin had his escape in flight, but for me the only freedom from this nightmare involved a life of deceit, of lies, of guilt, of utter loneliness. *Jaegerhalle,* once to have been a haven of peace, would be forever what it was now, a barren wilderness shared by myself and Erica. For I could never confide this secret to anyone.

And if I was caught, if there was any flaw in my plan, having concealed the body and the crime, then no one would ever believe I had not planned this. Erica's pathetic groping for her gun, her wild, amateur shooting in self-defense—this would be the truth for the jury, for Canada, for the U.S., for the world.

But did I stand a better chance if I told the truth now?

No. Better this. Just Erica and myself. She, beyond pain now, and myself left to cope in this desolation. I knew, then, that there could never be life nor warmth nor happiness for me again. No matter what the future should bring. This was not something I could forgive or forget, certainly it was not something God would forgive or forget.

I can never be with Keir again. I can never, never be with Keir again. I doubt if I could even look into his face.

I reached into my pocket and found the key to the barn. I went to the doors and unlocked them, found a spade and a large piece of old canvas. I dragged both around to the side of the barn.

I uncovered Erica with care. Even dead, and dead nearly eighteen hours, she was still beautiful. There was not as much blood as I would have thought, perhaps because she had died so quickly, or perhaps the snow and the frozen earth below her had absorbed it. The ax was horribly difficult to remove, probably because I was so hesitant, so tentative. Erica's snowflake-flecked eyes, even staring beyond me, seemed to accuse me.

Finally the ax was free.

The wound was terrible, even frozen by the cold it was terrible. Six inches long and hideously deep. I had to swallow several times when I saw it, and finally pulled her cap down low over it, arranged the hood of her parka over it. I checked her pockets, but there was nothing within them but a clean handkerchief. I tucked it around her cap to cover her face, the accusing blue eyes.

I took up the gun—definitely Keir's .25—after a brief struggle to prise it from the frozen fingers that loosely held it. My fingerprints would not be on it, as I wore gloves. And it didn't matter that I smudged them, for Erica, too, wore gloves, fine gray leather driving gloves. I tucked the gun into Erica's pocket, and removed her boots. For the moment I left them standing on the snow while I wrapped her body in the canvas. Thankfully, she had fallen with her arms not too far from her body, and though one leg was slightly raised, knee bent, her feet were quite close together, so she was not a difficult parcel to wrap.

The real difficulty was dragging her body into the barn. It was exhausting work, especially where the snow stopped at the doors, and I had to drag the body across the dirt floor. It was, thankfully, very cold in there, for I didn't know for how long she would have to be left before I could find a more permanent home for her.

And here, beneath the old Buick, was a bonus I'd forgotten about, a low trolley that mechanics used when fixing the underside of cars. With a struggle and much tipping off and readjusting, I managed to get Erica's body balanced on the trolley and was able to slide it, on its rusted and squeaking wheels, back under the Buick. Unless you bent and peered right underneath it, you couldn't see anything lying there.

I locked the barn again, took up Erica's boots, and, flicking as much snow from them as I could, placed them on the floor of the passenger side of the Mercedes. I went back to the scene of the crime and took up the ax, carrying it through to the laundry and scrubbing it clean. Then I scrubbed down the laundry tubs and washed and rinsed the brush I'd used to clean the ax.

But if the police came, finally, they'd find the blood. They have machines and special cameras or filters or some such thing that can find bloodstains no matter how small, how well scrubbed the scene of the crime . . .

But if the police got as far as the laundry, I'd have confessed well and truly by then. I had no illusions about my toughness under fire.

I checked that the answering machine was on and went into the bedroom to my closet. There, in a hatbox, I found my collection of blond wigs. I chose one that was as close to the length of Erica's hair as possible, found a ski cap in much the same mushroom and gray pattern as the one Erica had been wearing, and took up the bags I had packed.

I hid the key to the barn in the bottom of a drawer, took up the door keys and, after returning to my study to leave a light burning, left the house, locking it behind me.

Wearing the blonde wig, the cap, and a mushroom-gray pullover, placing my black parka on the seat beside me, I climbed behind the wheel of the Mercedes.

I drove away from the farm, and did not stop until just before I turned onto the main highway that would lead from Montreal over the border into the United States. Here, I parked the car, climbed into the backseat, and checked carefully through Erica's overnight bag and handbag. I also checked the car, all over, for any further clue as to why she would have come for me, but there was nothing.

I didn't know whether to be relieved or not. From my own handbag I took my dark glasses and put them on. I hid my handbag under the seat and placed Erica's bag beside me. Then I started the old car and turned onto the highway, my hands sweating on the wheel as I saw the checkpoint and the border guards before me.

Chapter Fourteen

My one consolation was that I had a plan. It was probably flawed, for I had worked it out during those long hours at the kitchen table, my mind tired, desperate, confused. I'd always thought killers were caught because they were arrogant; now I was beginning to think that their mistakes were caused less through a belief in their own superiority of intellect as through a desperate desire that everything would turn out well.

Did I think I could get away with this? I didn't care. Action—even dishonest, illegal action, such as hiding a body, stealing a car—was at least something to *do*. Taking control of my own actions, not waiting for the cold faces of the police officers, the safe, overpaid lawyers, to work out my fate. If I failed, so be it. But I must try to escape from it all. *I must try.*

And Erica had, herself, given me the idea of how I might succeed. Erica had, so to speak, written the script. It could benefit me, and it could benefit those who would, eventually, come looking for her. Those people, too, would be hoping for sensible explanations, easy answers. They had other cases to solve, reports to write, superiors to please, families to go home to.

Look at it this way, I'm doing all of us a favor.

"Driver's license, ma'am?"

I handed him Erica's driver's licence. This was the biggest risk, there in the gray, early-morning light. I put all my trust in Keir, in Keir's artistry with a scalpel, in the firmness of my jawline, my sculptured, perfect nose, the unwrinkled skin of my face and my full lips. It was not a very good photograph of Erica on the license, but still I said, with a touch of a Southern drawl and a wan smile, "I don't have anything to declare—except my exhaustion."

The guard smiled in return.

"Been touring?" he asked, looking at the license, looking at me.

"Checking the skiing lodges. Might come back in a few weeks."

Don't talk too much. You're talking too much.

"Oh, we've got some fine skiing up here. You should try it."

Then he was straightening, handing me back the license.

"Thank you." I dropped the license into my handbag and started to ease the car away.

"Just a minute, ma'am."

I stopped, paralyzed, feeling a silent scream building up in my throat.

He leaned on the window and frowned, his brown eyes serious.

"You look pretty beat to me, if you don't mind me saying so. Hundreds of people die each year on the roads due to driver fatigue. I'd like you to get some rest before you continue on to New Hampshire."

"I was . . . going to spend a day or two in Maine . . ." I squeaked, clearing my throat. "I *am* very tired."

"Good idea." He stood and waved me through.

* * *

I worried about the timing of this. How much time did I have before Erica was missed? There was nothing I could do, yet my hands sweated within the gloves on the wheel and my heart thudded sickly every time I thought of a missing persons report being filed, back in New York or New Hampshire. Yet my own timing had to be precise: this was crucial. So I forced myself to drive carefully, down odd highways, through strange towns, stopping for gas only at a crowded, busy outlet. I timed it pretty well. In the last rays of the winter sun I was in the little town of Green Bluffs, driving through it and past the turnoff that led to the Seahaven Estate. I was back in familiar territory, and not far, as the crow flew, from Erica's farmhouse, inland in the neighboring state of New Hampshire.

Yes, I thought grimly, parking the car in front of the little general store beside the deserted trailer park, I knew where I was going. So many summers had been spent exploring the coast round about here. Even the car was part of those memories, for we had driven up here, in those last days of Seahaven, when this car was new.

Later, they would notify Keir, and he would have to claim it. But he would no longer want to keep it. It would be tainted by Erica's tragedy.

In the car I found a half-empty packet of Virginia Slims. I felt smug. So that was how Erica had stayed so slim. I'd been able to wonder, through my terror, how Keir had felt about a wife who smoked, and smoked during a pregnancy at that. But now it was useful.

The woman behind the counter looked over at me hopefully, looked my expensive clothes up and down. I still had on the black slacks, gray woollen pullover and mushroom and gray knitted ski cap. My blonde hair was loose on my shoulders and I'd dispensed with the sunglasses.

"Can I help you?" the woman asked.

"A packet of Virginia Slims, please."

I still wore my own gloves, fitted, fine leather gloves of a dark gray color. I was able to pay for the cigarettes with confidence, opening Erica's handbag to find her purse and handing over the money. I added, "Can I have change for the phone?"

She wasn't happy about this, but she handed over some change.

"Where is the phone?"

"Just behind you. You passed it coming in."

I turned away—and my eye was taken, as I meant it to be—by the rack of new paperbacks for sale. Of course Erica's work was represented, amongst the Danielle Steels, the John Grishams, the Jackie Collinses. I picked up a copy of *Gaining:* I looked at it, grimly, setting my mouth in a hard line. The woman was watching me.

I replaced the book and turned to the phone.

"Does this phone take long-distance calls?" I asked

"Yes." More friendly. She was curious, now. She came from behind the counter, a large woman with hips so huge that her rump looked as if it were sitting in a spare tire inside her tight black leggings. A large red jumper covered her body to halfway down enormous thighs. She showed me how to use the machine, then went back behind the counter—and hovered.

"This is Beth Cosgrove."

Erica's voice was deeper than mine, but I didn't purposefully lower my own, the tears did that.

"Beth. Erica . . ." I was crying, couldn't have stopped if my life had depended on it. I forgot everything, the plan, the woman listening. Forgot everything but my friend, standing in her warm living room back in New York.

"Oh, Beth . . ."

"Erica? Erica is that you? Where the hell have you been, honey? I've been calling you for days."

"I . . ." Think, Sarah. Control yourself. The accent. Remember what Beth said, that when Erica was upset or angry, her carefully cultivated mid-Atlantic accent disappeared under her emotions, reverting back to her early years, in Mississippi. "I . . . I can't bear it . . . Beth . . . Keir's . . . he's . . ." *He's what?* "He doesn't love me, Beth. I can't bear it—"

"Erica, where are you? Where are you and I'll come and get you right now."

Dear Beth, darling Beth. How I wish she could. What I would give to be able to tell her, unburden myself, say, *This is Sally, Beth, and I've done a dreadful thing. Help me, Beth.*

But I couldn't say that. Because I knew Beth couldn't help me. No one could help me, now.

"I'm sorry, Beth. Oh, God, I'm so sorry. Ask Keir . . . to forgive me."

And I hung up on Beth's suddenly frightened, raised voice, *"Erica!* Don't hang up! *Erica!"*

Still crying, I walked out of the booth towards the car. The woman behind the counter stared at me, her mouth open a little, taking me all in, realizing that she knew me, recognized me. My photograph was on the back of the book I had just been holding in my hands.

I walked out of the store, climbed into the car, and drove off.

Lydia, the beautiful-but-not-as-beautiful-as-the-heroine character in *Gaining*, had, once she discovered she had Huntington's disease and had given up on trying to ruin the life and love of the naturally and very blonde heroine, Fern, walked into the sea. She had not had to drive very far to do so, as the house Lydia shared with the hero, Kyle, was on a headland overlooking Malibu.

It was a far cry from the icy waters of Shadow Bay, Maine. But if you had driven from Meadowsweet, New Hampshire, or had left New York to drive to Meadowsweet and had changed course at the last minute and headed for the sea, you would come out at the coastline very close to Shadow Bay.

It was all part of The Plan for the Erica whose last days I had to reinvent.

It was dark by the time I reached Shadow Bay, and very cold. The wind, however, was kind—it was about as gentle as could be expected for the coast of Maine in winter. That is to say, rough and cold. Rut not as cold nor as rough as I have known it to be. I'd have to work quickly, very quickly; if I did, I should be alright. I didn't know much about hypothermia, but I did know that I could not afford to be out in that wind—and wet—for very long.

I hadn't been here for ten years or more, but I knew the spot well. I parked the car among the trees, where, from the road, it wouldn't be seen immediately. I removed my boots, a black pair with a heel that had raised my height by three inches or so, and placed them in my nylon carryall. I pulled on Erica's boots. As I'd suspected, they were at least two sizes too large for me. I would have to watch my step very carefully on the path I was about to tread.

I sat in the car for a few, last seconds, arid tried to remember anything I might have forgotten. But I believed I was safe. I hadn't left anything of my own in the car, I'd kept my gloves on the entire time. There was the danger that I might have lost one or two hairs from my blonde wig, though I tried to brush the back of the driver's seat as best I could. When the police went over the car—as they certainly would—it was to be expected that they might find some of my hairs, long and dyed blonde, and hairs from my wigs, for it was only six months since I'd last been in this car.

I climbed out of the Mercedes for the last time, leaving the door unlocked and the keys in the ignition. I left Erica's handbag under the driver's seat, and took my own handbag and the nylon carryall. Then I headed cautiously through the darkened trees towards the edge of the slope, where it dropped sharply down, a hundred feet, to the sand and sea below.

Shadow Bay was so protected by the little, high arm of land that curved out from the shore and wrapped about it that the sun only shone here when it was directly overhead. The sand was clean and light, and the waves splashed rather than crashed, even in the stormiest weather. Because it was so narrow, so sheltered, the water at Shadow Bay was always dark, and on cloudy days it had an oily look to it. The rocks were often lichened; it was damp here, and always cool, if not actually cold. It was natural, unspoiled, unpopular. Keir and I had discovered it on a drive south from Green Bluffs. We had picnicked here, and made love on the sand in the dusk, for one cannot see the beach from the headland above it, the trees grow too thickly on the top of the slope.

To reach the sand, you have to park at the top and walk down a narrow, pleasant, rocky path. I wondered, as I made my way cautiously down, whether Keir would have shown this place to Erica. She had lived at the house in New Hampshire for three years, perhaps she had discovered it for herself. I had a feeling it would appeal to Erica; her books were filled with descriptions of isolated beaches and farmhouses and mountain cabins and chalets in whatever part of the world her writer's imagination took her.

I shivered as I looked about me, then back towards the slope above, at the dark trees and the square shapes of the two bathhouses, made of local stone, which stood like sentinels at the edge of the path to the sea.

They were the only buildings for two miles south along the seafront. Their twins were built beside Gull Beach, a more popular spot, where there was a restaurant, a gas station, a general store—and a bus stop on the route into Portland.

My feet in the too-large boots found the sand beneath my feet. I kept to the right, where the headland had spilled its scree of fallen rocks over the centuries, and groped along, using the sharp outline between dark rocks and lighter sand to guide me, until I heard the sound of the waves very close, smelled the salty fragrance of the seaweed, and saw the rocks to my right had leveled out into a low shelf.

Here was the water. It lapped about the soles of Erica's boots, and I took them off, and stood upon the rock shelf, dry here, and lowered the boots until they stood together on the sand. I didn't know what the tide would do, where it would take them, or if it would leave them there, to be found later. They were close enough so that it would be no surprise that there were no footprints leading to the shoreline. One thing I did know was that once a person swam out, far out, level with the arm of headland to my left, where the water of the bay ended and the sea proper began, a current would bear even a strong swimmer out to sea. But it was a long way to swim. A local fisherman had told Keir and me the story. Only those few people—and there had been a few—bent on ending their lives, swam that far away from shore.

In my carryall I had a pair of rubber-soled moccasins, and a pair of warm socks. I pulled them on, and began to inch my way back diagonally across the rock shelf, straining my eyes, as I drew close to the cliff, for the break in the rocks that marked the beginning of yet another path. This one led up at a tangent across the slope, and finished at Gull Beach, two miles to the south of where the Mercedes was parked. It was an unmarked but locally well-known nature walk, and I had to find it.

But I couldn't. It was too dark, I was too afraid, and I fumbled and fell and bruised myself many times, wasting precious time. In the end I was forced to do something I'd hoped to avoid. I took out a flashlight from the carryall, and stamped along the base of the cliff, risking being sighted from farther along the cliff top.

But there was no help for it. And finally, I found the gap between two large rocks, achingly, blessedly familiar, and started to climb once more.

It was damp, and slippery, and I had chosen these shoes especially because they had little tread and would, even if a footprint were found, not be particularly traceable. It was almost over, I told myself. Almost over . . .

And yet it was not. I was lying to myself, to keep my courage up, to keep my frozen legs moving. I'd slipped into rockpools on the shoreline, and my feet were wet and cold. I was terrified of frostbite, of falling, of being found frozen to death the following morning—or in a week's time. Who knew how long it would be before someone came this way? Hikers and nature lovers, fishermen and bird-watchers did not come out in weather like this.

I had spare socks and my high-heeled boots in my carry-all. I fantasized, as I walked, of sitting down, at last, and changing my socks. The world had contracted to just that. Sitting down and changing into warm, dry socks.

Only when I reached the top of the cliff did I turn the light off. It was a broad path, with a fence, wire and white-painted posts on the sea side. There was little risk of falling over. I walked fast, even ran a few paces. And when I was finally at what I believed to be a safe distance from Shadow Bay, I dropped to the ground and changed my shoes and socks, pulled off the blonde wig, regretfully, for it was extra warmth, and changed the mushroom and gray patterned cap for a dark cherry-red one. The damp shoes and socks, the wig and cap, I placed in the carryall.

The night was interminable. I still have nightmares about that walk. In the bag I had brandy in a flask, half a packet of cookies, and a chocolate bar, and I ate and drank a little as I walked, but still I had the feeling that I was walking in circles, that I'd missed the restaurant and the parking area that I was searching for, that I was doomed to wander all night, until I was found in the morning, either dead or gibbering with madness.

I saw the lights, first, and then I heard the music. I ran, then, and tripped and fell and picked myself up and ran again, stopping, finally, just back behind the trees. I clutched a fence post and cried, looking across a crowded parking lot to the lighted Gull Beach Restaurant. Through the windows I could see people dancing, while a band played a slow version of "There's a Small Hotel."

As I made my way past the silent cars, the music ended, and someone made a speech. It was, apparently, Eddie and Lorraine's twenty-fifth wedding anniversary. . . . Everyone applauded, cheered, and they played the Anniversary Waltz. My last sight of the festivities before I crept into the dark, rather foul-smelling women's room, was Eddie and Lorraine, alone on the dance floor, waltzing together.

This was the worst part. Even the nightmare walk along the cliff top had involved some action, some movement. Now I had to be silent, still. I couldn't risk being seen at the restaurant or the diner attached to the gas station. I had to remain hidden until morning, and the danger was of freezing to death. In my bag I had several small chemically activated heat pads and I eked these out, one per hour, as I spent the night crouched on the floor of the women's toilet, my buttocks on the woollen hat I'd worn for impersonating Erica. I stood and moved about when I dared, but no one disturbed me that night. That long night.

Yet I dozed. I wouldn't have believed it possible, for I wasn't tired. There was still so much to do, so many things about my future to consider, that I didn't think I could possibly sleep. It must have been the shock, which was still affecting me.

I had locked my cubicle door, and was seated on the floor, leaning back against the wooden door, when voices woke me. There was a dim light in the building, and for a moment I was confused and wondered what it might be, before I realized it was dawn, and two girls had entered the toilets.

"But if he really liked me he'd have asked me, wouldn't he?"

"Maybe he's, you know, asked someone else."

"Oh great, that's just great! Oh, damn—there's no toilet paper."

"I've got some in here."

Sounds of toilet paper being pulled from a dispenser.

"Can you reach it?"

"Yeah. Thanks. I mean, he has to ask *somebody*. And the reason I know he hasn't asked another girl is because—I mean, he's such a—"

Sounds of toilets flushing.

Much of the remaining conversation was lost under the sound of running water.

Finally, as they went out the door, "So I reckon I could ask him, like, you know . . ."

It was eight forty-five. I heard traffic, and the sound of a distant truck or bus braking somewhere nearby.

The world was awake.

I washed my face and applied makeup and brushed my hair at the mirror above the sink.

Outside, I crossed the road and joined a line for the bus. The voices from the ladies room turned out to be two girls of about sixteen, who continued to debate the actions of the particular young man and his choice of companion for next Saturday night all the way into Portland. In Portland I changed buses for one heading northward across the border.

I caught a taxi in Fredericton and had the driver take me home.

I had taken terrible risks, but by now I was so exhausted I would almost have been glad to be caught, glad that it could be over. It was now up to fate, to luck, to whatever one ascribed such matters, whether I was caught, and I was too tired to consider any more. The taxi came up the drive, past the gate with its copper name plaque, now weathering nicely, and up a drive that was . . .

Empty. No police cars. No ambulances. No official-looking gentlemen and women here to arrest me.

Yet.

I could see the light in my study burning, gold behind its drawn blinds. A comforting sight in the gathering dusk.

The taxi driver said, "You always take taxis? Living out here—you don't drive?"

The question could have been a leading one, but he was a friendly man, had chatted amicably all the way from Fredericton. I didn't think he was doing anything but making conversation.

"I was visiting the ophthalmologist," I lied. "The drops they put in your eyes for those tests—"

"Oh, the drops. Yeah, some people are bothered more than others."

I couldn't wait to get out of the car. I tipped the man generously, unwilling to wait for change. Part of my brain told me that perhaps it was a mistake, a large tip made someone memorable.

Yeah, I picked her up at the cab rank—took her all the way to St. Claude A funny little farmhouse up in the woods, looked like the house of the Seven Dwarfs. Yeah, I can point her out, Your Honor, that's her sitting in the front of the court. Yes, I m sure it was her.

Stop it, Sarah. If it happens, it happens. Live for now.

Now. Now, after thirty-six hours, I was back home. Snow had been falling. The tire tracks of the Mercedes had been covered, were now blurred forever with the obvious tracks left by the taxi.

I walked around the side of the barn.

A world of white; a blue-gray filtered light; a thin wind keening around the eaves and around the freshly banked snow. It was as if no one had ever walked this way, let alone fled this way, stalked this way, died this way.

There was no sign at all of the brief and deadly struggle between Erica and myself.

I turned back towards the house, passing the closed and locked doors of the barn.

No sign at all, except for Erica.

And I found I had to know, had to check if she were still there. I opened the front door, dropped my handbag, and got the key to the barn from its hiding place.

Returning to the barn, I had to fumble with my cold, gloved hands to fit the tiny key in the padlock. Finally, it turned and the doors swung open. Inside, the dusty old and rusting metal smells of the place assailed me. But beyond their familiarity I felt something I hadn't expected—a sudden and supernatural fear, looking into the darkness of that cavern-like space.

I groped frantically for the light switch and normality

returned. There was the old car, surrounded by the detritus of the Hahns' long years in this place.

I ran forward and bent to peer beneath the old Buick . . .

She was still there, a dark shape in the dim shadows beneath the car. Wrapped as she was, Erica did not look human at all; she was a roll of old, stained canvas. An overwhelming sense of relief flooded me.

I left the barn and locked it behind me, changed out of my clothes, and flung them into the washing machine. I lit a fire in the living room and heated the contents of a can of tomato soup—it was the closest to a real meal I'd had in the past forty-eight hours.

Forty-eight hours. It had been at about this time of day that Erica had driven up in the old white Mercedes with Keir's gun and a wild determination to kill me. Only two days ago . . .

I ate quickly, amazed that after all that had happened I still had an appetite. After I finished my soup, I took the packet of chocolate cookies from my bag and finished them off, sitting with a hot cup of coffee in front of the fire. It was almost cozy. It was almost . . . normal.

There were messages on my machine, but I wasn't ready to listen to them, doubted if I would ever be ready again.

And if it were Keir's voice?

Especially if it were Keir's voice.

Yet I couldn't hide forever. That, too, would arouse suspicion. It occurred to me that the rest of my life would have to be given over to Not Arousing Suspicion.

I switched the play button.

The messages: two from Merlin, "nothing important." Two calls from Perry McGarret—what did that mean? And one from his mother, Janice, asking me to dinner on Sunday. All of them would like me to call them when I had a moment, and hoped the writing was going well. I found, towards the end of the messages, that I was swaying a little with exhaustion.

I had a hot shower and changed into pajamas; I would phone everyone back in the morning. Now I wanted my bed, and crept to it gratefully. For the first time since I had moved to the house, I drew the rose-colored damask curtains around the bed. It was like a world of my own, tiny, ageless, comforting.

I kept waking through the night, despite my exhaustion, beset by bloody dreams. Erica howling around the house, Erica rattling pots and pans and leaving bloody footprints in the kitchen. Erica dripping gore from her head wound like a female Banquo, interrupting an editorial meeting at Brambles Thorne, terrifying a white-faced Sammy by raining blood from her blonde curls all over the board table, and gliding up to gibber at the head of marketing about her latest sales figures.

At one stage, I woke screaming and turned on the light, or tried to, frightening myself the more because in groping amongst the folds of the bed curtains I dreamt I was trying to brush past Erica, and she refused to move. My hands touched her shroud, her heavy, blood-soaked shroud . . .

And I was properly awake, found the opening in the curtains, turned on the light—and slept with it burning, all the rest of the night.

Yet my dreams of Erica persisted. She was tapping on my window, like Cathy in *Wuthering Heights,* pleading that she was cold, she wanted to come in. She was banging on the door, demanding to come in. I rolled over and told myself it was yet another dream.

But of course, it was not. Someone was banging on the door. I stifled a scream by biting the corner of my pillow— but there was no woman's voice calling.

The banging on the door persisted, a heavy kind of thundering.

Innocent. I'm innocent. I know nothing.

I pulled on a robe, found my rabbit slippers beneath the bed, and ran through the darkened house, turning on a lamp by the door as I neared it. "Who is it?" I asked.

"Perry McGarret."

Shit, shit . . .

Erica? I haven't seen or heard from Erica Tudor for more than six months. Lies, like that. You have to lie, Sarah . . . Lie to save your life.

I opened the door.

He was in his uniform, cap on his head, wearing a new navy overcoat that had replaced the one with the bullet hole through it. His face was set, as if the snow storm outside, keening past him into the house, chilling me where I stood, had frozen his features, turned the blue eyes to ice. He started to speak, above the howling of the wind, jerking his head towards the barn as he did so. It was hard to catch his words as the wind took them, blew them away. "Morning, I've come about that there body in your barn."

Chapter Fifteen

There are two commonly held fallacies about fainting. One is that you wake up not knowing where you are. You *do* know where you are, for most people aren't aware of fainting. Like coming out of an anesthetic, it seems you've been unconscious for merely the blink of an eye. The only surprise comes when you realize that you're suddenly on the floor, unless some kind person has moved you to a more comfortable place.

The second fallacy, indulged mostly in movie scripts, is that you can spring up almost immediately and address the pressing problem of finding those missing jewels, tracking down that murderer, escaping from those villains. In fact, you usually awaken with the dull ache of complaining blood vessels in the head and neck, and maybe a bruise or two, if your landing spot proved inauspicious.

In that dark, confusing predawn I went from gazing up at Sergeant McGarret in the doorway to finding myself lying on a settee with a rug draped over me, my aching head resting on a cushion.

There were two settees in my living room, both set at right angles to the fireplace. By lifting my head a little I could see, beyond my feet in the pink rabbit slippers, Perry McGarret down on one knee on the hearth rug, coaxing a fire into life. He had removed his coat and hat, but still looked very neat, very official, in the long-sleeved pale-blue shirt and navy tie, the navy trousers with their red stripe down the side. His head was turned away from me.

It was better this way, I thought, tiredly. Now I didn't have to lie, now there would be no more reason to plan. All I had to do was tell the truth. I was so tired, and so scared, that I didn't even care where it would lead.

Prison, Sarah.

Did women prisoners make license plates? Would it be hard on the nails?

I found to my surprise that I was glad they had sent Perry McGarret to bring me in. What I had to go through today, the arrest, the fingerprinting, the walk to the cells, would not be so frightening when accompanied by someone I liked and even trusted.

McGarret came back on his heels and turned to glance at me, gave a little half-take, and then a half-smile. "You okay?"

"Yes," I said, my voice croaking. I tried again. "Sorry I fainted. The stress, I guess. Do you want to leave straight-away?"

Gently, "Are you in that much of a hurry?"

"No. Oh, no."

His gaze was kind, comforting.

I said, "I'm glad it's you. I wouldn't have wanted it to be anyone else."

He rose to his feet, and came over to stand by my head, pushed the coffee table back a little, and sat down cross-legged on the floor beside me. He gazed at me intently; his expression patient.

Then he said, "I'm glad it was me, too. I'm glad I'm here now."

"We'd better . . ." I was about to say, *We'd better go now and get it over and done with*. But he had a hand on my shoulder.

"You'd better lie there quietly for a while. I've put the kettle on for tea—you don't mind?"

"Mind? Of course not. As long as I don't have to go out to the barn."

"That was just an excuse."

I stared at him, and he looked . . . he was embarrassed! His flat, high cheekbones flushed a little.

It was one of those terrible moments when whole worlds of the psyche collide, explode, changing time forever. And I realized that for some seconds his large, raw-boned face and those dark blue eyes were very close to mine.

"I think I m going to be sick," I said. but it was tears that came. Perry McGarret, trained for disasters, helped me sit up, and murmured, "Just do it any old where—on the rug—I'll clean up." And he sat on the settee beside me, his arm around me.

I was sobbing, panting. wanting to scream at him. Somehow I managed to say, almost calmly, "Why an excuse? What . . . sort of an excuse is that?"

"Well . . ." His arm was still about me; I half expected him to rock me like a child. I was confused: his nearness was disturbing, yet I liked the feel of another human's closeness. I liked the fact that he was so large that I had the illusion that I could hide against him, within the circle of these arms. Yet at the same time I wished he were a million miles away.

He was talking about the Buick. He'd always had an interest in old cars, but had never actually got around to buying one to restore. Now he had a place of his own, and a garage large enough and a friend who was a mechanic . . . Peter Copely, however, had said *he* had a friend who'd like the Buick, and since he'd staked first claim, so to speak . . . But then Peter's friend had since found another car. All this said in his careful, slow way, his arm still about me.

"That's what . . ." *Careful, Sarah. Carefully. But there was only one way to find the truth.* "That's what you said . . . when I opened the door. You came to offer to buy my car—

at . . ." I looked over at the grandfather clock. "At six o'clock in the morning?"

"Your light was on," his voice a little gruff. "I thought you must be up early working on your book."

I wondered how to get out from under his arm. He didn't seem to be in the least uncomfortable, didn't show the first sign of moving it.

I said, "You shouldn't be back at work yet."

"I wasn't. I'm not, officially. Raoul asked me out—there was a siege over at Fir Creek. The feller finally let his wife and kids leave the house and I talked him into surrendering. Been there most of the night . . . he's in the cells, now."

"Why does your boss keep calling you out on the dangerous jobs? You haven't recovered from the bullet hole in your shoulder yet."

He shrugged his undamaged shoulder. "I seem to be good at talking to them. Haven't had any training, no more than we all had at the Police Academy. Just something I've found out. Fellers like that—scared, angry—they'll listen to me, oftentimes. Don't know why. Don't have any way with words at all."

If I wriggled, would he move, take the hint?

He had been on his way home and had driven up the drive. He'd have thought nothing of it, he was the sort of man who'd probably be up and chopping wood by five-thirty each morning. And he'd seen my light burning, not knowing it was the bedroom, not the study; not knowing that I was sleeping with the light on to keep my demons at bay.

And his rather stiff, embarrassed words as I had opened the door. What he'd said hadn't been, *I've come about that there body in your barn*. It had been, *I've come about that car in your barn*, or something close to it. The wind had blown his words away as he had jerked his head towards the old outbuilding. *I've come about that car . . .*

"You got to stop working so hard, you know that? I bet

you're up most nights, all night. I bet you don't get near enough sleep."

I grated out, "Suppose not."

Then he said, softly, "What did you mean, earlier?"

"What?" the fear returning.

"Were you really glad it was me that caught you?" He had half-turned me around to face him. I gazed up at him in horror. "I sure hope you meant that," he said.

I had to turn away—first turn away, then break away—but his hand was on my chin, firmly? keeping my face turned up towards him.

He spoke seriously. "You won't admit it, will you? Not even to yourself. Won't admit you need someone. You hide behind your work, trying to do too much, trying to push everything else away ... You haven't eaten anything in days."

"How do you—?"

"The bread's stale, the milk's curdled."

"Have you been playing detective in my refrigerator?"

Calmly, "I play detective all the time."

I pulled my chin from his hand with a jerk of my head and stared straight ahead, into the hearth. His nearness was growing more threatening with each passing second. How had this happened? What had I said, in those first few minutes of regaining consciousness?

What had I said?

I'd said, *I'm glad it was you. I wouldn't want it to be anyone else.*

Oh, God ...

When once again his hand came up and touched my face, turning it upwards towards him, I knew what he wanted, what he expected. It was in his eyes even before his mouth came down, slowly, gently but firmly, on my own.

It was my own fault, really, I had no one to blame but myself. It was only a kiss. I could have borne that.

The problem was that *I enjoyed it.* And it was only halfway through the kiss, my hand raised to his head, my fingers touching the thick hair, that I realised I was not supposed to enjoy it. This was not Keir. And this was not just any other man. This was a police officer.

I broke away from the kiss, turned away, would have risen from the settee but for the fact that he sat on its edge, and to flee I would have had to scramble either over his lap or over the back of the chesterfield and across the broad refectory table behind it.

"I . . . you . . . this," I burbled.

He rescued me by standing up. "I'll get the tea," he said.

He glanced at the fire, which had settled down to a comfortable blaze between the three large logs he had set. He reached out and touched one of the long pink ears on my left slipper. "Love the bunnies," he said, in that ridiculous Southern accent, and left the room. I could hear him, even at this distance, clattering amongst the china and silver in the kitchen.

Lerv the buhnnies.

I began to laugh. I put my head on my drawn-up knees and laughed silently and long.

Which was really strange, for nothing about any of this was funny at all. Maybe I was just all cried out. Maybe I was losing my mind . . .

I had quieted down by the time he returned, bearing a tray with a tea service on it. He seemed to be having some difficulty, and I remembered his shoulder. The bank robbery had been only ten days ago. It seemed years; so much had happened in between.

I sat up, now, concerned for him. "You shouldn't have done that—I could have carried it."

He gave me a look that said *nonsense* and put the tray down, carefully, its weight mostly resting on his right hand. He'd somehow discovered my best Wedgwood behind the everyday dishes, found the boxed silver teaspoons at the back of the cutlery drawer, and arranged cookies on a plate with almost geometric symmetry. There was lemon, no milk. I hadn't shopped for some days. Despite his self-built persona as a redneck cop from Georgia, this was one of the Canadian McGarrets. This was Janice McGarret's boy. Beautiful things were not strangers to him, nor were manners nor etiquette, which he'd probably absorbed by osmosis in his childhood and early youth.

"Lemon?" he asked.

"No, thank you."

"Sugar?"

"One, please."

Oh, this was so bizarre. Thursday I kill a person, Friday and Saturday are spent concealing the crime, and Sunday I'm breakfasting with a member of the Canadian police.

When he handed me my cup, I took it, praying that my hands wouldn't shake. They did, and the delicate little cup rang in its saucer, musical as a bell.

I looked up and McGarret was spooning sugar into his own cup and pretending not to notice.

I tried to think of something to say.

I raised my head and caught a steady, unreadable look in McGarret's eyes.

"Can you talk about your husband?" he asked.

"Can I? Or will I?"

"Will you? I'd like to know."

I lowered my gaze to my teacup. Sometimes meeting his gaze gave a sudden shock, it disturbed me profoundly. I wondered if he noticed something of the sort, but decided he didn't. I hoped he didn't.

"I love my husband," I said. "I love him very much." And it was only when I looked across at McGarret that I knew I was partly using the words as a barricade, and in the unmoving face, the quiet depths of his eyes, I could see that he knew it.

"We were everything to each other for twenty-five years, and married for nineteen of them. We married while he was still studying medicine, against parental opposition. But I had no regrets. He was the first and only man I've ever loved. Or ever will love."

I should have looked at him at this point, but it was

becoming increasingly difficult. Not simply because of his large and disconcerting physical presence, but the danger of what I might say. All descriptions of my past, all talk of Keir would lead, eventually, to Erica. And how to speak of Erica to this quiet, watchful man without giving something away? Even now I felt at risk, afraid of my own secret desire to confess, to put my head into my hands and sob, *I killed her. I killed Erica. She's lying underneath the body of your precious old Buick in the barn.*

"You had twenty-five good years. Maybe, if you let yourself, you'll have twenty-five more with someone who'll love you for what you are, now, not what you were, twenty-five years ago."

"Thank you for your concern," stiffly, coldly, "but . . ."

And the telephone rang.

Before I could move, McGarret was on his feet and across the room, scooping up the phone from the table and bringing it back to hand it to me.

I picked up the receiver, balancing the machine on my knees. McGarret walked away, stood looking into the fire, his back to me.

"Sally?"

"Keir?" I cried.

"This is Bill Stanforth, Sally. How are you?"

Always the correct response. You could never really fault Bill. Or Barbara, or Katherine, for that matter. I thought for the first time, with a resentment that twisted inside me, that you could never take umbrage at anything they said. They were too clever for that.

"I'm well, thank you, Bill. How are you? And Barbara?"

"We're . . . we're very worried, Sally. I wouldn't be bothering you up there if we weren't . . . Both of us . . . all the family . . . very worried."

"What's happened ?" My voice was even colder than his. For I was braced for anything. Braced even to hear the worst, to hear the words I had denied even to myself, that Erica, with her little gun, had made sure that Keir could never come back to me.

"It's Keir, isn't it? Something's happened to Keir."

And Bill Stanforth, whom I had never known to be hesitant, unsure, was suddenly both of these things when he avoided my questions, answering obliquely, "When you answered the phone . . . you thought I was Keir. Were you expecting him to call you, Sally?"

"He often calls me, Bill."

"Yes. I see. But . . . recently? Have you heard from him recently?"

"If Keir wished to speak to you, Bill," I said, coolly, "I'm sure he'd call you."

Wicked Sarah. Smug Sarah. But where were you, Bill, when Keir disappeared with Erica, and I was left alone and frightened? What happened to twenty-five years of friendship—as I'd thought—between us?

"Yes he would call us—he calls us regularly, as you know. Before this . . . business . . . you know what a close family we were. You were part of it, Sally. We're all very sorry you're no longer a part of it."

"I think the relationship between you and your son doesn't have much—"

"Barbara and I haven't heard from him for a few days. Not since Erica came home from the hospital. We've called, but—"

"Erica's been in the hospital? What sort of hospital?"

Already I was presuming it was a mental hospital. She had checked herself out of some sanatorium after a breakdown. That would explain her state of mind when I had last seen her, crazed, obsessed, murderous.

Bill Stanforth was silent a moment. "You didn't know that Erica had lost the baby?"

I gave an involuntary cry, only just covering the mouthpiece in time. My head spun with an overwhelming sense of relief.

I hadn't killed the child. I hadn't killed the child.

"Sally . . . ? Sally?" The voice sounded tinny and persistent, but I could not, for a moment, speak at all.

I hadn't killed Erica's child.

A deep voice said, "You okay?"

I had forgotten McGarret. I looked up, startled, to find he had turned, was gazing at me worriedly. I tried to smile and failed, held the receiver to my ear once more and tried to collect my thoughts.

"Bill, I . . ."

But back in New York, the phone had changed hands.

"Sally, this is Barbara." The clipped, mid-Atlantic accent. The voice that could cut glass.

"Barbara, I last heard from Keir four days ago, on Wednesday night. It was only a message on my machine . . .

"Did he say where he was going, what his plans were?"

"Their plans, Barbara." I had to stop my voice rising in something that sounded even to my ears like a developing hysteria. "He'd just married Erica the week before. Is it likely he'd he making plans without his wife?"

Barbara was silent, hearing the unaccustomed edge to my voice.

She was a wise woman, Barbara. She said, only, "Sally, dear, we all love Keir. I know you love him as much as we do. Will you promise me something? If you hear from Keir, will you call us? Even better, get him to call us. But in any case, will you phone when you hear from him?"

"I'll phone you, Barbara, if you promise the same for me."

Again the silence, then, "Of course we'll phone."

"Barbara? How was Erica? I mean, losing the baby. Was she coping? Was she . . . very upset?"

"She was devastated."

I found myself holding the receiver at a very odd angle, against my forehead as if, any minute, I would start beating my head with it. The thought of McGarret as witness to my falling apart helped bring me to myself. But when I glanced up he was standing with his broad back tactfully towards me, seeming to study the brooding Scottish land-scape that hung over the mantelpiece.

"I'll call you, Barbara. Should I hear from either of

them. Perhaps he's taken Erica away for a few days to recuperate."

"He'd tell us." Bluntly. *He might not tell you, Sally, but he'd tell us.*

"Goodbye, Barbara." I replaced the receiver, and half-dropped the phone onto the floor beside me.

McGarret had turned, of course, was leaning his good arm on the mantel and gazing at me. "You want me to go or stay?" he asked.

He was a kind man.

"I m sorry . . ." I gestured rather helplessly towards the phone.

He said, "I'll stay if you like."

I looked up at him. Yes, he would. Just what I needed. An honest, kindly cop who wouldn't go away.

I smiled. "I'll be okay. Thank you for calling in. I'll . . . phone you about the Buick if that's all right."

"Sure. Whenever." He was pulling on his coat, reaching for his hat.

"Don't get up," he said, as I began to move off the settee. "I can see myself out."

The barn. Will he go to the barn . . . ?

But it was locked. Of course it was locked. And it had been McGarret who'd talked me into having the padlock fixed to the doors.

"I'll see you, then."

"Yes."

He nodded, his hat pulled low on his head, shading his eyes. And then he opened the door and stepped out.

There was an eddy of icy wind, even a few flakes of snow, with the cold air that replaced his presence in my house. One flake landed on the polished floor where the little mat had once lain and melted into a drop of water. I gazed at it, slightly mesmerized, saw how it reflected the glow from the lamp on the coffee table. Outside, beneath the whistling and keening of the wind, the motor of McGarret's car thrummed into life. The sound rose then faded, slowly, leaving only myself and my house and the wind.

And Erica.

I felt too numb to think, too tired to move. I dozed fitfully for a few hours. When I woke the room was filled with the gray light of a winter's day and the fire was ash. I woke with the same thought I had been grappling with as I'd fallen asleep. The single problem that had unexpectedly replaced that of getting Keir back into my life.

What to do with Erica?

Chapter Sixteen

I went home to the apartment on Central Park South and let myself in with my key. To my relief I could hear Keir's voice as I opened the door. But it was not Keir, it was his father, Bill Stanforth, standing in the center of the living room, with Barbara and their daughter Katherine. I stopped in surprise, for there were quite a few people here; Katherine's latest husband, Edward, and her two children Eleanor and Oliver, who looked at me with hard, unblinking little black eyes. No one, not even Keir's Aunt Clara, whom he privately called Dame Clara Cluck behind her back, was very friendly, though she used to be.

They stood back as I walked into the room, and I saw the coffin, then, down at the end of the room, where the light from the big windows fell full upon it.

Keir lay there, amidst the folds of white linen, his face pale and beautiful in death.

I screamed and jerked myself up from the pillow, gasping and tearing my mind back from the nightmare.

Here I was, at home in St. Claude, at home at *Jaegerhalle* in the four-poster bed. It was just a nightmare, no matter how vivid.

Was it? What if, now that there was no longer the tie of a child, Keir had told Erica that he wanted to return to me? And out of her mind with the loss of the child, the threatened loss of Keir, she'd taken the little .25 from her handbag . . .

No. NO!

At nine, when Clorinda was due in to clean the New York apartment, I phoned. But no one answered. I rang every half hour until eleven, then I gave up and called the house in New Hampshire.

The housekeeper answered, and was more friendly than on other occasions. It was obvious she was worried and under a lot of strain. Speaking about it—even to me—was some kind of release. "There's no news, Mrs. Stanforth. The police have been notified—Mr. Thorne did that, early this morning."

Sammy? He really must be worried about his prize author. I wondered that Bill and Barbara hadn't reported Keir and Erica missing, but then, their first thought would be the scandal, *more* newspaper headlines. Sammy didn't mind in the least about newspaper headlines of any sort.

"So there's been no news of either of them? Dr. Stanforth hasn't contacted you?"

"They've both gone. Dr. Stanforth arranged to go on vacation, but he disappeared two days before he was to leave. And Miss Tudor said nothing to anybody about going away. They were to come here for a week, you see, then they were going to Paris."

"I tried to phone the New York apartment . . ."

"Oh, Clorinda is only coming in once a week now. Mrs. Stanforth Senior—Dr. Stanforth's mother—she arranged that. Clorinda rang and told me. She asked me to call her if we heard anything."

Dear Barbara. Thoughtful of her, thinking of Keir's small economies. Neglecting to think of Clorinda with three teenage children to raise alone and needing the money.

"It was Clorinda who called Mrs. Cosgrove."

"Clorinda called Beth?"

"The place was . . . sort of untidy, messy. Not like them

at all, she said. And by the end of the week they still hadn't been in, she could tell, and the envelope was still there. It had all the discs containing the new novel. It was propped up on Mrs. Stanforth's desk as if for someone to see it, with Mrs. Cosgrove's name on it, and Brambles Thorne, and the telephone number. So Clorinda called. And Mrs. Cosgrove and Mr. Thorne came over, and they called Mr. and Mrs. Stanforth Senior to try to decide what to do."

"I see."

"We're all so worried, Mrs. Stanforth. Erica was devastated about losing the baby. And here we were thinking that Paris would be a change of scene for her, would help her get over it. But their tickets were left in the drawer of Dr. Stanforth's desk. The police came this morning and went over the place . . . so frightening, though they were nice about it all. And they found the tickets—for yesterday, they were."

"If you hear from them, would you have them call me? Either of them, there's some business I need to discuss with Dr. Stanforth."

"Yes, of course." Businesslike and tactful, grateful for the excuse, in case she had to relay my message for Keir in front of Erica.

My phone rang only five seconds after I replaced the receiver.

Please be Keir. Please, please be Keir . . .

"Sally? It's Beth, honey."

Strain in her voice, yet I was mad at her. She was there, in the thick of it, and she hadn't called me.

"Why didn't you call me, Beth? Why? I've been out of my mind."

"Do you think I don't know that? You were worried enough last week. Who'd have thought? Oh God, Sally, who'd have thought you'd be right, that something *was* wrong."

"*I did!* And you're my friend, and you should have trusted me."

"I'm sorry! I kept thinking, any hour, any minute, we'd

find something, and it'd be all so simple and easy to explain, and I would call you—or Keir would—and explain. You're so alone up there, Sal. I didn't want you to worry more than you already were."

"So why call me now? What have you found out? Is Keir alright? Is he . . . ?" Feelings of dread closed on my chest like a vice.

"I was just on the phone to Bill Stanforth. He told me he'd spoken to you, that you knew that they were missing."

"Where is Keir, Beth?"

"I don't know. What I do know . . . isn't good. They found the car, Sally. Up in Maine, parked on a headland overlooking a beach. They—the police—just notified Bill Stanforth. He phoned me. Erica's purse was in the car. Everything intact. There was no sign of Keir."

"What car?" I asked. "Erica's car?"

Unwillingly from Beth. "No, honey. That damnable old Mercedes." She was crying now, and I felt dreadful, helpless and so culpable that I would have given anything to blurt out the truth to her.

"What do the police think, Beth? Do they have any ideas?"

"They said . . . women who've lost babies, like Erica . . . sometimes do crazy things. She phoned me, you see, on that Friday night. I couldn't raise Keir. I called the police, but . . . we had no way of knowing where she was."

"They think she might have killed herself?"

"But she wouldn't, would she? She had everything to live for, Sally. She could have had more babies. She had everything any woman could want. It doesn't make sense. I can't believe she'd do it. I just can't."

I let a half minute or so go by, knowing she was crying, trying hard to regain her self-control. Maybe she blamed herself.

"I'm sorry, Sally, that I don't have any news about Keir. The police think it's . . . really weird, you know? Both of them disappearing like that. They . . . they won't *tell* you anything. You have to try to figure what they're thinking from the questions they ask.''

"Beth?'' Carefully.

Beth sniffled, blew her nose. "What?''

"Beth, is it possible . . . Is it possible that Erica was so depressed, so confused, that she . . . she killed Keir?''

A long, ragged drawing in of breath on the other end of the line. "Oh, Sally.'' Almost a groan.

"They weren't happy together, Beth. I've told you about the phone calls from Keir. I *wanted* him to be unhappy with her, Beth . . .'' And I was crying, too, crying, and angry, my teeth clenched.

"You loved him. You still loved him, that was natural.''

"I'm asking you, Beth. You knew Erica. They *weren't happy, were they*?''

That's why you came for me, Erica. That's why you wanted me dead and out of the way. One only hates what one fears, and you were afraid of me.

"I got the feeling . . . in the day or so after the baby . . . Well, even before she lost the baby, despite the wedding, things were a bit strained between them. Erica was tense, preoccupied. She kept talking about wanting to get away with Keir, out of the country, to Europe. And while at the beginning she was happy to have him come up to her in New Hampshire on weekends, she'd changed and wanted them both in New York. She seemed to need Keir around a lot.''

Was she smothering him? Clinging to him, even as he was trying to pull away? Oh, Keir, what did you do to her? Was it something as simple, as devastating as believing you loved her, then changing your mind and rejecting her?

"Beth, did you tell the police this? About your feelings that there was some tension between Erica and Keir?''

"I . . .'' miserably, "I had to, Sally. I couldn't lie. Clorinda would have told them, anyway. She often heard them quarreling, apparently. Though Erica never told me that they—''

"So . . .'' My mind was struggling to come to grips with

the possibility that it reared away from, for I couldn't, couldn't bear it. "So the police think she might have . . . have killed him? She would have known Keir had a gun, you see," I added. "A little .25 Beretta that he kept in his bedside drawer."

"I know." A strange voice.

"You *know*?"

"Clorinda told the police about it. Told them that it wasn't there, when she came in on Friday. She checked, and the gun was gone."

I was silent, thinking of my dream of the night before. Had it been a premonition? Was Erica so obsessed with Keir that she had to make sure that he wouldn't come back to me?

"Sally, I have to prepare you for this, because they were hinting around the possibility. Lots of these abandoned cars by the sea are sort of faked suicides, Sally. I think . . . I think the police believe there might be a chance that Keir murdered Erica."

Chapter Seventeen

She didn't believe this herself, Beth said. It was impossible. But then, painfully, so was the possibility that Erica could hurt Keir, or that Erica could do what it seems she had done, and drowned herself.

"Like Lydia in *Gaining*, just like Lydia in *Gaining*. Oh, God, Sal, I'm so *sick* over this. I'm on tranquilizers. *Me*, can you believe it? It's tearing me apart. Erica left the discs of *Catwalk* propped up on her keyboard for me. She could do *that*, but she couldn't confide in me."

Beth broke down, and I tried to comfort her. After talking a while we promised to call each other if there was any more news, and hung up.

I was still sitting by the phone, unmoving, thinking of all the lives I had wrecked, when I heard a car pull up outside. I decided not to answer the door and ran to the bathroom instead. I'd just stay here, and whoever it was would finally take themselves off.

But I hadn't reckoned on Merlin and Natalie's determination. Unsuccessful at the front door, they came around the back, tapping on the windows as they went, yelling that the car was in the garage and I was to open up immediately.

I flushed the toilet, dragged a brush through my hair, splashed my face with water, and went to the back door to let them in.

They stood on the doorstep looking sympathetic. Merlin carried a box full of groceries, and Natalie a casserole dish.

"We've heard what's happened. And Perry told us you still weren't well," Merlin said.

"And that you've been working far too hard," Natalie said. "And he thinks you're suffering from malnutrition, and that you're probably anemic." She grinned at the look on my face, then sobered with the words, "Looking at you, I've suddenly developed a healthy respect for Perry's ability as a diagnostician." They marched past me into the kitchen.

"My special casserole," Natalie said, placing the terra-cotta pot on the table.

"And a few staples. Perry said all you have in the refrigerator is moldy celery." Merlin opened the fridge door. "Wow," she said, over her shoulder, "he was right."

Natalie cooked brunch for us all from the eggs and cheese, among other things, that they had brought. Merlin put a cup of strong coffee—with milk, now—in front of me, and said, "What's happened with Keir?"

"He and Erica . . . they've disappeared. Their car was found abandoned in Maine. By a beach. Even the police are taking it seriously."

The bantering mood evaporated. We looked at each other soberly. Then Merlin moved to the bench to hand Natalie her coffee and, after returning to the table, said to me, "You didn't bump them both off, did you?"

A brief but horrifying silence, then I started to laugh, and they did, too.

From my hysteria came another sort of lie, by omission. *Keep it up, Sarah. You're getting good at this.*

They were so kind, it took ages to get them to leave, all the longer for not being able to convince them that there was no need to worry.

I insisted on paying them for the groceries, and promised to drive into town that afternoon to shop for myself. "I guess, between the novel and worrying about Keir, I let things get away from me. Perry was right, in a way," I said as I walked them to their car.

"Just remember that," Natalie said, as she kissed me on the cheek to say goodbye, "or we'll send him back here to check up on you—and your refrigerator."

She was already behind the wheel of the pickup when Merlin, after a glance at her, pulled back a little and lowered her voice. "He was really concerned for you. Perry really likes you, you know? I think he'd like to see more of you."

I stared at her, not capable of forming any words in reply. There was mischief in her grin as she ran around the car to the passenger side.

She climbed in, and they waved as the car set off down the drive. I waved back but didn't, couldn't, call goodbye, couldn't manage a sound.

Perry really likes you.

Because his kiss had meant nothing to me, I had presumed it had meant nothing to him, either. Just friendliness, affection, born of the cold gray morning, two independent, sometimes lonely people and a warm fire.

Now his sister was warning me. Of Perry's interest. Of Perry's possible attentions. Of Perry's presence. Here, on my little farm, in my little house. Near my little barn.

My knees felt weak. Close by at the side of the porch, was the woodbox; I went to it and sat down on it. The warm sunlight seemed colder, the brightness of the day suddenly more somber since Merlin's words.

The last thing in the world I wanted was a policeman hanging about the place. And he was too domesticated. I hadn't forgotten him making tea and serving it in my best tea service. His helpfulness would not, I felt, stop there: he'd want to chop the wood, shovel snow, clean out the attic, the garage . . . *the barn.*

Helpful Peregrine.

Curious Peregrine. Asking all the right questions about me, and my marriage, and Keir. He wouldn't be able to help himself; McGarret had a mind that had been trained to note, to assimilate, to record; a mind that would collect details without, by this stage of his career, even noticing he was doing so. He was a man of honor and honesty who could sniff out a lie like a customs dog homed in on the scent of smuggled drugs.

I found myself staring at the barn opposite me.

"It's only a matter of time," I told Erica, quietly, filled with an ominous sense of ineviatability. "He'll find you, and he won't be pleased with me at all. He's not the sort of man who likes secrets. Except his own, maybe. He wouldn't like *our* secret. It'd make him very uncomfortable. He'll want to off-load it as quickly as possible."

Regretfully, but coldly, he'd read me my rights. He'd drive me into St. Claude . . . in handcuffs? Surely he wouldn't use handcuffs. He *wouldn't*. He'd just have his great hand wrapped around my upper arm, and he'd lead me from his car, up the steps of the police station, through the glass doors . . .

I couldn't bear it if he used handcuffs.

I stood up and my eye was caught by the woodbox. It was more than six feet long. The lid ran the entire length. it was the perfect size: tall for a coffin, nearly three feet high, but I'd have to stack wood on top of the body, and this was temporary, after all, just until I could think of a better way.

"Before spring," I said. "It has to be before the spring thaw or she'll defrost. Though it's a pity, because after the thaw I could bury her."

I would have liked to have been able to bury Erica straightaway. Bodies should be buried, or cremated. A proper disposal was a sign of respect. I'd have hated to think that after my death I'd be floating around under old cars and wood heaps.

* * *

I made a lot of phone calls that day, several to the Bureau of Missing Persons in New York, asking, and progressively pleading, for news of Keir and Erica. But the response was consistent. I must contact Bill and Barbara Stanforth for any information. The bureau was in contact only with the next of kin, the Stanforths, in Keir's case, and by proxy, with her mother's permission, Mrs. Beth Cosgrove, in Erica's case. They were polite but firm: I was an ex-wife. I had no rights as far as Keir was concerned.

I phoned Barbara at the house on Long Island. She was polite, but cool. She promised again that she'd call if anything new developed. "Though you're just as likely to read it sooner in the tabloids," she said in a steely voice. Apparently the story had broken, it was front-page news on an otherwise quiet day. Barbara did have one small piece of information; one of Erica's boots had been found, washed up on a beach a few miles from where the car was discovered.

"So . . . she drowned?"

"Not necessarily," the crisp voice continued. "She'd not be likely to remove her boots if she were going to drown herself, would she?"

"I . . . don't know."

But no, the boot was one of those fleecy-lined, pull-on kind, loose around the ankle. Wet, it may have come off a foot, a foot splashing about in the water.

I reminded Barbara that the Central Park apartment was in my name, and that I'd be taking reponsibility for it until Keir returned. I don't think she was pleased, probably believing that Keir had been unduly influenced at the time of the divorce.

But still, we didn't quarrel. We couldn't afford to. This woman, so different from me in every way, was nevertheless attached to me as if we were Siamese twins, trapped together by our overwhelming love for Keir. Soon, because neither of us wished to believe that he was dead, he would call one of us.

I phoned Clorinda at her home, and told her I might need the New York apartment at any time and she was to continue coming in the three days a week. She was so grateful I was embarrassed. Her son had just received a small grant, not enough to help him through college, but enough to encourage him. I told her I would pay her for the days she had missed.

At three o'clock the following morning, when my alarm sounded, I almost reconsidered my plan for Erica. But no, it had to be done soon, so it may as well be tonight.

I dressed as warmly as I could, and from the garage I took my Christmas present from David and Janice McGarret, the red and blue sled. I left it by me as I emptied the woodbox. Fortunately it was only half full; I had meant to cut more wood but then ... Erica had come and I had avoided anything to do with the ax ever since.

Once again I was thankful that Erica had chosen to die in a reasonably graceful and dignified pose, the compact length of her body easier to maneuver onto the sled at the door of the barn, where earth floor gave way to snow. I pushed the mechanic's trolley back under the Buick, changed my mind, and pulled it out again to stand it against the wall at the rear of the building. It might come in handy for shifting firewood once the snow had gone.

Erica stayed remarkably well balanced on the sled as I pulled it the short distance to the woodpile. The sky was clear, as it had been all day, and by the light of the moon I unwrapped her a little, worried that she might already have begun to defrost, to decay.

But she had not, for it was very cold indeed on the earth floor of the barn, and Erica, in death, still looked very beautiful—like a fairy princess under a spell.

And now I had to put her in a woodbox.

"I'm so sorry," I said to her, scraping the last of the

bark and wood chips from the bottom of the box. "But you did start all this. Who'd have thought you'd have such a temper? Why couldn't you have asked to come in, to talk over coffee? Am I an ogress? Was I so unreasonable?"

The earth at the bottom of the woodbox was frozen hard—a safe but ignominious bed.

With great difficulty, for even dead and stiff as a store dummy she was a heavy burden, I managed to get her into the woodbox, though losing my grip on her clothing at the last minute meant that she tipped in rather violently and landed upside down, her feet poking over the edge.

It was lucky that the fresh air and exercise of my new life had made me stronger than I'd ever been in my life, despite the deprivations of the past few days. Otherwise I couldn't have managed, juggling and joggling Erica until she was face upwards and funereally correct at the bottom of the woodbox.

And there was another problem. I couldn't just stack the wood on top of her. What of the effect of all that weight? I didn't want her nose squashed, her teeth broken, by the weight of the logs. It would be a kind of desecration, as bad as putting the ax through her skull in the first place—at least I hadn't *meant* that to happen. I built a little three-sided shelf of logs around her upper torso and found an old piece of timber in the barn that just fitted over her upper body.

Then I had another idea. Running back through the house, I fetched the roll of carpet from the laundry, the little, blood-stained carpet that contained the sweater, jeans, and boots I'd worn at the time of the killing. I tucked these around the side of her body, and then placed the timber, a built-up shelf over her, and began to restack the wood.

What did it matter if the rug and my clothing were found with Erica's body? If they got as far as finding the body, I was damned anyway. And that way I didn't have to burn them in the fireplace and make the room smell of scorched wool and burning rubber. It was the sort of odor that hangs around for days and that McGarret would undoubtedly sniff out—and question.

I took the sled back and forth a few times to the wood heap by the barn and loaded it with more logs, stacking them around and over the shelf above Erica's body, and praying that Larry Carey, Merlin, Natalie, or any other helpful acquaintance—such as McGarret—wouldn't decide to fill up every wood basket in the house and find the fake bottom and the snow maiden beneath it.

By four-fifteen I had finished. I took the sled back to the garage and risked shining the flashlight around the woodbox to make sure it looked innocent enough if someone called early in the morning I wasn't worried about the sled marks, I may have had kindling stored in the garage, and using the sled to transport the fuel back and forth was a sensible idea in all this snow. Even the bits of fallen bark were nothing to worry about.

I returned to the cottage and my bed and once more overslept after a restless night. I was awakened by a phone call from a gently spoken detective from Missing Persons in New York. I answered a lot of questions, most of them truthfully. Yes, Keir had often sounded upset, tense, during our phone calls, but he'd never say why. No, I hadn't seen my husband for several months, not since we finally separated last September and he went to live with Erica Tudor. The last time I had spoken to him was the Thursday before last, the nineteenth, and he had left a message on my machine on the following Tuesday. No, the message gave no information, though in it he said he'd call back. So far he had not.

"And Mrs. Stanforth—I mean, the second Mrs. Stanforth—your husband's new wife?"

"I haven't spoken to Erica since last year, the same night my husband left me."

The detective, whose name was Weinstein, seemed to think there was nothing wrong with my seeming tense and unhappy when speaking of Erica Tudor. He said, "Well, if you hear anything of either of them . . ." and he gave me his number.

When we'd hung up, I thought, this will be easier than I expected. I don't have to be Sarah Telling Lies. I can put on a whole new personality: I can be Sally the Bitter and Aggrieved First Wife.

Let it out, Sal. Let it all hang out.

Perhaps there was a talent for being a successful killer, comparable to being a good spy, or a competent undercover cop . Something to do with thinking out all the angles, remaining cool under fire, and being able to lie through your teeth. I wasn't congratulating myself in any way, I still felt sick with guilt, still felt that it was only a matter of time before I was caught, but I was beginning to be surprised at my ability at all this. Keir used to worry when I'd get upset about an unkind comment made at work, "You have no killer instinct." Said with love, perhaps with pride. Keir loved me the way I was.

Was.

Would Keir love me the way I am?

I was changed forever by what had occurred, yet outwardly I went on about my life as if it was still the same.

I hadn't killed Erica because I wanted her dead; alright, I had fantasized about it, but I'd never have done it. And now that she was dead I wished her back to life again. I wished it had never happened. And yet . . .

And this was why I sometimes called myself a murderer—I had hidden the crime, I had not owned up. Because I knew I *looked* guilty and because . . . now that she *was* dead, now that no force on earth could bring her back . . . I couldn't help but feel . . . well . . . *relieved.*

For she was gone. *She was gone,* the woman who had taken my husband from me. Keir could not, now, stay with her out of pity, or pride, or a misplaced sense of duty and commitment. She was gone. She was never coming back. She was . . . out of the way.

Sometimes I wondered whether Erica would have suffered had she succeeded in killing me. I doubted it. No matter what her state of mind when she did it, Erica went to a lot of trouble, premeditated trouble, to kill me. She wouldn't lose sleep over my death, why did I keep losing sleep over hers?

But I did. And I do.

I'm sorry she's dead.

But I'm not sorry she's gone.

The newspaper coverage of Erica and Keir's disappearance was comprehensive. It described the car being found, the boot on the neighboring beach, it even mentioned the fact that the boot matched footprints on the sand that led down to the water's edge. The boot was identified by Erica Stanforth's personal maid at the house in Meadowsweet, New Hampshire, as belonging to her employer. A woman at a shop some miles from the scene had given positive identification of Mrs. Erica Stanforth, who had bought cigarettes from her on the night of January twenty-seventh. She had seemed agitated, and depressed. She had made a phone call, later verified to have been to her friend and editor, Beth Cosgrove, in New York. During the conversation she had been distressed and had cried. At one stage, before leaving, she had picked up a copy of *Gaining* and said to the shop owner, Ms. Delvene Gobbit, "It's a very tragic story, but life is tragic, isn't it? Life is full of tragedy." Ms. Gobbit recognized her straight away, knew she lived just over the state line in New Hampshire. She'd followed her outside when she drove off in that white Mercedes. Ms. Gobbit expressed regret at not saying something to her. But as she said, 'You never know these things at the time."

Ms. Gobbit had told police that she had a clear view of the car as Miss Tudor got in and drove away, and Miss Tudor was definitely the car's only occupant.

Police were still searching for missing plastic surgeon Keir Stanforth, Erica Stanforth's husband of only nine days, concerning his wife's last days and her disappearance.

On television, too, Delvene Gobbit made the most of her fifteen minutes of fame, and repeated what she had heard Erica say in the shop that night.

So history is written, I marveled. Why didn't *my* Erica think to say what Ms. Gobbit's Erica had said? I never was much of a one for overkill. James Hammel once told me that I put severe limits on his flights of hyperbole. Certainly if one of my writers had seriously presented me with, "Life is tragic, isn't it? Life is full of tragedy," I'd have written, *Puh-lease!* in the margin.

I was having a late breakfast on Saturday when I heard a car drive up. It couldn't be Merlin, I had just spoken to her on the phone; it wasn't Larry Carey, because he'd come early with his brother's snowplow and cleared the drive. It wasn't Alby Gresson, who, Larry told me, was in the hospital and had been for some time now, suffering from pneumonia. On hearing this, I had decided to send him some flowers, driven as much by guilt as by neighborly concern.

I peered through the curtains: a dark green Jeep Cherokee was parked by the front steps. If I leaned my head to the left I could probably see who had just been thumping like a creditor on my front door. I mean, there were a lot of green Jeep Cherokees in this part of the country . . .

And there he was, patiently waiting for the door to open, his big, expressionless, ugly face turned away a little, gazing through the ubiquitous dark glasses at the view of my snow-covered fields. His arm was in a sling—that was new. His police regulation overcoat was draped over his shirt and tie, but he didn't seem aware of the cold. He looked as if he were content to wait there a long time if he had to.

I opened the door, looked at him. "Who shot you this time?" I asked.

Chapter Eighteen

He removed the dark glasses and said, "I was hoping you'd come up with something a mite more original, being a writer. I got that question from just about everyone I met this morning, including the feller who did it."

Shot you?" I stood back to let him in, closed the door after him, and took his coat and hat.

"Nope. Broken bottle, down at the Grizzly Bar. Big disagreement over a pool game. Pete and I came in during the middle of it and talking just didn't seem to make an awful lot of difference to them."

I sat down on one settee. He sat beside me.

"I heard someone yell. 'Get 'im in the left shoulder,' and like an idiot I turned towards the voice. It was Jimmy Gresson—caught me real good. I had my hands full at the time," he excused himself.

"How big was this disagreement?"

"About twenty fellers or so. Raoul and Greg Cleaver turned up and we managed to book about seven. The rest lit out."

"Twenty drunk men fighting with broken bottles. And you and Peter waded into the middle of it."

He opened his mouth to speak, but I held up my hand. "No, don't tell me that a man's gotta do what a man's gotta do."

He watched me, a small smile on his mouth. "Okay," he said.

There was a short pause and I found myself wishing he'd sat on the opposite settee. There was something too friendly in his choosing to sit beside me in a room with three settees in it.

Suddenly, remembering, I said, "I haven't called you about the car. I was going to . . . but the roads were so bad. And . . . I've been busy writing, and I thought—"

"There's no hurry," he said. "My barn's been turned over to Patsy—more room for her there than being locked in a box stall. And my garage is full of winter feed for her. I don't mind waiting till spring."

I nodded, wondering why he studied my face. He *was* studying my face.

"I'm on my way home," he said. "They had to stitch me up again at the hospital last night, but when I came into the station this morning, my doctor had rung Raoul and ratted on me." He didn't look happy about it, glared down at the offending sling. "He'd sent out for this—I didn't arrive in it. Called me into his office and threw it at my head and told me next time I lied to him I'd be suspended."

I was trying to look serious. I said, because he obviously expected me to, "Would you like some coffee?" I didn't wait for a reply, but led the way along the hall towards the kitchen.

He followed me, more slowly. I was making fresh coffee when he said, heavily, from the doorway, "Sarah."

I looked over at him. He was gazing at me rather severely, but his voice held something like compassion when he said, "If you're kinda avoiding me because you don't want to be friends with me, I can live with that. But your reactions are all wrong, honey. You're acting dead scared, and that's the truth. Why?"

I wanted to say, *Don't call me 'honey.'*

I wanted to say, *Scared? Who's scared? I'm not scared.*

I wanted to say, *Get out of my house and never come back.*

I wanted to say, *Perry, I've done a terrible thing.*

His right hand had taken my left arm in a grip so reminiscent of the nightmare in which he arrested me that I almost fainted again. And when I looked up he was wearing his professional face, that closed, unreadable face, and his eyes were suddenly dark, opaque, like flat gray river pebbles. They told me nothing. Then he said, "We have to talk."

He hooked a chair out from under the table with one booted foot and pushed me gently down onto the seat. Then he turned to the percolator. "Coffee," I heard him mutter, "all we ever seem to do is drink coffee."

He cleared my cold breakfast things into the sink and took fresh cups from the cupboard. He went straight to the right place and I felt chilled, as I always did when he unconsciously manifested the fact that he noticed a great deal and forgot very little.

While the coffee was percolating he sat down at the table opposite me.

"Missing Persons have been in touch with you." A statement, not a question.

"Yes." My voice barely audible.

"You told them you hadn't seen your ex-husband or his wife since September last. That you didn't know where they were."

"Yes. I told all that to Detective Weinstein. I don't know what happened in New York."

It was hard to speak, hard to breathe. I had been wrong, I was not good at this. He sat quietly, across the table from me, and I looked at my hands on the table's surface and couldn't meet his gaze. Another two or three questions and I would crack. I wasn't cut out for this. *Keep the answers short,* a voice warned me. *Don't gabble.*

"Is that the truth, Sarah?" And of course I had to look

up at him. He spoke gently, but he was every inch a police officer for all that. "Did you tell Weinstein the truth?"

"Yes," I croaked.

He reached across the table with his right hand, and I watched the movement, was unsurprised when he took my left hand and held it. It could have been a kindly gesture, a supportive gesture. His hand was very large, my own seemed small in his grasp: two of his fingers lay casually, accidentally, against the inside of my wrist, and I felt my pulse beating against them.

I told myself, he could not be this smart, and then he said my name again, "Sarah." I had to look up at him and decide whether to leave my hand there or to pull it away, abruptly, and have him know that I dared not answer the next question with his hand there, just there, waiting for my pulse to race, waiting for the lie.

And he asked the wrong question.

"Sarah, do you know where Keir is?"

"No."

Our gazes were as locked as my hand within his. "He hasn't phoned you to tell you where he is?"

"No."

I left my hand there, loathing his touch. He was using me, the bastard. I was too angry, now, to pull my hand away, too angry to disguise the resentment on my face.

McGarret said, "You'd lie, though, wouldn't you? To protect him?"

"Yes," I hissed, careless. obstinate, "But I don't need to. Keir's done nothing wrong. And *you,*" I said, pulling my hand from his, "have no jurisdiction in this case at all."

"Oh, honey." That was all he said. Some emotion, at least, on his face, though I couldn't read it.

The coffee was ready. He got up and took the two mugs to the bench. "My interest in this case is because of you. You've been through enough. Don't you think I can see that? I thought . . . I thought I could help you."

I absorbed this, started to open my mouth to say, *Thank you, but I don't need any help.*

But he was saying, "You worry me, though. Saying you'd lie for him." He paused. I think he expected me to turn to him, but I kept my gaze on the door of the wall oven opposite me. In it I could see my own reflection. I could have been a suspect in any thousand police dramas, seated at a table in a straight-backed chair . . .

A drawer was opened behind me and I heard him hunting for teaspoons in the silver. "I made a few inquiries, through friends of friends of mine." Tinkling of spoon against cup sides. "Made some new contacts. Not official, and not to be made a habit of." He came back and placed a coffee mug down on the table in front of me. "You can expect someone to come and ask you more questions, Sarah. Something funny is going on down there. You ought to know. And prepare yourself. Think real carefully, honey, on how much loyalty you owe Keir."

I felt really, really ill. I put my elbows on the table and my face in my hands because I didn't want McGarret to see that I'd turned pale. I knew I had. I felt the blood leave my head, felt my temples turn suddenly cold and damp.

Something funny is going on down there.

I looked up at the big raw-boned face above me; he paused in the act of raising his coffee mug to his lips and returned my gaze.

And he wouldn't elaborate, the bastard. He seated himself at the table, and drank his coffee and watched me.

I said, "So you've been in touch with Missing Persons . . . Are you going to tell me what you found out? Isn't that why you came out here this morning?"

A small smile, calmly, "I came by to ask you for a date. I was going to tell you today, sure. Was gonna choose my moment, though. This . . . doesn't seem to be going all that well."

"I don't think there'd be a good time, sergeant. Tell me."

I couldn't quite keep the plea out of my voice. He studied me a moment, then relented. "Yesterday Forensic went over your apartment in New York. They found a lot of blood in the bathroom. I mean, a *lot* of blood. All washed off, very thoroughly. It shows up, these days, though. And your housekeeper doesn't know anything about it."

I sat still, my face unmoving. His expression, watchful, serious, didn't change either, as he continued, "There were tensions between Keir and his new wife. Quarrels. Loud. Nasty. Both housekeepers attest to that, the one in New York and the one at the country house."

He leaned hack in his chair and sighed. I started to droop a little, my mind trying to cope with this.

And McGarret said, without warning, "You made a lot of calls recently to the country house, the place in New Hampshire."

Taken aback by the suddenness of the statement, I looked up at him. He was gazing at me inquiringly.

"It was after that last conversation I had with Keir—he was so upset. I tried the New York apartment too, and all our friends, when I couldn't locate him. Everyone said," I finished bitterly, "that I was worrying for nothing. And the message he left on my machine on Tuesday—that was a worry, too."

"You still have that tape by any chance?"

"Yes. It was such a strange one." I scowled back at him. "I'm not giving it to you."

His dark brows shot up. "I wasn't asking for it. Last thing I want to hear, Keir whining to you."

I glared at him, but stopped myself from making a reply.

He got to his feet, took his coffee mug to the sink, and rinsed it out. "I was going to ask you out for the day—get you out of the house, away from your work . . ." He turned to give me a steady look, "Maybe stop you brooding, waiting by the phone."

"I'm not." But I didn't sound convincing at all, even to me. "Perry . . . the blood. Whose blood was it?"

He stood by the sink, drying his hands on a towel and

didn't answer straightaway. "They should know by late this afternoon."

He started to walk back through the house; I had to trot along behind him.

"Perry . . . ? McGarret? Will you call me? Will you let me know whose it was?"

We were back in the living room, he replaced his glasses and his hat and took up his coat, swinging it over one shoulder. He looked down at me silently, tellingly, and I understood the deal. I took an unconscious step back. He walked to me, bent to me, and said what I knew he would say, what he had to say. "I want your word you'll tell me if Keir Stanforth phones you, or tries to contact you in any way at all. I want your word that you'll tell me when and if he does."

"I don't think he will," I prevaricated.

"Oh, he will alright. Sooner or later. He was phoning you regular-like, all these months, with a new partner and a baby on the way. Now he's in trouble. He's in a *lot* of trouble—and he'll come to you."

"What if he's dead?" I blurted.

He looked at me, his gaze keener, more probing. But the voice was that same slow, unhurried voice. "If he's dead, where's the body, Sarah? And why did he withdraw several hundred dollars from an automatic teller in New Hampshire the day before Erica Stanforth was last seen alive?"

I gazed up at him, no breath left in my body. "You know more than you're telling me," I managed.

Quietly he said, "Don't let me have to say the same thing about you."

He turned to the front door and opened it. I followed him out. I made one more plea to the broad, obdurate back.

"Perry . . . if it's true you became interested in this case for my sake, then I'm grateful, but . . . I'd really like you not to concern yourself any more. It's—"

He had stopped halfway down the stairs, and turned

slowly. Two steps down and he was still a little taller than me. I finished, "I think it's best that you don't get involved."

I didn't immediately realize how the words sounded. It took a few seconds and the look on McGarret's face for me to see what I'd done.

"You'd walk to hell and back for him, wouldn't you?" he said. "Without knowing what he's done, without even trying to question what he might have done."

He leaned forward, his good hand on the porch upright near me. "Be careful, Sarah. Be very careful. If he's going to pull you into any kind of trouble, he'll have to cross the border to do it. And once he's in New Brunswick you can bet your sweet life I'm going to involve myself."

He turned and headed for the Jeep, down the stairs, past the woodbox . . . I didn't wait to see him go, but fled inside the house.

Chapter Nineteen

I went back to the kitchen, washed up my breakfast things and the mugs and spoons McGarret and I had used, my hands shaking in the sudsy water.

You'd walk to hell and back for him, wouldn't you?

I dropped a spoon with a clatter while drying it; the sharp sound of its contact with the stone floor making me cry out. I slowed my movements, dried the china with great care, placed each piece in the cupboard with deliberation. Then I made my way to the study, still trembling, feeling hollow inside.

I phoned a florist in town and had flowers and a fruit basket sent to Alby Gresson.

I phoned Beth, who was back at her desk at Brambles Thorne. She had no more information to give me, beyond the fact that Erica's mother down in Mississippi was taking the news very badly. "She's elderly and a bit frail, now. At least Erica's money has meant that she'll be more comfortable financially. Apparently Erica was drawing on experience for the early descriptions of the heroine's life in *Catwalk*. Some of it's the best stuff she's ever written."

"Can you send me a copy of the manuscript?" I asked.

"Well, I'm still working on it. It's very rough towards the end. Might be best if I send you the proofs."

All the warning bells in my head rang. It would take only the press of a button to print out a copy for me. What was there in *Catwalk* that Beth didn't want me to see—yet?

I found myself feeling resentful. She knew something, and she wasn't going to tell me.

I asked about Malcolm and the kids, and then told her I had to go. She seemed happy to hang up at that point, even relieved.

After the line went dead, I thought, *I should have asked her if Missing Persons had requested a copy of the new manuscript. Somehow I felt that they would have.*

I had shopped for groceries and was putting them away in the kitchen when the phone rang. Not one of my New York friends, not a worried Aunt or Uncle from Palm Beach. A brief sigh and a silence before the heavy, deep voice, unmistakable.

"I was way out of line."

"So was I. I'm sorry. You were only doing your job."

"I wasn't. That's the trouble. You were right. I have no jurisdiction. You told me my job, and I resented you for it." An exasperated sound, against himself, not me. "It came so close after Raoul having me on the mat that I overreacted."

He can admit he's wrong, I thought wonderingly. Wow.

A hesitation, then he said, "Sarah, can we start again?"

"Yes," I said, warming to him despite myself. "Of course."

"Can I come over? I've been in touch with my contact in New York. I'd rather see you to talk about what he said."

No conditions, no demands. Oh, God, he was being so *nice.*

"Come for dinner." I said, recklessly.

What are you doing?

"Really?" Even McGarret couldn't believe I was serious.
"Sure. 'Bout seven?"

"Seven," I said, and hung up.

*What are you doing? You have a dead body in the woodbox
and you ask a cop to dinner? Are you crazy?*

*I have to know. He can tell me what's happening in New York,
what the police think. I have to know.*

And it was only when I was opening the door to his heavy
knock that the thought occurred to me that I might not
be alone in my deception of this evening. Okay, he liked
me, but the Erica Tudor—Keir Stanforth case was headline
news in all the American and Canadian papers. And everyone, including myself, expected Keir to come to me.

To what lengths would an ambitious cop go?

I almost closed the door again; half open, it seesawed
back and forth a little in my grasp until I controlled myself
and opened it to McGarret's puzzled face.

He came in on a cold rush of air heavy with snow and
the scent of his aftershave. He wore beige trousers and a
soft leather jacket over a dark green shirt, his arm still in
the sling. In his other hand he carried a bottle of wine.

Wine. I had to control the sudden urge to shout at him,
This is not a relationship. We will not be making a habit of this.

But he looked tired; there were lines about his eyes,
the marks between nose and mouth seemed more deeply
etched this evening, and he was pale beneath the tanned
skin. I made myself consider what happened when jagged
broken glass was thrust into a healing bullet wound, and
winced. He'd probably spent hours last night having bits
of Budweiser bottle pulled out of him, shard by gleaming
shard.

"Come in," I said, meekly.

When I closed the door we regarded each other, warily,
almost shyly.

He said, "You look nice. You smell real good, too."

"Thank you."

This is not a date. Despite the wine and the fact that we both smell so nice. This is not a date, McGarret.

He was very helpful in the kitchen and insisted on cooking the steaks. I set the table in the kitchen, for it was a pleasant room and I'd feel less formal than at the huge refectory table in the living room.

McGarret poured wine for both of us, then went back to the steaks while I made the salad. He didn't talk much, and I was relieved about that. Time enough to talk of bloodstains. He was quietly cheerful, too, so there was no hideous news to impart to me. I drank a glass of wine and began to relax. Yet I didn't eat very much, and he noticed.

We talked about general matters; he told me that Larry Carey's wife, Marie, had given birth to a daughter that morning; that David and Janice were opening an exhibition of paintings at a gallery they had funded in Saint John; we discussed skiing, which we both enjoyed but had little time for since coming to St. Claude. He talked about the north of Canada and how, next spring and summer, I should make sure I visited Newfoundland and Labrador and the Yukon.

He washed the dishes, calmly, without asking permission or making a declaration of his intentions. I was struck, not for the first time, at his ability to make himself at home.

I took up a dish towel and we kept talking: whale-watching off the coast, whether I should get a few head of cattle to keep down the grass come summer; Otto and Frieda Hahn and why they would leave Canada to return to Europe. Hahn's works: which were our favorites, and why.

We took our coffee to the living room and he sat opposite me, on the other settee. I was relieved. The fire had been burning well and didn't need attending to. There were three baskets of firewood by the hearth; I was taking no chances that he'd decide to go outside to fetch more.

We were silent for a few minutes, both surprised a little, I think, that we'd managed a whole evening and not talked about Keir once. Both of us had something to prove.

I have my own life, McGarret. I am not obsessed. See me, relaxed in my fluffy pink sweater, so totally unobsessed.

"I hate doing this." The deep, lazy voice from the other side of the hearth.

My pulse began to beat uncomfortably fast. I looked over at him. *Here it comes.* "You hate doing what?"

"Talking about this business down south."

Our eyes met, locked, and neither of us smiled. So easily, so very easily the mood could slip, and we were back where we had been that morning, adversaries.

"The blood in the bathroom, Sarah—it belonged to Mrs. Stanforth."

I felt such a rush of relief that my fingers, holding my coffee cup, almost relaxed their hold. I had not dared to think about it too much. And now—it didn't matter any more that it had been Erica's blood. Erica was dead, but she'd left the apartment alive. We had Beth's phone call as witness to that, and Ms. Delvene Gobbit's testimony.

And McGarret said, "Some of it, anyway."

My eyes came up to his. I placed my coffee cup on its saucer and leaned forward to place both on the low table between us.

"Don't play with me, McGarret. We've had a very civilized evening, don't start playing policeman now."

He looked amused. I noticed he was handling his coffee just fine.

"What's so funny?" I asked him.

"You, I guess. Inferring that being civilized and a policeman at the same time isn't possible."

When I didn't answer, he said, in a conciliatory tone, "I get used to phrasing things a certain way. And I guess I am baiting you a little. It's hard not to, after what you told me this morning."

Here we go.

"But . . ." he shrugged, and winced a little. "I said we'll start again and we will. Erica Stanforth's blood was all over that bathroom. So was your ex-husband's—though to a lesser degree."

I didn't move, waited for more, but he gave me nothing, too busy watching me for my reaction. I dragged my gaze from his to look at the fire.

And it was easier, then, to speak, easier to frame my words, even forgetting to guard myself and speaking my thoughts out loud.

"What does that mean? What could have happened? Did they fight? Did she attack him? He didn't hurt *her.*"

"We don't know that."

I looked back at him, hating his inflexible code of behavior, his unwillingness to step outside what could be touched, smelled, *proved.*

"He'd never hurt her, or anyone. I know him! He's my husband, and I *know*—"

"He's your ex-husband."

Anyone else would have let it ride, would have seen that to me Keir would always be my husband. But this was Perry McGarret, and things would be done correctly, by God.

"Have you stopped to consider," I said, tightly, "that Erica might have killed Keir and then killed herself out of remorse?"

He thought about this; then, in his infuriating, detached voice, "It doesn't matter what I think. Homicide detectives in New York and Maine are looking into it. It's what they think that counts."

My gaze found my cup of coffee on its saucer on the table. My throat felt dry, constricted. I would like to take a sip of coffee but I didn't dare. I didn't dare move at all. Homicide. Missing Persons had called Homicide.

"Tell me," I said, and I hated the sound of pleading that had somehow crept into my voice. "Do you think Keir is dead?"

In the silence between us, the wind could be heard, flinging sleet-like stones against the windows. It was roaring high in the chimney, and beginning to keen around the eaves.

McGarret said, softly, "I don't know, Sarah. I think he

had something to do with Erica dying. But whether or not he's alive now . . . I don't know honey. I'm sorry."

What sort of passionate, violent relationship had Erica and Keir shared?

Maybe that's what he'd wanted, I thought now, suddenly frightened. Maybe I just wasn't exciting enough for him. Maybe I had been wrong about him leaving me for Erica's young, firm body. Maybe he left me for Erica's passion, the excitement of a volatile, even slightly unstable, personality.

She possesses me. Keir's words the; terrible night when he had admitted his love for Erica, the night he had left me, the last time I had seen him.

She possesses me.

As our gentle love, our tender lovemaking, had not?

I had forgotten McGarret, brought my gaze back to him, feeling myself flush already, knowing I'd find his quiet eyes upon me, patiently.

He doesn't know what you were thinking.

"One thing I can tell you," he said in measured tones. "If your ex-husband is alive, he's probably a very disturbed man."

I looked back to the fire and tried to see Keir, on the run, a very disturbed man. I'd painted a romantic picture of him, living alone somewhere, coping with his pain, his remorse. But through McGarret's eyes it was no longer romantic; it was tragic, and even ugly.

McGarret's deep voice was kind, so empathic that I could hardly bear it, wanted to hold my ears. "Do you understand, Sarah? You can't handle this by yourself. You aren't—trained for it."

I studied him, reading in his eyes all he was not saying. *Let me help you. Trust me. Tell me when he comes to you.*

And in my overwhelming weakness of that moment, I might have agreed.

You can't afford McGarret's goodwill, his friendship. You've got to keep him away from here.

Keir's secret life was the last of my problems. I had a worse one, a good deal closer to home—a very beautiful, very dead young woman, currently the name on everyone's lips the length and breadth of North America, lying in state in my woodbox, beside my front steps.

I looked hard at McGarret and said, "I've told you all I know."

The closed look came down like an iron mask over his features, softened with affection only a few seconds before.

But still he didn't look angry, or upset.

Get angry, McGarret. Wipe me out of your life and find a nice girl from good New Brunswick stock to give you babies and a normal life. Leave me alone with my woodbox.

He said, "I want you to call me, if he comes here, or if you hear from him."

"Are we back on that again?"

"Are you listening to me, Sarah?"

"Are you listening to *me*?"

"Promise me."

"I thought we were starting again," I said, tartly.

He gave a wry smile. "Aren't we? Seems I've heard this conversation before."

I studied his face, disbelievingly. "You *expected* that we'd go through all this again."

He placed his coffee on the table and leaned forward towards me. "I expected that you'd he sensible, once I told you what they found in the apartment."

I leaned back; against the settee, looked at him narrow-eyed. "I could lie," I said.

You won't or you'd have lied this morning."

Think, Sarah. Think.

He stood, suddenly, rose up and up and moved around the coffee table to stand over me. I had to throw my head way back to look up at him. And he reached down with his right hand and took my arm, pulling me to my feet. In the space between the settee and the coffee table we had to stand very close.

"It's getting late," I said, "I think you ought to go before the storm gets—"

"I'm not going anywhere until I have your word. Promise

me, Sarah, or I swear you'll never get rid of me. And I know that's what you want.''

Then something in his eyes stirred again. Some touch of twisted humor, I thought, furious.

''I promise,'' I said, glaring at him, wanting to pull my arm from his grasp, but I'd have to do it forcefully and there was no room here to step back, gain my balance.

''If he comes here—or if he phones or you get a letter or a fax, for that matter.'' Again the light stirred in the depths of his eyes, for he was winning, now, could afford to make funnies.

''I promise,'' I snarled.

He contemplated my face for a long moment, then his grip on my arm relaxed a little, and he smiled. ''I'll go home now,'' he said, and left the house.

When the engine had started, and the sound of the Jeep's progress down the drive had faded a little, I went to the window and looked over that part of the property. I thought I would be able to see the last of the crimson taillights, disappearing round the curve of the drive, but there was nothing. Just the snow thrown in the direction he had gone, as if the northerly gale had blown him away. Beyond the driving whiteness I couldn't see anything at all.

I slept little that night. The gale was terrifying in its intensity. I began to worry that McGarret was upside down in a ditch somewhere between my farm and his. Yet I hesitated to phone him. I had enough trouble with him as it was. And I didn't believe him when he said he didn't care about what was happening in New York. I might not hear about it, but I'd bet anything that he would. It would be filed away, any new development, within that rigidly tidy mind of his.

I blocked out the sound of the storm by placing my earphones over my head and lying in bed listening to a cassette of highlights from Wagner's *Die Meistersinger*.

Somehow Wagner suited my mood. He may have been an egotistical little racist but I had to admire his music, the drama, the passion of it.

The storm had eased a little by the following afternoon, but the wind kept me indoors. It blew like invisible specters bearing knives; even in the Colorado mountains I'd never known anything like it. It wasn't until Monday, when the wind finally dropped, that I stirred outside: I had spent the two days since my dinner with McGarret catching up on phone calls.

Every hour or so the phone shrilled.

Finally, unable to stand it any longer, I strapped on my skis and had a short but invigorating journey down the drive, over pristine snow, to check the letter box.

I was taking the letters and circulars out of the converted milk can and whistling the "Prize Song" from *Die Meistersinger* when a movement along the road made me look up.

It was impossible, but there he was, Alby Gresson slithering cautiously along the road in snowshoes, bending and picking up branches that had fallen onto the roadway since the plow had been through. Not making a job of it, obviously, on his first constitutional after hospital, but seeing something useful to do, and doing it. He had his head down, and seemed intent.

I waved and called out, "Hello, Mr. Gresson!" just to be neighborly.

He must have heard me. He stopped and stared at me; even at this distance I saw his narrow eyes narrow even further. He stood silently and still in that gray landscape, and I thought, so typical of him; he knew it was me, I was taking letters out of my own letter box, but too much to hope that he'd be well mannered enough to wave back.

I pushed my mail inside my zippered jacket and took hold of the ski poles, turning back towards the house—and only then noticed that he was sliding awkwardly over, towards my gate. He struggled up from the roadway onto the snowy bank and moved more confidently towards me.

We had the gate between us; McGarret must have climbed out of the car in the blizzard to close it after him, freezing his butt off, I thought fondly, exasperatingly, to Do the Right Thing.

"I'm glad you're feeling well, Mr. Gresson—but don't go doing too much, will you?"

I understood. then, the intensity that had been in his gaze, the sudden light in his very green eyes as he'd seen me.

I continued, "Well, I'd best be getting back to my writing . . ."

"Been home since Thursday," he said, before I could move. The things you sent to the hospital—they arrived at the house. Meant to come and thank you. I been reading about what happened, down in New Hampshire. Been on the television, too."

Then, unexpectedly, "Dark horse, aren't you?"

"Pardon?"

"Dark horse. You. That husband of yours." He waited. In the bright, reflected light from the snow his eyes looked as cold and green as the shadows between floating, shifting ice flows.

"Doctors," he said, "can't be trusted. That husband of yours was a bastard, eh?"

I should have turned then, and gone back to the house without another word. But I felt stung enough to reply, "He's my ex-husband, Mr. Gresson. And he's my friend. He had nothing to do with the suicide of his wife."

He shrugged, mock-innocent. "Her picture was on the television, and in all the papers. Your ex-husband's picture, too. Looked . . . familiar. Like I might have seen him around."

My heart skipped a beat, my legs in the heavy ski boots felt weak. I couldn't have moved, in that moment, even had I wished to. "When? You recognized my hus—. . . Dr. Stanforth? When? Where?"

He was laughing in earnest now, a dry sound like a creaking gate in a high wind. But his lungs, already laboring under the exertion of this walk in the snow, suddenly betrayed him, and he began to cough, a series of frightening, explosive, rattling coughs.

I remained where I was, I could not move.

Finally, wiping wetness from his eyes with a clean handkerchief pulled from his pocket, he managed, "I know what I know."

"If you've seen my husband about, Mr. Gresson," I said, withdrawing into a self-righteous tone in my fear, my excitement at his words, "then you should inform the police."

"You think so, do you?" he said. "I just might do that. I just might."

He turned and went off, on the snowy verge of the roadway, step-glide, step-glide, back in the direction of his own place. Had Keir been here, to *Jaegerhalle,* only four days ago, three days ago? I had been at home since Saturday, but before then . . . Thursday, and Friday . . . there had been visits to town, to the library, to the supermarket . . .

Alby had just come out of hospital, he couldn't have seen Keir . . .

From a car window? You know how independent he is. You know how he's always out-of-doors . . .

I had stopped my hard-won progress up the slope, the need to catch my breath in the icy air was overwhelming; but it wasn't exertion that made me pause. I needed stillness to think, think.

If I hadn't been at the cottage when Keir arrived, he'd have waited for me, wouldn't he?

Unless he didn't dare wait. Unless he was on the run.

What if Keir, wherever he fled to after his final—and obviously violent—quarrel with Erica. had at last picked up a newspaper. He'd find that Erica's car—*his car*—had been found abandoned. It looked like suicide, but the police were suspicious. And they had every right to be. There was no body. Even given the plot of *Gaining* and Erica's depression over losing the child, the setup looked phony. The car-abandoned-by-the sea was an old plot used by people who wanted to fake their own suicides.

And probably quite often by someone who had committed a violent murder and wanted the death to *look* like suicide. Someone who had a damaged corpse on their hands, a corpse which said as plainly as if it could speak, *look, someone murdered me.* I wouldn't have chosen that idea myself if I'd felt I had any choice.

I was in a quiet bend of the drive, out of sight of the road, and, for these few short meters, out of sight of the house. I was alone on a river of white snow, the woods leafless about me but for the greens of spruce and pine between the black trunks.

If I had faked Erica's death, why could not Keir? Keir was six foot one and slim, with a fine-boned face and neat, long-fingered surgeon's hands. And narrow feet that were a size eight.

My mind flung itself back from that train of thought, unable to believe, to consider . . .

I remembered that Delvene Gobbit at the store had recognized Erica, had sworn she had driven off alone in the white Mercedes.

But she could have met someone, they'd think.

She could have been followed, they'd think.

She could have driven back to New York and been murdered in the bathroom, the car driven away again, the body dumped, the car left abandoned—some time during the night of Friday the twenty-sixth. How accurate were they, these days, in dating bloodstains that were already several days old? The car hadn't been discovered until Monday, and Forensic didn't go over the apartment until after that.

What size shoe did Erica wear?

I hadn't noticed, knew only that they were enormous on my size seven feet.

I didn't know the difference between men's and women's sizing. I didn't know what size shoe Erica wore.

I can't believe it would come down to this. I can't believe it.

And I saw McGarret's face before me, his stubbornness, his anger, his exasperation, his caring; I saw, for the first time, in retrospect, what had been a kind of pain in the blue eyes when he looked at me sometimes.

He knew. McGarret knew. Probably the whole world knew, except me. In my blindness, my arrogance, my love for Keir, I had refused to see where this was leading.

If I had killed Erica and faked her suicide, then someone else could have done so.

The police did not suspect me. I was miles away and had no real motive. Keir had the motive, and the opportunity, and a history of violent quarrels with the deceased. Keir had also, conveniently, vanished.

I tried to escape the thought, but it bore down on me with a crushing force.

The police were looking for Keir. And when they found him they would probably arrest him for the murder of Erica Tudor.

Chapter Twenty

It took all my self-control, all my strength of character, not to panic. The steep, curved drive between the woods, then between the smooth fields that led to the house, had me breathless as I poled my way upwards.

I clambered onto the steps and unstrapped my ski boots. I threw poles and skis along the porch, careless, desperate, and rushed inside.

Why didn't they tell me? Why didn't damned McGarret tell me? Or had he, while I simply chose not to understand?

I poured myself a stiff brandy and sipped it while I lit the fire, not for the warmth but for the comfort.

The telephone rang. I ignored it, but listened for the voice of my caller when my message had finished. I wanted it to be Beth, I needed to talk to Beth.

"It's Perry McGarret, Sarah."

I whirled towards the machine, sloshing brandy. "You bastard!" And since the brandy was spilt already I followed the action through and flung the glass and its contents towards the voice. It shattered on the wall above the machine.

McGarret said, "Just wondered how you were. Ran into

Larry Carey this morning, he hadn't heard from you, but he can come out with the plow this afternoon, if you want to call him. Hope you're managing alright. Might come out to see you after Larry's cleared the drive."

"I don't want to see you!" I yelled at the machine. "I don't want to see your big ugly lying face again! Pig! You pig!"

"Well, that's about it." Mildly. "G'bye, Sarah."

"You lying, deceitful—!"

And I stopped, sobbing, realizing that any epithet I flung at the invisible McGarret also applied to myself.

The tape was rewinding. He was gone. I sat down on the end of the coffee table and stared into the small flames, still tentatively licking at the logs within the hearth.

And another nasty thought struck me. I'd told Alby Gresson to take his story of a sighting of Keir to the police.

What if he did?

Alby was lying. He was lying, trying to get a rise out me. *What if he wasn't lying?*

Alby could at this very moment be phoning the police station. McGarret, I realized, had been calling from the police station. I could hear voices, phones, traffic, a two-way radio in the background, and hadn't thought much about it. He was back at work.

What if Alby was phoning him right now?

"And Mrs. Stanforth told me I should come to you."

How would I know? I wouldn't, I thought, balling my fists on the table beside me. I sure as hell wasn't going to tell McGarret that Alby had maybe, *maybe* seen Keir.

If McGarret knew *I* knew, he would not be very pleased with me.

So what already? I should care what this big lug thinks of me?

I prowled up and down the room, wondering what, if anything, I could do. I'd forgotten about the spilt brandy—I slipped on it and fell heavily, taking a lot of my weight on my hand and knee. I lay there cursing, then picked myself up and stared at the blood pouring from my hand.

I went off to the kitchen and found antiseptic and a bandage—I'd put the heel of my hand on the broken base of the glass. The cut was quite deep, blood had all but filled my handkerchief. I wondered about whether I needed a stitch or two in the wound but decided not to bother. I wrapped it tightly, then set about tidying up the broken glass, wiping the sticky liquid off the walls and table and answering machine.

I brought in some more firewood, direct from the woodpile; these days I let the woodbox well alone.

Then I rang Larry Carey and asked if he'd come clear the drive, though in a way I was sorry. While I had enough supplies, I didn't mind being marooned, and after the plow had done its work, who knew what visitors would arrive?

Unless it was Keir. Keir with answers to my questions. I wanted that, very much.

The snow plow, driven by Larry Carey's brother, Dennis, was rolling back and forth between the house and the barn, and Larry Carey was clearing the stone steps when the phone rang. I'd turned the machine off, since the callers had slowed a little, so I took the call in the study where I could hear better. Still the noise from outside was loud, unpleasant.

"It's Perry McGarret, Sarah."

Great. Just great.

"I was wondering if you'd be home about ten tomorrow," he asked.

"Yes, probably, but I'm at a difficult part of the book. I'd really like to concentrate on that for a few days and not be disturbed."

He spent a few seconds absorbing this. As before, I could hear the noises of the police station in the background.

Let me never get closer than hearing these muted sounds through a telephone receiver, O Lord. Let me not ever find myself standing there in the middle of that scene, the eyes that belonged to those voices staring at me, McGarret's hand about my upper arm, and lost, lost.

"Sarah?"

"Sorry?"

"I said, it'll only take a few minutes."

"Look." I tried to find the right words, but there were none, only the truth. "Look, I gave you my word that if Keir comes, I'll tell you. Isn't that enough? Unless you've got something to tell me, in which case, could you tell me now, on the phone?"

In his usual low, measured tones, "I don't have any news for you about Keir."

"Then I'd rather you didn't come over tomorrow."

"Sarah, I wasn't going to be coming alone."

He had all my attention now.

He went on, "We've had requests from the police in both Maine and New York. They've asked us to send someone out to talk to you about Dr. and Mrs. Stanforth. Inspector Gerlain would like to ask you some questions."

Gerlain was shorter than McGarret, but that didn't make him short. He stood at about six foot two, was heavy in the shoulders, as McGarret was, and walked with the same slow deliberation up my freshly shoveled path at ten the following morning.

"I can cope with this. I can," I muttered to myself, trying to feel brave, trying to quell the fear that threatened to choke me.

This is the way they'll come, at the end. This is the way they'll come for you, shutting the doors of the robin's-egg-blue–and-white police car and strolling purposefully up the path, looking about as they go, noting things, not speaking.

I waited until they knocked before opening the door. I said hello, Gerlain nodded and smiled, McGarret nodded, touched the brim of his cap. With a glance at the man beside him, he said, "This is Inspector Gerlain, Sarah."

"How do you do." I put out my hand and he took it, his

smile widening. He had a broad face with blunt, irregular features, redeemed by the one thing that immediately took one's notice, a pair of very dark, very humorous black eyes that spoke of intelligence and a forthright, open personality. Despite graying hair, he looked to be about forty-five.

I led the way into the living room and towards the settees, asking them if they'd like coffee, which they both politely declined as they removed their hats.

Gerlain sat on one settee, his body angled forward, gazing at me with interest, a notebook and pen in hand, ready for business. McGarret leaned against the mantel: I saw him from the corner of my eye but avoided looking at him, avoided any glance that might hint at a plea for enlightenment, or an assumption that there was any friendship, any relationship at all between us.

Gerlain began in French, asking me if I'd mind the use of that language as it was the one in which he was brought up and Sergeant McGarret had told him I was fluent.

I glanced at McGarret, then, but he was looking somewhere else in the room. *What else have you told him?*

"Of course," I answered the senior officer.

Gerlain leaned back and gazed around the room, then spent five minutes commenting and asking questions about the ancient furniture before he settled, with Gallic courtesy and a sense of gravity, on the subject of Erica and Keir. He was a clever man; the conversation about the antiques helped us find a compromise between my Parisian French and his New Brunswick French and now he was confident we could move on.

"Do you have any idea, Mrs. Stanforth, where your ex-husband might be?"

"No. I haven't seen him since September twelfth, last year."

He smiled a little. "You're very precise with the date."

I looked at him seriously. "The date was important for the divorce. On the evening of the eleventh of September Erica told me she was having an affair with my husband. That night I confronted him with it. We spoke for some time about the state of our marriage, and in the early hours of the next day, the twelfth, he left me to go to live with Erica Tudor.''

"You were bitter?"

"Of course I was bitter. I hated Erica. She destroyed my marriage. She destroyed everything I had."

Out of the periphery of my vision I saw McGarret, leaning against the mantelpiece, stir a little. Somehow I knew this piece of body language was a warning. Be careful what you say.

"But the property settlement was more than generous," I went on, "and I have a new life here, new friends, and the publishing company I still work for is interested in seeing my first novel. So you might say that things have worked out for the best."

"Mrs. Stanforth." He looked concerned, kind. "For the record, so to speak—not for myself, but for those suspicious gentlemen in the United States who wish to leave no stone unturned—could you tell me of your whereabouts when your ex-husband and his wife disappeared?"

My face went white, then scarlet. I managed to croak, "You think I did it?"

"Did what, Mrs. Stanforth?" Quickly, still kindly, but very quickly.

"Killed Erica and Keir. Is that what they think in New York and Maine?"

"No, no, but you understand, an embittered ex-wife . . . If you could just tell me of your whereabouts on the twenty-sixth and twenty-seventh of January—and the twenty-eighth and twenty-ninth, if possible."

I stared at him. I couldn't think. Not a single thought entered my head.

Finally, "I . . . I don't know. I was here, of course. But . . . was that the time I had flu? I don't know. All my days here are the same."

Still benignly, Gerlain said, "Yes, it's known that you keep to yourself and often leave your answering machine switched on. We tried to contact you the day before yesterday.''

Don't look, guilt-ridden, at McGarret. Don't. "Yes. I often have the machine on for days at a time. Keir and I had many friends in New York. They all want to talk to me, to discuss the case. I find it . . . distressing.''

Like this. Like now. And to my horror, tears crept into my eyes so that I had to brush them away, angrily.

As if on cue, the phone rang. All three of us, myself and both police officers, stiffened and looked towards the machine.

My voice went on interminably, burbling in a friendly fashion that I couldn't come to the phone just now, but . . .

Don't be Keir, I prayed for the first time in all those long months. *Not now. Please, please don't choose this moment in time . . .*

"Sally. Beth says you often have the machine on while you're writing. Are you there? Can you pick up?''

Sandra Barton's aggrieved voice.

"No? Well, okay. I'm just ringing because Beth rang me last night.''

I sensed, rather than saw, the two officers exchange glances. I didn't look up from my hands, clasped in my lap. The cut on my wrist was throbbing, I was holding it too tightly.

"Darling, you *know* upsetting you is the last thing I'd do. I just thought that you'd like to talk about things, share your worries. And I am Keir's cousin. I'm the last person to think that Keir could have done anything *wrong*. I just wish he'd turn up. He's dragging the family name through the mud and he doesn't seem to care. Unless . . . I wanted to wait until I could talk to you, but I was talking to Sharalyn Camberwell—she said Jeremy said that everyone at the hospital noticed that Keir was really depressed, really down, in the last day or so before he disappeared. He even told Jeremy that he kept thinking how easy it'd be to end it all. Jeremy didn't tell the police that, of course, you know how doctors stick together.''

The temperature in the room fell about five degrees, the atmosphere suddenly as heavy as fog.

"Same with Andy. You haven't told anybody about what Andy said, have you? We don't want to get dragged into this."

I looked at Gerlain, and at McGarret. Neither of them were looking at me, nor each other. They were looking off into space, faint smiles on their lips.

"So call, Sally. This is the fourth message I've left for you. You have my number. Bye."

There was a complete silence except for the rewinding of the machine. I didn't want to look at Gerlain, but he cleared his throat as delicately as Hercule Poirot, and when our eyes met, he said, "A timely verification of your lifestyle, *madame.*" But the broad features did not smile.

I said, shrugging helplessly, "She's a relative of my ex-husband's. She's harmless."

"I'm sure. But an interesting woman. Her name?"

"Sandra Barton-Gregg," I murmured, unwillingly.

"Her address, Mrs. Stanforth?" And when I stared at him, appalled, he said, gently, "You see, she's such an interesting woman that I'm sure our friends in New York will also like to hear from her. As well as Dr. Jeremy Camberwell and his wife Sharalyn."

I rose to my feet to get my address book, grateful for the excuse to move, to get away from the intelligent penetration of those dark eyes.

There was nothing for it, I gave them the names, addresses, and phone numbers of both the Barton-Greggs and the Camberwells. At the end, putting away his notebook, Gerlain said, "Would you mind telling us, Mrs. Stanforth, what it was that Andy was so loath to pass on to the police?"

I was by now sitting back on the settee. "Sandra said that Andy and Keir were drinking at the golf club one day, and Keir said he'd made a mistake in leaving me, and would come back to me if he believed I'd take him back."

An interested silence.

"Your ex-husband was not entirely sure of his welcome?" Gerlain prompted.

"Why should he be?" I asked, coldly and, oddly enough, truthfully. "After all that had happened—with his new life, and me with mine—why should he think that? And," I leaned forward to gaze into Gerlain's eyes, though I was actually speaking to McGarret, "I didn't inform the police of Andy's conversation because I didn't think it mattered. Andy Gregg is a romantic, he exaggerates, and he drinks too much."

Gerlain nodded, slowly. "And if all turns out to be well with your ex-husband and he's declared innocent of any involvement in Mrs. Stanforth's death—if Mrs. Stanforth is indeed dead—and he is free to be reunited with you, what would you do, Mrs. Stanforth?"

I'd avoided that. All this time, since I had killed Erica, I had avoided confronting that question.

For it would break my heart. How could I accept happiness with Keir? Happiness with anyone, in any form at all, after I had killed Erica?

He's waiting, Sarah.

I'd lived day to day, since Erica's death, busy hiding it, always oppressed by it: and now he asks me what lies beyond . . . There was no beyond.

Sarah, he's waiting, even McGarret's loose, long limbs are draped there with an added tension . . .

"I haven't thought it out." The truth, as much of the truth as possible. "I never saw Keir asking me to come back. I never thought that far. I had a feeling—" I swallowed, glanced at McGarret, who, of course, gave nothing away in the blue eyes that rested on me critically. I shook my head, and it was as if the action loosened something within me, and tears leaked forth once more, unwillingly. "No," I said, wanting the question to be over, answered, finished with. "No, I wouldn't go back to him. Too much has happened. Erica . . . Erica will always be between us. Guilt and memories of her. Never knowing if he'd have chosen to stay with her—"

I stopped, unable to go on.

McGarret moved, walked out of the room, into the hall. Out of my jumbled thoughts surfaced the question, *Where the hell is he going?*

He came back with the packet of tissues that normally sat on the benchtop in the kitchen. What was interesting to me, watching Gerlain's face, was his total lack of surprise that McGarret knew his way around my house. "So I may assume, Mrs. Stanforth, that you had no reason to leave your little house and go to Maine or to New York and dispose of your ex-husband and his wife out of enraged jealousy."

I glared at him, then looked up at McGarret, thanked him for the tissues and, taking one, blew my nose. "I don't have an alibi," I told Gerlain. "I was by myself for most of the days you mentioned. But I didn't go to New York or Maine to murder Erica and Keir. I don't think Keir killed her, either."

McGarret had wandered away to a window. Gerlain said. softly, "You are emphatic with your answer, Mrs. Stanforth."

I said, "I'm becoming irritated by your questions, Inspector."

There was a faint sound from McGarret, but when I glanced over at him he was gazing out the window, a rather pained expression on his face.

"Mrs. Stanforth, shall I tell you why the United States police asked us to question you?" Gerlain, bland, impervious.

Oh God. Oh God.

"Yes," barely breathed.

"Mrs. Stanforth was a wealthy woman in her own right. In her will she leaves everything to her husband, Keir. And Keir Stanforth, *madame,* only the day before he disappeared, made a new will—or, rather, he reverted to the conditions of an older will. He left everything he owned to you."

* * *

From a long distance away I heard McGarret's bass voice rumble something. Gerlain said, in English, "A good idea, I think."

I had a crick in my neck; my neck wouldn't move. And then I rolled it, instead of trying to raise it, and that was better. I'd been lying with my head over the back of the settee. I'd fainted. Sitting there, looking at the man, and I'd passed out.

And then I remembered why.

"He's dead," I managed, rolling my heavy head, and managing to raise it, put my hands to my aching eyes. "He's dead, then. Dead."

"Mrs. Stanforth." Gerlain was beside me suddenly on the settee, his dangerous, kind eyes regarded me.

"How can they even wonder about it?" I asked Gerlain: *he* must know, he was a police inspector, he must know these things. "Isn't it obvious that he's dead? Keir killed himself. He phoned me, asked for my help, and . . ."

"He asked you for your help, in that last phone message?"

"No, no." Impatient with his sudden obtuseness. "But I should have known, should have seen. He needed to talk to me."

"Mrs. Stanforth, Perry told me about the tape—that you kept it. One of the reasons we came out here today was to ask you for it. Do you still have the tape with your ex-husband's message on it?"

I nodded, went to get up, but he put a hand on my forearm, gently enough. "Tell me where it is, and I'll get it."

I waved my hand towards the Elizabethan court cabinet against the far wall. "The top left compartment. The tape has *Keir* on it."

He left me. I put my head down in my hands. In a short while I sensed movement beside me and looked up to see not Gerlain, but McGarret, placing a mug of strong tea in front of me. Our eyes met, but we didn't speak: I didn't even have the energy to say thank you. He placed another mug on the opposite side of the coffee table, and took his own over to the window, where he stood with his head lowered a little, in order to look out.

"This is it, *madame*?" He held the tape in front of me. "Yes."

Gerlain held the tape out to McGarret. The big cop put his coffee mug on the window sill and took a plastic packet from his coat pocket. He slipped the tape within it, sealed it with a twist-tie, and scribbled something on a label on the packet's side. Then he brought out what looked like a book of receipts and gave me just that, a receipt for the tape. I accepted it, numbly.

Gerlain had seated himself on the other side of the table, was sipping his tea. He said, "Forgive me, Mrs. Stanforth, but do you truly believe that your ex-husband's dead?"

"Yes. I don't know." There was no emotion in my voice, no emotion left within me. "Why else would he do that, leave everything to me, unless he wanted to make sure I was taken care of?"

I looked up at Gerlain suddenly. "So I was under suspicion because I benefited from the wills? I don't need money. I've got a job."

For some reason this seemed to amuse Gerlain. He turned on his seat and gazed over at McGarret. McGarret met the look stonily.

"I see." Gerlain turned back to me, still amused. He drained his tea, and stood. "I think we have taken enough of your time, Mrs. Stanforth, thank you for cooperating with us."

McGarret placed his half-empty mug on the coffee table and followed us to the door. We all went out into cold sunshine. On the porch, as they replaced their hats and sunglasses, Inspector Gerlain said, quietly, "I'm sorry to have been the cause of distressing you, but it was necessary to ask these questions. I hope you understand."

Before I could speak, he hesitated, and added, "I wouldn't presume your husband is dead, *madame*. Erica Stanforth, well, it seems so in her case, though we'd all feel better if there was a body. A body would be able to tell us if her death was a violent one. But if she did, indeed, drown herself," regretfully, "by this time the tide, the sea, would have done its work. A pity."

A little more cheerfully, he said, "I don't think we'll need to disturb you in the future—not regarding your own part in any of this business. I'll inform New York and Maine of my belief in this matter."

I stared at him, puzzled. "I don't understand."

McGarret spoke up. "We don't believe you killed anyone, Sarah."

I gazed between the two faces above me. "Why not?" I asked, finally. "I could have lied to you."

McGarret gave a short, sharp sigh; the pained look was back on his face, but he was looking directly at me, this time.

Gerlain had his mouth held in a strange line, as if he were trying hard not to smile. Meeting my gaze, he said, "We don't believe you knew of the existence of the new wills, Mrs. Stanforth. And even if you could have faked that tragic faint back there, you passed the second test with flying colors."

I stared at him.

He went on, "Being told such news of the two wills, your first thought was that your husband must be dead. You didn't ask what ninety per cent of people would ask in those circumstances, 'How many millions of dollars are involved here?' "

I frowned at him. "I told you. I don't need Keir's money, nor Erica's. If this nightmare is true and they're both . . . gone, then I'd give it to their families, or to charity."

Gerlain headed off down the steps, "Thank you very much, Mrs. Stanforth."

I went back inside immediately. As I was closing the door I heard the unaccustomed sound of McGarret's laughter. For Gerlain had muttered something.

I couldn't be sure, but it sounded like, "You deserve each other."

Chapter
Twenty-One

There was only one way I could protect Keir—and myself.
I had to do something with Erica. I had to make her
disappear. And permanently. But in a dignified manner.

I felt I owed her that.

And the answer was there all the time, in the woods
above the house. It had been there ever since the night
of the storm, had I only known it; waiting there, yawning
there, the answer to all my problems.

It must have been one of the oldest pines in these hills,
before the storm felled it. It looked to be well over a
hundred feet long, as far as I could judge, and even then
the topmost branches had been broken off when it crashed
across the stand of yellow birches and came to rest against
a huge maple. The maple had somehow stood the blow,
though it, too, had lost branches. The roots of the great
pine had been ripped up—all but a few stubborn tendrils
on the lee side—and these had been snapped off brutally
and crushed by the tree's own weight. The rest of the root-
ball was exposed to the air: enormous, it towered over
me, the long roots like fingers clawing, bent with greed,
desperate in death, reaching back towards the earth from

which, for hundreds of years, it had drawn its sustenance, its life. Earth still clung to the gigantic root-ball, clogged between the gnarled fingers like a gardener's mud-caked hands. Even as I looked at it, a pebble or small clod of earth fell with a little rattle and a sigh, onto the snow that had fallen into the hole that was left behind.

The very large hole. I scrambled over to the edge: *the very deep hole.* Even with the snowfall it was more than four feet deep. More than ten feet in diameter and four feet deep.

What do you think of that, Erica?

I decided I hated Alby Gresson. All that morning I hated him, for unlike Perry and David McGarret, unlike all the other decent men I had met in St. Claude, Alby Gresson was a sneak.

Any time, day or night, I could never be sure if he wasn't watching my house from the shelter of the trees; maybe I was becoming paranoid—having a death on one's conscience does that—but he had a history of lurking about in the woods of *Jaegerhalle,* and I could never be sure that my displeasure and the presence of the new fence had brought any change in his behavior.

Erica would have to be moved in the middle of the night. Up that hill. Through the snow. So I spent the morning hating Alby Gresson.

I'd have spent the afternoon hating him, too, had I not been interrupted by McGarret.

He must have left Peter having lunch in town, for he was alone in the police car when he drove up. I let him in silently, watched him remove his glasses and his cap, knowing even before he did so that he would place them on the broad arm of the closest settee. I knew this because I had seen him do it before. Too many times.

"I just wanted you to know," he said, without preamble, "that the news of the wills came through with the request to interview you. I wasn't holding out on you, Sarah. Though," and he looked serious, "now that we're involved in this—even in such a small way—I can't go giving you any more information."

"Can't, or won't?"

"Won't because it's even less right than before, and can't because I'm not calling my friend's friend any more. Whatever I hear from now on is through official channels, and I'm not bucking that, honey."

Should I ask him not to call me "honey"? Would I sound churlish? Maybe everyone calls everyone else "honey" in Georgia . . .

I nodded. "You've done more than enough. Thank you."

There was a pause between us, and somehow I expected him to leave then, but he walked towards me.

"There's something else I wanted to ask you."

"Yes?"

I was watching his face, not his hands, so when he bent quickly to take my forearm in a firm grip I jumped in shock. Then we were still, and I found my bandaged wrist being held up between us, where I could see it very clearly. Just as clear was the question in McGarret's eyes, but it took me a little time to figure it out.

The bandage was seeping blood again, just a spot, a narrow line of scarlet perpendicular to the length of my arm, across my wrist.

"You're kidding . . . !" And I tried to pull away.

"How, Sarah?"

"A piece of glass. I cut it on a piece of glass. For God's sake, McGarret, do you think I'm *that* desperate?"

He still held my forearm, and carefully began to undo the bandage.

This is mortifying.

And I was pink. My face was pink, maybe even red, compounded as it was with the memory of how the glass had come to be on the floor in the first place.

"How, Sarah?" he said as he unraveled.

Say, *I heard your voice and threw the glass at the wall because you weren't there in person to throw it at?*

Say, *I was so busy shouting obscenities at you that I didn't care about broken glass and brandy on my answering machine, my walls, my carpet, my four-hundred-year-old table?*

Which would sound crazier? That, or a small bid for oblivion?

He was examining the cut. "Piece of glass, huh?"

"It was on the floor, I slipped on it and came down with the heel of my hand on the broken base of the glass."

He took a clean handkerchief from his pocket and pressed it on the wound, beginning to wrap it once more.

"Pass inspection?" I inquired.

He didn't lift his eyes. "Messy enough for a broken glass."

"You believe me, then."

"Guess so." He was doing an expert job of the bandage, not just around the wrist, as I had had it, but around my thumb as well: it held much more firmly.

"What was in the glass?" he asked mildly, and looked at me.

Oh, great, just great. I'm slipping on a sea of brandy, now.

I felt the flush coming back but held his gaze. "Hot milk," I lied, coldly.

The light behind his eyes was there, suddenly, surprising me as it always did. It came and went so fast, and yet I swear I never saw a muscle in that impervious facade move. He said, "You had a tetanus shot?"

"Tetanus? *Tetanus?* I'm a New Yorker, what do I want with tetanus shots? You'll ask me if I've been inoculated for rabies, next."

He was heading towards the coatrack by the door, and merely grinned as he took down my coat and held it towards me. "I'll drive you into town," he said. "Who's your doctor?"

"I don't have a doctor. I haven't been sick enough for one yet."

"I'll take you to John Tolliver. He's my doctor. Put your coat on."

When Sarah didn't come to the jacket, the jacket came to Sarah.

He looked down at my feet. "You'd better change out of your bunnies, too."

I would like to say I froze him out with my silence all the way into town, but I don't think he noticed my mood. He drove silently and without giving any sense of feeling that the quiet within the car was anything other than amicable.

I was thinking, crossly, that he was probably right, I did need to see a doctor—the damned hand *would* keep bleeding, and I needed it to heal as quickly as possible.

For I have promises to keep,
And miles to go before I sleep,
And miles to go before I . . .

"I figure he was setting out to kill himself, and then changed his mind."

I turned to look at McGarret, startled. He added, "That's just how it seems to me." Glancing at me the while. Then, eyes back on the road with a frown, "He's out there somewhere, feeling scared. He's only got the newspapers, the TV, he doesn't know if the bloodstains predate Erica's last known sighting."

I absorbed this. It made sense.

So Keir won't, can't, take the chance that he won't be believed. Like me. Like me.

"They're just my feelings," McGarret said. "For what they're worth."

"Thank you," I murmured.

He was quiet a moment, then said, in a harder voice, "There isn't anything to thank me for. It's just an opinion. I still think he'll come to you."

He had turned to look at me. I avoided looking at him, gazed through the windshield at lightly falling snow.

"Maybe not," I said. "Maybe he's in Mexico. Or France. Or Australia."

"He doesn't have the contacts that'd get him overseas

without a passport. Mexico's a possibility." And after a pause, softly, "Or Canada."

I turned to study him, more than a little disturbed. But he was pulling into a driveway. In front of us was one of the large houses on the Square that had been converted, this one to a medical center.

McGarret said, "Dr. John Tolliver. You'll like him."

I opened the car door. He asked, "You okay to take a cab home? If you want to wait till this evening, you could meet me at the station . . ."

"I'll take a taxi. I'll be okay."

Before I could move, he said, "Don't go doing too much. You need anything heavy done, firewood chopped, stuff like that, call me." His hand rested lightly on my arm.

I felt sick, turned, and looked longingly out the car door to a white, inviting, McGarret-less world. "Sure," I said.

"I mean it, Sarah."

"Great. I will. Thank you. Bye." I scrambled from the car.

"G'bye, Sarah. Take care."

I shut the door on the voice, the sight of him, and went up the drive, not turning back to wave.

He wants to cut my firewood.

I arrived home a few hours later with my hand comfortably numb and five of Dr. Tolliver's neat little stitches in my wrist. He, too, though he knew nothing of my friendship with McGarret, told me not to do too much over the next week. "Get a friend to lift anything, or chop firewood," He smiled.

Sure, Doctor, sure. I've just got this small chore of shifting a body from my woodbox up into the woods above my house, but as soon as I finish that I'll keep my lily-white little hands folded in my lap.

Of course, there was no hurry to bury Erica—she was frozen nicely, she was safe. But I wanted it, the funeral, as I began to call it, finished with. Then it would be over, all that part of my life: I could begin again, with this existence, this *post-Erica* existence, to find some way of learning to live with myself, with the enormity of what I had done.

There was a phone call from Beth on the machine when I got back. I phoned her, told her briefly of Gerlain and McGarret's visit. We were both subdued, both affected by it all. It was one of the things I found so hard to deal with, *what I had done to my friend.* At such times I had to tell myself that she would have been even more upset to be faced with the alternative scenario for that Thursday evening, twelve days ago; the news that Erica had shot me dead in my own front yard.

"I know you won't want to be here in New York at the moment," Beth said. "But afterwards, when it's all over . . . I mean, the apartment is yours, Sally. Why not come down here for a week, catch some shows, redecorate the apartment, make it yours. You know what I mean? It could be therapeutic, Sal."

"You think I need it?" I smiled.

"Yes, definitely," Beth said.

"I'll think about it. I'd like you to read the latest chapter I've written of *Scotty's Things.*"

"Yes," said Beth, with something like her old enthusiasm. "You could even send some more of it down to me now, if you like.

"And don't forget what I said: the apartment is yours. There are no ghosts there. It's your home. When you're ready. . . come home, Sally."

But I could never go home. I wouldn't even go home as a prisoner, extradited from Canada. I'd be tried here in New Brunswick where the killing had been committed.

And even if a miracle occurred and I was never "caught," never "apprehended" . . . how could I leave this place, where Erica lay? How could I trust some ignorant new owner not to disturb her resting place, buried with accoutrements like an ancient princess, as she would be, going into the Other World equipped with carpet, boots, slacks, gun? A cache of artifacts that might yet lead the authorities to me.

I had to wait for my hand to heal before I moved Erica from the woodbox. The stitches wouldn't be coming out until Monday, and I would have to wait several days after that. There were other reasons to hesitate; the fear that I would hear any day that a warrant had been issued, back in the States, for Keir's arrest. If that happened, I'd call Raoul Gerlain and confess everything. I'd show him Erica's body and the gun, and my ax. I must. I would not have Keir put in danger.

I kept steeling myself to the possibility, seeing myself being led up the steps of the St. Claude Police Station . . .

And there my thoughts reeled back. I found myself with hands balled to fists, teeth clenched, and the thought like a scream in my mind, *I couldn't bear it, I couldn't bear it.*

I went for long walks—even runs—in the woods when the weather permitted, building up my strength. I drove into town and bought a white ski suit. The color was not a good seller, the assistant told me, doubtfully. As I left the shop, she cautioned with a smile, "Don't get lost, will you?"

"I won't," I assured her.

" 'Cause they'll never find you," as the door shut behind me.

Lady, that's the idea.

I took my tensions back to my Macintosh in those days and worked on the novel. I felt guilty at how I was able to lose myself. I had my characters, now; I moved them around, brought them together and enjoyed their exchanges, their growth, developing there on the screen, in my mind. I spent a lot of time describing the town, the streets: it was set in Maine, but New Brunswick kept creeping in, the Square, a hedge I'd admired, a house I loved, a tire-swing attached to an old maple tree; all these began imposing themselves upon my Maine landscape.

I finished chapter fourteen on Monday. That afternoon, at two, found me in John Tolliver's office, gritting my teeth while his nurse plucked little black threads from deep within the skin of my wrist.

I kept the answering machine switched on, the volume turned up, and worked through the days and the nights until only the calendar on my desk told me which of those dark Canadian days was which. The voices from the machine beset me like demons, probing, questioning voices from New York, from here in St. Claude, and from Aunts and Uncles in Florida; everyone I knew seemed to be following the newspaper stories, wanting to know How I Was, Was I Alright?

Nothing from Keir. Why, *why* was there nothing from Keir?

Nothing from McGarret, which was a relief, and nothing from Beth, who somehow sensed I didn't want daily conversations. She was giving me space. Not so Jeremy Camberwell and Sharalyn. Not so Andy Gregg and Sandra. Messages from each of them, almost every day—including demands, not requests—that I phone them.

Sod off, as James Hammel would say.

Chapter
Twenty-Two

It was Friday, February sixteenth; the day of the funeral.

By now I knew my path very well, having planned it in daylight and taken it every evening after sundown to make sure I knew my way in the dark. From the rear of the house I turned right—towards the south—across a corner of snow-covered lawn, then up the slope of the wooded hill, traversing it at an easy angle.

The wind was virtually still, only a few errant flakes falling, and due to the cold of that morning, the deep snow was firmly packed. The weather reports promised no nasty surprises before dawn, no sudden storms and blizzards that might come upon me halfway through my grisly project. *A clear night tonight,* I prayed, just for insurance, *a clear night tonight, Lord, then like the song says, let it snow, let it snow, let it snow.*

I set my alarm once more for three-thirty in the morning, but in the end I couldn't sleep and got up at two, turning off the alarm and dressing warmly in several layers of silk and light wool before pulling on the white ski suit. My heart thumped.

Why? What's so different about tonight's dark doings? You

think Erica is going to resent being buried under the roots of a
pine tree any more than she resents lying in a woodbox?

But there just seemed to be a more comfortable feeling
to moving Erica around my front yard: our little perambulations between the house and the barn had been a necessary
stratagem and had the element almost of a game. Almost.
Until now, everything had been aboveground—most particularly Erica. At any time, I could have taken Inspector
Gerlain by the hand, led him to Erica's shroud, unwrapped
her, and said, *Look what I've done.*

I made a small thermos of coffee and placed it and some
chocolate bars in the pockets of my ski suit. From the spare
room, beneath the mahogany tester bed, I took the sled
and some ropes. I dragged them out front, and as quickly
as I could work in the cold night air, I unpacked Erica from
her log-made sarcophagus. Raising her body was difficult. I
needed the rope, looping it around her neck and over the
veranda railing, bracing my right boot upon the foot of
the woodbox and hauling on the rope with all my weight,
until Erica rose up darkly, stiffly, *scarily*, like something
out of *The Mummy's Curse*. I knotted the rope and ran to
her head, swinging her shoulders over the edge of the box.
Once again this was not done with the greatest dignity:
Erica ended up headfirst in the snowdrift against the woodbox, her stiff toes pointed towards the roof. It convinced
me, finally, that Erica had not, could not possibly, have
killed Keir and moved his body. I had grown strong on
simple meals and lots of outdoor exercise these past
months and just coping with Erica's 120 pounds was almost
more than I could manage.

Lying on the snow, wrapped in the dark oilcloth, Erica
looked like Count Dracula, having folded his bat wings
about him, having hung himself upside down from the
ceiling of his room, lost his grip, and fallen.

I had bothered to buy the snow-colored ski suit, but
Erica would still be a dark, torpedo shape, gliding without
apparent propulsion along the forest paths. I ran back
inside and fetched a king-size white bedsheet from the

linen closet. It was satin, half of my best set, but it was fitting, somehow. I wrapped her body in it and tied her, shoulders and head protruding from one end, feet protruding from the other, onto the sled. When she was secured I slipped the handles of a pick and a shovel—hidden three days ago under the edge of the porch—into the rope bands with her. I promised her, and myself, that this would be the last indignity.

Around the side of the house, the side furthest away from the drive, and then up my invisible path, long-planned, obliquely across what had been my summer lawn, into the trees to the southeast of the house.

I had expected the journey to be difficult, but had not realized what a literally dead weight Erica would be. It took an interminable hour and a half to reach the fallen tree with my burden.

It began to snow, sparse flakes that fell slowly, almost straight down from the dark skies onto Erica and me as we paused by the newly torn earth. I didn't wait long: I took the rope from around Erica's body and used one end to tie around my waist and the other end around a nearby tree. Only then, carrying the pick and shovel, did I dare climb down into the snow-filled basin: I was taking no chances on not being able to scramble out.

The heavy fall of soil from the tree roots above me had formed a dirty, easily shoveled mush that I was able to push aside before digging, as deeply as I could—and this was not very deep at all—a trench for Erica. It was the best I could do.

I stopped frequently for a few mouthfuls of chocolate and a swig of coffee from the thermos.

"This is the last move—I promise," I swore to Erica's shrouded form on the ground, level with my shoulders. Now that the ropes were gone, she looked impressive on the sled, very dignified in her silk wrappings, like a queen on her bier. "No one will ever disturb you here. And I'll plant another tree—and some flowers, if I dare. Bluebells.

I'll buy a couple of hundred dollars worth of bluebell bulbs and plant out the whole goddamned wood. And maybe crocuses, too. Everywhere, to make sure you have flowers every spring."

I had to slide Erica into the grave, but because the edges of the original hole weren't steep, her descent was not nearly as precipitous or ungainly as getting her into the woodbox had been. I joined her in the hole and was able to maneuver her without difficulty into the grave. With her, I placed the carpet, my bloodstained clothes from the day of the killing, and Keir's gun. Then I scrambled out of the hole. There was so much earth attached to the roots that in an hour I had the grave and the bottom of the hole itself filled with soil. I jumped down, then, and spread the slushy snow-and-soil mixture back on top of the three feet or more of dirt.

I stopped, then, leaning against the rough, damp side of the fallen tree, and stood mute.

The snow was falling faster now, its flakes were already beginning to cover the sled, the tools and ropes, and to fill the circular scar in the hillside. By tomorrow, except that the hole was not as deep as it was, there would be no evidence at all that a body lay beneath that gentle white blanket.

I packed up the tools and ropes and then hesitated.

I didn't know any Protestant prayers. Finally, I said, in a low voice that still sounded loud in that world of sighing snow, "Lord who made Jew and Christian, grant her forgiveness and rest. And I ask the same for me."

I left then, dragging a broken branch behind me to break up the marks left by the sled's skis. I didn't know if God had granted me forgiveness, wouldn't know until those moments after my own death.

And rest?

Somehow I doubted that. I doubted that very much.

* * *

I was braver about using a flashlight, now, and placed the sled and ropes away in the garage. I locked the doors and finally returned to the house, and to bed.

The grandfather clock said that it was five o'clock. Just before I turned out the light I looked through the window; the falling snow had already obliterated my footprints and the marks of the sled's runners.

When I woke at eleven the next morning, February seventeenth, there was no sign that anyone had ever taken a path through the snow, into the woods.

I should have felt more relaxed, at least a little happier— if one could use that word—to know that the evidence was literally buried. That day was a Saturday, cold but mild, as was the Sunday. On both days I went for a walk, meandering over the hills in no set pattern, but always passing, just once, the fallen pine and the snow-filled saucer where its naked roots had once been imbedded.

I looked around; the woods stretched out in every direction, but I was close enough to the top of the ridge to see, not only the land sloping down on my side, but, in the blue distance to the east, the hills of the national park that bordered my property, somewhere down there, out of sight in the valley.

The place was very peaceful. I went away contented enough—I could have done no better for Erica.

But she would insist on haunting my dreams. It always took the same pattern: I'd be going about my life and Erica's body, wrapped in white satin, her face clearly visible through it, would keep turning up. On a table of returned books in the library, making Stephanie cross with me; on the front steps of the St. Claude Police Station, just as I was walking past with my arms full of shopping. McGarret stood over it with a citation pad open, looking up at me with a scowl to say, "I take it this body belongs to you, ma'am?" And again at Brambles Thorne, this time lying stiffly on the board table throughout a staff meeting. This turned out to be quite a cheerful dream, with Beth saying now we'd be able to get a photograph for the cover of

Catwalk, and Sammy calling in a staff photographer and suggesting everyone have his or her photograph taken with Erica. Everyone kept thanking me for bringing her back to town, and no one seemed disturbed by the fact that she was dead.

I found I was worrying about Erica more now that she was buried than I had ever worried when she was occupying my barn and woodbox. She seemed so alone up there.

And I couldn't believe it was over. When Beth rang me, we tended to avoid mentioning Erica, and I began to feel, oddly enough, as if I wanted to talk about her, what she had been like, when alive. But I didn't like to ask, and Beth never volunteered. She talked of the company's plans for marketing the latest Erica Tudor book, due for publication this coming July, and of Sammy's growing panic that he had not yet managed to secure another writer to replace Erica. The only possible choice so far was to groom Leigh Holliwiss. She had hitherto written short romances under our Thorns and Roses romance label, and Sammy was attempting to convince her to write the large blockbuster novels Erica had made popular. We talked of Leigh's reluctance: her style was good and tight, her characters empathic, but she was daunted by the idea of having to produce two hundred and fifty thousand words instead of eighty to a hundred thousand.

"The millions will help," I said, and there was a silence from Beth.

"She'll get two hundred thousand tops for her first advance, and that's only if Sammy can't avoid paying her that much. Why are you so cynical Sally? It's not like you."

"Erica's not cold in her grave."

And neither of us spoke for a moment. Beth was still grieving; and I was thinking, wildly, bemusedly, *Erica is very cold in her grave.*

That was the only mention we made of Erica: Beth said nothing about missing her—not from any ill-feeling, but because it was dawning even on me that no one *knew* Erica. Not Beth, who had been jolted by the realization that she was regarded as Erica's best friend, and not, I felt, Keir, to whom Erica had given quite a few surprises, not all of them pleasant. And certainly not me: our relationship consisted of five minutes in a ladies' powder room, when she had made the announcement that had ruined my life, and a five minute chase around a barn when she tried to end it.

The Monday after I buried Erica I received my first phone call from a journalist. I hung up immediately, called the phone company, and had them give me a new, unlisted number. I notified Beth and a handful of friends and relatives and swore them to secrecy. And I notified Keir's parents, for I knew Keir would call them, or Beth, if he found my number changed. When he called. If he called.

The phone suddenly went quiet at about three that afternoon. It should have made me feel better, but I was coming to think that nothing would. I couldn't even concentrate on the novel. I was tired, but I didn't want to nap because then I wouldn't sleep that night—and the nights bothered me. I drank a lot of coffee, but I wasn't eating much: it was too much trouble to cook something, and I only pushed the food around my plate.

Was it over? Could it really ever be over?

You've done everything you can do. Erica is buried, literally and figuratively. Give yourself a break. Are you planning on going crazy over this thing?

If I only knew where Keir was. I even pulled out a map of the United States and studied it, town by town, state by state. But there was nothing to give me a clue. We had friends in many places, but none crazy enough to hide Keir if he were a fugitive.

Our cabin in Beaver Creek, Colorado? Too obvious. The police would know about all our properties, would know all our friends. How could I hope to find Keir where they could not?

When Keir himself did not want me to find him. And this thought hurt the most.

I drove into St. Claude to shop for supplies. I was out of bread and milk and orange juice: I needed postage stamps and I had to go to the bank. In my present mood I'd have preferred to stay home. It was a forced journey: I was worried about the state of my brain. I took particular care showering, dressing: even putting on makeup. I must not go crazy, I must not end up living alone and behaving in a peculiar manner, like poor Alby Gresson next door.

In the bank I ran into McGarret. I started when his deep voice said, without preamble, "No one's seen much of you lately; what've you been doing with yourself out there on the farm?"

"Writing, working," I muttered, flustered.

"Bit of thinking, too?"

What did he mean by that? *What?*

I forgot to move forward in the line; McGarret touched my elbow to gently nudge me.

"Have you heard from him?" His voice cool.

"Does that really concern you?" Gently, a small smile to soften my words. And seeing something harden in his face, "I haven't," I added.

"He's still listed as a missing person. New York will want to know."

"I'll let New York know. If I hear anything."

"How's the hand?" he asked.

I had to stop to display the small crimson scar. "Fine, thanks."

"I'm sorry," he said, his voice low, "about all the questions Raoul had to ask."

"That's alr—"

"In the end you had an alibi. Not that you needed it."

Don't go white, Sarah. Don't pale like a Dickensian heroine.

"I couldn't have," I said. That's it. Tell the truth. Tell as much of the truth as you can. "I told you and the inspector, I was alone during that time. I was working alone."

"I thought I'd go see Alby Gresson, see if he saw you about. He doesn't always stick to his own boundaries, as you know. He says he saw you. On the twenty-fifth."

And then I did go white. I know it because my knees were suddenly weak. "Spying on me? He was spying on me." And then relief, and I even smiled. "He couldn't have. I mean, it was nice for him to speak up for me, but . . . he was in the hospital all through that time. Larry Carey told me."

"Larry was mistaken." Bland voice, bland face.

We moved on a little. Slowly. So slowly. "He went in on the Friday—Friday the twenty-sixth. He'd been sick for a few days but wouldn't see a doctor. On the Thursday evening he took his dog for a walk—along Spring Mill Road, he says. Then the dog ran off through the trees, up towards your place. Alby said he saw you out near the barn, chopping wood."

I didn't speak. I couldn't have spoken if McGarret's next words were, *and he saw you put an ax through a woman's head.*

"I wouldn't be too upset with him," McGarret was saying, perhaps taking my white-faced silence as feelings of violated outrage. "He did get a case of pneumonia out of it."

I managed a kind of strangulated noise somewhere in my throat.

"He's always had people's respect around these here parts." I dragged my gaze from the middle distance back to the large features above my own. "But he is getting older, and we've had a few complaints from other neighbors—about him trespassing. He tends to think woods is woods."

Georgia had caught up with him, as it sometimes did, and I smiled. It was appealing, somehow, but McGarret actually flushed a little. He corrected himself ruthlessly. "Woods are woods."

I was thinking, *Trust you to go to Alby Gresson. And was it to check on what he might have seen of me around January twenty-fifth—or what the little sneak might have seen of Keir Stanforth?*

How can I know what Alby saw? I can't go and ask *the little bastard . . .*

The bank teller called "Next, please," and I would have moved forward, but McGarret had taken my arm, gently enough. "Have a coffee with me." His tone softer, his eyes warmer.

"I can't," I murmured. "Maybe another time," and I moved away.

"Sure," McGarret said, in his usual deep, serious voice. If I turned, his face would be serious too, I knew. "When you have more time to talk," he added.

I didn't look for him as I left the bank.

I didn't want to meet his gaze again.

There were marks in the snow. I could see them quite clearly as I came up the drive. I had to follow them, all the way to the house, and only then did I get out to examine them.

There were snowshoe tracks in the powdery whiteness of what had been my almost pristine drive. The only consolation was that there were two sets, one leading to the front porch of the cottage, and one leading away again, back down the drive.

I waited by the car. All seemed silent, all seemed normal.

But there on the porch was a small plastic bucket with a lid. A piece of paper was tied to it, with string, neatly, ending in a bow. The note was in very small, even handwriting, and it said, *We have plenty. Too much. Sweets for the sweet. Ha ha.*

It was signed, *A. E. Gresson.* I didn't even need to lift the lid to know what it was, the sweet, heady perfume of maple syrup hovered around the little bucket as I picked it up.

I looked around once more, but the world seemed silent, empty. He had obviously left, not finding me home. But why the note, the neat string? Did he know I wouldn't be home?

I looked at the snowshoe tracks disappearing back towards the front gate.

At least he'd come up the front drive.

Why wasn't I comforted by this?

Chapter
Twenty-Three

I was splitting firewood at dusk when the phone rang. I hurried inside, picked it up, and said "Hello," rather out of breath.

But no one answered.

"Hello? *Hello?*"

Finally, I replaced the receiver. It was probably a wrong number . . . Yet it was disturbing for all that.

They could have *said*, "Sorry, wrong number," couldn't they?

The next day, the wind had changed and blew from the southwest. It brought a false thaw: everything ran, and dripped, and the house seemed to gurgle to itself as if possessed, all that day, all the next night.

I pulled on my galoshes and plodded through the snowy slush like Christopher Robin. Each day, after hours working on the novel, I followed my usual paths through the woods, passing Erica's grave and noting with relief and satisfaction that once more it had passed another night undisturbed.

The cold settled in again, and with the renewed chill came McGarret. I found I was pleased to see him, but his

timing was bad. I had almost finished *Scotty's Things*, had
worked through the night until the print on my computer
screen was dancing about like microorganisms in pond
water before my eyes. Yet I was loath to stop, afraid of
losing my grasp on it, so I worked on through the night,
was still working at dawn, when a watery sun came up over
the hills above the house. I went into the kitchen for coffee
and fell asleep with my head on the table, in a patch of
sunlight, stricken supine like a cat by the brightness, the
warmth.

"Sarah!"

Deep masculine voice. I was back in New York, snug in
my bed, Keir was returning from a meeting. But why is he
knocking on the bedroom door?

"Sarah!"

"Yes?"

And only when I answered did I find that I was sitting
bolt upright at the kitchen table, more than six hundred
miles from New York, and that the voice was outside the
house, and not Keir's, but McGarret's.

I stood up hurriedly, glanced at my reflection in the
glass door of the wall oven, and groaned silently. My red
and black check shirt made my skin look the color and
texture of an underdone bagel, and my hair looked like
something one pulled out of the bathtub drain every six
months or so.

I opened the back door, and relaxed slightly when I saw
he was wearing jeans, a black sweater, and a parka. If and
when he came to arrest me, I knew he wouldn't be wearing
mufti.

He still wore his sunglasses, though. He peeled them
off to study me. "You haven't been to bed, have you?"

"If that's a comment on my appearance, a gentleman
would have kept his mouth shut." We regarded each other.
"That bad, huh?"

"Yep." Then, in a different tone of voice, "What are
you doing to yourself, Sarah?"

I decided I wasn't really all that pleased to see him. And

I knew that if I let him through the door I'd be in for more of the same. I stepped out onto the back porch, drawing the door closed behind me.

"This isn't really the best time for me. I've been working all night. I'm on the last chapter. And I want to send it off to Beth this afternoon."

"Can I have a cup of coffee?"

Say no. You can say no to Alby Gresson. You can say no to Eugene.

"Okay. But don't lecture me, okay? I'm alright. Writers often work all night. Writers often look ugly."

"Did you eat breakfast?"

"No, but I—"

"Did you eat dinner last night?"

I had to think. A bowl of rice crispies and an orange at about five the previous day. "Yes," I said.

He reached, easily, over my head and leaned on the door. It opened slowly into the kitchen, taking me with it.

I went immediately to the coffeepot, which was cold. Fetching fresh ground coffee from the fridge, I noticed my hands were shaking. Maybe I *should* have eaten something; *Scotty's Thing's* just wouldn't give me a break. It wailed like a silent siren at me, it howled in my blood, it competed with Erica in my dreams, calling for me to come, come back to the computer, punch out those few extra lines before I forgot them, before they were gone forever.

I drained the cold coffee into the sink, conscious all the time of McGarret's openly worried gaze upon me, knowing that he had been on the phone to Merlin and both of them had undoubtedly decided that I was becoming obsessive.

"Do all writers work like this?"

"Some."

"How come they don't go crazy?"

"Oh, they do. All the really good ones are a little crazy. A few of the really good ones are very crazy."

"Are you?"

"I am but mad north-north-west," I said, quoting Hamlet, "when the wind is southerly I know a hawk from a handsaw."

McGarret's expression didn't change, "Sit down," he said.

"Why?"

"I'll make us some breakfast."

"Are you hungry? I'll fix you some breakfast if . . ."

All six foot six of him was suddenly towering over me. "Sit down."

I pulled out a chair and sat. He found a pan and butter and eggs and grumbled at the lack of tomatoes.

I fretted on my chair.

"I can chop some onion if you—"

"Nope."

"I can't just sit here. I can—"

"Sit." He was breaking the first of what would be an unhealthy number of eggs into the pan. He took the broken shells to the kitchen bin, an old-fashioned metal one with a foot pedal, and was about to drop them in. Then he paused.

I was watching him through a fog, noticing his large foot on the pedal, his large hand holding the egg shells over the receptacle . . .

"There's nothing but coffee grounds in here." He glared up at me as if he took the state of my garbage can as a personal insult. "How much coffee have you been drinking? Do you know what it does to you?"

"Why are you always picking on me? Go home, McGarret. Cook your own eggs."

I was suddenly very tired, his very caring was weakening me. I put my head in my hands and blotted him out.

The table moved slightly, as if his weight was suddenly upon it. I half looked up, and heard, "Sarah," so close above me that I could feel his breath on my hair. He was on the other side of the table, leaning his hands to either side of me. If I threw my head back we would be very close indeed. "Sarah, you can't keep—"

The phone rang. I jumped to my feet. McGarret pulled

back only just in time to keep our heads from colliding. I left my chair so abruptly that it rocked.

In the living room I turned the answering machine off before my own voice on the tape had finished. "Hello?"

There was no reply.

This was the fourth call like this in the past week. It was getting ridiculous.

"Hello? Who is this?"

Still no answer.

This was getting spooky.

McGarret was burning toast when I returned to the kitchen. I'd hung up, finally, but stayed by the phone, unwilling to rejoin him in case he thought there was something suspicious in so brief a conversation.

I said nothing when I entered the kitchen, instead busied myself finding a cloth for the table and setting it. McGarret showed no curiosity about the call, for which I was grateful.

Yet I was beginning to worry. Might it be Alby Gresson, come by my new number, making a nuisance of himself?

It could be Keir, needing to hear my voice, not knowing how to approach me, what to say.

McGarret had come to some decision in my absence, had backed off a little. During the meal he asked me about my book, about my job, both before, as a full-time editor, and what it entailed these days, being freelance. There was no further mention of my state of physical and mental dishevelment. We ate our eggs on very brown toast and drank our coffee and stayed on safe subjects. He mentioned he'd like to see the old Buick once again, and we discussed ways of removing it from my property to his.

I found myself telling him about Geoff, and Uncle Zachary, and all the way back to my parents' death.

The grandfather clock must have gonged away unheard, several times, for when its sound finally penetrated, we'd been sitting there, opposite each other at the table, for almost three hours.

I sprang up and led the way through the house, grabbing the key to the barn off its hook by the front door. I didn't look at McGarret as we crossed the yard to the barn. It was snowing again, but lightly. I was annoyed with myself, really annoyed. There was no room in my life for exchanges like this, no room for the kind of friendship that required such honesty, such intimacy. Real friends didn't lie to each other, and my whole life had become a lie, and there was no changing it, no escape from it.

I'd been in the barn many times since Erica's stay beneath the Buick: I'd had to make sure that there was no telltale sign of her occupancy. I'd even tried to tidy the place a little, and had made several trips to the local rubbish dump with those useless things that had been light enough for me to carry to the Volvo and small enough to fit within it.

Now, entering the space with McGarret, I shivered, suddenly beset by feelings of dread, remembering those days of terror immediately after Erica's death when she had lain here, so close to where McGarret was now wandering, casually, his eyes on the old car and the snowflakes in his dark hair.

I almost said, *Let's not do this,* so strong was the feeling of Erica's presence still hovering, of something not being right. Had I forgotten anything? Had I?

My heart beat very hard, and I was terrified McGarret would turn and see the look on my face. How could I explain it?

He'd wandered around to the right of the car, I went to the left, and for something to do that would keep my head turned from him, I stood by the very dirty barn window. I should have cleaned it by now, I thought. But I have a horror of really dirty work, and tend to postpone it.

That made me smile. You put an ax through someone's head and bury her in the dead of night and shrink from cleaning a window covered with oily dust?

Except for making sure that the floor area was clean of

any possible trace of Erica, and preparing for a visit from either Copely or McGarret regarding the car, I'd had no desire to be in this place. Any thoughts I'd had of converting the loft to a studio had departed with Erica's short lease on the first floor. That's probably why I hadn't cleaned the window. I didn't want to be able to see in, didn't want anyone else to regard the little barn as particularly inviting.

Every other visit here had been for some purpose. I'd kept myself busy. Now there was nothing to do. Just wait for this man to stop his perambulations around the old car and get the hell out of here.

"Sure would like to buy her from you."

I looked over at him. He was just lifting the hood. With the engine gone he looked down into the space where, just a month before, he'd have been confronted with Erica's head encased in oilcloth.

He looked up at me. "Is that alright?" he prompted.

"Yes, fine," I murmured. "Come pick it up any time."

"How much do you want for her, Sarah?"

"Nothing. It's worthless, a wreck."

He replaced the hood and had opened the driver's door, saying, "She's not a wreck, she's a real beauty—she's just in pieces at the moment, that's all."

I don't know what changed the atmosphere. His words had something to do with it. I looked over at him. He'd had his head lowered, but now, as if confronted with another thought, he raised his head and looked at me. And he looked a little embarrassed.

If I could have, I'd have smiled, but it wasn't that funny. He hadn't been making some cleverly veiled allusion to me and our aborted conversation in the kitchen. But he thought *I* thought that's what he was doing. And I watched him struggle to find some way of getting out of the predicament without making things worse. But he couldn't.

I should have spoken up, made some comment about the car, something that would have made him more at ease, but I was feeling cruel. He had it over me in so many ways that I thought I could be forgiven this little bit of smugness. But I was reckoning without McGarret's own tactics.

Pull back, regroup, look at the facts, face them, and get the hell to the point.

"Sarah, I'm in love with you."

"Oh, goddamn you!" I whirled away and thumped the nearest thing at hand, the brown leather car seat, leaning up against the wall on its end. Dust flew everywhere.

"Sarah." The remorseless, deep voice behind me. "I'm serious, here."

I started to sneeze. This was no good at all. I headed for the door. *Erica did this,* I thought, wildly, blindly, sneezing as I tried to find the door with streaming eyes. This barn was haunted, cursed, the little bitch hovered among the dust motes and wreaked her revenge with unerring accuracy and a twisted sense of humor.

I reached the door and he was there, blocking out the sunlight, blocking out everything. I ran straight into his chest and he held me, and still I sneezed. I hoped I'd sneeze forever, for ten minutes, for long enough to get away, for I knew that when I stopped sneezing he'd kiss me. And I stopped, and he did.

"No," I said, when I could. "No." And I broke away— that's to say he opened those great thick arms and let me escape when I wriggled enough to show my displeasure. I stomped up towards the house, talking fast as I went.

"This just isn't right. It's all wrong. I'm sorry if I've given you the wrong impression. I do care about you, but not in the way you think I do. Though you shouldn't think anything of the sort because I've never given you any reason to. I mean, we've got nothing in common, no middle ground. You're New Brunswick and . . . and Georgia, and I'm New York . . . which is in the middle, I guess, but only in the strictest of geographic senses. I'm Jewish, and you're Protestant, and—"

"So was Keir."

I turned to look back at him and found him standing

so close he was almost on top of me. I couldn't read the look he was giving me, but I stepped back before it.

How did he know Keir was Protestant?

It'd be on a file, somewhere. He could have seen it.

Could have made it his business to see it.

And to cover my confusion I made my second mistake. With cold officiousness I looked at my watch and said, "I have to get back to work, now," and walked away.

"The hell you do."

He caught me as I reached the top step and held me by both my arms so I had to face him: one foot on the top step beside me, the other on the ground, and still he had to bend to me.

"How long do you think you can go on like this? Locking yourself away, brooding on the past. *Let go of it, Sarah.* Don't you know how worried everyone is about you? I've a good mind to call John Tolliver and see about a few days' rest in a sanatorium someplace."

"What?"

"You'll end up as crazy as Alby Gresson if you don't get yourself some help."

"You twisted bastard!" I yelled at him. "I tell you I'm not in love with you, and the next minute you're planning on having me committed?"

The big hands on my arms loosened their grip a little.

"I didn't mean ... They're unconnected. How I feel about you doesn't affect the facts of what you're—"

"Oh, gimme a break! If I'd fallen into your arms back there, you wouldn't be talking of calling in men in white coats. It smacks of abuse of privilege, *Sergeant.*"

McGarret went white. Suddenly he paled so much that the freckles on his nose stood out. Even his lips paled. But what was worse was what happened in his eyes. It was shock of a devastating kind, and I could see it there, and hated myself. *I've hurt him. I've really hurt him.*

With words, only words, and spoken in anger, rage. But I'd unwittingly—or had it been on purpose?—struck him in his only vulnerable place, struck at the heart of what mattered most to him. His honor. His job, too, but even his job was part of it.

He took his hands from me, slowly, and stepped back.

I felt my body lean forward a little to him, felt the start of tears and words of apology and screamed at myself *not* to react, *not* to speak. To let him go.

I have a dead body buried in my backyard, and you, sir, are a policeman.

I've hurt him. Hurt him.

You are too careful and ponderous and good at your job, and you watch me too carefully and read me too well. You'll catch me out, one day, some day.

I've hurt him. Hurt him.

He said, quietly. "You're good."

"What?"

"You're very good. You don't even know how good you are."

"I don't know what you're talking about," I said, my voice sounding subdued even to my own ears. I was teetering dangerously on the edge of an apology.

He walked calmly up the stairs and passed me, to lean against the wall, close beside the front door. I thought he was moving out of the wind a little, but there was very little wind. Then he said, "How long since you washed your hair, put on a clean shirt?"

I ignored him and went to go back inside, and of course his arm reached across and latched onto the opposite side of the door, effectively barring my way.

"I'm not bein' plain mean, here," the deep voice dispassionate. "We're facing facts. When did you last have a bath?"

I managed to open the door, was about to duck under his arm when he lowered it; I bumped my forehead on his forearm just as he said, "When did you last brush your teeth?"

Oh, God. Oh, GOD . . .

I felt as if I were dissolving, turning to water like thawing snow, lowered my gaze to the floorboards, lowered my head, couldn't breathe, and didn't dare.

Let the ground swallow me up. Let the ground just open and let me trickle away into oblivion. Let me die.

I became aware that his hands were on my shoulders, that he was shaking me gently, "Sarah, Sarah . . ."

I was pulled to his chest like a rag doll and held there with as little volition on my part, as little enthusiasm. I kept my head lowered, my lips pressed closely together.

The resonance of his voice through the large frame almost blocked off his actual words, spoken softly into my hair, "It's called tough love, honey. I gotta break through to you somehow." And the arms tightened a little, "What is it, Sarah? It's more than just Keir, isn't it? You're too sensible, you were coping so well when you first arrived up here. Why fall apart now?" And when I went to pull away, or tried to, "You know it's true. Why can't you tell me? Shoot, we were getting on so well over breakfast. You told me about your mom and dad, and Geoff . . . All these things hurt you real bad, and yet you could talk to me. Talk to me now, honey. Whatever it is, I can help you."

My heartbeat had slowed; listening to the voice rumbling through the body pressed so close to mine had me almost hypnotized, almost sleepy. I was in a warm and safe place, and for a long moment I forgot everything. I could even believe, *yes, I can tell him.* We'll go back to the kitchen table and make fresh coffee—

"Don't you think?"

"What?"

He pulled me away from him gently, and just as gently shook me so I had to look up at him. He was smiling a little, though it was touched with exasperation.

"Is anything getting through to you? I'll take you to dinner tonight, and we can talk."

"No!"

"There's a fine little restaurant in Fredericton—real private little tables. You have a bath and fix your hair and I'll call for you about six."

I lowered my head again, knowing my face must be as scarlet as the red check shirt that I was wearing for the fourth day running.

"I can't. I don't want to." Through a closed mouth.

"Sure you can."

"No," I mumbled to his boots. "I've got to get this next chapter finished and off to Beth in New York."

"Sarah." The voice too calm, too patient, and with my name the hands on my shoulders moved a little and his two thumbs positioned themselves beneath my chin and raised it willy-nilly until I was glowering directly into his face.

Kindly, he said, "I promise I won't go sicking John Tolliver onto you. But if you don't fix yourself up and agree to leave this house for a few hours tonight, then I'll send someone you'll appreciate even less. I'll send my mamma."

I stiffened in McGarret's grasp. Janice McGarret? Sailing with concerned and capable common sense into my house, my life?

McGarret was trying very hard not to smile. "And don't think I couldn't do it."

"I know," I snarled through clenched teeth. Janice was fashioned for crises like this. She'd respond like the lead dog in a sled team.

"Will you leave now, please?"

"I'm coming back at six."

I shrugged beneath the heavy hands. "Okay."

I relaxed as he stepped back and, after a long look, descended the steps. He spoke with his back to me as he went. "And don't try to hide out in the woods because I'll track you down and haul you into that bathtub myself, y'hear?"

He paused at the bottom of the stairs to look back at me.

"I hear."

"Six," he repeated.

When he turned I almost ran for the door, closing it behind him before he could issue any more orders.

This was Erica's fault, I thought again, grimly. I knew what was eating away at me, what was slowly destroying my life. I had killed Erica Tudor, and I couldn't forgive myself.

If it wasn't for Keir . . .

Standing there by the door, for the first time, I saw that there was going to be no end to the nightmares, the grieving, the guilt.

End it, Sarah.

There were two ways of doing it. Tell McGarret—or preferably someone from Fredericton—and go to prison. Or . . .

Or, Sarah?

Or end it completely. Once and for all.

You should have kept Keir's gun.

There are other ways.

Out of habit I drifted back to the computer in the study. I sat down at the desk with a mind more clear than it had been for a month. Looking at the last sentence I'd typed, I continued the paragraph. I worked calmly and well for several hours, stopping to curse McGarret occasionally for interrupting my day's plans. There was no way, now, for me to complete the novel and send copies of the discs to New York that afternoon. Not when I had to bathe and change my shirt and fix my hair and . . . *brush my teeth.*

I worked until four-thirty, and stopped only because I'd actually managed to do what I'd set out to do; I'd finished the twenty-four chapters of *Scotty's Things* and typed *THE END* triumphantly.

I made copies of my copies, so I had the discs ready to send off the following day. Then, hating myself, I bathed and washed my hair. I brushed my teeth four times and gargled with Listerine.

I will never forgive McGarret for this.

I will never forgive myself.

I went through my wardrobe, angry, and pulled out black trousers and a black sweater. For I'd decided I wasn't going anywhere. I was neatly dressed for an At Home. And that, by God, was where I was going to stay. How could I yell at

McGarret in a restaurant? And the longer I waited the more I wanted to yell at him.

I was all dressed. I sprayed myself with Giorgio and sat down on the settee to wait, clean and sweet-smelling and ready for war.

It was only five-fifteen.

I began practicing, imagining an obdurate McGarret—in a suit?—standing halfway between me and the door and determined to get the two objects closer. I practiced delivering arguments, cogent, appealing, to that unyielding face, and wondered what he'd do.

I just had to be firm with him. Somehow get him to leave me alone, not just tonight, but for the future as well.

I didn't have to put up with his bullying ways, I didn't have to stay and listen to his lectures . . .

I didn't have to stay.

I found myself in the spare room, at the wardrobe, taking out a couple of empty suitcases. I lugged them along to my own room and began throwing clothing and shoes into them.

Glancing at my bedside clock before I packed it, I saw that it was five twenty-five. Not much time at all. I tossed underwear and makeup into bags, collected toiletries from the bathroom, and hurriedly zipped up the cases, then carried them to the front door. Anything I'd forgotten I'd have to buy on the road.

I remembered the discs, ran back to the study, and fetched them, took paper and pen and began to scribble a note.

Dear . . . (what do I call him? Be nice, you're standing him up, remember) *Perry,*

I think you're right, everything's just getting a bit too much for me, so I've decided to go home to New York for a while. Merlin always said she'd look after the place for me—could you give her the keys, please? And apologize that it's such short notice. You made me realize I just had to sort myself out. Thank you for your concern. (That'll make him happy, putting the responsibility for my flight at his feet.)

Again my pen hesitated. Should I say, 'sorry'?

For what? I only agreed to go out with him under duress. Angry, I scribbled, *I washed my face and hands before I left.*

I made an effort at appeasement by signing the note, *Fond regards, Sarah.*

Big of you. Remember his kiss, out there in the barn? You nearly drowned. And you think all that pent-up emotion is going to be gratified to receive your kind regards?

It was ten minutes to six. I turned on the answering machine and looked around ... I propped the letter up on the arm of the settee where he invariably placed his sunglasses and his hat when he was in uniform. I anchored the paper with a copy of Erica's *Strings*—it was the closest book at hand on the bookcase.

He wouldn't get the connection, I thought, as I dropped the keys to the house on the settee arm beside the note, but it was significant for me.

I shut the door behind me without locking it and carried my handbag and suitcases to the garage.

I didn't start to relax until I was on the highway, headed towards the border. I had to stop myself, even then, from checking the rearview mirror for the sight of a dark green Jeep Cherokee in the traffic behind me.

Chapter
Twenty-Four

Beth was delighted to see me, and so, it seemed, was everyone else I knew at Brambles Thorne. Even those who had
been known to be malicious now smiled and welcomed
me with what seemed like genuine affection. But now, of
course, they could afford to be generous: I was no longer
a permanent part of the senior editorial staff and therefore
no competition in the subtle war for advancement.

People were surprised by the change in me. I'd warned
Beth several times that she'd find me a brunette, and
several pounds heavier than when she'd last seen me, but
she hadn't mentioned it to anyone else. The reactions were
invariably favorable. Sammy Thorne passed me in the hall
with an admiring look and it wasn't until I put my hand
on his arm that he turned, stared, and yelled, "Sally!"

He stepped back and looked at me, "You look great—
stunning! And . . . and healthy!"

"That's one way of putting it." I'd bought a new suit in
pale apricot silk only that morning and I knew I looked
good. I was staying at my beloved old Marlborough
Regency and had visited the hairdresser and had my hair
retouched and a protein treatment. McGarret should see

me now. When I got back I decided I'd have to thank him: he'd pushed me out of my safe little womb, back to the real world. I was feeling the pulse of New York through every fiber and was coming alive again.

"We gotta have dinner!" Sammy enthused, "tonight! No, not tonight, tomorrow. Yes! Beth, you and Malcolm come, too. L'Escargot, seven-thirty—okay? Marion will be dying to catch up with you."

I'll bet she will, I thought. Marion Thorne, Sammy's round, childlike wife, had been one of the many New York phone calls I had received during the really dark days after Keir's disappearance. Over the dinner table she'd undoubtedly be all agog to find out How I Was Feeling, If I'd Heard Anything, What I Thought Had Happened to Erica, to Keir . . .

Beth and I sat in a booth at the little bar near the Brambles Thorne offices. "Sales figures are up on all Erica's books. We're into a fifth reprint of *Gaining*," Beth said, and made a wry face. "Sammy has outdone himself in bad taste and put Erica's picture on the front cover. One of the Vaseline-lensed whimsical ones. And it mentions on the back cover that *Gaining* is the second-to-last book that Erica Tudor wrote before—"

"He didn't!"

"Before her life was so tragically cut short in what appears to be the same manner used in the novel."

"How can he do that? There hasn't been an inquest yet. And besides, it tells the reader how the story ends."

"Sally, everyone *knows* how the book ends. Haven't you been reading the papers and magazines? They've harped on the similarities between Lydia Diamond's death in *Gaining* and Erica's own. People aren't buying the book these days just because it's a good read, they buy it because Erica Tudor wrote it. She describes a woman's despair and how she walks into the sea when she can't gain the affection of the man she loves. The reader wants to know what she—Erica—was thinking, what she felt, right up to the last."

I shivered, and Beth noticed. "I'm sorry. I just want you to know when you see the new edition that I didn't approve."

"What about the new book?" I asked. "Can you let me see it?"

"Hm?" Beth sipped her drink, took a handful of peanuts, and put several in her mouth.

"Can I read the new manuscript? I asked you before, remember?"

But Beth's gaze was on the peanuts, the door, the wine list. "It's really not that good after the great beginning. If she'd lived I'd have asked her to do some substantial rewriting."

I felt a sudden chill. "Beth, what's the story? It's the second time you've tried to sidestep me on this thing. It's us, isn't it, her and me." A statement, not a question. "Erica and me and Keir. We're in the new book."

"No, no." Vaguely, looking above my head, then down at the peanuts, longingly. "Not exactly."

I felt light-headed, slightly sick, and it wasn't the martini I was drinking.

Beth said, "There are going to be changes, anyway. I've been arguing with Sammy and the board about it. As you can tell, the editing isn't finished."

I'd picked up on one of her first words. "Changes?" I said. "You're going so far as to *change* Erica's manuscript? That's a first, isn't it? Usually it was her poor writing that—"

"Small changes." She was looking once more at the door as patrons entered and exited. "Small . . . libelous . . . changes."

She still wasn't making herself clear, but I could catch the drift.

"Keir?" I asked. "Or me?"

She looked really unhappy now. "You."

Back in the office I coerced Beth into giving me a copy

of the *Catwalk* manuscript and took it back to the Marlborough Regency with me.

I read and read, all that night. I fell asleep about 6 A.M., woke after three hours, and read again until it was time to shower and dress for dinner with Sammy and Marion, Beth and Malcolm.

The heroine of *Catwalk* was called Russet Avenal, typical Erica fare. She was a self-made woman, also typical. She came from a well-bred Southern background—this was new, in the past Erica's heroines had always been born poor, usually in tenements, though exotic ones, Paris, London, Lisbon. No matter what the background, and Russet was no exception, the heroine always made it to the top of whatever her chosen career happened to be: an opera singer in *Traces of Heaven,* a cellist in *Strings,* and the owner of an international chain of diet and exercise studios in *Gaining.* Russet Avenal was a model, a victim of rape in her southern town, who goes to New York to have an abortion, instead has the child and fosters it out. She doesn't go home because she doesn't want to bring shame upon the old family name. She has a rough time in New York, is robbed and bashed when straying too late, naively, in Central Park. She's put back together—both emotionally and physically—by a handsome young plastic surgeon, Jonathan Whitney. Jonathan also happens to be the young intern who, years before, had delivered her child.

Jonathan was Keir's middle name and his mother was one of the Boston Whitneys. That should have gone, I thought, but perhaps Beth didn't know, or had forgotten. Maybe she'd been busy with other changes—she had been working on this since Erica's death. Maybe she'd already made as many changes to the manuscript as she dared.

For there was a subplot. Leaving the beautiful and vulnerable Russet in the hospital, awaiting the removal of her bandages, there is a flashback to a young Jonathan, on vacation in Hawaii. His wealthy parents have sent him there as a reward for graduating top of his class at Harvard Medical School.

In Hawaii the innocent Jonathan falls prey to a half-Hawaiian beach girl called Suzy. She is obsessed with him and follows him back to New York. As preoccupied with her own physical beauty as she is with Jonathan, she tries to make it as a model. She uses her sexual hold over him to get him to remodel her face, little by little, over the years, until she is regarded as one of the most beautiful women in the United States. It is at a cost. She takes drugs to remove the melanin from her skin, and when a fellow beach bum from Waikiki turns up and tries to blackmail her with her past, she murders him.

She does this by going to the commune in upper New York where he is living, and shooting him, then ransacking his cabin to make it look like a robbery.

Thank you, Erica. Now I know.

Desperate to keep Jonathan, she purposefully gets pregnant. Being an honorable man, Jonathan marries her from a sense of duty and pity, his mind still haunted by the beautiful Russet, whom he has tried unsuccessfully to trace since the birth of her child.

Suzy soon begins to make Jonathan's life a misery. He finds out that instead of losing the baby, as he'd thought, she had secretly had an abortion. She doesn't want children because they'd ruin her figure. Suffering from anorexia, bulimia, frequent nervous breakdowns, and suicide attempts, Suzy keeps her brilliant but increasingly unhappy young husband close to her by emotional blackmail.

She is not a nice person, Suzy. She is grasping, greedy, and adores jewelery, the pieces described lovingly and in great detail in some of Erica's best writing. To pay for her acquisitions, however, Jonathan has to perform face-lifts on aging, rich women, instead of performing the work he wishes; helping children with birth defects.

Part Three, and Russet is out of hospital and beautiful and well again. She and Jonathan, having found each other, begin to see each other frequently. Their meetings contained the best dialogue Erica had ever written. Jonathan Whitney's style was clever, witty, self-deprecating, and empathic; I knew Erica had recorded it straight from her memories of Keir and the first heady days of their relationship.

An affair begins. As Russet's career takes her from New York to Paris to London to Tokyo, she is touted as the great threat to Suzy's preeminent place on the catwalk. Suzy, who by now has her hair dyed red—she and Russet couldn't be blondes, Erica's heroine in Gaining had been blonde like Erica herself—realizes that she is growing older, and does not look good beside The Real Thing, the gorgeous Russet. When Suzy finds out about the affair between Russet and her husband she decides to fight back and hires private detectives to delve into Russet's past.

Suzy discovers the child and tracks her down to the farm where she lives with foster parents. She pretends to be Russet's estranged sister and convinces—and bribes—the couple to allow her to see the child frequently.

When Jonathan announces he is leaving Suzy to marry Russet, Suzy pretends to accept matters, but immediately drives to the foster parents' home and kidnaps the child. Russet and Jonathan, unsuspecting, are at that moment making passionate love together. Like the description of the jewelry, every nuance was specified.

When Jonathan and Russet discover what Suzy has done, a chase takes place across several states until finally Jonathan is shot by an insane Suzy. There, in a Florida swamp, Russet and Suzy battle it out, Suzy armed with a gun and dragging the unwilling child.

I was so intent on the story by this time that I was botching my makeup as I hurried for the dinner date and tried to read at the same time. It really was exciting; whatever else she was as a writer, Erica sure had pace.

I finished the manuscript in the taxi on the way to the restaurant, ignoring my chatty cabbie in order to devour the last few pages. Russet wins the fight despite Suzy having the gun, Suzy falls into quicksand and more than half a page is devoted to a harrowing description of her death while Russet tries—in vain, of course—to save her.

The child is safe, Jonathan is only wounded, and all three stumble out of the moss-grown swamp into the light of a new day.

The table of people fell silent as I approached them, clutching the heavy manuscript. I held it out to Sammy Thorne and said, "You've got yourself another winner."

The following day, back in the little bar near the office, I slid into the booth opposite Beth. She watched me nervously, knowing I was going to tackle all the issues I had kept to myself over dinner.

I fixed her with a glare. "A grasping, greedy, jewelry-loving *Hawaiian?*"

"We-ell . . ."

"Puh-*lease. You* changed it, Beth. In Erica's original, Suzy was Jewish, right? A home-grown New York–born Jew who gets her claws into Jonathan-stroke-Keir."

Beth said, in a rush, "She wouldn't let us see the manuscript, remember? You know how she usually took me to lunch—a lunch for every chapter—asking my advice, keeping me abreast of how it was developing."

"I remember."

"This time, *nothing.* I even tried to be firm with her, you know? But shit, she knew her power by then; she was *Erica Tudor.* I had a feeling something was wrong with the new manuscript, but she told me quite confidently—and she was right—that I didn't *have* to work on the book, Sammy could give her another editor if I found it 'distressing'; that was Erica's word, *distressing.* But if another editor worked on the book, how could I protect you? And if Sammy had stood up for you—yeah, yeah, I know—but if he *had,* she'd have just gone to another publisher and changed the modeling world for publishing and everyone would be even more certain of what she was trying to do."

"They can't miss it even now," I hissed almost violently.

"Everyone knows Erica broke up the marriage of a prominent plastic surgeon."

"I know, I know, but I couldn't very well make him a podiatrist, could I? You don't get a new identity and a healthy psyche from a *podiatrist*. She said it was semiautobiographical," Beth muttered, miserably. "She said it was a book she needed to write."

"I'll bet it was. She made up a world of lies and moved into it, as if it was reality. She had to convince herself I was a bitch in order to justify what she did." I made myself stop, I was on dangerous ground.

"I know, I know, Sally."

I thought Beth was going to cry. "Look, forget it. It's all over, isn't it? At least the Hawaiians will be very happy."

She looked puzzled. "They will?"

"In Erica's first draft, where did Keir meet his wife?"

In a small voice, "Her name was Shirley. He met her in Paris. His parents sent him to Paris when he graduated."

"Much more likely," I said, loftily, hiding the stab of hurt. "Have you had an offer for the film rights?"

"Paramount is having discussions with Sammy."

"They'll want to shoot on location. The Hawaiians will be delighted." I smiled at her. "It'll be a success, Beth. And you did a good job. Most people won't take it too seriously, they'll see any similarity as mischief or malice."

"You know, she wasn't really malicious. She was . . . sort of scared. The more I think of her—and I still think of her a lot—the more I come to see that she was driven by fear."

"I know."

"How do you know?"

"It . . . comes through in her writing."

Beth considered this. "Yes. Yes, it does, too, doesn't it?"

Then she said, "Keir never saw it—*Catwalk*. Erica told me she wasn't showing it to anyone. If he *had* seen it he'd never have let her finish it. He'd have stopped her, Sally. As it was, they . . . disappeared before it was printed out."

"Wait a minute. How do you know Keir didn't read it?

How do you know that wasn't the reason why they quarreled, that last time?"

"There wasn't a copy of the manuscript in the apartment."

"Maybe Erica took it with her and dumped it. Maybe
Keir took it with him."

"The police didn't think so, or they didn't mention it
to me."

"The police read *Catwalk?* In the original?"

"Of course. There were these discs left on her desk—
addressed to me, okay—but who knew what they contained? They were just looking for clues. When the lieuten-
ant from Missing Persons handed the discs back, he said,
'Miss Tudor didn't think much of the first Mrs. Stanforth,
did she?' And then he said, 'Was Erica Tudor ever raped?' "

"Was she?" I asked, suddenly interested. How autobi-
ographical was *Catwalk?* The description of Russet growing
up in the Deep South was obviously Erica: a romanticized
view of Keir was there, and a caricature of myself as his
Jewish wife. How much else was true and how much false?

"No, surely not. Not rape. It was just a device, like the
plane crash that nearly cripples the heroine in *Traces of
Heaven,* or the knife attack in *Strings.* It was just something
terrible for the heroine to pit herself against to prove what
she's made of."

"Oh," I said.

I called Merlin that night and thanked her for taking care
of *Jaegerhalle.* I didn't mention her brother, nor did she,
except to say, "Perry said you had to leave in a hurry—
nothing's wrong, is it?"

"No," I lied. "Just some legal matters connected with
Keir's disappearance." I told her I should be back in a
week.

There were no matters—legal or otherwise—that
involved me with Keir's disappearance except my own
grieving at his absence. I had the keys to the apartment

on Central Park South, but I couldn't bring myself to go there. The Marlborough Regency, with its mellow wood-work, old oil paintings, and elegant turn-of-the-century ambience, suited me very well.

Yet I stayed there only three days. I had dinner with Malcolm and Beth and brought presents for their kids and played with them, and had a great time. I went to the theater and saw two big-budget and forgettable musicals. And I brooded about Erica.

Erica had written *Catwalk* over more than a year, covering the months of her affair and finishing just about the time of her marriage to Keir. She had poured into it, into the character of Shirley-now-Suzy, all her hatred of me.

I drove down to Florida for two reasons. One was to visit The Aunts, the other was because it was relatively easy, in the southern states, to buy a gun.

And I wanted one, just in case things went badly for me. It would be good to know, comforting, somehow, that it would be there, close to me.

This would mean breaking another law when I smuggled it over the border. But what choice was there?

I spent one night each with Aunts Miriam, Shirley, Sadie and Uncle Gus. It was hard going, much as I loved them. Questions, questions, until I began to wonder if I really did have a life Up There in Canada. For I had no proper job, is that what I was telling them? I had no man in my life, how can that be, a beautiful girl like me? I was so pale—though it was good to see that I'd lost that half-starved look.

I escaped on March fourth with promises to phone each of them from New York and St. Claude to let them know I'd arrived safely.

But before I left Miami I proceeded to a narrow back street—yes, it really was a narrow back street. There I found a very casual young gun dealer, so casual that he barely looked at my driver's license and was simply gratified that

I saved him any paperwork by paying cash for the rather ugly and heavy .45 caliber Smith & Wesson revolver.

It was uncomfortable and awkward to hold after the little Beretta, but I was happy with it. I would get used to its weight and, after all, it would only be used once. I bought ammunition, too, and the young man cheerfully showed me how to load it. In case I forgot, I practiced in my motel rooms, each evening, on the long journey back to New York. And I wiped it down carefully with a bottle of disinfectant. After all, if you're going to put a gun in your mouth at short notice, you don't want to worry about germs. And who knew where it had been?

Chapter
Twenty-Five

I purposefully hadn't called Beth from Miami to find out how she'd liked *Scotty's Things*. Feeling very nervous, I wanted to wait and have a face-to-face conversation.

When I arrived back in New York I went immediately to Brambles Thorne. Beth was in a meeting, so I buried my head in the latest *Vogue* and tried not to mind. When she emerged, she looked flustered, gestured for me to follow her, and as we walked together towards her office, she took my arm. "We are *so* excited," she said. "I always knew you had it in you, but you've surprised even me. It's fantastic, Sal—it's just fantastic."

We walked past her office.

"Sally!" Sammy Thorne had appeared out of his own office, and was coming to greet me, to usher me in. "Welcome back. This is so wonderful, I can't tell you."

"You like what you've read so far?" Bemused, I turned from Sammy to Beth, who was closing the door behind us.

Before Beth could speak, "Yes!" Sammy almost yelled. "We've got to get to work. I'm looking at simultaneous publication. We'll blitz the market. What a coup! You little dark horse, you! You genius!"

And Sammy Thorne hugged me.

Over his shoulder I looked at Beth. She was smiling, but something in her smile made me cautious, as did Sammy's surprising, boyish enthusiasm. Over a little book of barely eighty thousand words, a leisurely paced novel that would in no way cause a ripple on the surface of New York's publishing pond?

One arm still draped around my shoulder, Sammy ushered me to a chair.

I couldn't have heard him right. "Simultaneous publication—with what?"

"Sally," Beth said quickly, *"Scotty's Things* is just such a wonderful book. When I finished it, when I could see where you were going with it, saw it as a *whole* . . . It's very exciting for me, Sal, to discover such a book. I gave it to Sammy and he agrees with me."

"That's wonderful!" The shock was passing, my elation was growing: all my work, all the pain I had put into the manuscript. And I'd succeeded! They liked it. They *loved* it!

"This could be one of the greatest—"

"Sammy, you said I could handle this." Almost curtly from Beth. To my amazement, Sammy lapsed into silence, like a little boy who'd been chastised.

Why?

Beth pulled a chair closer and sat down facing me with a smile. "We're rushing *Scotty's Things* into print, Sally. Pub date is twenty-eighth of May—"

"That's only . . . that's less than three months away!"

"Yes!" Sammy exploded into the conversation. "We've got to get to *work!* I've had a cover designed." He disappeared behind his desk, opening drawers. "It's only supposed to be a rough, but I'm really pleased with it, I think we might go with something like it—"

"Sally," I dragged my fascinated gaze back from the top of Sammy's head to Beth, who had moved her chair even closer to mine and was gazing at me very earnestly. "Sally, *Scotty's Things* is more than a good novel—more than a *brilliant* novel. It's accessible. It makes you *feel*. I haven't read anything like it for years. Sally, I know you only expected a small run of—"

"First print run will be five hundred thousand!" Sammy looked up to crow at me. "Lead title—well, co–lead title—and fine presentation. It'll be a collector's piece. National tour and—"

I stood and faced them. "What are you talking about? This is a little book! A simple little story—"

"So was *Jonathan Livingston Seagull*. So was *Love Story*. So was—" Sammy was cut off in mid catalogue by Beth.

"There's nothing wrong with these books being successful, Sally."

"No, I know. It's just . . . I just . . . I never saw *Scotty's Things* like that. I don't want it turned into another *Bridges of Madison County*."

"I was going to mention that next," Sammy said resentfully. He looked over at Beth. "You were right," he said. "I didn't believe you, but you were right." Back to me, and he tossed a cardboard rectangle into my lap. It was covered with tissue paper. I lifted it, and felt my heart stop. "I suppose you'll say you don't like that, either."

It was a small watercolor, and it was really quite beautiful. Two young people, naked, in a gold-and-mote-flooded attic, standing close, but not too close, the wonder of fresh passion evident in their bodies, their faces. It really was a lovely painting, misted, timeless. One could respond to it on several levels . . . And I caught myself up. I knew why it appealed to me. But I'd be damned if it would be used for the purpose Sammy had planned.

Naked people—no matter how beautiful the illustration—had no place on the cover of a book like *Scotty's Things*. But that was not the worst of it. In striving for a young, handsome, perfect specimen of manhood, the artist had, unwittingly perhaps, depicted Keir. The face was Keir's. And the girl . . . she had honey-brown hair and gray eyes, but the features were such that it could have been a young Erica Tudor—or myself, had I possessed at eighteen or nineteen those features that Keir had given me with his sculptor's hands.

"No," I said tightly, and my throat had closed. I spoke through rising tears. "No."

"It was an accident, Sally." Beth came to me, took my arm. "I only saw the illustration yesterday. It was a fluke— I rang the artist and he said he'd been given the basic descriptions by Sammy. He just used artistic license to create two beautiful young people."

I swallowed my tears and turned to Sammy. "You can't honestly expect to put this on the cover of my book!"

"How was I to know they'd end up looking like that? But it's a beautiful cover, don't you think? Tasteful, attractive . . ." he coaxed, trying to appear sympathetic to my feelings, but sales figures kept appearing behind his blue eyes like figures on a cash register.

"But there are no sex scenes in *Scotty's Things!*" I almost howled at him. "Deborah and Piers don't sleep together! That's the whole point—the *innocence* of all of them— Scotty, Piers, Deborah! The love between Piers and Deborah is real and it haunts their lives and when they meet again after all those years—"

"This is what I have to talk to you about." Sammy seated himself behind his desk and there was a subtle change. It was more than the distancing of himself behind the mahogany barrier, it was his ease in the way he leaned back slowly in the high-backed, leather-upholstered chair. He was suddenly serious. He was suddenly The Publisher.

"We have to have Piers and Deborah make love, Sally. The book needs it. It's crying out for more *intimacy.*" And before I could gather my thoughts, he went on, "I believe they should make love as teenagers, during that first summer at Greycliff—and in the later summers—during that long walk along the beach when they talk about Piers going to med school, and during that storm when they shelter in the lighthouse."

"No, it's all wrong, that's not what I was trying to—"

"Didn't you and Keir make love before you were married? Don't tell me you spent all those summers on the beach at Maine and—"

I felt a sudden rush of blood to my head. "What the hell do you—"

"Sally." Beth beside me, her voice calm, her expression willing me to be calm. "What Sammy is trying to say is that some physical expression of Piers and Deborah's love for each other would add depth to their characters, would add depth to the book."

"It's plenty deep enough," I defended grimly.

"We need to know that these are two *passionate* people. We need to *see* that passion," Sammy said.

"*Who* needs to see?"

Sammy said, coldly, "I don't need to tell you this, Sally. You're a pro. *The Reader* will want to see."

"I *am* a pro, Sammy. I've had twenty years in this business and I can tell you this. Just as it is, with no groping, no *smut*, this is a good book. And *The Reader* I wrote it for will agree with me."

There was a pause. Sammy shifted his weight a little on the throne and leaned his elbows on the arms. He said, "Then let's put it this way: *I* need to see it, Sally. If you agree, I can make this book a great success. I'm going to spend millions doing it. I'm going to give you two and a half million dollars for the privilege of seeing your name on the bestseller list. I am also, at this moment, waiting to hear back from every big gun in Hollywood on the film rights. You've got to trust my judgment on this, Sally. Do you trust me?"

Two and a half million dollars and *big guns in Hollywood* and *film rights* swept across my mind like so many dry leaves. "Trust you? Trust you? I should trust you, when you're sitting there effectively blackmailing me?"

"Sally." Panic in Beth's voice, but Sammy didn't change expression, not a muscle moved. We understood each other perfectly.

Beth was saying, "Sally, you're such a fine writer, you can do this—you can make it gentle, beautiful. You don't have to have details, just . . . an extension of their love for each other. Oh, you know how to do it! Doesn't she, Sammy?" Desperately turning to him, "Sammy? We can leave this with Sally, can't we? To think about? We know you'll do a great job, Sal, if you decide we're right—"

"She knows we're right," Sammy said, with a small smile, as if he had already won.

"I don't," I said through clenched teeth. "What I've written isn't the sort of book you want to publish. I'm not an Erica Tudor."

There was a funny silence, then Beth said, "Of course you're not! You're a much better writer than Erica ever could be!"

And there was that silence again.

Sammy said, "You could sell as many books as Erica Tudor, Sally. Fine, well-written books. Not crap. I'm a good publisher. I'd like to sell lots of finely written bestsellers." He leaned forward. "That's what I think you can do for us."

I stared at him, openmouthed. Then I turned to look at my wretched friend Beth, and back to Sammy again.

I managed, "You want to groom *me* to replace Erica Tudor?" Then, with dawning horror, "This other book you mentioned, that I'm sharing lead title with, come May twenty-eighth . . . It's *Catwalk*, isn't it? You've brought Erica's last book forward to be published with mine. You're crazy!"

"For God's sake, Sally!" Sammy stood, began perambulating around his office, as he does when he's very excited or distressed. "This is a marketing opportunity like no other! Erica is dead, she's killed herself, or she's been killed by your ex-husband. No, let me finish, please! You've written a book that's almost semiautobiographical. Can't you see how the general public will want to read both books and compare?"

"Semiautobiographical?" I almost shrieked. "Where did you get *that*?"

And I whirled suddenly on Beth, who was so startled by

my expression that she almost stepped back. "I didn't tell him anything, Sally. You know I wouldn't. It's the newspapers, the magazines. We've got a clipping service, remember. Keir Stanforth is very big news—"

"He's America's version of Lord Lucan—" Sammy began.

"Sally," Beth continued, more gently, her face full of pity, "everyone in the country knows all about Erica's background, and Keir's. And Keir's story is so close to yours, you met so young. Sammy's not alone, Sal. We can see you in Deborah, we can see Keir in Piers. And Piers's wife, Jennifer . . . it's Erica. It's all very sympathetically written—especially Jennifer's pregnancy and Piers's decision to go back to her . . . But it's *all there, Sal*. There's nothing wrong with it, all good writers draw on their own experience—"

I felt suddenly cold, and sick. Was it so obvious? I hadn't thought it was obvious at all. "Let's forget about this," I said.

"What?" Sammy stared at me.

"I've changed my mind. I don't want the book published."

It was like taking a toy from a child. Sammy's face worked a little, he looked at Beth, who was staring at me with a strange expression. "You're kidding, right?" Sammy said.

"Tell him I'm not kidding, Beth."

"He couldn't believe you'd feel this way. But I understand, Sally. You feel we're asking you to compromise your work—"

"We're asking you to accept two and a half million dollars and an international career—"

I said to Beth, "I will not make money out of Erica Tudor's death."

Sammy said, "Someone's going to."

"Shut up, Sammy," I snapped.

Sammy turned from me to Beth, and then back again, like one of those carnival clowns that you force-feed with ping-pong balls. I would have liked to force-feed Sammy Thorne with ping-pong balls.

He said to Beth, "You hear this? You hear what she said to me?" He turned to me. "We have already started on this project, Sally. My reputation and the reputation of this company are at stake—!"

"It's *my* book, Sammy!"

"In the eyes of New York and Hollywood it is *our* book, Sally!"

"Write your own fucking book! You become the next Erica Tudor!"

"Don't you fucking swear at me in my own office!"

"Sammy—" Beth began.

"Give me back my manuscript, Sammy."

"I'll go to court if I have to! All I'm asking is that the characters get intimate. Agree to that, and we can all be very happy. You, me, and Hollywood. Very happy."

I headed for the door.

Beth rushed across the room to hold the door before I could slam it. "Sally, all our plans, the promotion, the tour, might take you to England, Australia—"

Beth and I wrestled with the door. She finally got herself on my side of it and gained possession of it. I was halfway to the elevator when I heard, behind me, "I'm taking her to lunch, Sammy."

"We are not paying for it!" Sammy screamed. "This company will not buy lunches for a traitor who bites the hand that feeds it! *Do not pay for her lunch!*"

Over lunch, Beth talked. She talked and talked and didn't touch her food, while I said nothing and ate stolidly, crunching through a salad I didn't really want because with a full mouth I wouldn't be expected to pass comment. Beth didn't want comments anyway, she wanted acquiescence, and I couldn't give it to her.

At one stage, she said, "Me, personally, I love the book just as it is. Like you say, they were innocent, all of them—"

"They were innocent times," I told her, through a mouthful of lettuce and apple and walnut.

Beth went on, "I watched your face, back there in Sammy's office. You were horrified that people would see too much of your own life and Keir's in *Scotty's Things*. It just might be," she said with what looked like genuine unhappiness, pushing her baby tomatoes into a line and knocking them off the edge of a lettuce leaf like so many orderly lemmings, one by one, "that you're using Sammy's request as an excuse not to let go of the story. You feel too involved, too . . . exposed. Like many of the best novels, Sally, you wrote *Scotty's Things* mostly for yourself."

"And now it belongs to the world," I said, tartly.

But Beth didn't grimace, Beth didn't smile. She said, "Yes. Yes it does."

I think Beth was beginning to take my silence for agreement, or at least for consideration.

"Let me talk to Sammy," she said. "Once he's calmed down, he'll see that losing you as a writer isn't worth a couple of pages of interpolated sex, and tits on the dust jacket."

I was suddenly tired, tired of New York, tired of Beth's frightening professionalism, tired of her knowledge of me that enabled her to push all the right buttons.

"I'm going home to New Brunswick," I said.

I had planned on calling in to check on the apartment while I was in New York, but found I couldn't bear it, knowing now that it contained as much of Erica's presence as it had once contained my own. And Keir's things would still be there. I wasn't ready to face the poignancy of Keir's clothes, books, Keir's pajamas, Keir's toothbrush and aftershave—and no Keir.

I headed for Route 95, and home, stopping occasionally at small inns with views overlooking various stretches of the Atlantic. I was in no hurry to arrive back in St. Claude.

As soon as I arrived I'd be beset by calls from Sammy and Beth: *Had I decided yet? Had I?*

Had I?

It was a strange thing. I couldn't sleep, kept mulling over and over what Sammy had said, where he had suggested I place the scenes of Sexual Intimacy. He probably got it from Beth, he wasn't above purloining ideas from his staff and passing them off as his own. But I found he—or they— were right. The scenes on the beach would be wrong, but the lighthouse, it was unmanned, empty, cold. We moved closer together for warmth . . .

I was sitting up in bed, writing in my notebook. Writing the scene Sammy had wanted. The next day, driving north, I thought about it some more, and that night I wrote another scene. Piers and Deborah as adults, finding each other again.

It was good. It was really very good. Kind of funny, and kind of . . . innocent.

Finally here was my mailbox, the white-painted gate, my trees, my drive, the barn, and my little house, all wearing a covering of fresh, light snow, the air still, the day clear and blue, as if to welcome me home.

I'd expected to find Merlin at the house, but she'd left a note saying that I'd be tired and would undoubtedly like the place to myself, but I was to come to dinner at the farm that evening.

It was good to have the house empty, to explore it anew, reacquaint myself with the life I had created here, with New York still fresh in my mind.

No, I thought, walking through the rooms, I hadn't made a mistake that day I passed through St. Claude, without a past, without a future, and chose this house. No matter what I did with my life, write novels, or simply continue as a freelance editor, I wanted to be here.

My answering machine was full, calls from Eugene and

the Dufours, from Perry McGarret and from his mother, Janice, mentioning something about a ball to be held in three weeks' time in St. Claude. There were calls from all the Uncles and Aunts, impatiently wondering if I'd arrived back in Canada and why hadn't I phoned them to let them know I was safe?

I made my local calls first, and chatted with my friends, but Perry McGarret's phone didn't answer.

Then I rang The Aunts, and—as would be expected—it was nearly three hours later before I replaced the phone after the last call and was able to walk, in the fast-descending dusk, up the hill through fresh-powdery snow, to visit Erica's grave.

The scene was pristine, as undisturbed as if no one had set foot in this part of the forest for centuries. I stayed for a long time. And then I came back to the farmhouse and typed a copy of the two scenes I'd written. Was there too much of Keir and me in them? I didn't know. But writing them had brought him closer, for a little while.

I faxed the ten pages to Beth. An hour later she phoned, full of praise and enthusiasm. And Sammy had decided to compromise on the cover—"something to do with those tiny toy soldiers" would grace the cover of *Scotty's Things*.

Along with the check for the agreed amount for house-sitting, I gave Merlin and Natalie a gift I'd picked out for them in New York, a small bronze statue of a dog, dating from around 1850, and bearing an uncanny resemblance to their small terrier, Rat, down to the fatuous grin.

"I thought of buying you a piece of Lladro or Wedgwood, but ..." I looked up tellingly at the mantelpiece, bare except for two sleeping tortoiseshell cats, tails hanging over the edge and lolling in the warm updraft from the fireplace.

"Our days of possessing fine porcelain are long gone," Merlin laughed.

* * *

When I got home there was only one message on my machine.

"Hi. Sarah. Perry McGarret." A long pause. "Welcome home. Call me when you get a moment." Another pause. "G'bye Sarah."

I went to bed, but despite my exhaustion I didn't sleep well. I dreamt confused dreams of Seahaven, and Keir, waking with a nameless sense of loss to realize that the phone was ringing.

In the dark I stumbled out to the living room and picked up the receiver. There was no reply. I pleaded, I demanded, to know who it was, something I had never done before. Perhaps it was just the memory of Keir still so close to me, but I began to wonder if it wasn't Keir, out there, somewhere, unwilling—or unable?—to talk to me.

Or was someone tormenting me, phoning me only to torment me? Who would hate me that much?

The only person who had hated me that much was rotting in a grave in the middle of the forest.

I was heading down the slope towards the house when a flash of red caught my eye. Alby Gresson was just rounding the corner of the barn, laboring up the drive, also headed for the cottage.

I cut down the slope towards him. He paused on seeing me and waited, shoulders hunched in his red parka, slapping gloved hands together. I found myself thinking that his elderly bones would be happier beside a fire on cold days, but I wouldn't be the one who suggested such a thing to him.

"So you're back," he said, when I was within a short distance of him.

"Yes, yesterday. How are you, Mr. Gresson?"

"When are you going to call me Alby? Call me Alby."

I smiled, not knowing how to reply. I knew—just knew—

that I couldn't call the man by his first name. It was hard enough keeping him at a distance as it was.

"Were you coming to see me for a particular reason?" I asked.

He had been smiling, but it faded, slowly, in the silence after my words. When he spoke his voice was terse. "No," he said, "no particular reason."

His words hung in the air. I shuffled my feet a little. Why was it I felt so uncomfortable with this man? It wasn't that he said anything truly offensive, yet I always felt defensive, wary, always had to control the urge to move back, away from his intensity, a kind of silent demanding that was as palpable as a gnarled hand on my arm.

"Well . . ." I didn't know what to say. "What can I do for you, Mr. . . . Gresson?"

"You can't do anything for me. I only came to pay a call, like good neighbors do round these parts."

"Look," desperate to amend matters, even if it meant asking him in, I started to move towards the front porch. "Why don't we go into the house and have some coffee."

He followed behind me as I walked, but I doubt if he heard anything I'd said.

"You're trying to fit in here, I can see that, but you won't do it, I can tell you right now, miss. Not with that New York attitude of yours. 'What can I do for you?' Nothing! I don't want nothing from you! You should be asking what it is I can be doing for you! That's what you should be asking."

We were at the steps and I paused; I was suddenly loath to have him within the house. I had to make a conscious effort not to retreat a step.

"There is something I can do for you, Miss Smarty-pants New Yorker. There's something you want from me really bad."

He edged closer still and this time I did edge back until my heel struck the lower step and I faced him fully, glaring at him, daring him to make another move.

His voice low, as if someone might have been listening,

he said, "You'll want me to keep my mouth shut, that's what you'll want."

I had been expecting some horrid, clumsy sexual advance, and his actual words shocked me so much, terrified me so much in their implications, that I felt the blood leave my face.

"You've gone pale," he said, his handsome, narrow head cocked in sudden and sympathetic concern. "Let's go inside and sit down." He placed his hand on my arm in a gesture that was as confident as it was familiar. Repulsed, I quickly pulled away. And in that dangerous moment, as Alby's face contorted, I heard the car engine.

Overkill. That's what it was. I almost laughed, but there would have been hysteria in my laughter. Bright against the snow, the robin's-egg-blue and white of the police car nosed its way up the drive, and even from that distance I could see McGarret behind the wheel. Only McGarret. It was just after midday, he had probably, once again, left Peter Copely to have a solitary lunch in town.

Had McGarret seen Alby Gresson grab for me? At any rate, he wasn't smiling as he unfolded his considerable height from behind the wheel. He nodded to the old man, "Alby," and touched the brim of his hat to me. "Ma'am."

I nodded, "Sergeant."

Then the three of us stood there, McGarret leaning easily on the open door of the police car. I thought he'd say he had some news for me, or wanted to ask me further questions, but he just leaned there, the brim of his cap low over his eyes, and, it seemed to me, those eyes fixed on Alby.

In a growl, "I'd best be going," my neighbor said. "You two got things to talk about."

He moved off, passing McGarret with the car between them, heading for the shortest route past the barn and down the drive.

McGarret shut the car door, said to him, voice flat and meaningless, a formality, "Good to see you."

"Yeah," Alby Gresson muttered. "Be seeing you."

I watched McGarret walk towards me with some relief and even pleasure; his presence strong enough, welcome enough to make me able to push Alby's words to the back of my mind.

We didn't move inside straightaway; I wanted to see Alby Gresson disappear down the drive. I glanced at McGarret but he didn't appear to be in any hurry, stood quite close to me, but not too close, hands resting easily on his hips, eyes on the expanse of pristine field that sloped away down to the trees. A dark shadow and a low roar testified to a truck going past, heading towards town, barely discernible through the trunks and branches of the trees, leafless though they still were.

I had to lean forward slightly, peering around McGarret's sizable bulk, to check on Alby's progress down the drive.

But Alby had made very little progress. He was, in fact, staring into the backseat of the police car, and even as I looked, he began to swear.

He looked up at us, then, his face a mask of undisguised fury, and still the obscenities streamed forth in a low, congested voice that nevertheless carried quite clearly to where McGarret and I stood.

Or where I stood, for McGarret was already walking towards the older man, and it was only then, watching Gresson face McGarret directly and raise his voice, that I realized that the torrent of foul language—vile, obscene, indiscriminate in its use of sexual terms—was being flung not at me but at McGarret.

The big cop moved forward, quickly. I held my breath. McGarret stopped in front of Alby and said calmly, "Don't ever, ever talk like that outside your own house, Mr. Gresson. Or despite your age and what you did for Canada during the war, I'll haul your ass in front of a magistrate so fast you'll be winded. Do we understand each other, sir?"

Alby backed away, but the look on his face wasn't fear

or even nervousness. He said, "You're a fool, boy. You don't know what you're getting into."

I didn't wait to see Alby leave, didn't wait for McGarret to move, but walked away myself. Not towards the house, I didn't want to leave the daylight for the darkened rooms of the cottage, knowing McGarret would follow. I walked instead the short distance to the gate that led to the field before the house, and leaned there, the snow chilling my arms through my jacket sleeves, my mind already chilled.

Gresson was mad. That was it, he was mad.

Wasn't he?

He had nearly said something to the police sergeant. What?

You're a fool, boy. You don't know what you're getting yourself into.

You'll want me to keep my mouth shut, that's what you'll want.

I heard the squeak of snow beneath McGarret's boots and turned towards the sound, my head still down, unable, unwilling to lift it, in case I saw questions in the dark blue eyes. I felt the top of my head graze his chest, saw the boots, the dark trousers, the gun belt, and closed my eyes. Through his jacket the top of my head gradually warmed. I felt his hands on either side of my parka hood, felt them close on either side of my face, and stepped back, stepped away. But not before I'd noted the smell of his aftershave, the faint fresh odor of his sweat, and puzzled at the fact that I found them comforting, that I wanted to stay there, smelling the smell of him, feeling the warmth of him, hearing his breath come faster, more shallow, the longer I stood there against him.

"Thank you," I turned to say to him. I thought we were walking almost side by side but he was gone from beside me, had his back to me, heading for the rear car door, opening it and taking out a dozen dark red roses.

This was what Alby Gresson had seen as he'd passed the car, what had stopped him in his tracks, provoked the stream of abuse.

I began to be frightened. Alby Gresson was obviously

not only a disturbed man, he was becoming dangerously obsessed.

I must have been looking at the roses with something like horror, still deep in my own tangled thoughts. Finally, I looked up at McGarret. If he was disappointed at my lack of pleasure in his gift, he didn't show it, but simply twirled the cellophane-wrapped stalks in his hand like a tennis pro would a racket and headed for the porch. With his other hand, he took my arm in a gentle, possessive, unbreakable grip and ushered me into the house.

As if I were being arrested, I thought.

You'll want me to keep my mouth shut, that's what you'll want.

You're a fool, McGarret. You don't know what you're getting into.

Chapter
Twenty-Six

McGarret couldn't know how shaken I was, nor could he know the cause of it, but he was wise enough not to present me with the flowers. He placed them, instead, on the hall table beside the phone and then pretended they didn't exist. "Welcome home," he said, meeting my gaze and holding it. "Was Alby Gresson one of the reasons you lit out of here so abruptly? I know it was partly me, but I'd kinda like to think I didn't scare you all that much."

I went to the roses and took them up, burying my face in the blooms to cover my confusion while I tried to frame a reply.

"You don't scare me," I lied, looking up from the flowers with what I hoped was a smile. "And Alby . . . well, he's just Alby, isn't he?"

"Quite a few folk are saying he's more than just tetchy," he said. "Remember, I had to take his gun down there on your fence line few months back. Alby's in cahoots with at least two of the magistrates, and he got it back." He finished with a scowl, then added, "Any trouble from him, you let me know, hear?"

"Yes. I will. But I'm sure he'll be fine. I hardly ever see him. He keeps to himself, mostly."

McGarret gave another of his half nods, and there was a silence.

"Well, I expect you're in your lunch hour, or I'd ask you to stay. For coffee. Or lunch. But. So . . ."

Nothing. I mean *nothing*.

I'd just come from a couple of weeks of real exchanges with real people; enthusiastic, self-opinionated New Yorkers who talked over the top of each other in the good-natured belief that if you had the courage of your convictions you'd speak louder.

I'd forgotten this aspect of McGarret, that he could at times be a kind of . . . walking, conversational black hole.

He took his hat off his head in one movement, and with a flick of his wrist it went spinning like a Frisbee into a corner of the settee. He didn't follow it with his eyes. His eyes were on me. "Sarah, we have to talk."

I snuffled at the roses. "These are so lovely I'd like to put them in water right away."

"We have to—"

"Of course. Talk. Of course we'll talk. But I'll just put these in water." And I sailed into the kitchen before he could object further.

I was braced for the sound of his booted feet following me down the hall, but they didn't. Alone, relieved, I dropped the roses onto the table and leaned upon it, my hands grasping the table's edge and trying to cope with scary—but *scary*—emotions.

I like him. I really like him.

You're attracted to him. He's big and kind and male and here—and Keir isn't.

I could keep him as a friend—everyone needs friends, a friend is okay.

Oh yeah? A cop? As a friend? People with bodies buried in their backyards don't have cops for friends.

"Need any help in there?" From the living room.

"No, I'm fine!" I ran about putting coffee on, thrusting the roses willy-nilly into a vase.

Get rid of him, Sarah.

In the living room, McGarret had begun to toy with the sound system. I heard music, an introduction that was unfamiliar, maybe it was the radio . . .

He's too much at home here, too much at home.

And I recognized the music, now. He'd rifled through my CDs and found Johnny Mathis—it had only been played once, at my birthday twelve years ago, when Uncle Ira, who was a rabbi, had given it to me.

We've only just begun . . . to live . . .

I didn't know how to handle McGarret; I only knew I was doing it badly. I was obviously giving him the wrong messages, somehow. But were they wrong? I had come to like him and respect him. And more, somewhere through the long months I'd come to see the subtle shifts of emotions on that face, even to look for the smile that deepened the lines about his mouth, the changing expressions in the shadows of his eyes. I'd begun to wait, to hope, for the laughter that I sensed, but never heard, in the deep voice.

But he's a police officer. A *police officer*.

From the CD player in the living room, Johnny Mathis was crooning "A Certain Smile."

Shut up.

I carried coffee and cookies back into the living room. He was standing at the window, taking up most of the light. His eyes on the view of the fields, he was lost in thought; I didn't want to walk into any scene he was playing in his head.

"Coffee's ready," I told him, and he turned and looked at me, and at the coffee on the table, but didn't move forward.

What scene was he playing, there at the window? From that window one had a view of a corner of the barn: was he thinking of Erica? Did he suspect something?

Stop it.

"I was away longer than I expected to be . . . in New York. We've been discussing the book I've written."

He moved forward, looking at me.

"And . . . it's. . ."

He bent to the table and picked up his coffee, then stood and moved across the room once more. To my relief. I found I could speak more clearly, think more clearly, when he was at a distance.

"So you're going to be a writer," he said. "Like Erica Tudor."

"No! Well, yes, but—" and I found myself saying, "They think the novel's going to be a great success, it'll make my reputation. . . . But they want changes I don't agree with. I have to go along with them."

He hadn't moved, not even one tiny muscle around his eyes, fixed on me with their usual bland inscrutability, but a wave of disapproval came from his big frame, and I stood braced for the words that would follow.

I sat down on the settee and stalled for time by reaching out for my coffee.

"How can you write well if you don't believe in what you're doing?" he asked.

And he doesn't know the half of it. What does this say about me, about what I've become?

"You don't understand the world of publishing," I informed him coolly.

"No." He drawled out the word, not at all put out. "But I understand you."

I found I'd stopped breathing. "You can't," I whispered.

But he could. We were friends. From that inauspicious beginning five months ago, when I'd run the Volvo into the back of his Jeep, we had grown closer. Even avoiding his voiced feelings for me, I couldn't deny that we had become friends. Close friends.

One can dismiss a lover, even a potential lover. But how do you dismiss a friend? So I felt driven to say, "I'll have to travel back and forth to New York a lot from now on. And I'll be really tied up with the writing for the next six months, plus my editing work. It'll keep me busy." I petered out.

He had seated himself during this, on the broad arm of one of the settees, sideways, one booted foot crossed over the other. He watched me quietly and I knew he was waiting with another polite phrase, until I had talked myself out.

So I shut up. And waited. I could be silent, too. For perhaps it had been my very defenses, my I-can-chatter-away-to-you-because-we're-just-good-friends, that had given him the wrong impression of my feelings, made him warm towards me more than he should have. I didn't chatter to Alby Gresson, did I?

"Sarah," he said, "what are you trying to do?"

Well, how do you answer *that*? I didn't.

"Are you attempting to inform me," he said helpfully, "that you don't want to see me again?"

"No!"

Yes!

"No," I repeated, "no, but . . ."

Yes, you idiot!

"Well, yes. In a way. It's just that I'll be really busy."

Don't prevaricate! Don't quibble! *He's a policeman.*

The volume of the sound system was too loud. How come I hadn't noticed before how loud it was? Johnny was singing about walking hand in hand by the sea.

McGarret sat quite comfortably, his booted foot swinging a little in time to Johnny's eulogizing, *"And I say to myself, it's wonderful, wonderful . . ."*

McGarret spoke easily, "When I ran away from home I kicked around a lot—experienced a lot. Done just about everything a man could do and still call himself a man. In all those years I've known a lot of women, Sarah, but you got me beat. Help me."

"It's wonderful, wonderful!" Johnny sang ecstatically, *"Oh, so wonderful . . ."*

Help him.

"Exactly what do you mean by that? How do you want me to help you?"

"Help me," he said gently, "understand what you're doing. Why you're running."

His words have nothing to do with Erica. He can't possibly suspect anything about Erica . . .

But his words made *me* think about Erica, and when I retorted, "Running from what?" my throat was constricted with my sudden fear.

"From me." Quietly. "Because of what's happening between us."

"Nothing is happening, Perry, Nothing *can* happen."

"Why?" came the deep voice.

"Because." Irritable in my desperation, my fear, my lies. "Because I don't feel . . . that way . . . towards you. I can't feel that way anymore."

He said, "I don't think that's the truth."

I said, trying to keep my tone cool, "You're my friend, I couldn't—" *Uh, no?* "I wouldn't," I amended, "like lying to you."

He stood up, and such was my nervous state that I started a little. He didn't see, having moved across the room to switch on a lamp. My face must have been lost in shadows, there by the fireplace, and he wanted to see me, see my face.

From affection, from caring?

This is what they do to suspects. One day, it will be just like this, in some gray room with a table and two chairs, at St. Claude Police Station. And someone—not McGarret, please God, not McGarret—will be scanning my face. And not from affection, not from caring.

"It's getting late," I said pointedly. "You could have scoffed the contents of an entire McDonald's outlet by now. Shouldn't you be back on duty?"

He stood still suddenly, aware that I was right, but awkwardly determined to finish what he had to say. "I heard the message on the tape you gave to Gerlain."

Was he psychic? And how dare he? *He* was just a provincial sergeant in a small Canadian town, he had no right to listen to that tape, to Keir's voice, to Keir's pain. "Where is my tape? I want it back if New York has finished with it."

"They have. It's back at the station. I forgot it, I'll bring it out next time."

Next time? *Next time?*

And he went on, still in that low, patient voice, he who had listened to Keir's tape along with Raoul Gerlain and Peter Copely and who knew how many other cops, with emotions ranging from amused to dispassionate.

"Keir might have been phoning you that night as a friend. You've known each other twenty years. It was a good divorce, as divorces go. Amicable. Sometimes ex-husbands and wives can be real friends to each other. That doesn't mean they'll get back together again. Usually they don't. What's dead is dead."

"Perhaps," I said, hearing my voice wavering in my efforts to keep it controlled. "I'll keep all that in mind. Thank you for your concern."

"Oh, honey!" Again I started, but his abrupt movement took him past me, to the mantelpiece, where he leaned, his back to me, his big hands made into fists. I could hear him breathing from where I sat on the settee, nervous as a prairie dog, on the tips of my haunches, ready for flight.

What could I do, what words were safe, guaranteed not to provoke another outburst? I had never seen Perry McGarret angry, and I never wanted to. So I merely watched him, and waited. The broad shoulders were bent forward a little, and as my fear and anger gradually dissipated, I felt a growing pity for the man. No, it was more than pity. He was my friend, and I was hurting him.

"I'm sorry," I said, and meant it. "I'm very fond of you, you know. I never wanted to hurt you." I took a deep breath, bracing myself to be honest with him. "You're right. It is Keir. I still believe he loves me."

I stopped, apprehensive, seeing the shoulders tighten a little, the big head come up, but he didn't turn. And I thought, there is more than one lie here. I don't believe Keir loves me. He couldn't. I hurried on, "I can't . . . form any relationship with you, or anybody, until I know for sure that . . . that there's no hope for Keir and me."

He turned abruptly. "And what if he's dead, Sarah?"

"Stop it," I said.

"No, I won't." And as I moved a little, "I'll leave here soon, but not before I make you face this. There's been no sign of him. Do you realize how hard it is for someone to drop out of sight like that? Especially a man with a career and commitments like Keir has. He hasn't used any credit cards, hasn't called you or your parents or *anyone* since the quarrel with Erica."

"What quar—"

"Ah, come on, now! You know they quarreled! They were always quarreling! And the blood in the bathroom, Sarah. Either they tried to kill themselves or each other."

He paused, then said, "She had a lot of money, Erica. There's this possibility, too—that she might have had him killed."

My wrist dropped a little, coffee plopped onto the rug. Carefully, very carefully, I leaned forward and placed the mug on the low table before me.

McGarret continued, "That's pretty far out, maybe, but the boys in Missing Persons are thinking more and more that it's a possibility. There's been nothing heard from Keir after his phone call to you."

"Why should she kill Keir? *Why?*"

He watched me, pained. "Because she loved him. Or . . . what passes for love in a disturbed mind."

I looked up, sharply, but didn't dare speak. So the police—this policeman, anyway—believed Erica to be mentally disturbed. And why not? She'd killed herself, hadn't she?

The look on McGarret's face was one of deep pity. "Sarah. Honey. Whatever happened, he's gone. You got to let go."

"I can't." I must have looked wide-eyed, staring, for he was suddenly moving towards me, concern on his face. "Stay where you are!" I yelled at him.

He stayed. And after a moment's consideration, he said, "That's it, isn't it? You don't dare let me close."

He was right. That's what it came down to. Not for the reasons he thought, but what did it matter, when all was said and done?

And I liked to have him close, that was the sad part. Out there by the pasture gate, as Alby had retreated down the drive, close to McGarret, I'd felt a sense of comfort in his closeness. Thinking of it now, I felt my throat constrict, my eyes burn. "It doesn't . . ." I tried again, "I don't . . . Oh, *please*. You don't understand!"

And I had to look up at this. He waited for me to look up at him. He was still standing by the fireplace, but facing me fully now.

"You're wrong," I breathed, reading his gaze, panic rising even higher. "I'm sorry if I've led you on."

"Sarah, you haven't led me on." A touch of exasperation in the voice. "It's just *happening*."

I shook my head. "You're wrong, McGarret. You're wrong."

"You think that's so? Honey, if I came over there and took you in my arms and kissed you, you'd be telling me with everything within you that I was right."

I said coldly, "You'd be wrong."

"I don't think so." His voice heavy, thick with emotion suddenly.

A second's desperation, then I stood and backed away to a clear space in the center of the room. "Okay," I defied him, making a pantomime of rolling up my sleeves. "Okay, what have I got to lose except a kiss? Come on, I'm ready for you! You want a kiss—I'll give you a kiss."

And he was smiling at me, and I started to smile in return, for the man had a smile that could break your heart, and something happened to mine, in that moment, looking at him.

"And after the kiss, when I've proved my point," I continued without pause, "I want you to leave. I want you to leave and not to come back. Understand?"

Slowly the smile left his face, and it was almost worse to see that happen, and I hated him for it.

And he said, "One kiss ain't worth that." And I saw that the smile hadn't quite left his eyes.

There was a silence. We were across the room from each other.

"Some quiet evening, I sit by your side and we're lost in a world of our own . . ."

Over Johnny's rhapsodizing, McGarret said, "Don't take too long, Sarah."

"Don't wait, McGarret. It's not—"

"That's up to me—"

"It's not worth it. I'm not worth it."

"You are to me."

Moving at the same time to fetch his cap from the settee, he said, "I'm a pretty good judge of character, Sarah. Although," and he paused to look at me with his large head to one side a little, the gaze critical, "if someone had told me a year ago that I'd fall for a sassy, smart-mouthed, city woman with a chip on her shoulder and big eyes that give everything away . . ."

We were very close. I gazed at him and hoped he was wrong, *wrong*.

I followed him to the door. He opened it, pulled his cap on, squinted out at the white glare on the snow, and sighed a little. It was obvious he didn't want to leave.

"Wonderful, wonderful!" sang Johnny behind us.

"G'bye, Sarah," McGarret said, and stepped through the doorway.

"Goodbye," I murmured, and was about to shut the door when he stepped back.

He said, "One of the things I admire about you, one of the things that made me fall in love with you, is this real stubborn attachment that you have to Keir. I admire it, even while I recognize it as wrong thinking."

And before I could speak, his tone sobered: "I hope to God he's alive, Sarah. I pray to God he is. Because in the middle of all this pain you've been going through since

he left you, the one thing that's kept you going is the
thought of him being out there, somewhere. You've been
holding onto the thought of him, of what you had together,
like it was a life-jacket holding your head above water. If
he *is* out there, honey, he's got a whole lotta problems of
his own. He can't help you. No one can ... though I'd
like to try."

"Thank you," I murmured, looking at his chest at eye
level, not wanting to meet his gaze, to see what was in his
eyes.

And his voice hardened then, the words forced out of
him. "And I got my own reasons, too. I want to ask him
what the hell he meant, putting you through all this. I
want to hear his answers—if he has any. So don't you
worry, I want Keir alive. I can't fight him if he's dead. I
can't fight a ghost."

He left me then, and I shut the door behind him.

Inside the house, Johnny was asking me What I Was
Doing for the Rest of My Life?

Early in the morning, there was a knocking at the door.

But it wasn't McGarret. It was Keir.

He wore a dark suit, the sort of suit he always wore to
the office. He looked as handsome, as impeccable as ever,
unruffled by the long trip. But what had I expected, I
wondered, as I flung myself into his arms with a cry. Some
change, something ...

But he was the same, his arms around me the same, the
scent of him the same, his lips against my ear, my cheek,
upon my lips, drawing forth the old, warm familiar
response. It had been so long. So long.

"Where were you? Where have you been? Oh, Keir."

"I had to sort myself out. I was in Africa when I heard
about Erica. I couldn't bring myself to come home. I've
been in Rwanda, working in a clinic. Oh, Sally."

At that moment, Merlin and Natalie's dogs appeared

around the side of the house, growling. I moved towards them, telling them to stay, to be quiet.

They were growling in enjoyment, in play. They were having a tug-of-war with a ragged gray coat. I watched as they flew back and forth across the lawn. But it wasn't a coat, it was Erica's limp, rotting body they held between them, shaking it, dragging it about.

No!

No!

I woke, screaming *NO* over and over again.

Night. I was sitting up in my bed in my darkened bedroom, not at the door, facing Keir and the horror. Here in the safety of my little four-poster bed, feeling very alone, I lay down once more and listened to the silence.

This isn't the way I planned to end my life. I had always believed I would grow old with Keir in our New York apartment.

How did it happen, Keir? I asked, the dream of him, the scent, the feel of him still so close. *How did this happen to me? And what has happened to you?*

I woke to the morning sun glowing dimly through the drawn blind.

The dreams disturbed my thoughts for most of that morning. I went for a walk after breakfast, up into the hills, and I paused by Erica's grave, as usual. My dream last night had been born of my own guilt and fear. No dog would have any interest in Erica's resting place. I had buried her too deep, it had been too long.

But for me she would never be buried deep enough.

The phone was ringing, and it was very late at night.

I didn't think of the silent caller. It had been a long time since I had been summoned to the phone to hear his—or her—waiting presence at the other end of the line. Not since a week or so before I had set out for New York.

"Hello," I said.

And no one answered.

And only then did I think of Keir. Only then did I think, *Who is doing this to me?*

"Why are you doing this to me!" I fairly yelled into the phone. "You gutless bastard!"

Nothing.

I waited, the caller waited.

"Who is this?" I asked finally.

A sound. Some kind of breath, or sigh. But it was too short—and the caller replaced the receiver.

Chapter
Twenty-Seven

Something was moving, out there in the dark outside my bedroom window.

I'd woken, suddenly, without knowing why, lay in the silence for a moment, then picked up my bedside clock. It read 3:25.

I heard it, then, the crunch of a pebble underfoot.

And again.

Someone was out there.

Bears? I thought hopefully. Ever since I had arrived up here I'd wanted to ask a local about the danger of bears, but I knew they'd either laugh at me outright or tease me to the point where I'd be afraid to go out my front door in case I became a takeout snack for a passing grizzly.

No, this was danger from a two-legged predator.

I lay there, my heart thumping, and avoided action. Action meant rising, confronting this intruder in some way. I didn't want a confrontation, I just wanted to be mistaken.

Skrt. A pebble ground against another, ground together beneath a certain weight. No raccoon made that noise.

Out of bed reluctantly, I crept to the side of the window

and pulled the edge of the blind away, just a little, from the window trim.

Nothing but darkness. The shadows of the trees—my bedroom faced the back of the house—were lost, mingled with the black expanse of lawn. It was like pulling back a curtain to find a blackout blind behind it. A flat darkness, without form.

But it did have form, didn't it? For there was the faint ground-pebble sound once more, off to one side. I'd have to go to the next room, the spare bedroom, to peer out the window.

And what would I see?

More darkness. A different view of darkness. I moved silently along the hall to the kitchen.

The wide flagstones of the kitchen floor were cold on my bare feet. I moved to the back door, took a deep breath, and quickly, quietly, opened it.

In that moment I remembered the gun.

I hadn't seen it since I'd pushed it to the back of a drawer in the study. I hadn't looked at it since, it wasn't even loaded. I'd purchased it to kill myself, not someone else. I never considered it in terms of hurting someone else.

This is what guns are for, Sarah. Guns are for just such moments as this.

I stood in my nightdress in the open doorway, dithering. There was nothing but silence and darkness out there. I moved back inside, closed and locked the door.

For the rest of the night I lay awake with the gun on the bedside table beside me.

Later that night, it began to rain. I remembered, then, that the weather reports had predicted days of heavy rain. I lay in bed, listening to the increasingly heavy deluge, and thought of the tracks that might now be washed away.

In the morning I walked around the house in the sleety rain. I found one spot where the leaf litter on the forest floor had been disturbed, and a few twigs had been broken off the lower bushes. That was all.

I went back to the house. On the way I wondered whether I should have notified the police. But the answer was still the same. I didn't want the police nosing about up here on the slopes.

And I didn't want McGarret to think that there was further trouble from Alby Gresson. It might not have been Alby. And McGarret, if he knew about last night, would feel he should go talk to the man. I wanted to get to the bottom of matters myself, I didn't want McGarret asking the questions.

Alby had answers. The wrong answers, but in a rage, to hurt me, to hurt McGarret, he might give these answers anyway.

No; the police, whether McGarret, Copely, or Gerlain, should be kept as far away as possible from this farm— and Alby Gresson.

I came into the house from the front porch. As I walked up the front steps, something white caught my eye, beside a flowerpot of spindly, frostbitten geraniums near the door. I hadn't noticed it earlier. How long had it been here?

The pot was not a heavy one, and had been lifted and placed upon the envelope to hold it down. It was a white self-sealed envelope, one that could be purchased any-where.

I tore it open. On a single piece of cheap, lined writing paper was written,

Murderess. I saw what you did. Murderess.

It must have been placed there last night. The old man, burning with his precious hatred, smarting at the way McGarret had humiliated him, had struck back as best he could, at the only person he knew who was in a worse— and weaker—situation than himself.

We'll see about that.

I drove too fast and swung too wide on the last curve of the drive, the back wheels spinning out, so for a moment I thought I was going to crash into the fence. But I gained purchase again and slowed, shaken, leaving the white-painted gate with its copper nameplate at a demure pace.

I had never been to Alby Gresson's home and was surprised and disturbed at how close the actual farmhouse was to mine. Out of sight, yes, but five minutes by road and less than that on foot through the woods, if one was fit.

Two men were working on a tractor in an open shed as I drove up. One was Alby's build, with dark hair grown long on one side and brushed greasily over to the other to cover the bald head. The other was stockier, with a belly that strained at the waist of his overalls, but he was not much taller. Both had Alby's looks, the small even features that could be called good-looking but for the intangible *something:* the expression in the eyes, or the movements of the mouth, or the ducking, sideways motion of the head as if in a primal gesture of looking for the best opening to attack.

Neither of them gave me any welcome, and I ignored them, parking the car and climbing out to run up the steps to the house.

Alby took some time before he opened the door, and I was surprised to see him still in his pajamas and dressing gown. It put me off my stride a little.

"Been sick?" I said to his surprised face. "Caught another chill while out walking in the woods?"

His face closed, yet he stood back to usher me in to what I could see was a pleasant and scrupulously clean living room. "Come in."

I held out the page of the letter to him. He had to pull back a little to focus on it. "You were creeping around my house last night to put this under the front door, but it's draft-proof, so you left it on the porch."

He was silent.

"If you've got anything to say to me, say it to my face—or say it in court."

"Clear enough, what it says there," he said. "I know what I know."

"So you admit you wrote this."

"Maybe I did, maybe I didn't. Maybe there's someone else who knows what you did. Maybe there's someone else that seen you swing that ax."

I felt myself pale. I'd have liked to sit down. But I didn't dare give in, didn't dare show any sign of weakness. "You're insane."

"You want to talk business, come inside." He stood back once more.

I didn't move. I wanted an unimpeded route of escape, back to the car.

"You'd better have proof of your allegations," I said, "or you'll be the one to go to jail. There's jail terms for perjury and defamation, not to mention harassment. Sergeant McGarret has already had to warn you about that. You try to bring a trumped-up criminal charge against me and everyone will know it's from spite, because I wouldn't accept your advances."

"My advances." He was remarkably calm. "I gotta admire you. You got more gumption than any woman I've ever known. But I'm equal to you. All I've got to do is get them to dig up that barn of yours. Then we'll see about proof."

"You'll find *nothing*." I don't think my expression changed, but he could sense something, sensed my sudden confidence, and wasn't pleased. "You'll look a complete fool."

"Maybe. I saw what I saw. The police are bound to investigate. That big boyfriend of yours—dumb as a post, he is, but he'll have to take me seriously. I'll have 'em dig up your entire farm. They'll find something, sooner or later."

"Maybe they'll find something on *your* land."

His eyes widened slowly, then narrowed abruptly. He shifted from one foot to another, just slightly, just enough for me to realize that this thought worried him.

"And I'll tell you something else," I pressed home my advantage. "If there was a crime committed by someone—

anyone—months ago, and you saw it, and said nothing, you're an accessory after the fact. That means jail. And blackmailing someone—that means even longer in jail."

He didn't move. Even the cunning, the malevolence in his face was gone. The features, for once, were still.

I turned and went down the porch steps into the yard. The two men, his sons, had moved across from the shed and the tractor. Not close enough to hear our conversation, which had been conducted in low, almost conspiratorial tones, but close enough to sense that it was a hostile confrontation.

I opened the door of the car.

"And stay off my land," I threatened, turning back to Alby, "day *and* night."

The two sons looked at each other and at their father, then at me with what seemed to be sudden understanding. I wondered, as I started the car and drove past their still, silent, hostile figures, what he had told them.

Would my threats be enough? I asked myself, driving home. The rain had paused, but now began to fall once more; sullen, heavy drops on the roof, the windshield.

I turned on the radio and further storm warnings, even flood warnings, were predicted. Good. This would be one night when I wouldn't be receiving any unwelcome visitors.

He arrived the following afternoon, after another night during which the lightning and thunder played across the earth and sky. The morning was little better, settling down, if it could be called that, to rain of almost tropical intensity, the hills, the fields, even the garage and barn obliterated by torrents that turned my drive into a river. I needed more firewood and was there, at the woodbox, in a rusty-looking old slicker and sou'wester of Otto Hahn's, the hat pulled low over my eyes, when McGarret drove up in the Jeep.

He was in uniform, but looked even wetter than me. So much so that he was able to saunter almost casually over to me, rain running down his face, dripping off his clothes. His police-issue boots squelched noisily. "Afternoon," he said, and touched the brim of his cap. It made a small river of rain that leapt off the brim and ran down his sleeve.

"Come inside," I grinned, as he tried to flick it away. He took the wood from me.

"Where've you been?" I asked as we sloshed our way back to the house, unhurriedly, blinking at each other in an effort to avoid the stinging drops flung at our faces by the wind.

"Directing traffic," he said. "The bridge is out, the one 'bout ten miles upriver of town. And Spring Mill Creek, and a few others. Been out there waving my arms around and arguing with motorists half the night and all day."

He paused politely at the front door, looking down at his wet clothes and boots. "You can't be wetter than me," I pointed out.

I lit the fire for extra warmth, turned up the heating a little, and helped him out of his coat.

I didn't remove my own rain gear, not straightaway, for I remembered that I hadn't brushed my hair; in fact, I hadn't brushed my teeth that day. I had also been drinking too many cups of coffee again, and brooding about what Alby Gresson would do next.

"Excuse me," I said, and stomped wetly down the hall. I brushed my teeth, washed my face, and put on some mascara. I left the sou'wester and oilskin coat hanging over the railing and changed my sweatshirt—paint-spattered and stretched almost out of shape, but a favorite for working in—for a lambswool sweater. I dragged a comb through my hair, then returned to the living room.

McGarret had made coffee. Two steaming mugs stood on the coffee table before the fire. I glared at them resentfully.

He was seated on the edge of one of the settees, apparently so that the lower, soggy legs of his uniform trousers wouldn't wet the settee. "I'm stuck," he said, wryly.

"Oh?" I said, wondering what the hell he meant.

"Spring Mill Creek being out and all. I can't get home. I'll spend the night at Merlin's."

"But you didn't go to Merlin's."

"No."

"You came here."

"Came here first," he said, stolidly. "Heard that Jimmy Gresson told folks in town you drove to his place and threatened his father."

Oh great.

I looked at him. He was calmly sipping at his coffee, but that didn't fool me a bit.

"Someone was prowling outside two nights ago."

He put his cup on the table, then he stood and all pretense was cast aside. "Why didn't you phone me, Sarah? After what happened—"

"There was no need to panic."

"You should have called me."

"I can handle myself." And this was such a *dumb* lie in the circumstances that McGarret stared at me with his mouth open long enough for me to change the subject.

"Look, you'll catch your death, don't you think—" I was going to say, *Don't you think you ought to be heading for Merlin's?* But he looked so big and wet and miserable and concerned I found I could forget about him being mad. After all, he'd called in here to check on me, despite his discomfort and exhaustion after a double shift. Outside the rain had settled in like a wet sponge around the house.

"Don't you think you ought to take those wet boots off? Come to think of it, would you think I was after your honor if I offered to loan you a bathrobe?"

"I'd hoped you would. And no, I don't suspect you of being after my honor. But I don't think you'll have a robe that'd fit me."

"I've got one of Keir's," meeting his gaze. "His shoulders were pretty broad."

This wasn't true, but Keir—and I—always liked oversized bathrobes. This one was new, it had hardly been worn. I had bought it on impulse in St. Claude several months ago; because I was sure Keir would come, one day, and I wanted him to feel at home, wanted him to know that I had expected him.

I gestured for McGarret to follow me, and I fetched the robe, along with fresh towels from the hall closet, and led him to the bathroom.

"All the soap and talc is Giorgio," I explained, gathering up the oilskins from the shower curtain railing. "I mean, not the masculine Giorgio, the feminine one. I mean," it was a very small room indeed when shared with a large policeman, "you'll be smelling of perfume rather than aftershave."

"I can live with that."

He smiled at me. I backed out and closed the door on him. Another imprint I didn't need, McGarret in the middle of my peach-and-white bathroom, unbuttoning a pale blue shirt stained dark by rain that had run down his collar and halfway down his chest.

I made fresh coffee and carried it into the living room. I was just putting the tray down when a soft *thrummm* sound came from the back of the house: the clothes drier.

"Hi."

I jumped.

He was padding towards me from the hall in the white bathrobe, upon large bare feet; I tried not to look at him. Even my Giorgio smelt different on him. I caught the scent of it as he moved past me to reach his coffee, seated himself on the opposite settee.

Looking like a stranger in the fluffy white robe, McGarret smiled at me.

At least he hasn't come to arrest me. Not today.

When he does, when he comes, you'll see it in his eyes. You know him too well, now. You'll see it in his eyes, when he knows the truth about you.

"Why didn't you phone me when the prowler came, Sarah?"

I squirmed a little. "I scared him off. Look I . . ." And I said his name, to soften my words, "Perry, I can't depend on you."

An infinitesimal, tight pause, then, in his normal tone, "I'm not asking you to depend on me. I'm asking you to depend on the police force. I'm asking you to depend on the law.''

I tried to swallow, and couldn't.

The room was in shadow, the only light came dimly through the windows and more brightly from the fireplace. I reached out and turned on a lamp. The shade was an apricot-pink and it spread a warm glow on the room.

I looked back at McGarret and felt a little more at ease. He was less threatening in the soft terrycloth robe, as if he'd been wrapped in a cloud. His long hairy legs hung out from beneath it and were crossed comfortably. He leaned back against the settee cushions; I felt part of a domestic scene—and yet removed, as if I were watching some favorite TV rerun, with good family values. And this was so deceptive. I had to make my brain work.

"I don't think I'll have any trouble with . . ." I stopped. "Whoever it was," I said carefully.

"You can't go around threatening people, Sarah. If Alby gives you any trouble, we can take out a restraining order."

"If you're going to lecture me, you can just pull on your wet clothes and slosh off."

"If I wasn't so tired I'd come over there and tan your hide. You're an intelligent woman, Sarah, but sometimes you behave like you don't have a lick of sense."

I tried very hard not to smile. It was hard to take him seriously, with his fluffy cloud of bathrobe and hairy legs.

He said, "I'll drive over there tomorrow and have a talk with Alby."

"No." The smile left my face. "No, Perry."

"Why not?"

"Because . . ." desperately, "I already talked to him, *reasonably*. I told him that . . . people were laughing at him and he was making a fool of himself."

"Honey, you don't tell that to obsessive personalities!" He leaned forward. "Don't you know how fine a line there is in the minds of men like Alby? They can snap just like that!" He snapped his fingers and, to my consternation, stood and crossed to me. He pulled me to my feet, making me spill my half-drunk coffee. He took it away from me and put it on the table and held me by the shoulders.

"I want to move in here for a while, keep an eye on him," he said.

"Absolutely not!"

"No strings. Separate rooms. Just until Alby loses interest. If it is Alby hanging around."

I looked up at his face, and read more there than his words told me. He didn't mean to *lie*, he was trying to believe his own words. But how long would it remain separate rooms? How long would it take Alby to find another hobby?

And what happens when Keir finally comes?

Keir. What would Keir think, finding McGarret's toothbrush in the bathroom, McGarret's clothes in the drier?

Or was it Keir that McGarret would be waiting for?

"I can't have you do that," I said coolly.

"Try it. My intentions are honorable."

"I know that." And my voice still betrayed me. I tried to think of Keir, of Keir coming here, but—it was his hands on my shoulders, that was it, it was the fact that instead of staring at his badge or a button on his shirt I was looking at his bare chest between the crossed-over edges of robe. "I know that," making my voice firmer, "but I don't think it's a good idea."

His voice a growl, "We've had this talk before. I'm not talking about you and me, here. I'm just talking about you, and your safety."

I made myself look up at his face, into his eyes. "I don't think so. There are other things at work here. It's never simple."

He held my gaze a moment, then he said, "It's Erica Tudor, isn't it?"

If he hadn't been holding me I think I would have collapsed.

"Sarah?"

I tried to speak, but no words would come. My eyes filled

with tears of weakness and I hated myself even while I was grateful that the expression in his eyes softened a little.

"Oh, honey . . ." I was held close to that massive chest, felt his kiss on the top of my head, my ear, my cheek.

"No, McGarret, *no.*"

His arms were a vice around me and I couldn't even look up at him. His heart thundered against my ear, his voice rumbled around and above the sound of it, "You can't go on blaming yourself. It was Keir who sent her over the edge, rejecting her the way he did, just after she'd lost the baby."

I squirmed, but he held me tight. "Hush up, I'm not letting you go now. . . . And she was high-strung anyway, Sarah. She wasn't a strong girl. I've seen cases like her time and again. They just don't have any real fight in them. Faced with problems—bad problems, but not *real* bad— they kill themselves and leave their families asking what they could have done to stop it."

"I should have told Keir," I sobbed against his chest. Oh God, I had been alone for so long, without the touch of another human being for so long.

"Told him what?" when I couldn't finish. "Go back to Erica? You loved him, you're only human. He was your husband, after all, till she came along."

He shook me a little, gently, side to side, without letting me out of the embrace. "Sarah, Sarah, just promise you'll try to put it all behind you."

"I want to. You don't know how much. But I can't."

"Sure you can." And his hot mouth was once more against my scalp and I had to fight the desire to raise my face to his lips, expose my throat, expose—

"You should find someone else," I said in a hard voice. "Find some girl in her twenties, get married, have babies."

"I don't want babies. If I was a family kind of man I'd have married a Southern girl and settled down in Slow River."

I had to smile. He sensed it and bent to peer at my face, puzzled that I thought his statement, made honestly, sensibly, was amusing. He saw nothing unusual in his unconscious acknowledgment of the superiority of *Southern gals.*

Misreading me, he felt driven to add, "Plenty of girls in Slow River would've had me."

Tiredly, "Then why?"

"World's an ugly place," he murmured, holding me close once more, resting his chin on the top of my head, "and cops die, lot of the time. I never was one to hang back." I remembered that he'd been shot twice. So he hadn't wanted to leave a wife and children.

"Can I spend the night?" he asked. "In the spare room," he added.

I looked up and thought I saw amusement there at the back of his eyes. But I also saw a man I had come to trust. It seemed churlish to send him to Apple Tree Farm now. I hesitated.

"This isn't the start of anything," I warned.

"Oh, I know that."

"And it isn't the middle, either."

He merely smiled a little, then he let me go, and wandered off towards the hall. "I'll cook—as long as it's pasta."

We cooked pasta together and washed the dishes, and it was then that the phone rang. I answered it in the living room. "Hello?"

No answer.

"Who *is* this?"

Already McGarret was moving down the hall towards me, purposefully. I hung up, quickly.

And he saw me hang up quickly.

"What'd you do that for?" Crossly, for him.

"It was a wrong number."

"You don't say, 'Who is this?' to a wrong number, not like that."

"I presume it was a wrong number. Nobody actually spoke."

I knew it was a bad idea to have him here. I knew it.

He took my chin gently in his hand and turn my face up to his.

"I swear, nobody answered."

"Do you know who it was, Sarah?"

"No!"

"Has it happened before?"

"Well . . . a couple of times. There's no heavy breathing or anything. I'm sure it's just a—"

"When did the calls start?"

"Three weeks ago."

"How often are you getting, them? The truth, Sarah."

He was suddenly all cop, despite the bare feet, despite the toweling robe. He was looking at me as it I were avoiding this conversation, would evade him if I could. And he was very right in this. *Are you crazy to have him here? Only a crazy person would behave the way you do.*

"Only one a week or so. Look, it's probably—"

"Tomorrow we'll put a tracer on your phone. When he rings again—"

"No!"

The word hung in the air, and he looked at me, looked down at me, and I could see his thoughts forming. *She doesn't care about catching Alby Gresson making nuisance calls, she's afraid that we'll trace calls to Keir Stanforth.*

What excuse could I give for that *no?* There was none. I waited for him to make some comment, but he played his usual tactics and waited. So a ridiculous amount of time was spent with us standing there by the phone table, looking into each other's eyes and neither of us wanting to be the first to give way.

And finally, I said, "I'll make up your bed," and walked past him, braced for the feel of his hand on my arm, but he let me pass without comment.

I took clean bed linen from the closet and went to the spare room; I could hear him padding along behind me in his bare feet.

I thought wildly, defensively, it doesn't matter. If this has taught him anything, then it's all to the good. Maybe

I am protecting Keir. I have a right and a duty to protect Keir.

He helped me make the bed, and we worked as coolly as a couple of chambermaids in a motel. It was still early, so we watched television, sitting at either end of the settee. We didn't talk much.

Again, I could sense him thinking, hard, and I didn't like it at all. Keir stood between us like a specter whose name, like members of some primitive tribe, we dared not speak.

McGarret wasn't confronting me now because he was using what he knew, he was storing it away. He didn't even ask me, straight out, *Was that Keir Stanforth on the phone?*

Chapter
Twenty-Eight

Alongside the spare toothbrushes in the pantry, I found a cake of Yves Saint Laurent soap that had found its way into my belongings when Beth had packed my things for me, back in New York.

It was Keir's and, as he thanked me politely, McGarret's eyes told me he knew as much when I handed him the soap and toothbrush as we parted in the hall that night.

He thinks you're preparing for Keir to drop in. He thinks you're expecting Keir.

So what, already?

It was now quite late, but I knew I wouldn't sleep for a long time. I changed into striped cotton pajamas and a robe and sat up in bed reading James Herriot's *All Creatures Great and Small.*

When the soft knock sounded on my door, I was prepared. I had almost expected it. "Come in."

He did, still dressed in the toweling robe. He sat on the edge of the bed, looked up at its ornate bedposts and canopy admiringly, and then, turning to me, "I had to say this before I went to sleep. If Keir comes back, and he hasn't broken the law, and he can make you happy . . .

that'll be fine with me. You won't get any trouble from me at all. But even if he does come hack, and you get together with him again, you'll still have to do a lot of forgiving, a lot of forgetting.

"You've already started real well, you've made a good life for yourself here, 'mongst people who've come to care for you. You'll keep getting stronger, and the . . . the pain of what's happened will fade some. Eventually it'll pass. I know what I'm talking about, I been hurt too.

"But the pain passes, and then you can remember the good times. What you gotta do is, not brood about the bad things, you gotta turn your mind to other things, and get on with life, till you're ready to face what's happened. That's the only way."

He looked embarrassed, suddenly. "You understand what I'm saying here?"

"Yes." And I did. But *he* didn't understand. *He didn't understand.*

"Promise me, then, you won't go brooding on Erica's death, and what Keir had to do with it, and making yourself crazy, 'cause you'll probably never get to the bottom of things. And you got better things to do now."

"I know."

Like what, Sarah?

"Promise, then."

"I promise to try."

"You know I'm right 'bout this."

I lowered my gaze to my book. "I know."

"Well . . ."

I looked up at him.

"Well . . . goodnight, Sarah."

"Goodnight."

His kiss was warm and friendly add I had to stop myself from closing my eyes to pretend it was anything more, and made myself the one to pull away first. He touched my face, fondly, and left, shutting the door behind him.

And then the house was silent but for the steady rain on the roof.

* * *

I dreamt that McGarret and I were walking on a beach, miles from anywhere, and he turned to me, actually laughing, and swept me up in his arms and kissed me. Then we were lying on the beach and . . .

I had always thought it would be impossible to make love on a beach without a blanket underneath, but this was wonderful. This was . . .

I woke up with reluctance, my body almost to the point of climax, and lay gasping in the darkness.

I had never made love with any man but Keir, had never wanted any man but Keir. Until now.

I was lonely, that was all. It was taking Keir so long to get back to me. Where *was* he?

Maybe those phone calls were from Keir, maybe he couldn't speak to me, couldn't let me know where he was, in case I would be implicated. In what?

If Keir had done something wrong, was afraid to go to the authorities, yet still loved me and needed to hear my voice . . .

I was comforted by that thought. Comforted, too, to know that McGarret and his police-issue revolver slept in the next room. The very house seemed to breathe more easily. *I wonder how it would feel,* I thought, and it was the last conscious idea I had before sleep claimed me once more, *to feel this safe all the time.*

I was woken from a deep sleep by the sound of my door opening. By then McGarret was already in the room . . . in his trousers, bare-chested and very, very angry. By the time I struggled to a sitting position he was standing at the foot of the bed, one hand resting high on either bedpost and saying in a voice of ice, "You lying little . . . witch."

I looked at my clock—it was only one forty-five, he hadn't long left the room to go to his own bed. Why was he dressed?

And then I thought, he was preparing to leave. He's so

cross he was dressing in order to leave, but came in here to yell at me instead.

He was a very scary sight, never to be called good-looking, his big body was even more frightening, now I could clearly see the angry, only partly-healed wound in his left shoulder, and the puckered, scarred flesh of the old wound in his right upper arm, in the center of a four-inch incision, white against his broken skin.

"I was looking for something to read . . . was finding it difficult to sleep . . . and they were lying there in full view on top of the bookcase, couldn't help but see 'em."

"What, *what?*"

The house wasn't the tidiest lately, I had loose papers lying on quite a few surfaces. What was on the bookcase in the living room?

It was the pages Sammy and Beth had me write to include in *Scotty's Things*.

I felt my heart sink.

McGarret was shaking his head in a kind of despair, repeating, "You lying little . . ." Words failed him. "It's your story, isn't it? Yours and Keir's. This book you've written that they're so excited about. It's all about Keir Stanforth."

"No it's not—"

"Piers Danforth? Doctor Piers Danforth?" he accused. "Is the rest of the book as hot as what you've written there?"

"No! You've taken those scenes out of context—"

Dryly, "This is what you meant when you said you had some changes to make."

"I didn't have a choice in the matter—" I began but he shouted, he actually shouted,

"Oh, come on! I know you well enough by now, Sarah. Those big operators in New York couldn't force you into writing that stuff. You're strong. You'd have stood up to them. You wanted those descriptions of sex—you were re-living you relationship with Keir—"

"Stop it."

"And here I was," in a calmer tone, as if wondering to

himself, running his hands through his hair, "here I was last night, talking to you about putting the past behind you—"

"I want to, Perry . . . You don't know—"

"Don't give me that. All the time . . . all these months, you've been writing the story of you and Keir Stanforth. Those publishers force you into inventing a happy ending too?"

"You don't understand the publishing business. My career was on the line, McGarret! I didn't have any choice!"

He looked at me, stony-faced. "You don't need them, Sarah."

"I do! I need my editing job, I need to have *Scotty's Things* published—I really need that, I do!"

I had my face down in my hands by then. When his voice came it was calm, and slow. His normal voice, but somehow that was worse. "But you get to write about Keir, about you and Keir, you get to go over and over, everything that happened."

"I have to!" Without looking up.

A pause, then, "You'd see it that way, I guess. What your publishers are doing, is, they're making you do something you already want to do."

I raised my head to look at him. He seemed suddenly beaten. I wished I didn't know him so well that I knew when he was unhappy. I wished it didn't matter to me so much.

"Oh, Perry," I said. But there were no words, none I could find that would make him feel any better.

After a pause, he prompted, "What," into the silence.

"Nothing," despondently.

Another pause.

"You were going to say something."

My dream, his presence here, his censure, perhaps, most of all—and tiredness—brought tears to my eyes, in quantities enough that hiding them was difficult. I lowered my

head, and told him, "It's all been said before. I haven't
lied to you. I've meant everything I've said to you."

"I sat here on this very bed not two hours ago and you
promised me you'd forget about the past . . ."

"I can't! Why won't you believe me? I want to! But I
can't! It won't let me! Not ever!"

Something was happening in his face. It contorted a
little, his eyes became, suddenly, very dark. He didn't speak
for a long moment, and when he did his voice was matter-
of-fact, as if some decision had been made. "You know
what rape is, Sarah?"

I stared at him.

"Do you?"

I stared at him.

"Do—you—know—what—rape—is?"   Each   word
calmly, carefully enunciated.

"Sexual . . ." I swallowed, "intercourse without con-
sent."

He nodded slowly, "That'll do."

"McGarret . . . Perry . . ." But I couldn't go on, not in
the face of that look.

"Say no, Sarah."

"What?"

"Say no. That's what you do. You say, 'no'." And, still
looking at me, his hand went to the buckle of his trousers,
and pulled at his belt.

"What are you doing?!" I drew up my knees, still crying
but half-laughing, feeling hysteria wobbling inside my head
as if I'd been invaded by a large bowl of Jello, distorting
everything, making everything unreal. I buried my head
upon my arms upon my knees.

"Listen, McGarret . . ."

I heard the sound of the zip on his trousers.

"I'm not looking, McGarret!"

A pause. The deadly voice, "Say 'no', Sarah."

"I . . ."

"Say 'no'."

"This is crazy!"

"Shoot, I know it's *crazy*. Saying it's crazy don't count. Say *'no'*."

I kept my head down, my eyes closed. Even when the blankets were pulled, not un-gently, out of my grasp, and his naked body slid between the sheets beside me.

The voice came from below me now, from the pillow beside me. "Say no, Sarah," the voice gentle, now. "Say 'no, I don't want this'."

"I . . . I can't . . ." I lay beside him, sobbing against his chest, my fingers already touching his shoulders, feeling the warmth of him.

"Then say yes." His lips upon mine. "Honey? Say yes."

His lips were gone and I leaned hungrily up to them. "Yes . . ."

"That's my girl . . ."

"Oh God, no!"

"Sarah—!"

"I'm sorry, I'm sorry! I'm really sorry, but no. No!"

"Sarah, honey—"

"It's not your fault—it's my fault! I should have thought! I just didn't think!"

"Sarah, you'll fall off the edge of the bed. Just come over here . . ."

"I just never—! It never occurred to me! I mean, you're what? Six feet six? I'm only five feet five and a small build—you know? *Small.*"

"Sarah, I won't hurt you—"

"You . . . I . . . Oh, God, this is embarrassing! I should die! I should die of embarrassment! But I wasn't to know! Who thinks to check these things? I mean, it's not the sort of thing—"

"Honey, I'm used to this. I can control—"

"You don't understand, this is a basic matter of physics, like those problems in high school math, you know?"

"Come here, Sarah—"

"Listen to me, McGarret—"

"Come here, Sarah—"

"It's not that I don't like you—God, I like you! And it's not that I wouldn't want to if I . . . If you were only . . . Oh, God. You've got the wrong girl, McGarret . . . oooh . . . it's just one of those incompatibility things that no one ever talks about . . . oh! . . . It's not your fault, you're just . . . six foot six and . . . ooo."

"That good? That good for you, sugar . . . ?"

"Oooo."

"Baby? You see? You see . . . oh, honey . . . !"

"Yes . . . Oh. Oh!"

"Sarah . . . ? Now, sugar? Oh, Sarah . . . Now?"

"Oh . . . Yes . . . !"

"Oh, baby . . . Oh, sugar . . . Oh, Sarah, I love you, honey! Oh, Sarah!"

"Oh, baby! Oh, sugar!" yelled this good Jewish girl from Brooklyn, "Oh, honey! Oh, oh, oh!"

Chapter
Twenty-Nine

I awoke in the morning lying on my side, facing the window, and the bed was so still that I thought at first I had dreamt it all. But when I moved, my body ached, it was sore in places I couldn't remember being sore since . . . well . . . a long time. And then I thought, he must have left, for a milky morning light was visible from the edges of the curtain blinds. I rolled over, gingerly.

He was still asleep, on his back, his head resting in the crook of his left arm, bent beneath his cheek. I would have thought he'd snore in such a position, but he breathed gently, silently.

In sleep there was a kind of beauty to his face that I hadn't seen before. His features were never really mobile, there was always that stillness to him, even on the few occasions he had seemed angry. But in sleep he looked so unguarded, even vulnerable. I could see in him the boy he had been, who had been so unhappy that he'd run away at fourteen. I could see the man who had been so hurt by the world that he wouldn't allow himself to love, to father children.

What does he want from me?

Quietly, I climbed out of bed: I couldn't find my pajamas—they were undoubtedly in a tangle at the foot of the bed, somewhere near McGarret's large feet. I pulled on my robe, dropped unceremoniously by the bed in the heat of passion, and padded over to the window.

Very gingerly, I raised the blind, gazing over my shoulder at McGarret all the while. He didn't move as the blind clicked upwards, and the dimness in the room gradually lightened to the translucent gloom of the day outside.

Still McGarret slept, looking like a downed Roman statue after the Goths had used it for spear practice.

I stood at the window and wondered what to do. Crawl back into bed beside him? Go make breakfast? Have a shower and get dressed?

If I woke him, he might want to make love again. I shivered pleasurably, then scolded myself

It can't go on.

Why should that cause such an ache inside me? There was, already, a sense of loss, and he was still here, for heaven's sake. It needn't end, perhaps I was overreacting. I lived between his place and St. Claude, he could call in on the way home, on the way to work.

It can't go on.

What if he's really in love with me? What if I break his heart, as Keir has mine?

He deserves more.

Let him take care of himself. He can find any number of women.

He loves you.

But I love Keir. Maybe the romance writers are wrong, maybe you can care about more than one man at the same time. But you can't live with them both; what are we, Mormons?

No, Mormon men collected wives, the women weren't allowed more than one husband. And even the Mormons, like the Jews, finally found that polygamy was just too much of a strain.

Tell him now. Tell him as soon as he wakes up.

Tell him what? Tell him how?

I looked over at him and he was awake. "Don't even think about it," he said.

"What?" My voice too small.

"Excuses," he said. "Stop hunting around for ways of getting out of this. You're not getting out of it."

Was I that transparent? "Why not? What do you mean?"

He didn't answer. He locked his hands behind his head and lay there, looking at me, studying me as if I was something pretty special, but perplexing. All his feelings for me were there on his face, and if I'd gone to him, he'd have taken me in his arms.

"You know," I said, "this can't go on." And I was pleased with my firm voice, my kind tone.

McGarret was silent.

I had the next sentence formed in my mind, the next several sentences, actually, and then I stopped. I knew, just *knew*, that I'd end up sounding like a badly written monologue from an off-off-Broadway play. He had that effect on me.

"You are supposed to contribute here," I told him, tightly. "You're supposed to say something. *You* say something, then *I* say something, then *you* say something. It's called conversation."

"Sure. But there's lots of times," he said simply, honestly, "when I just don't have anything to say."

"That's not the point."

He looked skeptical. "So we just keep yakking until—"

"Until one of us convinces the other of the superiority of their argument," I explained, and then thought, *How did I get into this?*

"I don't," he said, frowning thoughtfully, "see anything to argue about. What is it you want to argue about?"

"I don't want to argue. I want to . . ." I stopped, helpless. He gazed at me, perfectly willing, as he always was, to listen to me.

I made several false starts, then said, finally, "I don't

love you, McGarret. I don't know what happened last night
. . . but I don't love you."

"Shoot, I know that."

"Then why?"

He sensed all there was in the word. He said, "Because
you will." And he climbed out of bed, began to walk around
it.

"No! Don't come any closer!" I turned from his naked-
ness, his approach.

When I looked at him, he was standing still, at the foot
of the bed, arrested in the process of reaching for his
trousers, draped over the headboard. "I was going to the
bathroom," he said, with almost a note of apology, and
with his trousers over his arm he walked, naked, out of
the room.

I watched him go and sat heavily down upon the window
seat. While I sat there I heard the toilet flush, then the
shower start running.

I pulled on my slippers and padded through the house
towards the kitchen. Behind me, in the living room, the
phone rang. I half reached for the phone receiver, but
found McGarret had caught up with me. He leaned past
me on the off side, took my wrist, and held it.

It was McGarret who lifted the receiver, shaking his head
warningly at the same time when I looked at him in outrage. He wore only a towel wrapped around his waist: his
shoulders were still damp and the hand on my wrist was
cold. I moved, and he held firm.

I heard the clear voice at the other end of the telephone
say, "Sally? Sally, is that you?"

"Who is this?" McGarret said.

A silence from the other end of the line, then, "Who
the hell are you, buster?"

Calmly, "Who are you, ma'am?"

"I'm Beth Cosgrove, Sally's editor, who are *you*?"

I saw his mouth tighten at the word *editor*. In a tone only
a few degrees warmer, he said, "It's Perry McGarret."

"Oh yes?" I could sense Beth's bemusement, her growing interest.

"I'll put Sarah on." He handed the receiver to me.

I took it, glaring at him, but he met my gaze with a mild look of his own and went off towards the bathroom once more.

"Hello."

After a mischievous pause, Beth said, "I lo-ove that accent."

"He's a friend, Beth, that's all. A really good friend."

"So you're not sleeping with him?" Musically.

I tried to figure out how best to lie. I knew I'd never hear the end of it from Beth if I admitted to anything resembling a relationship.

And she said, "It's okay, Sally. Don't answer. Tell me all about it some other time. I was just ringing to tell you I've nearly finished the edit. The new scenes are *great.* I'll have the manuscript back to you by the end of next week. Okay?"

"Great."

She chatted on, discussing the manuscript, then said, "Sally, you wanted to publish under the name Sarah Feldman. Sammy feels you should use your married name." And, before I could interrupt, "I tend to agree with him; it's going to be partly your name that sells this book. It's just a fact of life that people will want to read your perspective."

"Maybe. Yeah. Yeah, you're probably right."

She was silent a long moment, then she said something McGarret had already told me. "Maybe we won't ever know what happened to Keir."

I took a deep breath. It hurt a little. "Yes," I said. "I know that."

"But . . . we'll get over it, Sally. We will. Once you've finished the book and it's on the stands, we can forget about all this, maybe."

McGarret came out of the bathroom, wearing the white toweling robe, and stood in the hall, looking at me.

"Yes, Beth. That'll be real good."

"And Sally?"

"Yes?"

"I'm glad you've got that guy, whoever he is, in your life. Start living again, honey. I don't . . . I don't know— somehow I just don't believe Keir will come back. And I know he loved you, Sally, and I know he'd want you to be happy."

We hung up, soon after that. I looked at McGarret. He said, "I was wondering where you kept your ironing board."

He asked for a clean pressing cloth and after setting up the iron, I left him pressing his trousers and shirt. Going back and forth to the bathroom before I had my own shower, I could hear him. He had the small radio turned on, tuned in to some country-and-western station. He sang *Doo-doo-doo* along with the wailing singer, in a basso profundo that was pitched so low as to be almost a non-noise.

After breakfast he left the room to phone the station. He came back to say that he was needed, the floods had not receded. I stood in the doorway of the spare room as he buckled on his gun belt and shrugged into his jacket. I followed him to the door, where he pulled on his hat, turned, and kissed me goodbye, gently, tenderly.

I went for a walk, the usual path, pausing—and I had other spots where I paused, made myself pause, equally long, equally pensively—finally, at the fallen tree. I always made sure I never stood directly over the grave, now indistinguishable from the surrounding forest floor. A few weeks before, I'd seen a small, lone pine seedling growing in amongst the roots of a yellow birch. I eased it out and up with the aid of a stick, and, not feeling too hopeful for its survival, placed it in the center of what I knew to be Erica's grave. It had clung tenaciously to life, and now stood taller, its uppermost tip putting out a kind of toothbrush of new growth. I hoped in fifteen years or so its roots would cradle Erica, and no one, then, could disturb her.

Its immediate ancestor, the fallen pine, once the needles had died and fallen, now provided a rough seat in one of its branches. The trunk provided a comfortable place for one's back, so it was a natural place to sit, to look down the slope at the sunset through the trees. And I needn't look directly at the grave: I knew Erica was there, from the periphery of my vision I could see the little pine tree, about ten yards to my right, its brighter tips of new growth moving a little, back and forth, when the wind blew.

McGarret was a problem, but Alby was a more pressing one. I had to face the fact that he still might decide to go to the police. I realized that it would be a relief. I couldn't bring myself to turn myself in, but if someone else found out . . .

That was why some criminals made stupid mistakes. Of course, some criminals *were* stupid. But some, like me, particularly your unpremeditated kind of lawbreaker, must feel a sense of release when the suspense is over, when a higher power grabs us and says *You'll pay for this.* For some of us are ready to pay.

It occurred to me that I could, still, tell the truth. At least that way Erica could have a decent funeral in Mississippi.

And McGarret would understand, then, at last, why I had avoided a relationship. Maybe—and it was a sobering thought—maybe it would take the truth about me before he would stop loving me.

But it was all too late. I still couldn't face them all, the knowledge of them knowing. McGarret, Beth and Malcolm, Merlin and Natalie, and all the precious and foolish Aunts and Uncles . . . the list went on and on. And Keir. Of course, Keir. Wherever he was.

And I couldn't face the seedy, disinfected institutions that would house me, the rough hands of policewomen, the loss of my freedom, my *life.*

It was too late for the truth. If retribution came to me it would have to be fate that brought it.

Fate in the shape of Alby Gresson.

And from the dammed well of my thoughts I allowed a polluted trickle to struggle through to my consciousness.

I could kill him. I could find a way. Kill him before he spoke to anyone. . . . The thought was carried on a rush of anger. *That would fix the old bastard. Blackmail me, would he?*

In my mind's eye I saw his figure before me, in a winter's landscape as I had often seen him, shoeing his way along the road, seeing my car coming, fast, purposeful.

The lascivious smirk on his face replaced by a look of fear. A satisfying *thump* and the little wretch would fly up in the air like . . . like the dwarf in the fairy tale of Rose White and Rose Red, when the bear had swiped him, and he'd flung up, up into the air, up and up and up and was never seen or heard of again.

I spent some minutes enjoying that prospect. That's what I wanted for Alby, just such an ending. *And he was never seen or heard of, ever again.*

I somehow expected McGarret to phone that evening. Instead he turned up at eight, in jeans, denim shirt, and his leather jacket, carrying a small carryall and two uniforms, obviously straight from the cleaners, on hangers and in neat plastic bags, slung over his shoulder.

"No," I said.

He walked forward and I was moved out of the way like a bobbing cork when a yacht sailed by. "Just for a few days," he said. "Gotta few days off. I'll camp in the spare room if you like." He wasn't even looking at me, but was walking through the house, knowing just where to go. I didn't know how to argue with him so I went back to my study and shut the door, in denial.

I worked for an hour, just mundane household accounts, but was forced to pause when I became aware of good smells, rich food smells creeping in from under the door.

A radio was playing, distantly, a lugubrious country-and-western song; every now and then a tap would be turned on or off, the pipes ran through the walls of this room and it was audible, the hum, the clunk of water under pressure.

I wasn't used to it. Normal sounds for a household of more than one. Domestic sounds and smells. Barricaded here, I tried not to acknowledge the sense of comfort they gave me.

I got up and went to the kitchen, finding him spooning up some kind of seafood and pasta dish onto two plates. "Knew you hadn't eaten," he said. "The stove was cold."

We ate at the old refectory table in the living room. He had lit a fire. And I found I was relaxing, was finding it hard to fight each of McGarret's new incursions.

When the phone rang, towards the end of the meal, he looked at me steadily as he rose to answer it and I didn't even make an attempt to move.

Did he really think I was in danger?

Or was this just another way he was taking over my life?

I heard McGarret say. "Hello," and that was all. When he returned and picked up his fork I asked, "Who was it?"

"They didn't answer," he said, his eyes on his plate, as if this was of no consequence.

And I began to be afraid. I began, for the first time, to think that this man, who knew so many more of the faces of evil in the world than I did, actually might know something I didn't. And he seemed to know what he was doing.

I began to be glad he was here.

"Eat up," he said.

I found that I'd been staring at him, my fork held forgotten in my hand. "Sorry. It's really very nice." I made an effort to eat.

Afterwards I insisted on washing up alone. When I joined him in the living room he was watching a cop show set in New York. He moved a cushion so I could sit beside him, and he draped one heavy arm about my shoulder, pulling me silently in towards his body.

Beneath his wing.

The explosion was deafening, terrifying, but what stayed in my mind ever afterwards was the room exploding into points of light, the room exploding into diamonds, into a million stars.

The suddenness of the pain was so startling that at first I didn't know what hurt. Then I discovered that it was almost everything. I had no breath, I couldn't move, and my whole body felt bruised. Opening my eyes, I found I was lying on the floor parallel to the settee.

I wasn't able to breathe because McGarret was lying on top of me.

"Sarah," his breath, his voice close to my ear, "That was a shotgun blast. Do you understand? I don't want you to move. No matter what happens, don't move from this spot until I come back for you."

Come back for me? Where the fuck did he think he was going?

As he moved, I must have moved, for the full weight of his two hundred and twenty pounds was suddenly upon my rib cage once more.

"Grnfg," I said.

"I mean it, Sarah. I swear I'll wring your neck if I come back and find you've moved an inch."

McGarret was gone. His receding feet were the last thing I saw before the lights were switched off.

Chapter Thirty

In the darkness I heard the faint grinding crunch of broken glass beneath McGarret's boots. The television set, the only light and color and sound in the blackness, suddenly extinguished itself with an unhealthy *tck* and the sound of its cord being wrenched out of the wall socket.

I heard McGarret move again. He was treading away carefully along the hall, *towards the spare room, towards his gun.*

He didn't come back. It was very quiet here, lonely, and very scary. My terror was so absolute that even my arm, twisted awkwardly and painfully beneath me, was no incentive to wriggle to a more comfortable position.

Alby Gresson wants to kill McGarret, too. McGarret had been back in St. Claude, a grown man, and a cop, for seven years, and Alby Gresson had borne him no illwill. Until I came along.

If McGarret dies, I thought, imagining him out there in the darkness, alone . . . if he dies, it will be my fault.

Don't let him die, God. I've already promised I'll be good. I'll make up for Erica's death, I swear I will. Don't take McGarret, too.

He had only a handgun. Alby Gresson had a shotgun. I risked a look upwards, towards the window through which the blast had come. The drapes hung in tatters, there was a huge hole in the blind, the batten at the lower edge dragged on the floor, its scalloped edging pathetically still attached. It moved a little in the chill wind that blew through the shattered diamond panes.

I waited, continuing my litany, *Keep McGarret safe, God, don't let him die, Lord . . .*

And I listened. I listened very hard, but it was silent outside, silent within the house.

When the front door burst open I sat up abruptly with a half-strangled cry. The lights came on suddenly, blindingly.

It was McGarret, striding over to me, his revolver held loosely in his hand, pointing at the floor. He placed it on the settee and hauled me to my feet, "You okay?"

"Yes."

"You've cut your face." He peered at my forehead. "Not deep, though."

"Yes, but who—"

"You gotta stay here, honey, don't leave the house." He was already scooping up the Smith & Wesson, backing away, "I'll be gone for a while."

By the time he'd finished speaking he was in the hall, moving fast. Stunned, slower, I moved after him. We collided as he came out of the spare room into the hall once more. "Okay?" he asked me, and didn't pause for a reply. He had his gun belt and car keys in one hand, his gun still in the other.

"McGarret?"

He paused, and looked at me with his cop face, as if he didn't really see me, or if he did, I didn't matter. He had moved away from me, into that parallel universe of his, dark and elemental, where I couldn't follow.

"It was Alby Gresson, wasn't it?"

"Yeah," he said, almost unwillingly. "He'd used both barrels, so's it was empty. But he swung it at me. He fell and hit his head when I grabbed it off him. He's out there, cuffed to a tree—I gotta get him to a hospital."

He came back to me, held me briefly, awkwardly, his hands full, kissed me, his lips cold on mine, and was out the door without looking back.

I stood where I was and listened to his car driving off. It paused at some distance, engine idling, then a car door slammed, then another, then he was gone.

I don't know how long I remained there. I was thinking of his voice as he'd told me what had happened outside. There had been something in his tone beyond the emotionless reporting manner that I knew to expect. There had been regret, distaste, even a kind of sadness.

This was hard for him. This wasn't just any crazy old man, this was a man who had been a hero to thousands, even, perhaps, to the young Perry McGarret.

And it had come to this.

I looked around the room, then fetched the vacuum cleaner and turned it on.

Thankful to be busy, I vacuumed the floors and window ledges and furniture for a long time, long after any twinkling shard of glass had been sucked away from sight.

I still hadn't finished to my satisfaction when a car pulled up with a protesting shriek of brakes. I stood, frozen with fear, in the center of the room. But then there were light footsteps on the porch, soft voices calling my name—and Merlin and Natalie were pushing through the front door.

I stared at them, they stared at me. Did I look like them, I wondered, white-faced, wide-eyed? I held the vacuum cleaner hose tightly in both hands; I think I'd been planning on using it as a weapon.

"Perry called from his car," Natalie said, approaching me very quietly now, as if I were some frightened animal, out in the brush somewhere.

It was almost funny. I could have said, *Hey, I've been shot at before. What's more, I've killed a person, I've dragged a corpse up hill and down dale and shoved it in a pit. I've lied to your precious Perry and to a police inspector. You think a few shotgun pellets through my living room window is going to rattle me?*

But still I found my smile of welcome a bit forced, my voice a bit unsteady, when I said, "Come on in the kitchen—would you like some tea or coffee?"

Alby was in the hospital for two days. At the end of that time he was taken to the courthouse and charged. I waited at home during those days, locked in my study, trying to ignore McGarret's worried eyes upon me when he returned from town, trying to ignore my own fearful thoughts.

If Alby was going to talk, he'd have done so by now, wouldn't he, surrounded by all those policemen? Or . . . in the court when the charge was read out, then, *then* would have been the time, the most satisfying and dramatically appropriate time, McGarret there in front of him, and witnesses to McGarret's baffled horror. That would have been the moment to stand up and shout, *Yes, I shot at her, your Honor, but she's a murderess! I saw her kill a woman with an ax!*

And McGarret had thrown the book at him, being in the position of holding it, so to speak. Alby's lawyer pleaded that his client was not fit to stand trial, but Raoul Gerlain had had enough: the town was divided, but the judge ruled that the police had a case, despite Alby's continuing refusal to speak since his arrest, despite petitions from many prominent people in the town.

At first I'd thought even McGarret was leaning towards clemency; the charge was to be the unlawful carrying of a firearm, but then he explained to me that this carried a maximum of a two-year sentence if Gresson was found guilty. What I would have thought was the more serious charge—discharging a firearm—carried a maximum of only six months. He could be let off with just a warning, McGarret glowered.

I didn't particularly care one way or the other, vacillated

about it in my mind, even hoping, some days, that Alby got off altogether—anything to keep him happy, anything to keep him quiet. The next minute I was thinking, *Two years? Two years max? He tries to kill us both and they can only keep him away from me for two years?*

But most of the time I didn't want to think at all. My Macintosh was very quiet, and through the closed door McGarret, when he was home, wouldn't have known if I was working or not.

I wasn't. I'd sit in the armchair in the study and look at photograph albums of Keir and me. I'd lose myself in the past, and try to avoid any thought of the future.

Any time now—perhaps even as I sat there—Alby Gresson might be telling Raoul Gerlain of the day he went for a walk through my woods, on the evening of January twenty-fifth, and how he had seen me put an ax through someone's head . . .

But Alby stayed silent, so silent that McGarret—and even Peter Copely, when he came with McGarret and a tow truck to remove the Buick from my garage at last—said with cynicism that Gresson was going to make a plea for diminished responsibility.

Stay quiet, Alby. Stay very quiet.

In one matter, at least, he did. From the night Alby put both barrels of shot through my living room window and was taken away, there were no more strange calls. So it had been him tormenting me.

And yet, safely behind bars, he was still tormenting me, with a silence as profound as those frightening phone calls had been. Would he speak? When would he speak?

But the days went by, and I heard nothing, read nothing in McGarret's eyes but warmth and welcome and affection, each time I'd see him. Maybe Alby wouldn't speak at all.

And I found I was able to face down the stares, the questions, of some St. Claude residents. However disliked Alby had become over the years, he was still a native son, and I was the newcomer, the catalyst, the troublemaker.

I retired more and more to *Jaegerhalle,* would have liked

to have been alone at *Jaegerhalle*, but McGarret was around a lot. And I couldn't stop myself: each time he'd come off duty I'd study his face as he came in the door; had today been the day? I felt driven to ask him about Alby, to probe, and McGarret wasn't the most forthcoming of companions.

"Has he talked to anyone? Is he having visitors? Does he talk to them?"

"Has visitors. Don't talk much, so I hear."

"Do you think he's prevaricating?"

"Sorry?"

"Is he pretending, do you think? Could he really be insane?"

"Don't know. I'm no psychiatrist." He scowled. "He's cunning, though. Always was. I think he knew just what he was doing. I think he still does."

One night I dreamt of Erica. She came walking down the hill from the direction of her grave, wearing a Lincoln green parka, suede trousers, and suede boots—an outfit she'd worn in a photo shoot in New Hampshire two years before.

I met her at the back porch. "Erica," I said with delight, "you're not dead!"

"No, isn't it great!" She came up the stairs, her fair hair tossed by the wind. She flicked it out of her eyes as she had when she came to meet me, across the room at the Brambles Thorne offices. We grinned at each other.

"That's wonderful!" I cried, hugging her. "You don't know what this means to me! This changes my whole life!"

And then I woke up. I woke up and realized the truth, and burst into tears, trying to hold onto the dream, closing my eyes tightly and willing her back into my mind, into my sight, healthy, beautiful, smiling at me—alive.

"Erica!" I cried out for her. "Erica!"

And it took several minutes before I discovered that McGarret had his arms about me, that we were lying there, in the dark of my bed, and McGarret was cradling me like a child in his arms, while I sobbed Erica's name aloud.

Chapter
Thirty-One

The following morning I was woken by McGarret seating himself on the edge of the bed in jeans and check shirt. He brought with him the smell of the forest.

I smiled sleepily, and thought he'd return it, but he was serious. *Erica. It had to be Erica.* We hadn't talked last night, and I didn't want to talk now. Surely he'd see that it was just a dream, and meant nothing.

"Anything wrong?" I murmured, stretching. McGarret took my balled fist when it was at arm's length from my body and brought it back to himself. Disturbed, I watched him hold it gently imprisoned in his own large hand, and it was an effort to remain smiling, while I waited for him to speak.

"Sarah, I want to stay here. Legal-like. Will you marry me, Sarah?"

I stared at him while the words penetrated, saw the obdurate look on his face. I went to pull my hand away, abruptly, but all tentativeness was gone from him now. "Just listen."

"No. It's out of the question."

"We should talk about it."

"No."

"Okay." A sigh. "We can live together if that's—"

"No, McGarret. *No.*"

He stood then, slowly, and gazed at me a long moment. Then he left the room.

It was McGarret's day off. When I showered and dressed I found him drinking coffee on the back porch. I went back inside to pour myself a cup and came to sit beside him. I didn't pull my chair closer to his, I needed a little distance.

Somehow I knew he was leaving, there was an emotional withdrawal from me, I sensed it.

"You're going home?" I asked, just to be sure. "Don't you want to stay for the day? Since you're already here?"

"I don't think that's what you do, in shallow, meaningless relationships," he said, seriously. "I'm going home to feed and exercise my horse and do my laundry. You can visit," he paused, "anytime."

"I don't know your address," I said, hedging a little. There were different kinds of intimacy, I was finding, some more threatening than others. I was beginning to know McGarret's body, I wasn't all that eager to know his world, the secrets of where he kept *his* coffee mug, *his* towels, *his* ironing board.

"Fifteen, Stoney Creek Road," he recited. "Go on up past Alby's place and it's the second road on your right, just after the Spring Mill Creek crossing. Two miles on your left along there and you come to a gray stone place with a chestnut mare in the field in front. Close the gate as you drive through."

And he left, to feed his horse and do his laundry.

The house was very quiet when he'd gone.

In New York, I'd never noticed spring much. Up in the sealed world of our apartment above the fairy-tale lights by night, the fairy-tale green park and forest by day, it meant Keir and I would be planning our trip to Paris rather than our trips to Beaver Creek, Colorado. Down there, in Central Park and on the streets, it had meant the sight of daffodils and crocuses, and the scent of freesias beneath the trees and the florists' awnings.

I found McGarret's place easily enough. I saw the horse, grazing down by the gate, before I saw the number, or the house, sitting by itself on a small rise.

It looked like a perfect little Georgian cottage, two windows, with blinds half drawn like sleepy lids, and a door in the center topped by a little gabled porch like a turned-up nose. An odd, whimsical place in which to find McGarret.

Inside, the furniture was sparse, rustic in style, and beautifully made. When I commented, he looked a little embarrassed; it had been a gift from his mother when he told her he was moving to St. Claude permanently.

We stood there, gazing at each other. "Show me around outside," I suggested.

He showed me the outbuildings. In the garage I found the old Buick, in even more pieces than it had been in my barn. From there we went down to the fields, and he introduced me to his horse, Patsy Cline.

"She's my favorite singer," he volunteered. "I was with a friend at a horse sale down in Georgia a few years back. Heard the name being mentioned as part of a sale. Then I saw her. She was down in the ring, being ridden about— never saw anything more beautiful in my life. Cost me almost a year's wages . . . but I had to have her. Kept the name, too. If Miss Cline was alive I don't think she'd mind."

She was indeed a beautiful animal. She nuzzled at my hand, lipping it, and breathed into my ear in a friendly fashion.

"I don't think she'd mind at all," I agreed.

We stood there for some minutes, companionably silent, then he draped a large arm over my shoulder, casually, fondly, and we walked back to the house. It began a loose kind of routine. Not one that I think he was particularly happy with, but he was wise enough not to pressure me.

He'd phone me, and ask it he could come over; and as t was never more frequently than once or twice a week, I always said, yes, drop by. Once in a while I'd get into the Volvo and drive to his place. Whether he was home or not didn't bother me. If he wasn't I'd feed the carrot I always brought to Patsy and go home, and say nothing to McGarret about calling in. If he was home, he was always home alone, and here, or at my place, we were lovers. But there remained that little double standard in my favor. I never called to ask permission to visit; he did. He was a gentleman, McGarret, though I think he'd have been embarrassed if I'd told him that.

Alby Gresson went to trial. He sat stone-faced throughout, and bad as it must have been for him, it was equally harrowing for me. Every time he opened his mouth to speak, I thought, *This is it, here's where he'll tell them.* I sat with sweating palms through all the questioning.

"And what was Sergeant McGarret doing at your house at that hour, Mrs. Stanforth?"

"We were watching television."

"Would I be correct in saying that you shared a relationship with Sergeant McGarret? That you were, in fact, lovers?"

"Objection, your Honor," the prosecuting attorney spoke up. "The witness's relationship with Sergeant McGarret is of no bearing on this case: the fact that he was there at the time is what is most to the point."

"I would like to know, your Honor," Alby's lawyer pointed out, "if a visitor to Mrs. Stanforth's farm would find Sergeant McGarret's car outside at other times. At midnight, perhaps, or three in the morning. This would lead a susceptible mind such as my client's to presume the object of his obsession had her own affections engaged elsewhere. This knowledge would have a considerable effect on a mind that was, *at this time,* unstable."

"You will answer the question, Mrs. Stanforth."

"Yes."

Alby's lawyer came up close to me, turned to face the court, and raised his voice. "Could you speak up, please?"

"Yes. Sergeant McGarret and I were lovers."

Hmmmm, the court went, collective heads a-bobbing this way and that, and *hmmmmm* it said.

Sergeant Peregrine David Willingham McGarret was superb. He took the stand in his best uniform, stated the facts in his sonorous, unemotional voice, and remained in total control of himself throughout. He looked at Alby only once, to identify him as the man he had seen running into the trees, carrying a shotgun. He was very helpful in answering the defense's questions: in fact the whole court seemed to be in agreement, the trial a formality that must be indulged in, justice not only to be done and to be seen to be done, but to be done with a restrained, almost British propriety and courtesy.

And in the end, the result—a guilty verdict and a sentence of six months in prison—divided the town in the same way the arrest had.

The police seemed satisfied; even McGarret seemed satisfied, but it was hard to tell with McGarret.

But I wasn't satisfied. I don't know what I expected, but what I had was a date—a date six months into the future, when Alby Gresson was free. And I had to hope he'd changed his personality, his character, his morals, and his ambitions by the time we met again.

It was a big ask, and I was scared.

As we left the court, McGarret and I found ourselves surrounded by his family, the Dufours, and Natalie, Stephanie, and Eugene. It was suggested by someone—not McGarret, and not me—that what we needed was a drink, so we straggled down the road to the Loyalist Arms and sat in a booth with a large table and extra chairs drawn up to it. I don't remember the afternoon; it blended into evening, and still everyone was talking, talking, making suppositions, giving opinions. I drank whatever was put in front of me, and then someone—David, I think—suggested we make it dinner, so we ate, though I can't remember what.

McGarret drove me home in my car and kissed me goodnight at the door of my bedroom. I was lying in the dark for some time before I realized that unless he took my car, he had no way of getting home.

I got up and padded through the house to the spare room. He was in bed asleep, his uniform hung neatly on hangers, underpants and socks folded neatly on a chair above his neatly placed boots. His gun belt and keys on the dressing table.

I looked at him sleeping, on his back and for once snoring softly.

I couldn't bear you to know. I couldn't bear it.

What if Alby Gresson told the prison psychiatrist?

I was crying silently. I felt unbearably alone. I crept into bed beside McGarret and he woke, and held me. I cried, and he held me. He held me all night, until I fell asleep. When I woke, he was still holding me.

In the morning I felt very hungover, but I wanted advice, I wanted his opinion. Not having drunk much at all, he was chipper enough to decide to fix the leaking tap in the kitchen. I took two aspirin and prowled about the room.

"What if Alby doesn't learn anything in prison? What if he comes out crazier than when he went in?"

"He'll be fine," McGarret said calmly.

"And what if he's not?"

"I can handle him."

"You're not always here."

He looked up from the greasy, decapitated tap. As our eyes met, I turned away. I fiddled with the ornate carving and knobs on the seventeenth-century Danish dresser. "And even if you were," I continued, "he might do just what he did last time, only this time he'll aim better."

"I think he meant to scare us, scare me off, that's all."

"He might have meant to blow our heads apart like

melons. He's probably out in the melon patch at the prison farm right now, lining them up on the fence posts, sighting down a broom handle . . ."

One of the pieces of carving was loose. I pushed at it. I didn't immediately hear what McGarret said. My back to him, I'd found that part of the front of the cabinet moved. One of the small panels—I'd been pushing at it while I twiddled one of the knobs.

"Sarah?"

"Sorry?"

"Hand me the washer off the table. And do me a favor, honey? Stop talking like that. If you'd seen as many head wounds as I have . . ."

"Sorry, sorry." Stricken. For I, too, had seen head wounds. What was happening to me?

I left the cupboard alone. For I suddenly thought, if this is a secret panel, with a secret space behind it, I could put the gun there. I was nervous of McGarret finding it. Maybe he'd go to the study one day, looking for a postage stamp, and there it'd be, my hefty Miami-bought .45.

McGarret was saying, "After all those months in prison, I think you'll find that Alby will just want to get on with his life. He'll have accepted . . . things."

I looked over at him. His head was bent, screwing the pieces of tap back together. *Things* had not been his first choice.

"You were going to say, Alby will have come to accept us."

He would have liked not to answer, but he knew me by now, and muttered, "Maybe."

It was getting worse and worse. He wasn't making me feel better at all. I tried to think of what to do, felt trapped here, waiting, just waiting, for these six months to pass and Alby to decide what particular form of revenge he'd like to take.

"Maybe I should move back to New York."

McGarret straightened, turned to face me.

"Not now," I added.

He came over and put his arms around me, holding his hands, dark with grease, away from my body. "I don't like the idea of you going back to New York."

And in his arms, increasingly, neither did I.

I waited until he'd returned home before I padded back to the kitchen. The dresser loomed there, looking somehow sinister, though it held nothing more suspicious than a sixty-piece dinner set.

I twiddled the knob and pushed at the little carved panel. With a smooth *click* it swung in a little. I pushed it further open.

The cavity was at the left of the cupboard, taller than it was wide, so that, peering inside through the main carved doors you didn't immediately notice that a space of about five or six inches was missing from the left side of the interior.

There was nothing inside the secret compartment. I was disappointed. The cupboard predated the recycled convent cupboards by at least a century and a half. I'd thought there would be *something* there—a letter, perhaps, or a diary. I didn't go so far as to hope for jewelry or *gelder*.

I fetched the Smith & Wesson and the box of ammunition from the study. The gun was loaded, now, and ready for whenever—if ever—I needed to use it. Both gun and box fitted easily into the secret cavity, then I closed the little door. This was more fiddly than opening it had been; I had to pull the door—on a small, beautifully constructed invisible hinge—towards me, using only the high-relief carving as a handle. It was lucky I didn't bite my nails. I could imagine some sinister Danish nobleman in 1640, chipping his polished nails and cursing the cabinetmaker, as I did now.

The door was shut at last. I could safely leave the gun here . . .

I could, now, safely leave McGarret here, here in my house, when I left to go on tour to promote the book.

That afternoon he returned. He seemed tense, more quiet than usual. But he stayed close to me all evening. Even watching television he'd turn to gaze at me. When he reached for me it was with an unaccustomed passion and possessiveness. "I've got phone calls I need to make . . . I'm a bit tired. I don't think I need—"

"I know what you need."

And he was right. Always, before, and then afterwards, when I lay in his arms, half across his chest, I wondered that I was here, with this man with whom I had so little in common. It had always been Keir who took me to those dizzying heights and depths where I could forget, forget *everything,* for a brief, short while.

But while it was happening with McGarret I forgot even Keir, and that was strange, and disturbing. What was most disturbing was that I seemed to be taking it so calmly. Accepting this dangerous relationship. He was here often. Too often.

The following morning, as he was dressing for work, I asked him, gently but honestly, not to come back that evening. "I have Collette Palmer's new book to edit. I really have to be single-minded about it. I won't be much company—I'll probably work half the night."

He was pulling on his trousers, tucking in the light blue shirt, doing up his fly, and frowning as if these small everyday actions took great concentration. He smelled good, his compact movements still brought his woodsy talc and his own clean scent to me where I sat on the edge of the bed.

"Okay," he said, fastening the belt of his trousers, reaching across for his gun belt from the top of the dresser. "I've got a few things here. I'll take them with me this morning."

I said nothing, not being able to retrieve the companionable mood between us without the words he wanted to hear. *Don't go.*

He was fastening the buckle of the gun belt, settling the weight of its gadgetry upon his hips, gun to the right, cuffs behind it, mace on the left. I always enjoyed the ritual, his thumbs within the belt, maneuvering it about a little. I was always reminded of Gary Cooper strapping on his six-guns in *High Noon*.

Dew not forsake me, o my . . .

The thumbs were still hooked in the gun belt. He was facing me and not smiling, but on the whole he was taking what must have seemed like a rejection very well. And then he said, "Missing Persons in New York have located Keir."

Chapter Thirty-Two

I stared up at McGarret. He looked very large and official and if I hadn't been sitting there, still sticky with our love-making of the night before, I might have taken him seriously. And yet I couldn't smile at his joke. It wasn't amusing at all.

"You *are* joking." Just to make sure.

"No, Sarah."

I wondered why he kept his thumbs in his gun belt, it was an odd time for such a gesture, and rather an aggressive stance, or maybe merely a determined one.

"How do you know?" It was all I could think of to ask. I was avoiding the question, *Is he alive?*

"They called the station. Raoul left it to me to tell you. He's okay. The Maine police have cleared him of any involvement in Erica's death."

He was alive.

I felt weak with relief. Until that moment, coming from an unimpeachable source such as McGarret, I realized I hadn't quite believed it could be possible.

"Why," I said, coldly, "did you tell me now? Why not last night?"

Nothing moved in his face, in his stance. "I suppose I wanted to see if you'd ask me that."

I was coldly furious, but through my rage I understood. "Is he in New York?"

"I don't know."

I stared at the impervious, professional face. He must look like this when he comes to someone's house and confirms their name and mentions a relative and says, *I'm afraid there's been an accident . . .*

He's not really cold, I reminded myself, torn between wanting to rake his mask away with my claws and a terrible pity for him and the thousand questions I wanted to ask about Keir.

"I know this is difficult for you, Perry—"

Nothing.

"It's hard for me, too. You must know I'd want to talk to him. You must have an address, a phone number."

Some emotion flickered across the grave face. "I wouldn't lie to you, Sarah. Missing Persons aren't permitted to pass on information that the subject of the investigation would prefer withheld."

"Talk English!" I shouted, frightened, not understanding, hating the immovable, unshakable granite of the man before me.

"Sarah . . ." The hands came out of the gun belt, almost made a gesture towards me, then fell to his side. Calmly once more, "He doesn't want anyone to know where he is."

Impossible. Ridiculous.

From somewhere far away, after what seemed a long time, I heard McGarret murmur, "I'm sorry, honey." As if he really meant it.

I didn't feel quite real, though I knew I was still sitting on the side of the bed in my robe and my bunny slippers. I was looking at the polished toes of McGarret's boots. I *watched* the highly polished toes of his boots, and it was somehow easier to do this with great concentration than to think.

When the boots suddenly moved, I jumped.

He pulled me to my feet and held me. "Far as I'm concerned," he said, carefully, "this doesn't change anything. You've got to sort out your own feelings for him. But until—and if—you want Keir in your life, I want to keep what we've got. And we've got something here you never had with Keir, can't have with Keir, because it's you and me."

Us.

"Sarah?"

I looked up into the hooded blue eyes.

"God's honest truth, now; you really want me to leave?"

God's honest truth?

"No," I said, and brought my own arms around him. "But I'm hurting, McGarret. I'm hurting."

"I know."

I found it hard to believe, in the days that followed, how little difference McGarret's news actually made to my life. I had always thought that when Keir was found he would come to me, that I would, in fact, be the first person that he contacted.

Arrogance, Sarah. He can live without you.

Hadn't he proved that already? You need proof? How much proof do you need?

Still, sometimes, I found myself lying awake at night, finding excuses for Keir; an accident, amnesia . . .

Get real, Sarah.

McGarret was staying at *Jaegerhalle* nearly all the time. The day after he told me about Keir he drove up with a shiny aluminum horse trailer sailing along behind the Jeep Cherokee. He had brought Patsy Cline to stay. It was all I could do, standing there on the front porch, not to scream, *Take her home.* A toothbrush is one thing, a few clothes maybe—but a man's *horse?*

Yet if I said, *Pack up your gun and your hoss and be out*

of town by sundown, he'd *know* that part of me, despite everything, was waiting for Keir.

He saddled Patsy and rode her about the big fifteen-acre front paddock. He sat well, easily in the saddle, but the big mare seemed determined to show off, her action very high, the tail held like a banner. If she could have spoken, she'd have been yelling, *Look at me, y'all.*

If this had been any other man, I thought, watching them, he'd have left me by now. But there was so little friction between McGarret and me, except for the Keir conversations, except for the *us* conversations, that we shared *Jaegerhalle* with the companionship of lifetime friends. And this despite the constant ferment of my emotions, and whatever cool plans went sliding in and out of McGarret's quiet brain. We shared the cooking, the washing up, the laundry, and the housecleaning. He'd tended for himself for so long he wouldn't have expected anyone to wait on him.

Down there in the field, McGarret dismounted, and I stiffened as I watched him hunker down to examine something minute in the grass, something he picked up, and placed in the breast pocket of his shirt.

The bullets had gone that way. Some of them, past me, past the side of the barn, off into infinity, I had thought, off to be lost forever in the snow.

Snow melts, Sarah.

But the spring grass was growing greener and thicker each day and would have covered a bullet . . . For God's sake, it was beginning to cover Erica's grave, up there in the hills, where the break in the tree canopy since the pine had fallen now let sunlight into the tiny glade. If the grass was kind enough to hide Erica, it would hide a tiny bullet, wouldn't it?

Wouldn't it?

He hadn't remounted the mare, he was wandering around looking at the ground . . . Once he looked back at the house, saw me standing there, raised his hand, and waved. Waving back was hard, and I hoped he didn't notice my lack of enthusiasm.

And he bent once more, his hand enclosing *something*, and that something, too, was placed in his shirt pocket.

I moved inside to the dark coolness of the house. I was afraid to remain on the porch, afraid something in my stance, even from that distance, would give me away.

Inside I was alone with my fear, my thoughts skittered around like small animals in a cage, but there was no escape; I had to wait until McGarret unsaddled Patsy, had taken his saddle to the barn, and returned to the house. I met him on the porch, two beers in my hands, a smile on my face. We sat on the porch and talked about Patsy, and he said he'd like to buy me a horse so we could go riding together.

How jolly.

"By the way, what did you pick up, down there in the field? Not glass, was it? You shouldn't put Patsy in there if there's glass."

He reached into his pocket, took something out. He wasn't smiling. He placed his beer can on the narrow arm of the porch chair and took my own fist. I wondered if he noticed how oddly cold it was. He opened my reluctant fingers . . . and placed a four-leaf clover in the palm of my hand.

I looked up; now he was smiling. I smiled, too. He said, "We'll keep an eye on the papers, see what horses are for sale. Patsy was at a purebred sale, but I think it's best, usually, to buy privately."

I wanted to say, *I don't need animals, more ties.*

I wanted to, but couldn't say, *Don't plan on us being together and sharing things.* I wanted to, but couldn't say, *What's the other thing you have in your shirt pocket?*

In the morning, there was a knock at the door. I answered it and Raoul Gerlain and Peter Copely pushed past me into the room. Everyone seemed to be talking at once.

Peter Copely had taken hold of me and had nudged me up against the wall beside the door, had pushed my hands to the wall high above my head and now ran businesslike hands of his own down my body.

I started screaming.

Raoul said they'd come to arrest me for the murder of Erica Tudor. Peter Copely pulled my hands behind my back, the handcuffs were cold and they pinched my skin painfully as they closed.

"McGarret!" I screamed.

"I'm here, honey . . ."

"Tell them!" as he came through the door from the hall. "Tell them—!"

I woke in the darkness, warm darkness, McGarret's arms around me, his face next to mine, saying, "Hush, now, hush now. I'm here."

What the fuck had I been saying? "Oh," I said. "I was dreaming."

"Some dream."

"Was it? Was I yelling?"

"Only blue murder. Then you started calling my name. What was it about?"

It was fading, fading slowly, gratefully.

"I was sinking in quicksand," I told him.

Beth faxed the new cover illustration to me at ten the next morning. It was simple, a fallen toy soldier. It was evocative, interesting. I phoned her and told her how pleased I was.

The following evening Sammy called, back to his old ebullient self. He'd sold the film rights for three million dollars.

McGarret was with me when the call came through, at about seven-thirty. He'd just come from the station and had changed his clothes, and we were drinking a glass of white wine together to celebrate when the phone rang once more.

I picked up the receiver, and the voice said, "Sally?" before I could say hello.

It was Keir. *It was Keir.*

"Sally?" he repeated.

"Yes." I found myself leaning a little on the phone table, my eyes unfocused. I was aware, then, of McGarret, turned to look at me.

"Sally, I've just come back to New York. I'm at the apartment. I couldn't call you sooner. I wanted to. Will you talk to me?"

"Yes, but . . ." I stopped, because I didn't know what to say. When I glanced at McGarret he was looking fixedly at me. Even the news highlights showing a gunman being arrested in Toronto didn't take his attention from me.

"I know you have no reason to want to talk to me," Keir was saying. "I don't blame you if you slam the phone down. But Beth said . . . Beth said that you'd talk to me."

"Yes," I said.

There was a thoughtful pause, then, "Sally, are you not alone? Beth said . . . there was someone else in your life now. I'm glad, Sally, if you're happy."

"Thank you." Trying not to look at McGarret looking at me. He stood and went to the coat pegs and took down his jacket. Without speaking he walked out the front door, and I knew he knew. The door shut behind him. "Sally?"

"Yes, Keir."

"Am I causing trouble for you?"

"No. No, Keir, talk to me, I have to know."

A sigh then, "I want you to know. I . . . I killed Erica, Sally. I killed her."

Chapter
Thirty-Three

"I knew I'd made a mistake soon after Erica and I moved in together. But I felt committed, Erica was so dependent on me. She wasn't a strong person, Sally, despite her looks, her career as a model and as a writer. She was very insecure. She needed so much, and I . . . I was so full of myself, thinking I was *important* to someone. There's no excuse," in a harder voice. "But I was going to wait a few months and tell her it was over.

"I was making plans to move back to the New York apartment, when she announced she was pregnant. And that was that."

We didn't speak, and it was as if the telephones didn't exist, as if the miles between us didn't exist.

"Did I bother you, phoning during that time? It was all I could do not to call you every day. I wanted to so badly."

"And Erica?" I said. "You didn't tell her how you felt. You didn't, did you?"

"She was finishing *Catwalk* at that time, working really hard on it. She wouldn't let me see the manuscript. I didn't mind, I was only happy that she had something to occupy herself with. Until then she'd been wanting to meet me every day for lunch, wanted to go out every night. She was afraid I'd get bored with her. And you know the pressures of my work. I'm so tired I can hardly *see* at the end of a working day. I never realized it until Erica. You and I . . . we lived so quietly up there in our little world."

I didn't speak. He cleared his throat and went on, "When Erica lost the baby . . . matters worsened between us, the situation became intolerable. And no, Sally, I didn't tell her I still loved you, I didn't even tell her I was unhappy, I was stupid, but I wasn't cruel.

"Erica kept insisting I was phoning you when she wasn't around, when I was at the office, or the hospital. She then became convinced that you were back in New York, that I was seeing you . . . *I wished she was right, Sally*.

"If I'd really loved her, I'd have tried to help her. And she needed help, I see that, now. I was so wrapped up in my own misery, in what I'd done in losing you, that . . . I just didn't read the signs with Erica. One night, when I couldn't stand her suspicions, her jealousy, the *poison* she'd been spewing out about you, I told her I was leaving her, I was going to a hotel that night and I wanted her to go home to New Hampshire in the morning.

"She listened to everything I said very calmly, and then she asked me if I was going to go back to you, and . . . and instead of saying *no*, I . . . I was stupid enough to mutter, 'Sally wouldn't have me back, after what I've done.'

"Erica sat there for a few seconds, then she calmly got to her feet and went off to the bathroom.

"Minutes went by and I didn't hear any sound, and I started to get worried. She hadn't locked the bathroom door. I walked right in and found her standing over the basin with a razor blade in her hand. When she saw me she made a slash, several slashes, up and down her forearm. None were deep, but she was screaming all the time, even while I was struggling with her, trying to get the damned razor blade out of her hand: *What about what I'd done to her! What about what I'd done to her!*

"Eventually she dropped the blade on the floor, and

efore I could stop her she'd stooped after it, grabbed it
n the other hand, and slashed out at my face. I dodged
ack, but she caught me across the neck, quite deeply."

"Oh, God, Keir."

"I slipped, fell, and smashed my forehead on the corner
f the shower stall. I was bleeding, too. The police told
ne they found almost as much of my blood as Erica's.
They said it puzzled them."

"Were you knocked unconscious?"

"No, just stunned for a few seconds. When I looked up
t Erica she was beating her fists on the walls, on the mirror,
nd sobbing that she wanted to die, she wished she was
ead, over and over again.

"I gave her a couple of tablets to make her sleep and I
tayed with her until she drifted off, promising I wouldn't
ave her. It was the only thing that calmed her down.

"Later, when I knew she was sleeping, I cleaned the
athroom with paper towels and toilet paper and put it
ll down the chute straightaway. I didn't want poor Clo-
inda to find all that blood in the morning and think
here'd been a massacre." His voice lower, "But in the
nd she was put through a lot anyway, wasn't she?"

"We all were, Keir. We all were," I said, then, "Did you
o to a doctor?"

"When I knew she was sleeping, I called Jeremy Cam-
erwell; he came over and put two stitches in my head,
ive in my neck."

"Oh, God. And Jeremy knew, that bastard. He knew all
his time what went on and said nothing . . ."

"Sally, *please*. Jeremy has been a very good friend—I
ave to protect him from this."

"Okay," reluctantly.

"You see, I told the police I sewed myself up. It's not
ard to do, the cut on the neck is beneath my ear, and
unning vertically. I could have done it myself, but I didn't
ave any instruments or suture in the apartment.

"I phoned you late that night, but you weren't home.
o I left a message. I never meant it to be the last . . ."

The tape. *That tape,* that had gone to the NYPD via ever
police officer in St. Claude.

"In the morning," Keir continued, "I found Erica wri
ing me a note. She seemed quite calm, just determined
She said—and the note said—that she was going home t
New Hampshire to think about our future together. Tha
was typical of her, you see. *She saw only what she wanted t
see.*

" Well, if her pride made her want to seem the instigato
in this separation, I didn't mind. I was relieved. I didn'
think further than that, didn't want to.

"Erica's car was at the mechanic's, but I was so . . . *please*
that she'd gone . . . I didn't care that she'd taken th
Mercedes. I didn't think any more about it, beyond th
inconvenience.

"As the morning wore on, I began to worry about Erica
I should have phoned her at Meadowsweet, but I decide
she wouldn't be there yet. And then I thought that I shoul
talk to her in person, try to gauge if she was really beginnin
to adjust to it being over between us . . . So I called Jeremy
and he met me at his place, to loan me one of his car
and give me the key to his cabin in Beaver Creek.

"I wonder, looking back on it, whether I really ha
any intention of confronting Erica at all. Because once
reached the turnoff to Meadowsweet, I just kept going
turned the car round, and headed for Colorado. I took
lot of money out of the bank in Concord—as if I knew I'
be staying away awhile. I knew Erica couldn't have m
traced if I didn't use my credit cards."

His voice was heavy, "I was at a motel on the road whe
Erica died. I had receipts for the motels I stayed at—bu
no one came forward, no one told the police they'd see
me—and I just couldn't bring myself to come back, whe
I heard. There were supplies in the cabin, and I hunted
When my beard grew I risked a trip into a small town fo
more supplies. *I couldn't come back, Sally!*" he repeated. "
think I was crazy with my sense of guilt, of hopelessness

I just . . . panicked. I couldn't decide what to do—so I stayed put."

"Jeremy helped you, didn't he, Keir? He knew you were at the cabin."

"Yes." Reluctantly. "He brought me money, books. He drove down to see me, said it was the closest thing to an adventure he'd had since college."

Jeremy Camberwell, with his supercilious smile, his secretive, quietly arrogant personality behind his blond, Ivy League good looks. How he must have laughed: at me, the Stanforths, the police. He'd gain a sly and gratifying sense of power from all this. "An adventure" for him—but what of the heartache for those Keir had left behind?

"When I'd call you," Keir said, "you sounded so strong, so content with your new life. I couldn't believe that you'd forgive me. I couldn't forgive myself for betraying you the way I did—and then Erica. I should have called Hal Abraham to her that last night. I just . . . stopped thinking clearly. I wanted her gone, Sally. God help me, but that night, that last night in the apartment together, wiping the blood off the walls, I wished she was dead. When I found out she was, when I was at the cabin . . . I think it pushed me over the edge."

We were silent. I could relate to all he said, but I didn't know how I could say so, or whether I should.

"Sally," Keir said, "you will let me see you some time?"

"Yes," I agreed. "I'll see you."

"I never stopped loving you, Sally." And I knew he was speaking the truth.

"I love you too, Keir," I admitted reluctantly. He needed to hear the words, and as I spoke them I knew that they, too, were the truth.

And just like a nasty scene in a movie, I turned around, the smile and the tears on my face, and was confronted with McGarret, standing quietly in the hall, unbuttoning his jacket. He hadn't crept up on me, it wasn't his style: I'd simply been too intent on Keir to notice him.

"Keir, I have to go now."

"Can I call you again?"

"Yes," I said, and replaced the receiver quietly on its cradle.

McGarret said, mildly, "You didn't have to hang up in such a hurry."

"Did I do that?"

"You were making plans to see him again."

"You misunderstood." I went to turn away but one big arm was suddenly leaning on the wall in front of me, blocking my path.

He said, "It sounded pretty clear to me."

"Some time. He asked to see me *some time.*"

"Sarah, are you lying to me?"

"No!"

" 'Cause there's no need to lie. What you say to him is your business—but I won't have you lying to me. Hear?"

His arms were about me.

Why can't I love this man? I thought. *He is so goddamned lovable. What is the matter with me?*

McGarret made love to me that night, and yet he seemed somehow, for the first time, to want to detach himself from the proceedings. He took a long time about it, seemed to toy with my mind as much as my body, and the warm darkness between our flesh came alive with the sounds of my voice pleading for him, pleading for release, pleading for more . . . when I discovered it was my voice, and what it was saying, I fell silent. And only then did he take me thoroughly, completely, and yet with the knowledge now between us, that I had called for him, had needed him.

But it had been nothing more than a moment. Just a moment. And moments would not be enough for this man, I knew it. He wanted more than moments.

*   *   *

In the darkness of the following morning, I found him in his uniform, tiptoeing around the room by the light from the hall, packing his belongings.

I pretended to be asleep, but there was such a *finality* to the small, suppressed sounds, that I got up once he'd left the room, and followed him.

In the spare room, that he'd always used as a dressing room only, he was packing calmly, methodically, and did not look up. He was as unemotional as if he were clearing out drawers at the end of a holiday.

"So you're leaving." I leaned in the doorway.

"Had to happen sometime, I guess."

"Yes." Heavily. I wondered how much I had hurt him. It was so very hard to tell; but whatever the extent of it, he didn't, at the moment at least, seem intent on hurting me back. I wanted to say to his bent back, *I never meant to hurt you at all.*

I wanted to say *something*. But there were no words at that time that wouldn't have sounded clichéd. I watched him, feeling more wretched, more miserable by the second. I didn't even have the consolation of knowing that in McGarret's absence I'd be free to embrace happiness and a bright future with Keir. There was no bright future, no happiness, for me. An eye for an eye and a tooth for a tooth. A life of youth, fame, love, and riches—all these things Erica had lost when I'd killed her, and I could not accept them by default.

I wanted suddenly, rashly, to say all that to McGarret, just so I could tell him: *I'm just as miserable as you, for a different reason. I'm just as hollowed out and bereft as you are. You may* believe *you'll never know love again, but I* know *I won't.*

He said, "I'll come back for Patsy tomorrow."

"Sure."

He had finished packing. It was surprising how little he had when compressed. The carryall, his suit-bags of uniforms.

I stood away from the door. As he walked past me into the hall, I said, "Will you promise me something?"

"Depends."

The voice was cool, but when I looked up to his eyes, looked deep into his eyes, there was humor there, or tolerance, or fondness; it was enough for me to continue. "Promise me you won't cut me dead on the street."

"Shoot you?"

This was hopeful. This was almost a joke. "You know what I mean, promise you won't look through me, promise you'll always say 'Morning, Sarah.' "

"I promise," he said, "unless it's afternoon."

Both of us almost smiled. But it was hard, harder by the moment, looking at each other.

I turned away and said, "I *will* see Keir again. But I'm not going back to him." Beside me he gave a small sigh, or maybe he began to speak and then stopped. When I looked he was gazing over my head at nothing, the wide lipless mouth held hard. "I'm not," I said.

"Don't hold yourself to promises you can't keep, Sarah." He put down his bags and reached into his pocket. I watched as he took the key to my front door from his key ring and handed it back to me. I took it, feeling its weight like lead in my palm.

I didn't see him leave. When I next looked up, when my eyes had cleared, he was gone.

I heard the front door close.

I heard the Jeep drive away.

I sat on the edge of the bed and thought: he didn't say, *G'bye, Sarah.*

The following morning I drove into Fredericton. I stayed there until late, needing a change of scene from St. Claude, somewhere where I wasn't well known, where I wouldn't have to greet people, stop and talk with them, and answer the question, "How's Perry?"

I drove home trying not to hope that I'd find McGarret

at *Jaegerhalle* when I got there. After all, I'd left the house all day to avoid him, hadn't I?

He wasn't there. I went to the barn. It was empty.

The house looked dark and unwelcoming. Just as I put the key in the lock I heard the mailman drive past, heard the little truck pause at the gates. Grateful for something to do, to avoid the empty house, I walked back down the drive to check the mailbox; it was just on dusk.

Letters from Aunts, a fat envelope from Brambles Thorne, which I presumed was my travel itinerary for the tour. Nothing from Keir.

A car came past; I only looked up because it seemed to accelerate as it drew near me, coming from the direction of town. It was a wheezy old pickup, one I'd seen but never really noticed before. It went past quickly, the driver, balding, dark lank hair, looking grimly ahead. But out the passenger window a gremlin peered through the steaming glass.

I stood frozen in shock, couldn't take my eyes from the pale face behind the window that was disappearing down the road in the gloom.

Alby Gresson had come home.

Chapter
Thirty-Four

There was a message on the machine from McGarret, asking me to call him at the station or at home. I reached him at the station.

"Sarah, there was some kind of glitch in the red tape. Alby Gresson was released from jail early because of his health. We weren't notified until today."

"I just saw him."

"What? Where?"

"Just passing by in his son's pickup."

"How did he behave?" His professional tone.

"Just . . . looked. No emotion. He seemed," and I was telling the truth, here, "old and tired, Perry."

McGarret was silent, and I could hear the voices, the phones, in the background. Then he said, "I want to come back."

He spoke so low that it took a second or two to decipher his words from the station patter behind him.

"No," I said, my eyes shut tight, trying not to see his face in front of me, the big hand holding the receiver, his big head bent, the line of his neck . . . "No. The restraining order would still be current, wouldn't it?"

"Yeah, but—"

"I'll be alright."

"Sarah, I don't think we really thought this through."

"About Alby?"

"I . . . Yeah, about Alby *and* about us."

"Alby won't try anything more. He's been judged as okay to return home. I'll be fine."

"Sarah, I shouldn't have—"

"And regarding us. There *is* no us. You said it yourself when you were leaving, it had to happen sooner or later."

"I was talking through my ass. Sarah, let me stay in the spare room—just a few weeks."

I couldn't bear it. I was feeling as torn apart as he was. And this was not fair to him. It wasn't *fair* to him.

"No, McGarret. I can't keep you as a bodyguard forever. I've got to show Alby that I'm not afraid; I'm going to live a normal life, like I did when I first came here."

I could almost hear McGarret's thought processes: should he try to frighten me? Would it be fair to frighten me if I remained obdurate? Was I likely to remain obdurate?

He made up his mind. "Okay." A deep growl, like an unhappy bear. "Just call if anything—anything—happens. Or if you're just plain scared, or if you . . ." he stopped, again the growl, "Just call me, Sarah."

I moved through the house, his words echoing through my mind.

I'd forborne saying to McGarret, "So you collected Patsy and the last of your belongings." And he hadn't said anything. So I thought he must have left a note. I looked in all the rooms. The greatest affront was the spare room. He'd been in here, alright, and dusted the now empty dresser-top, and stripped the bed and put the sheets in the laundry basket, the blankets in the now-empty closet.

"You were hardly in here anyway!" I shouted at him, as if he were in the room with me.

Then I sat down in a heap on the carpet and cried. I wept for McGarret, the only man who had ever loved Sarah Feldman-Stanforth, forty-three years old. I wept for a man who was wise enough to see all my faults and kind enough to love me anyway. I wept for what might have been, if it hadn't been for Keir. If it hadn't been for Erica.

Somehow the months, the weeks had passed, and while the thought of the imminent publication of *Scotty's Thing* was exciting, I had other thoughts on my mind. The years of ambitious dreams were finally culminating, *soon,* in the reality of a career as a professional writer, yet I found my moments of anticipation crowded out by my sense of vulnerability, living here alone—with a dangerous enemy once more only a few hundred yards away.

So Alby Gresson had been home for over a week and I hadn't known he was there. I had a feeling his sons, happy to be known in the province as brawling misfits, nevertheless took exception to having a father who was crazy with guns. Maybe they were taking really good care of the old man.

Or so I told myself.

Yet I left the gun where it was. It was insurance of a different kind, and I had become superstitious about it, after I had placed it in its secret compartment. That hiding place had been made for security of one kind or another—perhaps even skulduggery of one kind or another—more than three hundred years ago. It was created for someone who, like me, had secrets. I found I didn't like checking on the gun, didn't like opening the cunning little door. I didn't even like *looking* at the heavy weapon, reminding myself of why I had bought it, imagining the day when I would be forced to open the compartment for the last time . . .

I knew it would be safer, now, if I kept it in a drawer by the bed, but I didn't *want* to shoot Alby Gresson. I had already killed one person, and I was tired of killing people.

o I left the gun where it was, figuring if I ever *really* was
nder attack, I'd have time to get to the kitchen cupboard.
fter all, who'd expect me to run for *that*?

'he phone calls grew more and more frequent, from Bram-
les Thorne with last-minute queries, from journalists, and
rom friends, the ones in New York wanting me to stay
vith them, arranging parties—or trying to—for my return.
'hese I wriggled out of, having a long memory of the time
fter the divorce when so many of them seemed out of
own, until they smelt blood—perhaps literally—and
vanted to close in on the pathetic remains of Keir and
Erica's marriage.

My friends here in Canada were a different matter. I went
 little silly and attended a lot of impromptu celebrations,
nidday meals at the Brunswick Inn that Stephen Sondheim
night have used for inspiration for *The Ladies Who Lunch;*
arties at *Jaegerhalle,* or the McGarrets' white palace, or
Merlin and Natalie's place, or the Dufours' house. McGar-
et was always invited, but regretfully declined to attend
ny of these gatherings.

And I set up the Zachary Feldman Foundation of New
Brunswick. The money from the sale of *Scotty's Things* was
o go to cardiac units at hospitals within the province; in
ny will I bequeathed the sale of the furniture at *Jaegerhalle*
o benefit the Foundation also. The house itself would be
urned into a writers' retreat and be dedicated to Otto
Hahn.

Except to visit my friends, I didn't often go to St. Claude
hese days. I was afraid of running into Alby Gresson—or
ven one of his boys—in the supermarket, and people
vere too friendly and asked too many questions about the
oming book, and about Perry McGarret.

And seeing him was hard. Across the street, driving past
n the police car ... He'd smile with his eyes, and raise
is hand, or tug down the brim of his cap, should he be

wearing it. And I'd think, *Would he be doing that, if he hadn*
promised?

Yes, he would. *He would.*

But every time I saw him, it ruined my day.

Natalie had friends from the hospital who were betwee
houses at the time of the book launch, so some swappin
went on at this time. Two days before I left, her friend
came to the farm and looked after their cats, and Merli
and Natalie came to *Jaegerhalle* with Chloe, Olaf, Hone
and Rat.

I phoned McGarret to say goodbye, and he said: Wel
the big day's almost here. And I said: Yes. And then h
said: You take care of yourself down there in the big cit
you've probably lost your edge. And I laughed and sai
Yes. And then we were quiet. And I asked: How's Pats
Cline? And he said: Real fine, but getting fat. But it wa
hard to talk after that. And the silence was very long indeed
Finally he said: I have to go, we've got a call. And I sai
Yes, of course, sorry. And he said: No, I just wish . . . An
I said: It's okay. And he said: Come back, Sarah. And
said I would, and then I said: Goodbye, McGarret.

And he said: G'bye, Sarah.

I hadn't heard from Keir, and though I knew how to get i
touch with his parents, or Jeremy or Andy, I was reluctan
If Keir wished to talk with me, he'd do so. How long ha
I waited for him, prayed for him, grieved for him?

And then, the day before I was to leave, I received a fax
Staying with my parents. Beth says your tour finishes in New Yor
on June fourteenth. Can I meet you at the apartment? Fon
regards, Keir.

I found I was nervous. I found I was scared. That was a
far into my feelings as I dared to look.

* * *

he apartment, our old apartment, did nothing to make
1e feel better. I was grateful to find Clorinda had waited
) welcome me. She made sure I knew there was food in
1e refrigerator, and then she left, saying at the last, "I
ope you and the doctor can . . . talk. I think you both
eserve to be happy, Mrs. Stanforth."

I smiled and thanked her, but after she left I turned to
1e only familiar thing in the room, the view of Central
ark from the windows, and thought, *happy?*

The apartment seemed an extension of what I'd seen
1 photos of the house in Meadowsweet: comfortable, cozy,
ry expensively furnished with country-style antiques. The
ofas were floral-covered, with flounces. Even the cushions
ad flounces. The king-sized bed in what had been our
edroom had flounces, as did each of the beds in the other
iree bedrooms, including the one which Erica had used
s a study, with the third best view in front of her desk.

I sat in her chair, looked at the blank screen of her
Iacintosh, and thought, *Something isn't right.* I got to my
et and walked through the apartment, through all the
alls and both reception rooms and the huge living room
iat was half the size of *Jaegerhalle* in itself. I couldn't work
out.

Something is wrong.

I even made myself go into the main bathroom, and
poked at the walls, sparkling clean, now, as if I'd find the
lood still there . . . I shivered.

Something is wrong.

I found I didn't like being here, for I looked around
nd discovered that nothing in this apartment, this home
iat Keir and I had shared for so many years, was mine.
nything that was ours I had left for Keir when we sepa-
ited. As for the rest—all the furniture, ornaments, drapes,
ie very color of the paint on the walls—it was Erica.

The book launch was that afternoon, the following

morning I would fly out on the first leg of the tour. Wa
it worth moving to a hotel, just for this one night?

Yes it was.

I phoned the Marlborough Regency and booked a roo
for the night, and for the night of the fourteenth of Marcl
the day the tour ended. I'd been foolish to think that th
was my home, even though I owned each and every horrib
expensive square foot of it. And I realized, waiting fo
Keir, that I should *not* be waiting for Keir. No matter wha
happened, we shouldn't be sharing the apartment. W
could be adult about this, we *could* be mature about it . .
but we weren't. I felt like a lost child, and somehow I kne
Keir was as lost as I was.

Living in New York most of my life, I had become accu
tomed to crowds. I'd slowed down some in New Brun
wick—maybe McGarret was more right than he knew—
maybe I *had* lost my edge. For I was unprepared for th
success of *Scotty's Things*. I was unprepared for the gushin
talk show hosts, the size of the headlines, the bestselle
list, the sales figures, the constantly changing hotel room
and hotel staff—and the crowds.

I was used to crowds—but on New York streets in pea
hour, in New York stores at sale times. I wasn't used t
crowds in *bookstores*. I wasn't used to crowds that crowde
around *me*.

Beth had asked for leave and was on tour with me, an
even she began to worry. "You don't eat," she pointe
out. "All you do is order a salad and play with it. We ma
as well get room service to send up a game of Scrabbl
and be done with it."

We finished the tour in Washington; exhausted, I tol
Beth I wanted to hire a car and drive north by myself.
needed a little time without people, I said, I never wante
to see another airplane. Beth reminded me I had a literar
lunch on the eighteenth. She'd allowed for me to have
few days' break from the minute we arrived back in Ne

ork, but if I felt like spending long hours driving . . . Then
e added, "I think you're putting off seeing Keir."
I thought of lying and then rethought. "Yeah," I said.

he past has a way of following you. It wasn't all that restful
drive; I kept going over and over what had happened in
ese past months. I thought of Alby Gresson, and the fact
at at least I didn't feel haunted by him as I did in St.
laude.

I drove into the underground garage below the apart-
ent block on Central Park South—and only then did I
ome out of my daze and remember that I didn't live here
nymore.

The past owns one. There isn't any escape. And I kept
riving, found my old car space, and parked the rented
ar there. For a long time I sat in the car, thinking: how
any more of my reflexes are so conditioned?

Like, will I be able to see Keir, and not want to hold
m, forgive him?

How could I come here? I was staying tonight at the
arlborough Regency, the literary luncheon scheduled
or one o'clock was to be held at the Marlborough Regency.
hy was I here?

To see Keir.

I should phone first.

But I knew I wouldn't. Knew even before I climbed out
f the driver's seat, taking up my handbag and briefcase
d leaving my cases in the trunk.

A car came down the ramp from the street level, and
rned towards me. It was a very battered and dirty little
dan of unfamiliar make and model, looking out of place
the company of the Mercedes, Rolls-Royces, and other
p-of-the-range cars that sat complacently about the large
arking area.

And my heart, bumping hard with my fright, faltered a
ttle, for I knew it was Keir.

I *knew*, though I almost didn't recognize him. How thi
he was!

"Sally," he said, in that voice that had lodged in m
heart for twenty-four years, since I'd first heard it besid
me on the stairs at Seahaven.

He moved towards me, his arms went around me, an
his body pressed into mine, mine held close in his embrac
And after all the heartache, the terror, the grieving o
the past nine months, our reunion took place in a gra
cavernous garage below Central Park South, our embrac
of which I had dreamt for so long, took place between tw
parked cars.

Chapter
Thirty-Five

I want it to be as it was between us. Is that asking too
much? I have to know."

"Keir, we have to talk. We must *talk.*"

He sighed, pulled back from me, and I straightened
from where we had ended up, half reclining on the settee.
He gazed down at me tenderly. "I'm being selfish. There's
plenty of time. I'll stay in the spare room . . ."

"No, Keir. I'm staying at the Marlborough Regency."

He could think I'd sleep in *that* bed? It wasn't *our* bed,
it was a *new* bed, made to look like an old bed, and he
had made love to Erica in it.

Keir had always been sensitive, quick. "Of course," and
he looked up and around the room. "I'll . . . arrange the
sale of all this, send the proceeds down to the Tudors."

"Okay. Good." It was the first broaching of the serious
matters that lay between us.

And then I found I couldn't discuss it. Suddenly I knew
if we once began to turn back, to talk about what had
happened, then my newfound trust in him would have me
confiding in him. I knew I would tell him everything.

* * *

Keir wanted to attend the literary luncheon with me, an
I phoned Beth to see what she could arrange. It wasn
any problem, she said, there would be a spare seat besid
me at my table.

"Are you happy, Sal?" my friend asked.

I thought, and then answered truthfully. "I think I woul
be, very much—if I could let myself."

"Then let yourself, Sally," Beth said. "Life's too short.

We weren't any real distance from the Marlboroug
Regency, and we decided to walk. Hand in hand, Keir an
I strolled down the street we knew so well, and I foun
myself wondering if I could live here anymore.

I had ties in Canada. I had Promises to Keep. But at th
moment I pushed the thought away and did what half
lifetime had taught me to do when confused or sad.
moved closer to Keir, and he put his arm about me. W
walked like that the rest of the way to the hotel, not speak
ing, not needing to speak. And his nearness dispelled m
confusion, my desire to think, my need to form the que
tions that I had to ask him, the incidents I had to tell hi
about.

But something about the apartment still bothered me
something stayed with me, reminding me just as I was o
the point of another thought, reminding me that some
thing wasn't right, something . . .

"Raging Studs, sir?" The young man behind the des
asked Keir.

"I beg your pardon?"

"Are you part of the Raging Studs entourage?"

I had to bite the inside of my lip. Keir's face forme
what he would not like to have known was a very Stanfort
expression, and he said, calmly, "No, I'm Dr. Keir Stan
forth, and I'd like to book into a suite close to my wife's.

Our eyes met. I could have objected, but I saw in th

rk depths that I had not been the only one who was
unted. Keir did not want to spend a night in the apart-
ent either. And certainly not alone.

"I have only a room—" I began to inform the young
an, who was having trouble with the computer. At that
oment the hotel's owner, Hortense, saw us, and came to
ur rescue. Of course two adjoining suites on the seventh
oor were available, she said, and beamed between the
o of us. "Kelly," she commanded, "the keys to Suites
01 and 702, please."

A pretty young blonde woman handed our keys to Keir.
hadn't occurred to her to hand one—and certainly not
oth—to me.

I thought, oddly, *I'm not a single woman any more. I'm an
appendage to Keir. I always was an appendage to Keir. Someone's*
fe.

The young woman hadn't taken her eyes from Keir's
ce as he chattered with Hortense.

She's read the book, I thought, suddenly. She knows
ho he is, for the poor girl was finding it very difficult to
ep her mouth quite closed, and she leaned forward,
owly, until she was standing at an odd angle against the
esk as if she'd spent too many long and unsuccessful
ours at a singles' bar.

To my amusement, I realised that I was responsible. I
ad labored long and lovingly over Piers's childhood, his
obringing, the forces that shaped the man, and then the
an himself, for I had missed him so much that writing
out him, describing him, brought him closer to me.
he Piers Danforth in *Scotty's Things* was my Keir, and
cognizable.

This young woman, this stranger, knew him. Or felt she
d. She had given me one look of frightened respect and
en forgotten me; she was leaning over the desk with her
os slightly parted.

Hortense was saying, "The young musicians—I hope
ere won't be too much disturbance. They're nice enough

in themselves, but the media . . . Let me know if you hav
any problems.''

We made our way to the elevator, for the staircase, th
wonderful curved cedar staircase, was packed with youn
people in jeans and parkas and journalists wearing h
rassed expressions. The doors to the restaurant wei
closed, and from inside I could hear the sound of lou
laughter. Through the heavy cedar doors with their pane
of etched and beveled glass, I saw a large table of longl
aired, rather scruffy-looking young men having a boiste
ous lunch. They seemed to be the restaurant's only patron

When we entered the elevator I saw the young receptio
ist back away down the desk to talk to another woma
Hortense having already sailed across to the stairs to ti
to move the people who crowded there for a better viei
into the restaurant.

''Have you heard of the Raging Studs?'' Keir asked n
as we entered the elevator. I shook my head; my last viei
of the women at the desk was of not one, but two ope
mouths, two pairs of hungry eyes.

The elevator attendant had heard Keir's question abou
the Raging Studs. As he closed the doors of the orna
iron cage and we clanked upwards, he said, ''Hottest thin
on the rock scene at the moment, sir. Three number on
hits in a row.''

''Good sound?'' Keir asked.

''Horrible, sir. And I speak from experience, having tw
daughters who play their albums night and day. They'r
supposed to be in town incognito—only arrived from L./
this morning. I'd brace myself for some excitement if th
news spreads that they're here.''

I was tempted to ask if he'd told his daughters, but we'
reached the second floor, and stepped out.

A woman with a child in a stroller was waiting there.

''Going down, ma'am?'' the elevator attendant aske
and she nodded and pushed the stroller into the elevato
The child, in a yellow jumpsuit, had a sweet, bright face

We'd attended functions in the Marigold Room befor

nd knew it was across from the elevators, around the
urve of the balustrade that led to the great staircase and
verlooking the first-floor lobby below. I was still thinking
f the child, the stroller . . .

Keir stopped in the middle of the wide expanse of carpet.
: was quiet up here, there was nothing on this floor to
nterest the fans and journalists downstairs. Keir turned to
ne and said, "Sally, there is some hope for us, isn't there?"

I looked at him, finding it hard to concentrate on his
ords. My mind was racing with other thoughts. Strollers.
lots. Bassinets. *Baby things.*

"Sally?"

"Um."

"What's the—?"

"Keir, where did the furniture go? The furniture for the
aby's room. Erica had decorated one of the—"

"Back to New Hampshire," Keir said. "No. She sold it.
: upset her. I left the details to her. I think she sold it
ll."

He was walking towards the great cedar doors on the
ar wall; I could see a crowd of people, mostly women, at
ables inside. Outside the doors, on a large sign, were the
ords, *Literary luncheon for Sarah Stanforth.*

He was lying. I knew him better than I knew myself and
e was unwillingly, desperately, lying.

I said, "She'd just come out of hospital after losing the
aby. She wouldn't have had time before you quarreled.
nd she wanted another baby, she'd have wanted to try
)—"

"Let's talk about this after—" His hand was under my
lbow but I pulled out of his grasp.

I knew what had been niggling at the back of my mind
t the apartment. The waiting nursery. Keir himself had
old me about it. *And it was gone.* It would have to have
one *before Erica had lost the baby.*

"What hospital did she go into?"

"What?"

"What hospital?"

"For God's sake, Camberley, alright? Jeremy was looking after her."

"But Jeremy is half-owners in Camberley."

"So? For heaven's sake, Sally, we're late as it is. Look they're all waiting for you."

But they weren't. A woman sitting near the door had turned and seen us and was hurrying out towards us.

At the same time there was a commotion downstairs. "Look," Keir said, leading me to the balustrade to see that the Raging Studs were trying to make their way out the restaurant doors, and were being mobbed.

"Keir, was Jeremy looking after Erica?" I asked, feeling sick, beginning to feel really quite sick. "How did he look after her, Keir?"

He glanced at me, and away again.

"Usual thing. He gave her a curette afterwards, it's standard practice."

A shrill excited voice called, "It's you, isn't it?" The woman bore down on us, addressing us both, but her eyes were on Keir. "Mrs. Stanforth and . . . and—"

I said, "Afterwards . . . or *before*?"

Keir, so handsome in his dark suit, looked a little desperate. He gazed from the woman—a rather fat, bright-eyed woman who reminded me of the good-natured little baby we'd seen into the lift—to me.

She was saying, fluttering a little at some distance, "Oh, this is so exciting. This is just a thrill—to actually meet you both."

"Afterwards or before?" I demanded in a low voice.

No nursery. No sign that a child had been welcomed or planned. It certainly wasn't planned, except perhaps by Erica. And it certainly wasn't welcome.

"Jeremy's helped you out a lot, hasn't he?" But it was a statement, not a question at all. A statement, in a small cool voice, as I studied his profile. For he was unwilling to look at me.

I spoke his name, and he turned to me, then, with a

ook of haggard wretchedness that I had never seen before.
Ie spoke quietly and firmly.

"I tried to tell you on the telephone. And then I thought,
'll wait and tell you when I see you. But when I saw you
again; I didn't know how. How could you forgive that?
Iow could anyone? But I did try to tell you when I phoned
ou in Canada: you can see now why I couldn't face
eturning to New York after I heard she was dead. I killed
ier, Sally. Because the child was in the way. It stood
oetween me and having you back again."

And despite my feelings of horror for Erica, for what
he must have gone through, I found myself pitying Keir.
t was an overwhelming feeling, and completely new for
ne. "Keir," I said, "it was all for nothing. I couldn't have
:ome back to you. How could I be so happy in St. Claude,"
pointed out, as he began to interrupt, "if I were only
narking time for you to come back to me? I made myself
i life, Keir. Without even being aware of it. It was only
vithout you that I realised that I didn't really need you."

His jaw tightened. "You're lashing back at me because
hurt you so badly—"

"No, Keir—"

In the periphery of my vision I saw that the fat little
voman had entered the Marigold Room and had come
out again, more people, mostly women, in her wake. We
iad to stop this conversation, this was no place for a conver-
ation like this . . .

Keir took my arm. His face was contorted with emotion,
iis voice constricted. I could only stare at him. I had never
een him like this.

"You can't forgive me, can you? For Erica. You can't
inderstand that she meant nothing to me! She was a pretty,
:mpty shell, Sally! She meant nothing!"

"She did!" My voice pitched as low and as vehement as
iis, a sudden, unaccountable rage rising in me. "She loved
ou, Keir, really loved you. More than I ever did!"

"I can't believe that. I won't."

His stubbornness, his dismissal of the girl who had been

driven to kill for him, made me furious. "All she wanted was to be your wife! And by then, I didn't want that any more, though I didn't know it. I'd come too far, Keir, to go back to that life."

"You were happy in that life!" His voice broke with desperation, for he looked into my eyes and saw I meant every word.

"It wasn't a life! *Now* I have a life! And I'm not giving it up to go back to being Mrs. Dr. Keir Stanforth!"

"Keir Stanforth . . ."

"Piers Danforth . . . !"

The two names commingled and whispered and grew and all around us the respectful crowd, no longer at a distance, pushed forward.

Other people had left their seats and had come out the doors. It was hard to speak, now, for books were being thrust at me, and pens, and I couldn't tell, through my tears, which pens belonged to which books, and all I could do was say to the blurred faces, "I'm sorry. Just a moment, I'm sorry . . ."

Women were thrusting between me and Keir, as if we each had a following. I had to reach out for him, found his hand reaching for me—but we were jostled apart.

I heard him speaking my name, but it was lost to me amongst the other voices. "Omigod, it's him!"

"He's back!"

"Omigod, he's gorgeous!"

Where was Keir? He was gone, lost in the crowd. It was like one of those dreams where you try to move, and find you can't. There were hundreds of people, all rushing out of the Marigold Room, fanning out through the doors, and I found myself being edged sideways by the flow, sideways and backwards. People were beginning to be as uncomfortable about the crush as I was, a voice from within the room, as distant as one of Alice's doors in *Through the Looking-Glass,* screamed, *Is it a fire?* And someone else yelled "Fire?" and someone else yelled "Fire!" and a lot of people were yelling a lot of things, and all at once. Above

hem I heard Keir's voice calling my name, but I wouldn't
urn towards him.

It was so hard to move against the tide; it had become
quite clear, until the panic, that it was not really me they
had rushed to see. People glanced at me, recognized my
face, but most were looking about for Keir. Now they still
eemed to be pressing towards Keir.

An elderly woman close to me murmured, "I feel faint.
feel faint." But I couldn't reach her, I couldn't move. I
was beginning to feel really frightened, the physical pain
of being hemmed in so closely made me forget even my
pain for Erica. Keir was still shouting for me, and I tried
to turn around, to see where he was, somewhere behind
me . . . I *couldn't* turn. I *couldn't*.

"Keir?" I cried out. But I don't think he heard me, so
many people were shouting, so many women were screaming. "Go back!" I yelled at the people in front of me, to
the hundreds of people in front of me, not to anyone in
particular, for there seemed to be no single individual, it
was a swaying canvas of terrified faces before me. I shouted
again, and that was a mistake, for there was suddenly no
room to take a breath to replace the one I'd just exhaled.

This wasn't happening. It couldn't be happening.

Above all the noise, because I was listening for it, I could
hear Keir's voice, "Sally! *Sally!*"

Gradually, inch by inch, I was being pushed to the right
of the doors, and turning my head alone, for I couldn't
move my body, I could just see Keir above the sea of jig-
gling heads, panicked faces; mouths were open in terror,
all mouths were open, gasping; I couldn't tell who was
screaming and who, like me, could not. There was a dreadful fecal smell from somewhere close; a woman directly in
front of me looked blankly into my face and vomited on
my shoulder. Then her eyes rolled up in her head and she
seemed to turn her face to the ceiling. She stood still,
pressed up against me, her head lolling back and forth
like a marionette with a broken string.

From somewhere a siren began to wail, adding its scream
to all the others.

"Sally! I love you! I love you, Sally!"

His face was white above the heads of the crowd, for he
knew what I did not know.

Keir! I tried to say his name—but it was already too late
for Keir vanished. He vanished, before my eyes, like a cruel
magic trick—and then the floor shifted and threw us all
to the ground.

It's an earthquake, I thought, *here in New York.* I couldn't
see, I couldn't breathe. I had been buried alive in living
bodies, heavy hot bodies squirmed and screamed in blackness. My last memory was the smell of vomit and perfume
and the sweat of terror. And I thought, *God forgive me all
the wrong I've done.* I thought, *I should never have left Canada.*

Chapter
Thirty-Six

Beth and Malcolm flew back with me to St. Claude. Frank and Nanette Dufour met us at the airport and drove us to *Jaegerhalle*.

There were quite a few people at the house. I was embraced, kissed on the cheek; everyone gazed at me with concern. I didn't mind. I barely noticed. Perhaps the tablets had something to do with it.

Someone had cooked. Stephanie was there. And Eugene Boillot. A subdued Janice McGarret told me kindly that I was to call her if I needed anything. Merlin and Natalie hugged me close, Louis and Marie-France Ambroise from the Brunswick Inn both took my hands, and—the biggest shock—Aunt Sadie, Aunt Miriam, and Aunt Shirley were all there, all the way from Palm Beach.

I thought McGarret might have come, but I looked about the room and didn't see him.

It was his mother who, after a warm clasp to her ample bosom, said with a frown, "He left for Europe only two days ago. He said he had to go, that you didn't need him right now."

Wise McGarret. Cruel, wise McGarret.

"You will forgive him, won't you?" Janice peered into my face. "He's an odd boy, always was. But he seemed so much more . . . approachable when you and he . . ." She stopped. I felt I had done all my talking in New York. I was all talked out. I gazed at her helpfully but couldn't think of anything to say. Lately, words just didn't come.

"Perry and I will always be friends," I said finally, and left her. A few people looked after me worriedly, but they thought I was going to the bathroom. I went along the hall to the kitchen, opened the door, and shut it behind me.

I went to the Danish bureau, and twiddled the left-hand rosette—I slid the little panel, and found McGarret's note.

That was all.

I recognized his writing, and started to grin, despite myself. So he'd left me a note after all. He'd stolen my gun, the varmint, but at least he'd left a note. I sat down at the kitchen table to study it. It said: *As you see, there's nothing here. If there was something here, there'd be TROUBLE.*

But there isn't. So there won't be.

It wasn't signed. He'd simply added, at the lower end of the page:

Don't let it happen again.

I put my head down and laughed a lot.

And then I heard voices and footsteps in the hall and only just managed to get the note back in the compartment and the compartment closed and to get myself in a position against the edge of the sink.

"Sarah?" Stephanie Atkinson, her blue eyes round and worried behind her glasses.

"I'm okay," I said, calmly. "I just wanted a glass of water. Let's go back to the guests, shall we?"

In my sense of unreality I wasn't even disturbed when Raoul Gerlain called in briefly with Peter Copely. But it wasn't news of more tragedy. How could it be? What else could happen? Gerlain had called in merely to tell me that If There Was Anything He Could Do . . . He left the sentence hanging.

Aunt Shirley had been standing there all the while, gaz-ing up at Peter Copely. "Such a cherub," she sighed, when she was sure he couldn't hear. "If I was twenty years younger . . ."

"Try fifty," Miriam said. "This isn't the time nor the place, Shirley."

"I can pass a comment. Can I not pass a comment?"

And just then Alby Gresson arrived, and I was almost pleased. In some strange way he seemed a face from a better time, and he was well, now, wasn't he? Perhaps we could all be friends. I wondered why everyone was suddenly so hushed, so still—except for The Aunts, who kept their whispered discussion going until they realized the rest of the room was quiet.

I thought how rude everyone was not to welcome Alby. I had always felt rather badly about him. He had spent so many years alone, grieving for the one woman he had ever loved. That, of all things, can make a man mad.

I started to walk towards him, and Janice McGarret, standing near me, for some reason put her hand on my arm and held it there.

"Wasn't going to come in, but I saw the inspector was here, so I changed my mind," Alby said. "Decided to do my duty."

Yes, I thought, with a feeling of sudden relief that swept my body almost like a feeling of joy. *Yes.*

"Alby . . ." Raoul Gerlain began.

"You just listen to me!" He was shouting. "Just listen," Alby said, more calmly. "I've come to report a crime." He glared at me. "I don't care if they send me back to jail for this. It was seeing what I saw that sent me in there. And we can make a deal, Gerlain, can't we? If I gave information about a murder, we could cut a deal, couldn't we?"

Gerlain didn't answer. His broad face was as impassive as McGarret's would have been.

Alby licked his dry lips. "I saw her kill someone." And he thrust his hand out, the index finger pointed directly at me. Somewhere in the room behind me I heard a little suppressed squeak, and found time to pity my poor aunts. They should have stayed in Florida.

Alby went on, "It was about the time that writer and her doctor husband disappeared. Well, I can explain some of it. I saw *her*—" again the finger jabbed towards me, "take an ax and bury it in the skull of an innocent . . ."

The room erupted, everyone was crying out, Gerlain had stepped forward, and so had Peter, his face pale, gazing between the furious Alby and his grim-looking superior. Hands grabbed at Alby; hands, kinder, grabbed at me, for support, for solidarity? Or were they making a citizen's arrest while Gerlain and Copely were busy?

Alby was screaming, now, over the raised voices. "She's a murderess! A murderess!"

"It's true," I told the room. "What he's saying is true."

"I saw her! From the trees down by the roadway. No provocation at all!" But his eyes slid away as he looked at me, for he knew he was lying. Erica had had a gun. But he was not going to tell them about the gun.

"Cold-blooded, she was. Never gave the man a chance! Hit him from behind with the ax. Buried it in the side of his head, she did. Saw them both as clear as day, I tell you! Dr. Keir Stanforth it was, I saw everything! He's buried in the barn. Go dig up the barn, Gerlain, and you'll find him! Go dig it up, if you don't believe me!"

It was Aunt Shirley's voice behind me that whispered loudly, shakily, "Who? Who's he saying is buried in the barn?"

"I saw it!" Alby shrilled. "I saw her kill her husband! I knew his face from the TV and the pictures in the newspapers! I'd know him anywhere! It was him, alright. Saw her kill him in cold blood, I recognized him from the television! She killed him with the ax! With the ax . . . !"

He had to scream this last, because Raoul Gerlain and Peter Copely were dragging him towards the front door. Gerlain was trying to talk through Alby's shouting, saying in a tight voice into the little man's face in an effort to make him listen, to silence him, "Shut up, you old fool!

Her husband died a week ago. Haven't you seen the newspapers? Her husband was crushed to death when that balcony railing collapsed in New York. He was one of seven
people who died . . . Alby? For God's sake, Alby, Keir Stanforth died a week ago."

"But . . . he's right," I said to Gerlain, following him.
'What he said is right! I didn't mean to . . . but . . . he's
telling the truth, I *did* commit murder! I *am* guilty of
murder."

"Hush, Sarah." "Hush, Sally." So many people telling
me to be quiet, all the worried faces looking at me with pity
and embarrassment. Eugene, his soft brown eyes gazing at
me, said, "You can't blame yourself for what happened to
your husband."

"Inspector!" I began, but Gerlain was still edging the
wildly flailing Alby towards the door. He looked at me with
apologetic regret. "We'll take him in, Mrs. Stanforth. I'm
really sorry about this."

"But he's right," I told them, had to tell them, could
not wait another day, another minute; for what did it matter
what happened now? "I killed Erica Tudor! And I killed
Keir, too! Don't you understand? I killed Keir, he'd be
alive except for me!" They were staring at me, the whole
room, in expressions of shock and worry and such pity
that I wanted to shake them, each of them. Were they
stupid? Were they deaf? "I killed both of them," I told
them all. "It's all my fault! It is! It's—"

The room was turning slowly to the right; it was a horrible
feeling, bringing back to me the sensation of falling, falling
in a stifling crowd, as when the balcony balustrade had
shattered, and Keir and all those people had toppled out
into space, down into the crowd of people in the lobby
below . . .

I heard one of The Aunts sobbing, I saw David Mc-
Garret's dark blue eyes, full of concern, bend over me.
'Perry . . . "

It was David who caught me as I fell.

Chapter
Thirty-Seven

I visit Erica's grave quite purposefully and openly now. The crocuses and bluebells are a blur of colour around the baby pine. If my friends don't find me at the house, they know they'll find me here. For Keir lies here. Alone, they think, but we know better, Keir, Erica, and I.

Confronting Keir's parents to ask for his ashes was a bad experience. Beth drove me there, and waited in the car while I walked up the drive of the Stanforth mansion and frightened their butler by marching right past him. There was a large gathering of family in the living room, and standing there I realized that every single person in the room hated me. They may not always have hated me, but they hated me now.

And the polite masks worn by the immediate family since Keir had stubbornly insisted on marrying me were gone. The resentment and the naked dislike were there on their faces and in the hostile silence.

"Is she coming to the funeral tomorrow?" Keir's sister Katherine demanded. "She killed him. She's not going to be allowed at the funeral, is she?"

"Katherine!" From the look on Bill Stanforth's face

his warning was less because of Katherine's feelings than because she had spoken of them.

"She's right," said the harsh voice of one of the Boston Stanforths, the one Keir had always called Dame Clara Cluck behind her back. He would have appreciated the sight of her this evening; she stood, rustling and bristling in her favorite brown taffeta, her enormous shelf of bosom heaving. "Bill, there must be something we can do." And to me, "We'll fight that will, too, my girl, don't think we won't!"

There were murmurs in the collective throat of all the room and I almost stepped back in the face of their hostility.

"Be quiet, Clara." It was Barbara who spoke. I looked at her, and realized for the first time how alike we were, the more so as I grew older. Beneath the blonde hair in its faultless chignon, her face was set against her pain, as mine was set against my own. Only her eyes betrayed her. "What do you want, Sally?"

"I need to speak to you and Bill alone."

In the library, I said, "I'll renounce any claim on Keir's estate—not anything that'll come from Erica, that goes to her family. But I'll give you Keir's estate—in return for his ashes."

"No!" Barbara was almost frightened. I realized I had always frightened her, because I could take her son from her. Now he was beyond both of us, and still she was afraid. "Tell her no, Bill! It's our boy! Our son! She's only Keir's ex-wife! She has no rights! God knows what she'll do with his ashes."

I said, "There's a young pine tree in the forest on my farm in Canada. I want to take his ashes there."

"Say no, Bill!"

Bill gazed at me. "You're talking a lot of money, Sarah."

"I don't need money. I had Keir's love. You know it, both of you, in your hearts."

Barbara looked really distressed. Bill gazed at me with that same look of consideration.

"I won't go to the funeral," I said.

It was then he nodded. "Come to my office in the morning, I'll have my lawyer draw up something."

"I'll want to collect the urn myself from the crematorium; I'll want seals on the urn, and documentation."

Again Bill nodded, slowly. "You have my word."

"No . . ." Barbara moaned. Bill took her arm and hissed something at her as he drew her away a little. He was enunciating so clearly in his frustration with her that I could easily read his lips, *Six million dollars, Barbara . . .*

Barbara was trembling, but remained silent. Then she said to me, "Just don't show your face at the funeral."

As I left the library with them, Katherine was waiting for me. Sandra Barton-Gregg stood a little to one side, trying not to look interested in whatever was happening. She placed a restraining hand on Katherine's shoulder, but every atom of her being was egging her on.

"I hope you're satisfied! You weren't content with stealing him away from his family with your lies and your tricks—you little whore! God, we used to laugh at you at Seahaven, with your blonde hair and your French clothes! We laughed at you because you were so desperate to be one of us, and you never were and you never could be! Never!" Her voice broke, and she was weeping wildly. Her husband pushed through the gathering crowd and held her tightly, glaring at Sandra, then drew his wife away.

"This way, Sally." Bill was ushering me out, and I went, gratefully.

Behind me I heard Katherine's voice screaming, "You weren't content with ruining him! You had to kill him! You killed our Keir! *You killed him!*"

And I had. This was the horrible irony. I had created Piers Danforth to remind myself of Keir, to relive our life, our love, just as Perry McGarret had accused me.

I should have listened to him. Perhaps if I had, Keir would still be alive. I am a better writer than I ever thought possible: I loved Keir, every aspect of him, and I had made him come alive for my readers. They had loved him, too; they had felt they *knew* him. And hadn't those women in the Marigold Room recognized him?

I can never forget the looks on their faces, their delight, as if recognizing an old and dear friend. *It's him! It's him!* Could I blame them? I might as well try to blame the rock band, struggling to get up the stairs away from the fans and journalists who had poured through the hotel's front doors. Or blame the hotel itself, whose solid railings had never been meant to support the press of hundreds of bodies unable to descend the stairs and, anyway, intent on getting closer, closer, to Keir. My Keir. Their Keir.

In my dreams Oscar Wilde's words echo, I catch the traces of them even in my waking moments, their terrible truth, that each man kills the thing he loves . . .

Keir lies at rest, now, with Erica. Perhaps he wouldn't have wanted it quite this way, but I'm sure Erica would be pleased. And this way, I'm close, to tend to any weeds and take care of their resting place.

I'll never sell *Jaegerhalle,* now. I have to stay, if only to take care of Keir and Erica, and I don't mind in the least. There's a contentment to my days, now, that rivals anything I've ever known in my life. I could almost think I was happy, but if so, it's amazing, a great gift that has come gently without my being aware of it.

I don't hear from Alby Gresson. He spent days stalking Inspector Gerlain, telling him an ever-increasingly garbled tale of my killing Keir with an ax and burying his body in the barn. He still tells anyone who'll listen, but few people do. One of his sons is always with him these days. He needs looking after. He gets confused and talks of a man shooting at me; I destroyed him for shooting at me, but I deserved to be shot at.

Everyone feels very sorry for him.

Now spring is turning to summer, and the world would be just about perfect, except for the letter I received from McGarret.

I'm sorry about Keir, Sarah, he writes, *I truly am.*

He's in Kilkee, in County Clare, Ireland; he'll be flying home out of Shannon Airport on Tuesday.

It would have been good to see McGarret again, but at the end of his descriptions of Ireland, and how everyone took him for an American, and how he'd discovered Guinness, he told me that he thinks we should get married.

And he says the house at *Jaegerhalle* is a bit small, and we should build a bigger one.

You always said that the cabin would be a writers' center one day—you could do that now. The new house should be built up the southern slope, where the fallen pine tree is. I know how attached you are to that place. The little pine tree could be moved to the front garden of the house.

I also know how careful you have to be, digging for foundations up there. Steel pole construction would be best. You can leave it to me to see that everything is done right, so it's all safe.

Sarah, I know you'll always be unhappy, but you may as well be unhappy with me.

And then the postscript to his note:

I've put in a real lot of thought, here, and I don't think I should take no for an answer on this one.

Hour after hour I sat there on the settee, reading and rereading McGarret's letter. Then I placed it on the fire, mushed up the ashes very carefully, and doused the flames. Then I went into my study and wrote about a thousand words on what had happened the night Erica Tudor died; that's how I began it, *This is what happened, the night Erica Tudor died . . .*

I was really calm about this. I saw things a lot more clearly than I had for some time.

I switched my answering machine on and then I faxed

the several pages to Beth's home in New York. It was late at night both in New York and here. I wondered what time it was in Kilkee, County Clare.

I could imagine McGarret walking thoughtfully along a shingly beach in a mild Irish spring. He'd bend occasionally and pick up a pebble and skim it across, the water. Why did I somehow know that McGarret would be good at skipping stones?

He had worked it out. He had finally Worked It All Out. Had Alby helped him? Had he found something I'd missed? I'd never know.

And now he was coming home, and he expected me to be able to look into that ugly, honest, and beloved face and read there his knowledge of what I had done: he expected me to let him, *him* live the kind of life of deceit that I had built for myself.

Nice try, McGarret. Nice try, my love.

I locked the door behind me and left the house. The fax machine must have woken Beth, back in New York, for my phone started ringing as I headed for the car. I could hear Beth's voice when my own voice stopped, like a shriek across the distance between the house and the garage, *"No, Sally! NO!"*

I drove into St. Claude, and parked the car a little way down the street, so I could walk, and collect my thoughts. The streets were quiet and cold. I passed the cobbled street that contained Eugene's bookshop; I passed the library, and the park . . . And there on the corner was the police station.

I'd be allowed one phone call, wasn't that how it worked? I'd call Merlin and ask if she and Natalie could look after the farm, that was more important than a lawyer.

I had only one deal I wanted to cut with Inspector Gerlain. I wanted Perry McGarret kept right away from me. And because he was McGarret's friend, and would protect

McGarret even from himself, I realized he'd help me on this.

It was odd how many dry leaves blew along the empty street, stubborn leaves that had held on until the new growth had pushed them off the tree. They hissed in little eddies around me. The lights in the foyer of the police station were almost the only signs of life in the town. I could see a young policewoman at the front desk.

And in the end it was like nothing I had imagined: there were no hard hands pressing into my upper arms, no handcuffs on my wrists. Only the dark night and the empty street behind me, and I was able to walk all by myself up the stairs to the brightly lit office behind the heavy glass doors.

Veronica Sweeney was born in Sydney, Australia. After failing first year Law at the University of Tasmania, she went on to a career as a scriptwriter, actress, and novelist. Her first book, *The Emancipist*, was published in 1985, and her second novel, *South Lies the Valley*, in 1988. *A Turn of the Blade* is a departure from the historical settings of her previous books and the first of her novels to be set in modern-day North America. Veronica lives on the north coast of New South Wales, but travels extensively to research her work.

THE MYSTERIES OF MARY ROBERTS RINEHART

THE AFTER HOUSE   (0-8217-4246-6, $3.99/$4.99)

THE CIRCULAR STAIRCASE   (0-8217-3528-4, $3.95/$4.95)

THE DOOR   (0-8217-3526-8, $3.95/$4.95)

THE FRIGHTENED WIFE   (0-8217-3494-6, $3.95/$4.95)

A LIGHT IN THE WINDOW   (0-8217-4021-0, $3.99/$4.99)

THE STATE VS.   (0-8217-2412-6, $3.50/$4.50)
ELINOR NORTON

THE SWIMMING POOL   (0-8217-3679-5, $3.95/$4.95)

THE WALL   (0-8217-4017-2, $3.99/$4.99)

THE WINDOW AT THE WHITE CAT
                                (0-8217-4246-9, $3.99/$4.99)

THREE COMPLETE NOVELS: THE BAT, THE HAUNTED
LADY, THE YELLOW ROOM
                                (0-8217-114-4, $13.00/$16.00)

ROMANCE FROM FERN MICHAELS

DEAR EMILY   (0-8217-4952-8, $5.99

WISH LIST   (0-8217-5228-6, $6.99

AND IN HARDCOVER:

VEGAS RICH   (1-57566-057-1, $25.00